OUT OF SERVICE

ALSO BY JOSEPH HEYWOOD:

Fiction

Taxi Dancer (1985)
The Berkut (1987)
The Domino Conspiracy (1992)
The Snowfly (2000)

Woods Cop Mysteries

Ice Hunter (2001)
Blue Wolf in Green Fire (2002)
Chasing a Blond Moon (2003)
Running Dark (2005)
Strike Dog (2007)
Death Roe (2008)
Shadow of the Wolf Tree (2010)
Force of Blood (2011)
Killing a Cold One (2013)
Buckular Dystrophy (2016)
Bad Optics (2018)

Lute Bapcat Mysteries

Red Jacket (2012)
Mountains of the Misbegotten (2014)
Beyond Beyond (2020)

Short Stories

Hard Ground: Woods Cop Stories (2013)
Harder Ground (2015)
Upper Peculiar (2019)

Nonfiction

Covered Waters: Tempests of a Nomadic Trouter (2003/2015)
Limpy's Adult Lexicon: Raw, Politically Incorrect, Improper & Unexpurgated As Overheard & Noodled (2023)

A WOODS COP MYSTERY

OUT OF SERVICE

JOSEPH HEYWOOD

LYONS PRESS

Essex, Connecticut

LYONS PRESS

An imprint of The Globe Pequot Publishing Group, Inc.
64 South Main Street
Essex, CT 06426
www.globepequot.com

Distributed by NATIONAL BOOK NETWORK

British Library Cataloguing in Publication Information available

Library of Congress Cataloging-in-Publication Data
Names: Heywood, Joseph, author.
Title: Out of service / Joseph Heywood.
Description: Essex, Connecticut : Lyons Press, 2024. | Series: Woods cop mystery ; 12
Identifiers: LCCN 2024022872 (print) | LCCN 2024022873 (ebook) | ISBN 9781493085675 (cloth ; alk. paper) | ISBN 9781493085682 (epub)
Subjects: LCGFT: Detective and mystery fiction. | Novels. Classification: LCC PS3558.E92 O98 2024 (print) | LCC PS3558.E92 (ebook) | DDC 813/.54—dc23/eng/20240517
LC record available at https://lccn.loc.gov/2024022872
LC ebook record available at https://lccn.loc.gov/2024022873

∞™ The paper used in this publication meets the minimum requirements of American National Standard for Information Sciences—Permanence of Paper for Printed Library Materials, ANSI/NISO Z39.48-1992.

This series is for all my DNR solo partners in trucks over more than twenty years.

And to all the other DNR law enforcement personnel who suffered my presence in various and sundry goat rodeos around this wonderful state of ours.

And to all those men and women who have proudly served our state in gray and green, or any other state as game wardens.

And to all those officers who willingly shared personal stories and experiences with me.

And to all those spouses and significant others who were so kind to me over these past two decades.

I thank you one and all.

CHAPTER 1

The Copper Island

KEWEENAW COUNTY

> Like a wild goose flies, unclaim'd by any man.
>
> —William Shakespeare, *As You Like It*

Operating undercover, you could swim only so long in cesspools of assholes, accidental criminals, major felons, psychopaths and sociopaths, and hordes of clueless, petty scofflaws without losing a part of yourself.

This case, Grady Service hoped, would not continue to drag on much longer. The stretches with this latest band of yahoos were wearing him down and pinching at his nerves, a piss-poor state of affairs for one operating so deeply under the radar he had pretty much reduced his life to an occasional phone call. This might technically be called a life, but as a way of life it was the polar opposite of living.

Making personal course corrections had always been difficult for him, and this time the distance between here and there seemed to be lengthening, at least in his mind, which was, whether they knew it or not, where all people lived their lives, and undercover cops even more so, and with far greater intensity and much more danger than ordinary citizens would ever have to face.

It had been a long nineteen days since his last visit to his camper, and he was sick of MREs and hungry for his own food, meager as it might be here. But even more than food he needed sleep.

He had a couple of days off and it was his plan to use them to unspin his head and his soul. There would not be enough time to physically get back to the family, but he hoped there would be enough time to sort things out here, and unwind.

With time off he should already feel the first wave of relaxation, but his damn inner spin was roller-coastering, and why this feeling again? Last time here he had been bothered by the same creepy feeling, and here it was again.

The feeling didn't hit him in his unmarked Ford or even during the walk-in, but only as he reached the camper door lock, and kept fumbling with the damn combination, as if something was warning him he was on the verge of a weak spot, and perhaps a threat, and maybe he should step back for a minute and assess the situation and his feelings. As usual, however, he plunged forward, laughing at his foolish self. What could be a threat here after all the bullshit he had been dealing with almost daily for going on six months?

Maybe this uneasiness had come down to him through his old man's genes, but his whole life he had possessed a sort of early warning system that alerted him to threats, and so far it had proved reliable. But when he stepped inside, he was too tired to even hit the light switch and, instead, stripped down, and collapsed onto his sleeping bag on the bed, not bothering to open it, thinking sweet, dreamless sleep would work its magic, as it always had and, he was quite certain, always would.

And it did.

Briefly.

"Worm's been watching on you, goin' six month, Mister, and Worm can't tell if you be the most private man ever come to these woods, or the most paranoid. Mister never park Him's old truck in the same place twice in a row, and Mister never walk to Him's house-trailer by same route, or direct A go B, A go B—oh no, never that! One time Him made two-damn-mile loop to cover quarter-mile start to done, and Worm ain't afraid to tell you, that scared the Bejeezums out of Her."

Startled awake, his hand gripped his .357 and he blinked repeatedly trying to see his intruder in the damn dark. He was moving too fast as he tried to clear his brain of sleep-fog and he told himself to slow down so he didn't make a dreadfully stupid or tragic mistake.

He spoke to the clearly female voice who he could not see: "Worm? That would be . . . you?"

"Worm not say this Her if not Worm. Mister kinda made Worm go uh-oh, whoopsy-doodle Mister bargin' in the way Him did, and crashin' so fast. Worm hopin' mebbe we talk like town-people, yack-yack, yada, yada, how's them little grandkids? The fish bitin' today? Your golf gettin' any better? How come you don't sleep with me no more? And all like that, but Worm, Her havin' watched close-like how Mister live and, knowin' how Worm live,

Her guess town-talk ain't for the likes of Mister or Worm. Listen up: Worm tell Mister this straight out: Worm don't like the smell of civilization."

"You know there's a Colt pointed in your direction, right?" Service told her.

"Sure Worm knows and this fit what town folks and cops call profilin'. Worm plenty-plenty times seen Mister jaybirded, but Worm don't see Mister jumpin' off that fartin' sack so can wave Mister Willy-Willy and his Colt-gun at Her."

She could see in the dark that he was undressed? No, it seemed more likely she had heard him shed his clothes, but this also meant she had been inside and waiting for him and how the hell had she done that? The combo lock was closed tight. And why was she here? "Worm's living a dangerous life, breaking into other people's property," Service pointed out.

"Worm thinks risk calculation is what Her pretty good at, if Worm can get into any place she want, any time She want—and this always been so, always, always—this mean low risk low, right, Mister?"

How did one talk rationally with someone who addressed themselves in the third person and employed some vocabulary idiosyncrasies that reminded him of Limpy Allerdyce? *Paranoid*? Good grief. But one thing was certain among all the uncertainties in this, whatever this was, she was uncowed and sounded far younger than such confidence warranted.

"Worm knows Mister layin' there, wonderin' if Worm really seen Him nekkid is what Him wonderin', after tryin' figger out how Worm, She gets inside house-trailer camper house without him knowin'."

"Nobody can see in the dark," he told her. "And this is real dark, with not a speck of light."

She chuckled. "Worm think nights for Worm like days for Mister."

"Worm is a philosopher?" he said.

"Worm is damn realist is what Worm is—same as Mister, two realists, sittin' here in black dark."

Astonishing realism and punishing detail for a dream, but then this, whatever it was, seemed more like a nightmare, albeit with some very almost-funny wrinkles. Was she armed? Did she have all her marbles in her package? Breaking in like this, way out here in the boondocks especially, ranked somewhere on the scale between braindead and brilliant. "Are you like one of those superheroes with superpowers, like some breed of Batgirl can see in the dark?"

"Worm think this thing what seem super to Mister, not super. Worm, She born this way, and Worm don't make no excuses for how She can see or look."

How she looks? Had she just flashed a chink in her armor? "Being only one of us can see in the dark, I've got no way to know what Worm looks like and that seems unfair for town-talking."

"Worm thinks ain't no reason Mister see Her until Her decide it time. Worm think Her and Mister don't need to eye-see each other to make understandin'."

"Worm breaks into my RV and now she wants us to reach some sort of understanding?" Service said. "Worm may see in the night like it's day, but her sense of realpolitik ain't on the same shelf with her unique eyes."

This seemed to earn him another chuckle. Whoever she was, she seemed preternaturally calm and poised—given the circumstances. "How about I get up and make us some coffee and breakfast," he suggested. "You hungry?"

"Worm always hungry, but Worm don't eat when strange Mister march 'round with Him's pajoggler swinging in breeze. Worm Her think Mister should slip on duds he shed earlier like a snake chasin' a new skin."

"Somebody breaks in like this, I wouldn't make her for someone with a streak of prudery."

"There's a whole heap of real an old guy like Mister wouldn't make," she said back with a chirp.

"Batgirl got something against old folks?"

"Worm, *not* Batgirl. Worm Her name, Mister! Worm, okay?"

"In fairness we didn't really formally introduce ourselves, but what you said suggests to me that my ways scare Worm like a hungry bird bouncing over her. Worm, *that's* your actual, legal name?"

"Names like clothes, Worm thinks. Don't wear same ones all time. And yes to question."

"Which question's that, Ms. Worm?" he asked, confused.

"Worm's name is Worm, and yes, Worm armed too, sawed-off Remington, 12-gauge, fourteen-inch barrel, double ought buck."

"A walking anti-personnel weapon is Ms. Worm."

"Don't call Worm no Mzzz thing. Worm's plenty."

"Or?" Service asked.

She let loose a deep, loud sigh in the dark. "Worm ask, what reason Worm needs this? Are we not two ships passin' in night, that awful and nutmega, mebbe make the zipless boinky-boinky?"

His turn to laugh. "I'll be: Worm's also a bibliophile! Not to mention, a pip."

"Worm says Mister got no idea," Worm said.

"There's a nub beginning to form," Service told her. "Want to explain what Worm is doing here, inside his camper? He can call cops, if Worm wants, or She can talk to me."

"No cop ever run Worm down. What behind that Second Door, Mister?"

The *Second Door*? She *was* a pip. What institution had raised her? Something inside told him her brag on eluding cops wasn't an idle one. Very strange girl, very odd behaviors, almost animal-like and a semi-automaton who knows language but does not know it. The U.P. tended to be a magnet for human outliers of all sorts and no doubt she had an interesting story to tell, if she could, or would. "I'm listening."

"Her sees Mister got two of hearing skin-flaps. People don't palaver this way."

"Sure they do. I'm settled here, and you're settled where you are, so why stir up a new working formula?"

"Mister is very careful man," she told him.

"Nor careful enough. He let Her get by Him."

"You jokin' Worm how Her talk?"

"No insult intended," he told her, "cross my heart."

"Worm sees you not cross heart!" she yipped.

Oh shit. She *can* see. He quickly slid his hands down to his junkal region.

Worm laughed with obvious glee. "Mister is careful *and* funny."

"I think we'd define our comedies differently."

"Worm wonder Why Him never bring no Hers here. Him a Him-Him?"

"No, and it's none of your business."

"Out here, all is Worm's business," she said. "To stay alive and free. Worm not think Mister bad to bring him-her here. Him *have* a her?"

"Mister thinks Worm's a philosopher at heart."

"Worm rather do than yack-yack, and last thing Worm want do, is tell others how live. Tell others how Worm thinks, and soon they telling Worm how she live."

"Will Worm ever get to the point of this surprise visit?" Service asked, abruptly.

"Mister ain't going nowhere. Worm have no hurry."

"Mister wants to sleep, which he can't do here in the dark with Her blathering like a banshee. He suggests Worm make Her point, and git."

"So Mister can call cops?"

"What does Worm care if they can't catch Her."

"Worm think Him should make food, make coffee, and pay Worm for keep look over Mister's place, keep safe. Worm be Mister's crow. Can't sneak up on crows, Mister."

"Or else?"

"Worm think woods full of sneaks and snoops and jerk-woods on loud putt-putts. Thems steal anything them come across, even locked up."

"Not much here to steal," Service countered.

"Worm know ain't thieves the only thing Mister want worry about. Mister got the lookers-about."

"Like Worm?"

"Worm ain't look-about. Worm is watcher."

"There's a difference between watchers and look-abouts?"

"Look-abouts ain't *of* here, them."

"But watchers are . . . *of* here?"

"Worm say okay, yes."

"Worm going to tell Mister more about look-abouts?"

"Different fellows lollyganking, lookin' for somethin', and finally Worm thinks one day, Them lookin' for Mister!"

"That's a pretty strong conclusion based on sparse and feeble data."

"Worm got gut with chord of spine to brain, Her. Them's looking for somebody, and same two keep comin' back 'round, comin' back 'round, here one day and not here one day, and one day they here again, Worm think: Must be Mister Them wants!"

"She sure it's not Worm they want?"

"For Boy-Men Worm she be just small amusement, them, mebbe use her boinky-boinky to pass time, but Worm sure main event be Him."

"Him being me?" He was beginning to drown in her sea of third-person pronouns.

"Yes, Worm knows this."

"Have the snoopers seen this camper?"

"Not yet, Worm thinks. Mister got it hid real good way up here. Took Worm long time find here, and like Worm, Thems keep comin' back by and comin' back by, lookin'-lookin' for somethin'."

Service said, "Let me understand this proposition, if that's what it is. For remuneration Worm proposes to disrupt these look-abouts?"

"Him says, okay deal?"

"I didn't say that. How much is Worm thinking?"

"Worm think a lot, much thinkin'."

"No, how does she want to be paid . . . remunerated?"

"Worm not think like that. So Mister also think Them is looking for Mister?"

"I never said that. Stop jumping to conclusions."

"Worm, her not jump on nobody, 'cept got Her reason."

"Restraint and self-discipline are good traits for Hims and Hers."

"How much Mister want pay Her."

"I never said I wanted to pay you. That was *your* idea."

"But Mister right away think Her want pay, so must be in Mister's mind Him want pay Worm."

"Your logic eludes me," he confessed.

She chuckled. "Confuse Worm too, sometimes."

"This whole thing is some stupid game and I'm tired of playing. Get out. I need sleep."

"Okay, Worm go, but Worm think Him want security more than sleep. Her got to be right: Worm seen Mister always sneaky-sneakin' in here. Mister don't want nobody know Him here, Worm think, Him think?"

She was a weasel, this strange girl, and weasels were smart and calculating and wise in their own ways. "What do these two look-abouters look like?"

"Pictures make better words," she came back.

"You have pictures?"

"Worm have trail cameras."

"Aren't you afraid they'll be stolen?"

"Worm know how hide in places mans won't look."

Arrogant, confident, full of bravado. "You mean *most* people."

"Mister want look pictures, or keep try put Worm on back foot?"

"That what I'm doing, putting Worm on her back foot and off-balance?"

She giggled. "Not likely, old Gus like Him."

"I'm getting out of bed," he announced. "I'm feeling cramped."

"Free country," Worm said.

"I'll make us some coffee and breakfast, you do drink coffee, yes?"

"Worm don't turn down coffee never."

Service quickly pulled on his trousers, got up, stalked over to the light, flipped the switch, and turned to look at the chair where he assumed she was sitting, but it was empty. What the hell? Was he losing it?

"Worm here," the voice said from directly behind him and he turned and saw her, rangy, thin with knots of muscles, stark naked, and sure as hell no kid.

"Even Tarzan wore a damn loincloth," he told her.

"Her speck not in bedroom make boinky-boinky with Jane," she retorted.

"That's your name is it, Jane?"

"When Worm say her name Worm, her name Worm. Where coffee?"

"I've gotta make it first."

"Worm not stop Him."

"Put some clothes on," he told her. "I find this too distracting."

"Him not like Her's natural?"

"That's beside the point. Civilized people wear clothes."

"Worm likes air on skin. Mister don't like how Her look?"

"You look just fine, but I am not comfortable with this."

"Why Him put on Him's pants?"

"Please," he said. "Clothes. You want some of mine?"

"Her never figure Mister be prude," she said. "Seen him many times all-together."

She was a peeper? Was that what he had sensed recently whenever he came here?"

"How old are you?"

"Guess."

He laughed. "That's a game a smart man learns to never play with a woman."

"Worm thinks Mister was a-laying there in dark thinkin' Her's sixteen or something, right?"

"Maybe."

"You think Worm some kind of mooncalf?"

"Wouldn't say that." What did she mean by mooncalf?

She laughed. "When Mans hear word Worm, them think fish, fuck, or ruin mebbe."

"Not every man."

"Her think Mister get old, change Mister's order. Where fuck fall in Him's order now?"

She was a pain in the ass. "It falls where it aught, when it aught."

"For Worm too," she came back. "When time come, Worm make move, or if Him prude and can't handle, Worm say 'move-time arriveth.'"

"No offense, and not to change the subject, but where the hell did you learn English?"

"Same place English people learn English—from Him Mister Shakespeare."

"You learned English from Shakespeare—at what school?"

"Worm, Her think six grades plenty for Her, and since then . . . "

She didn't finish her thought. "Worm *needs* coffee!"

"They don't teach Shakespeare in grades one through six," he pointed out.

"Learn later, on own. Where coffee?"

"I'm working on it. Sit down, and stop hovering like a damn vulture."

The strange girl's voice dropped an octave and she said, "More pity that the eagles should be, while kites and buzzard prey at liberty."

"What the hell is *that*?" Service asked.

"Shakespeare. Mister said vulture. Shakespeare him got many birds in Him's work."

She could call up Shakespearean lines, but talked in the third person about herself and made a mess of pronouns. What was the deal with her?

"Peeping's a crime, you know. They put people in jail for looking where they're not supposed to."

"Worm not worry, think that all go bye-bye now Her work for Him."

"We've made no such agreement," he reminded her.

"You like Him-Shakespeare?"

"I don't really know him."

"Worm teach Mister. Buzzard from Richard Third, bad, bad, bad man, kill babykin and all, smother 'em dead with feather pillows."

"I barely know our own country's history," he told her.

"Englanders are cousins," she pointed out, "and Her teach Mister history too, Him want?"

"I don't need you to teach me anything."

"Worm think Mister wrong and Her know Him-Her got deal now."

"There is no deal."

"Worm knows when Him and a Her make naked together in small space, there is deal, bargain is struck, only the price to be spoke."

"How do you like your coffee? I think there's some milk."

"Hot and hard, like Worm's men."

"I, that am rudely stamp'd . . . To strut before a wanton ambling nymph," he said.

She stared at him, her mouth hanging open, part-pout, part-grimace, surprise in her eyes, and then slowly . . . a smile with dimples for parentheses. "More to Him than meets one's eyes, Worm thinks."

"You concluded that Worm's the only one who ever read Shakespeare?"

"*Nyet, Her bet,*" she said, her smile widening. "Worm hear Mister Him swear sometimes in Russian-talk, out loud like Mister in state of most pissedoffedness."

Her own place couldn't be far from here, he reasoned as he poured coffee. She was extremely odd, but when he was honest about his own life and ways, the word seemed quite apt for him as well, and recognizing this similarity both amused and annoyed him. Decades of shoveling human detritus for normal, law-abiding citizens. What kind of life was *that*? Look where it had led him.

"How much you think watchin' over Mister's place is worth?" he asked his strange visitor.

"Worm wants be fair, and unless you Mister Moneytags, which Mister's way of livin' don't look like Him is, Her ain't lookin' to empty Him's piggy bank. What Mister, Him think fair?"

"Let's Worm and Him get something very clear. It will *not* be Worm's job to confront looker-abouters and snoopers. We will call the law for that."

"No call cops when Worm about."

"Does Her have a problem with the law?"

"No wants, no warrants, if that's Mister's question, and no record beyond juvenile, which is now moot as lawyer-mans say. Mebbe Worm don't like them that wear shiny tin. Her gets near them types, Worm's head hurt."

"Your head okay right now?" he asked.

She nodded. "Worm's head good."

"How about three hundred a month?" Service proposed.

"Three hundred what?" she came back.

"Dollars."

"Cash?"

"If that's what Worm wants."

"Three hundred a month: Okay, cash." She thrust her hand forward, and said, "Match Worm skin."

Which he did and as he turned to make breakfast he heard her go out and come back in and when he looked up, she was fully dressed.

He put a plate of scrambled eggs, some crisp bacon, and green peppers in front of her, and anise and caraway rye toast, then watched her attack the food.

Outside the wind had risen and was speed-bagging the sides of the trailer-camper.

"Worm think Mister got funny schedule. How long Mister think this go on?"

"Mister is not at all certain."

"Want tell Worm what Mister do?"

"Mister does not, but this thing could last a week more, or a month, or even longer. It will be what it will be."

"This thing Mister do is food for Him's soul?"

"What does Worm mean by soul?"

She shrugged. "Think on this much, and don't know. You got a name, Mister?" she asked.

"Pick one you like and I'll try to abide. One name's as good as another."

"Mister think evil's real?"

"As real as dirt and fire and water."

"And air?"

"That too, for sure, and sometimes I think it's hot wind that blows over people and makes them do greedy, stupid, thoughtless things."

"All peoples got souls?" Worm wondered out loud.

"Can't say all any more than we can say none. Far as I know, nobody's ever seen a soul they could describe so others might know one if they saw one."

"Everything got souls," Worm came back, "even rocks."

"You sound like an Indian."

She sniggered. "Who you think sins most, the tempted or the tempter? What if we all dead and this is heaven?" she asked, changing direction again.

"More likely it's hell," he said.

"Orion," Worm said.

"The Hunter," Service said, "belt of, it's a constellation, a connect-the-dots in the sky."

"Uh-huh," Worm said. "Orion with the belt and sword, and while she ain't seen Mister's belt she sure seen his sword. . . . Worm think temptation make the doing more sweeter. This work Mister do is dangerous?" she asked, quickly shifting directions the way investigators were trained to do. Either that, or her mind was totally unstable and all over the place.

"I never said anything about work. It was you who called it a schedule or job or whatnot."

"Worm thinks Mister is prude and very careful listener."

"Mister tries to be," he said. "And I ain't much of a fan of Orion, but if he's Worm's hero, so be it. Free country and free choice."

"Worm spend night?" she asked.

"Sure," he said. "It's too damn late to be out and about in the bush."

"There is bush, and bush," she said.

"I mean the woods," he said by way of clarification.

"Worm's libido takes 'nother drubbin'," she said. "What Mister and Worm doing tomorrow?"

He looked at her and thought she was perhaps one of the most naturally beautiful women he had ever seen. "Worm will be leaving to do whatever it is that Worm does, and Mister is going to get some damn work done around here."

"Shall we then to bed with kind embracingments and tempting kisses?"

"To bed is right even if the we part is wrong. You take the bed. I've got a couch rollout. All that's from Shakespeare?"

"Taming of shrew. They had great sex," she added.

"Not on stage they didn't," he pointed out.

"Back then them call dressing rooms tiring rooms. Why Him think that was?"

"Him doesn't know but thinks Her wants to enlighten him."

"Can't dress unless undress first," she explained. "And once undressed, all is possible."

He smiled.

"What?" she asked.

"All the actors in Shakespeare's day were men."

"We not *in* Him Shakespeare's time," she replied. "Her and Him are Here Now, Not There and Then and Back When and we are alone as were Adam and Eve, and got any apples in this rig?"

"Let us to bed," he said. "I'm beat."

"Worm loves it when Orion talks this way."

"In that hit you miss," he said.

"Her heart skips happy. Him knows Bard's work!"

"Narrow prying tires me."

"Vituperation lights Worm's heart," she said softly.

"Douse the light, Worm."

"Put out, as in dampen and extinguish, or put out as in give it up ant let it all hang loose?"

He turned out the light and crawled onto his bunk and she was immediately beside him trying to wriggle her way in and he pushed her down onto the floor.

She laughed. "Worm welcomes the rude hand."

"Worm needs to put it out, any of it, all of it."

"The poisonous damp of night doth disponge on Worm."

"Anything is fine as long as Orion is not part of it," Service said. "If you get a chance, take it. If it changes your life, let it. Nobody said it'd be easy, they just promised it would be worth it."

"Not Shakespeare," she said.

"Nope, it's Seuss."

"He was friend of Shakespeare, this Seuss?"

"I'm pretty sure he would have been."

CHAPTER 2

Camp ROCK

KEWEENAW COUNTY

O, that I would call the dead to life.

—William Shakespeare, *Henry VI, Part I*

"We only take dead men," Colonel Histah "Sane Zane" Harlikin told Grady Service the very first time they had met. "If you join us, you're either OTGOL or NOTGOL, off the grid of life, or not. The kind of work we plan to do for patriotism and freedom makes it critical that nobody get snared by stray paper."

Service stared at the man's slightly yellowed hue and kept his lip zipped. The colonel was seized by soliloquy and anyone in such a state, the undercover detective knew from decades of experience, would not tolerate interruption, and clearly the colonel was on his soapbox. "The dead get little attention from the living," the man explained, and stared at Service with a gleam in his eyes. Power tripper? If this man was the one called Sane Zane, what was the rest of his family like?

"Feds," Service thought bitterly. It had been the FBI and ATF who landed him among these wingnuts and his own governor, whom he had met but once, who heavily supported such infiltration, and endorsed *him* as the man to do the job. Undercover work was dicey, but as a general rule, fish and game violators were one thing and little Napoleons and wannabe Pattons were of a very different, and far more dangerous breed.

Called Camp ROCK by outsiders, this place to its wingnut insiders was known as Fort ROCK or The Fortress but Service did not take such people lightly. Had it not been a couple of helmeted hemorrhoids from a now-defunct Michigan militia group who had destroyed the Alfred P. Murrah Building in Oklahoma City back in 1995, killing 168 people, including nineteen children, and injuring close to seven hundred others? The number of potential domestic terrorists in the country was unknown, but most such groups were taken seriously, and needed to be. One slip-up could prove disaster. Look what happened with 9/11 when fed agencies were not talking to each other and sharing relevant intel.

"Your guys handle the details of the death, or is that my play?" Wyndham Vold, aka Grady Service, asked the colonel whose jaundiced pale yellow flesh had the faint white striations of a vampire, and the patient demeanor of a hired personal Latin tutor in a fancy private school.

"Your death," Harlikin said, "is your show all the way and how you handle it will help us determine your suitability."

"Even, if I came out on a dishonorable?"

"The last thing this country needs, or cares about, is honor."

"How long do I have to make this happen?"

"There's no real rush or set time frame, but if you want in and started on your way to a meaningful new life, you may not want to dither about. Perfection in pulling this off is the goal here, not speed. It is not like we're panting over a new recruit, even one who looks to be on paper just the sort of man we seek. The truth is, and you ought to be aware of it: There are lines forming to get into this outfit, long lines, but we like to be sure of what we're getting, and we prefer unattached males with previous military service. Combat experience moves candidates up the preference list."

"What're we called, our outfit?" Service asked.

"It isn't yours son, not yet, but I admire your thinking in this matter. Many seek the true gold of God's glory. You like glory, son, you seek the light of fame?"

"Nossir, what I seek is to be left alone and not treated like a pariah. I just want to know what my job is and for others to stand back and let me do it."

Harlikin closed his eyes, nodded, and issued a cartoony snuffling sound. "This is the nose of a predator, son, and the thing a predator smells first is another predator. You're one of us, aren't you son?"

Pure rhetoric here, no expectation of a response. Service looked past the man and said again, "You never said what we're called, Colonel."

Histah Harlikin tightened the muscles in his neck. "First, we never address each other by ranks unless we are in uniform, and even then sparingly if we are not in fully contained security conditions. Most of the time, like now, we're in mufti and its given names and nicknames. We are true-blue citizen *soldati*, not the paid whores the country tries to fob off as patriots."

"Those fobs are well paid for their soldiering," Service pointed out.

"In a true patriot army, each man is expected to be financially self-sufficient and if not, he'll not be one of us. You employed now, son?"

"I work six to nine months a year as a bird counter."

The colonel whistled and looked at his middle-aged body-man who stood by his side as he sat. "Now *that* occupation is not something we'd ever heard of before this very moment. Bird counting? How does that work? All birds, certain birds?"

"Been a raptor counter for several years. I started in DownEast Maine, and spent some time along the headwaters of the Mississippi."

"You are the first of your kind to try for our ranks. Don't be startled or offended if you get tagged by the boys as Birdman."

"Been called worse," Service allowed.

"You tag these birds you count, Birdman?"

"Nossir, just count them and report my counts daily for a period of time."

"You good at what you do?"

"Good enough to keep getting hired. It's hard to catch on with the networks that sponsor this work, but once you do, you're in."

Harlikin came back, "If you don't mind my saying so, you are definitely not a spring chicken, son. The job you do, seems to me, would want young, strong eyes."

"Young eyes today often can't see any further than a smartphone in their left hand," Service retorted.

"Right you are, but there is linkage between eye strength and the aging process," the colonel said.

"There are exceptions to every rule," Service pointed out.

"Guess that makes you one of the exceptions," Harlikin said.

"So far, always not being always when it boils down to biology."

"I'd like sometime for us to talk more about this bird work you do—if you pass selection, and can make the jump." Service was listening as he studied a gray metal filing cabinet behind the colonel. Sitting on top was a two-gallon jug filled with live ticks. What was *that* shit about? "Ready when you are," Service told the man, and not caring if they ever talked about it. He'd spent two weeks with the feds, watching birds from a tower looking out on part of Galveston Island in Texas, predator counting being the feds' idea of a terrific legend, and the Galveston gig part of the background development, on the ground experience being critical to having an unbreakable cover. Ironically, the outfit that ran the Texas birdwatch offered him a job at the end of his two-week stint. "Got the eyes of a sniper," one of the Texans declared, "and such eyes are not common, even among we Texans who are overall uncommon among all other types of men."

"Some of the men are talking about initiation fees," Service told the colonel, and waited to hear his reaction and explanation.

"Don't call it an initiation fee!" Harlikin corrected him. "We operate the way citizen armies are supposed to operate. You equip yourself on your own dime and you get paid a pittance while in uni, or on official duties for the regiment."

"Funny how you can attract men when the real Army's had to drastically upgrade pay for active-duty troops for recruiting and retention," Service pointed out to see what reaction he would get.

"The so-called real Army is as clueless as a horse you give a hambone to gnaw. The British regimental system was and remains the ideal organizing principle for assembling fighting forces. Personally, I think that the United States Marine Corps grew out of the regimental philosophy, which is a few well-trained, highly motivated men ready and able to handle anything, and even when the time comes to hang up their swords, the men of the regiment remain an emotional support system for their comrades. Building such a force is expensive and we are on our own, not sucking at federal or state troughs. There is no fee here, only the K and C, which is twenty-five thousand dollars a man."

Service whistled softly. "Twenty-five K *per man*?"

"Every man must be equally equipped, trained and garbed, but we want quality control, so each man contributes K and C, and we issue unis and equipment, which he then owns and maintains, and we oversee all training to make sure it meets our standards, which are far more exacting than what the government expects."

"K and C," Service said. "That's something to grab a man's attention."

"As well it should and must," Harlikin said. "There's nothing fancy-schmancy about this outfit. We say what we mean, and mean what we say."

"You haven't yet said what you're called," Service reminded them again.

"Regiments of Christian Knights," the colonel said. "ROCKs."

"Regiments, plural, there's more than one?" Service asked.

"We aim high, son."

Which was no answer at all. "What is it you do to sustain yourself financially?" Service inquired, already pretty sure what answer would come back to him. "If I'm not stepping out of bounds with that question."

"I proudly trade in the Second Amendment's sweet, cold fruit."

"You're a gun dealer?"

"We prefer HSWD Marketing and Distribution."

High speed wireless devices, a euphemism invented somewhere in the fringes and shadows of the guntopian National Rifle Association. The Feebs and ATF said they had yet to encounter a civilian militia that was not in some way connected to firearms sales, usually its founder the gun-dealer in chief, and enriching his own treasury at the expense of his recruits.

"I can handle the twenty-five K ante," Service told the colonel, who bristled.

"This is neither gambling nor a gamble," the self-appointed colonel insisted. "You have adequate sums in the bank?"

"I certainly do not, but plenty of banks have twenty-five K in *their* vaults."

"We ROCKs admire audacity. You ever rob a bank?"

"You think I got the dishonorable for beating my meat in front of the CO's wife?"

Service thought the colonel suddenly looked paler than his usual yellow.

"How you choose to raise your K and C is wholly your concern, Birdman, and has nothing to do with us. You choose to swim onto the Reef of Trouble, and cops show up here, we don't know you, have never known you, have never heard of you, and will never know you or hear of you in the future."

Service grinned. "See, like I said, for me this *is* a gamble!"

"You need to think this through carefully, son."

"I want in and I'll do whatever I have to, to get there."

"We'll be in touch, or we won't," the colonel said. "If you qualify, we will call and if not, you'll never hear from us again, and I do sincerely wish you luck with your bird-counting."

The ROCKs summoned him to report back three days later, but he told Harlikin in a text on the phone they had provided that he had a three-week birding job starting in a few days and needed to fulfill that before he could take care of ROCK business, and after that he called the FBI and the team met to figure out what his next step would be. That had been six months ago, and now he had dropped twenty-five grand and was brought in at what they called the entry path phase and now the colonel was after him for *more* cash.

Nobody in the Army or Pentagon had any record of inquiries about Service's alias, and the FBI said it would continue investigating the ROCKs from without while he went inside, but he was pretty sure the claim of record-checking was bullshit. The question was why, and there was no ready or obvious answer.

CHAPTER 3

Marquette

MARQUETTE COUNTY

But all hoods make not monks.

—William Shakespeare, *Henry VIII*

Captain Lisette McKower, newly promoted head of DNR Special Investigations (fancy titling for detectives), had the face of an angel and the eyes of an executioner. Everyone in the room was law enforcement and connected by badges and oaths, but if they were a family, Grady thought, it was a dysfunctional one on its best day, which clearly was not today.

"We're reluctantly agreeing to this operation *only* because there is a vague, and theoretical CITES violation and therefore a wildlife component, for our state," McKower said in her practiced honeyed voice, which she could turn to razor wire with no more than a blink.

CITES was an almost half-century old international, multilateral treaty used to protect endangered plants and animals. At present more than sixty-six hundred species of animals and thirty-four thousand plant species were on the protected list. Of more than sixty kinds of eagles in the world, the bald eagle, the US national symbol since six years after the Declaration of Independence, was one of the many bird species. Under 50 CFR 22, the Migratory Bird Treaty Act (the Bald Eagle Protection Act), not only were live eagles given full protection, but it also was illegal to traffic in parts of deceased eagles.

To support the legislation the US Fish and Wildlife Service Office of Law Enforcement created the National Repository in the early 1970s, its job to make sure that Native Americans (who were with few exceptions the only Americans entitled to eagle parts) got them. Those not entitled were pursued and prosecuted. Typically, this was done in concert with a state where infractions were taking place.

Service looked around the table. "I see FBI and ATF. Where's Fish and Wildlife?"

"It is not in our mandate to question team membership," FBI Special Agent Jeckyl Coldbeg said curtly. The man was now one of the FBI's two resident agents for the Upper Peninsula, but he lacked Special Agent in Charge (SAC) credentials. Despite lacking an SAC's authority, the man was running a multiagency task force. It defied explanation. Coldbeg's predecessor, Busby Adair, had been a good guy and fine colleague, and eventually a friend, with no claim on turf and his eyes only on justice. So far, Coldbeg was not emitting vibrations of playing nicely with others.

"Pardon me," Captain McKower said, "but *screw* your mandates. Detective Service is right to question this. Fish and Wildlife's feather cops out of Colorado were created for just this sort of operation, yet they are not here. *Explanation*?"

"I'm just following orders," Coldbeg offered.

"Custer's grunts in saddles followed their goofy colonel's orders, and look what happened to that lot," Service said and immediately felt the captain kick his foot under the table.

Fred Stairs, the U.P. regional manager for ATF, held up his hands. "We neither want, nor need sand in our axles and gears. We need grease."

Service liked Stairs well enough, but had not worked enough cases with him to form a picture. Stairs and Adair always seemed to have gotten along.

"My nose is itching," Captain McKower carped. "And it only itches when it senses bullshit and obstruction. Let it be on the record that law enforcement for the Michigan Department of Natural Resources is involved in this for one reason only: Detective Service will remain inside only until he can verify eagle feathers or parts in the suspect's possession, and when that happens, our detective is, and I mean right-fucking-now, out of there and it will be up to you people to figure out the road from that point. Copy that, Detective Service?" she finished, not glancing at him.

"Got it Cap'n, loud and clear. Verify and boogie."

"Roger *that*," McKower said forcefully.

ATF's Stairs said, "We've never been able to get a man inside before now, and this outfit carries the stench of potential bad news from local to national. This is a good thing you've done, finding a way in," Stairs complimented Service.

"I'm not *all* the way in yet," Service reminded them. And this was true. The target group seemed rather hinky and cautious. He wanted to further add that it pissed him off to be pulled from undercover in the field to meetings in public buildings in the U.P.'s largest town. Being too much in towns risked blowing his cover. "Would be better if you folks had these meetings without me," he said diplomatically. "My captain will keep me in the loop and be my link back to you and vice versa."

McKower again said, "Feathers verified and my detective is out the door."

Service still had a significant issue. "Okay, exactly how much *latitude* do I have with these jamokes?"

"That's your call, Detective," Special Agent Coldbeg said. "You know your limits and the legal limits for undercovers."

"Felony involvement, if unavoidable?"

"The upper limit is always homicide and the like," the special agent said, "but you'd better have unimpeachable legal grounds for exceptions."

Homicide and the like. What the hell was equivalent to *murder*?

Coldbeg reportedly had transferred from the FBI's Minneapolis office, which immediately cast some doubt on his competence. The U.P. was booniedom, and while certainly not a plum FBI gig, neither was it Devil's Island, and Coldbeg's predecessor Adair had been around a long time, and had done a great job, Adair being the sort of man who brought glue to teams. Coldbeg gave off no such vibes.

On the plus side, the FBI had been great in helping him build his cover for the undercover job, but that part of the FBI had no idea what his assignment was and could not enlighten him about the group to be penetrated, and Coldbeg had been less than helpful, which was partly why Lis brought her chip-on-the-shoulder act to the table.

"Is this group implicated in any homicides?" Service asked.

"That's for you to determine," Coldbeg said. "We have reason to believe they have their noses in a wide array of activities."

"So . . . the answer is yes, or maybe, or you have no clue?"

Coldbeg held out his hands in mock supplication.

"This meeting is *over* for us," the captain said and kicked him hard in the boot again.

"There is no need for your presence here," Coldbeg told her.

"Which is exactly *why* I *am* here," she retorted and stood up. "*I* will see you gentlemen soon," she said, shot a look at Service, and they both headed for the door.

• • •

They drove to the south end of town to the Huron Mountain Bakery, and Service ordered coffee and a pistachio muffin that felt like it weighed a pound.

The captain ordered only coffee. "How do you stay so svelte when you eat crap like that?"

"Not crap, soul food. WTF was it with the shots on my age?"

"Your limit is feathers, end stop," McKower said emphatically.

"Undercover doesn't work that neatly," he said. "You know that," the longtime detective reminded her.

"Damn right I *know* the business. I'm just making sure you do too," she said, and she certainly did. She had been the division's first female detective when the general rubric said women couldn't do such jobs. But some of her cases and sheer risk-taking bordered on legendary.

"What's Tuesday think about this gig?"

"We don't comment on each other's work," he told the captain. Tuesday was Tuesday Friday, the Michigan State Police homicide detective for the U.P., stationed in Negaunee, and his longtime partner.

"She won't like it," McKower said of her close friend.

"She's a pro. She gets it, Lis."

"Allerdyce still living with you two?"

"He comes and he goes, but I guess, yah, he is, sort of."

"You keep that asshole out of this deal, copy?"

"These militia types are *his* kind of peeps."

"Ixnay with this crowd and that asshole, and that is a direct order."

"I like knowing he's nearby," Service said.

"He's not your toy teddy bear," she said with a snarl and a smile. "Too much risk with this crowd, Grady. I don't get why yet, but these jerks seem to creep out the FBI and that's not something we often see. Why doesn't the Bureau have someone inside?" she asked.

"Why me?" he replied, though he understood what she was getting at.

"Our new kids lack your experience and frankly, eventually I want us entirely out of the UC business so we can make our mission more advisory and consultatory within each of the twelve districts. We want to teach others how to fish, not do all the fishing ourselves."

"The fishing is the *fun* part, not holding hands with our cubs," he exclaimed. "You ever question your own sanity as you went into a new case?"

"Almost every time. You?"

"Same. The power of perpetual novelty gets old fast."

"This deal is not something you're accustomed to, and not what we're built for. I mean: militias? Jesus, Grady. These guys are whackjobs and when I say verify feathers and get your ass out, that's just what I mean."

"Because I'm old?"

"No, you jerk, because I want to see you older, not dead."

"Is that a compliment?"

"I would hate to lose you this close to your retirement."

He bristled. "*What* retirement?"

"It is inevitable for all of us," she said and took a slug of coffee. "Even legends."

For someone so petite and feminine, she drank coffee like a Marine in a trench. "Knock off the retirement shit," he told her.

She poked his massive arm. "Tell Tuesday I'll give her a bump. Now I've got a meeting at the Roof and then I'm heading BTB." Meaning Below The Bridge, into the state's Lower Peninsula. In the minds of most Yoopers, Service included, lower also meant lesser.

The Roof was the DNR's regional service center adjacent to the max security Marquette Prison. The DNR building looked vaguely like some sort of exotic pagoda, and had been called the Roof since its dedication. Decades ago Service thought the place a dungeon. He hated desk work and offices.

"Again, my friend. Keep that damned Allerdyce out of this, or any DNR business, and *be* careful."

"We'll agree to disagree. There's a place for him with us."

"Never," she said, "and I mean it when I say keep him out."

"This eight-ball outfit is operating in the Yoop. What if somebody recognizes me?"

"That's ever a risk in undercover," she said, "but less likely in this deal. The intel on them is that they deal almost exclusively with people from other states, especially from the Mountain West, and then mainly out of the Northwest's eightball political sanctuaries and redoubts. Truth is, they trust us Yankees less than the Butternut bozos from the Deep South. They think we're morally deficient," she said, with a smirk.

"Morals are relative, variable and negotiable," Service said. "We should have hung the Rebels when we had the chance. You don't give amnesty to buzztails who like to bite."

"That's history," McKower said, "and those options aren't open to us. Eagle feathers, and out, *capisce*?"

"Yes, ma'am."

She shook her head and grinned. "I've never figured out why so many people, especially women, think you're charming."

He shrugged.

"Feathers and out," she repeated, this the theme for the day.

"Drive carefully, our highways are filled with assholes," Service told her.

"Your concern is really quite touching," she said, smiled, got up and left him with the bill, which made him laugh.

CHAPTER 4

Copper Island

KEWEENAW COUNTY

Scale of dragon, tooth of wolf.

—William Shakespeare, *Macbeth*

At first glance one might not understand who or what they were meeting when they encountered Limpy Allerdyce for the first time. The man almost always wore a deadpan mask, like something out of a kabuki play, rarely raised his raspy voice above a whisper, and perhaps worst of all, spoke a form of English that was pretty much his own, a language by one, for one, and did such a thing even make sense conceptually? Could there even *be* a language if there weren't two to palaver equally in it?

Language aside, like a sly dog, the old violator had a way of making himself understood.

The weather was hotting up in ways Yoopers abhorred. Let the mercury bob along at 30 below 0 Fahrenheit for three consecutive weeks, and you'd hear nary a complaint. But let it hit 80 one day, and Yoopers would be tearing out their own, and each other's hair. This late surge upward was making social life risky. "Been five months youse been under da covers, sonny, since seen youse. Pipples startin' gotten dere worries-up. All dis hot weather sucks. Da Kevinaw she allas get too bloody much shit weather. She hot one day, and snow, da white dirt, she come down da next. Why pipples live dis place?"

If Allerdyce was carping, it was a fair indication that he was happy enough.

"Everything so far is under control. Does the Peeps' grapevine [meaning Allerdyce alone] think I'm dead or alive?"

The old man squinted and cackled happily or dementedly. It wasn't easy to distinguish which.

McKower had wanted no part of involving the felon in the current UC operation, but both the FBI and ATF, accustomed to dealing with massive scum-balls and multiple major felons, were not only supportive, but in fact had brought Limpy's name forward back in the late fall after Service's stint in Texas prepping his biographical cover story for this case. There he had worked with someone who actually counted birds and raptors for a living and who efficiently taught him the rudiments of the job.

Special Agent Coldbeg had approached him in mid-December. "We understand you have a man, a special asset, Allerdyce. Do you think he could handle some special work in this case?"

"He's neither my man, nor the Michigan DNR's," Service said, "but he has certain skills that make him a world-class skulker."

Coldbeg said, "Once you're in deep with this entity, they will sniff your every orifice like a new dog in the pack, and if they approve, they'll want you to kill yourself to prove you belong. They believe that a new identity will put you off the grid of law enforcement."

"Sounds insane." What was Coldbeg talking about?

"They see it as practical, *de dicto* and *de re*."

What the hell was the man trying to say? "Okay?"

"They figure that dead men under new identities are less vulnerable to any and all authorities, and having died and disappeared once, they figure they can repeat such magic as often as needed."

"Normal people have no idea how to do what that requires," Service said. "Does the group assist them?"

"As far as we know, not so far."

As far as they knew from whom, and how and when? "Sounds screwy."

"Each man is on his own and can't fully join or even be seriously considered for full, permanent membership until the deal is done, and then the outfit evaluates his performance, and if the potential candidate has fucked the pooch getting it done, oh well, he's already dead and on his own, and somehow they make those facts and make-believe marry."

Death was the price of failure to measure up? What the hell? "I assume you guys will assist me with this?"

"We do this all the time with witness protection, but after you're officially dead, we'll feel better if your guardian angel is Allerdyce rather than one of our razor-cuts in a dark suit."

No argument here, though he guessed McKower and some other mucky-mucks from Law Enforcement in Lansing might wig out to find out

Allerdyce was a hand-puppet for the federal government. At some point he was going to have to level with his captain, but not yet, not this soon. "Tell me again this group's main sin other than they want to be soldier boys and dragon killers?"

"You've been told numerous times. Do you have a problem with your hearing, comprehension, or information retention?"

"Oddly enough, I have the hearing acuity of a bat and the memory of an elephant. I'm just having a very hard time getting my mind wrapped around a bunch of losers in play-army clown suits who you guys think may be a real threat to overturn our government and the American way of life."

"Cack-handed social clowns such people may be, and emotionally disturbed, Detective, but most of them also appear to have some rather impressive skills and backgrounds. And Sane Zane Harlikin is an extraordinary charismatic, whose main selling point seems to be Christian libertarianism, leave us alone to worship God our own way, blah blah, wah wah."

"There's evidence of something greater than disgruntlement?"

"Harlikin doesn't make many mistakes, and those he does make, he fixes fast and permanently."

Permanently, as in dead? Why couldn't Coldbeg talk plain English? "Where's the evidence? Show me something to put my fork in."

"We have documentation, but not nearly enough."

"So I dive into this shit with Allerdyce as my umbilical?"

"You don't think the man can handle it?"

"I know he can handle *his* part. It's you people I wonder about."

"That's just pre-op jitters."

Grady Service looked at the man. "I don't get pre-op jitters."

"The plan's the plan," Coldbeg said.

Some plan, Service thought, and now that the infiltration was a few months deep, his progress seemed strangely, aggravatingly slow. He'd managed to kill Wyndham Vold and give birth to John Eben Batanovich, Jeb for short, and what was next? Harlikin seemed a very careful fellow, and ruthless from what Coldbeg seemed to be hinting at.

The assignment was a screwy one in that part of the time he was at the ROCK camp and other times not there, but out doing his fake birds jobs while other ROCKS also came and went like he did. Some of their time together was spent in intense training, some of it familiar, and akin to basic military or police training, and some was make-work and a waste of everyone's time. How the hell others balanced their time intrigued him.

The bird counter cover story seemed to be both holding and buying him plenty of time away from Harlikin's Keweenaw compound, but so far he'd gotten not a whisper about eagle feathers, or any other feathers for that matter. All Harlikin's men wanted to talk about were guns, and animals they'd killed, or would kill, or scoring with women like it was an endorsed sport. The men closest to the colonel seemed the emotionally withdrawn type with fierce eyes and few words, their exact jobs not at all clear.

So far he'd met one with the colonel only once. As with other times and more in the meetings, Harlikin always had a body-man in the room, usually adjacent to one of the colonel's shoulders. Paranoia? Or had Harlikin legit reason to be nervous?

He'd so far given Limpy a dozen names to push to the feds for follow-up and, so far, ten of the twelve were identified from gravestones, which was interesting, but lacking any significance for anyone other than the Feebs, and probably the rest of the feds had access to some very strange databases. He and the DNR did not.

Allerdyce scowled. "Dis ain't no good, bein' messenger boy," the old man complained.

"We each have a job to do."

"Don't like mine, Sonny. Do better inside, wit' youse. Be real team dat way, side by each."

"No way in," Service told the man.

"You give 'er look-see, find one, okay dere?"

"Okay," Service said, without intending to.

"What dat big girlie doin' creepin' youse's camper?"

Worm. "You've *seen* someone?"

"Plenty time. She a looker dat one, tall as tree, and she real good in da woods."

"Why were *you* at my camper? How did *you* find it?"

"Can always find youse, Sonny."

"And there was a woman there?"

"Ya sure, youse betcha. Cedar savage, wood-tick wildwomyn."

"You followed her?"

Allerdyce grinned his crooked grin. "She don't never got no idea Limpy's even out dere."

"You know where she hangs out?"

"Mebbe," the old man allowed.

"Spit it out."

"Ain't ready. Wait."

"It's not your choice." If she was somehow part of this deal, he needed to know, how and why.

"Youse t'ink she in dis same t'ing youse in?"

"Don't know," Service said. Which was true, but his gut said she was with him, not the ROCKs.

"Trut' is, I ain't founded 'er place yet. But Limpy's gittin' hot-close."

Was the old man lying, playing games, and if so, why? "When you know, make damn sure she doesn't know that you know."

"Youse making skroink-skroinks wit' dis girlie?"

"That is *not* your business, Old Man."

"Youse got woman an' kid. How come youse don't make dickteckative Friday youse's wifey, eh?"

Good question. He had no answer reasonable or otherwise. "Maybe you and I are too set in our ways to get married."

"Youse ain't never gone be like da likes a me," Allerdyce said.

"Maybe more than you know," Service said.

"I ain't letting 'at chit 'appen," Allerdyce said determinedly. "Saw yer ol' man fall, Sonny. Won't let youse do same t'ing."

CHAPTER 5

Near Champion

MARQUETTE COUNTY

A wolf, nay, worse.

—William Shakespeare, *Comedy of Errors*

Even in a messy, complex undercover case, one had to find an occasional way home to normalcy and what passed for sanity.

"Karl, Grady Service." Karl Bonak was the legendary, longtime Marquette Channel 6 weather guru and author, a walking encyclopedia of Yooper weather, now, tomorrow, and yesterday. They had known and respected each other for years.

"The man impervious to weather. Been a long time, Grady."

"I need some advice."

"Name it and I'll do what I can."

"I want to take my granddaughter and son someplace special. But I need a mixed sunny and cloudy day this week."

"You don't want advice, you want a miracle. Even Ike didn't ask for this much from his weather guys for D-Day."

"I know and I'm sorry, but they're kids."

"Well normally I don't trade in miracles, but what part of the U.P.?"

"Near Champion."

"Champion . . . okay give me a minute."

"Still there?" Bonak said, returning to the line.

"Yessir."

"If I were a betting man, I'd say there is a possibility, and even a pretty darn good one maybe, but not a sure thing, for Wednesday afternoon between two and three-thirty. And I'm guessing it's not going to look like it until the very last moment. All clouds and rain the rest of today and tomorrow, but there could be a nice little Wednesday window for you."

"Thanks, I owe you."

"Hope it works out, Grady. We should have coffee sometime."

"We'll do it, Karl."

• • •

Granddaughter Maridly and son Shigun sat in the bucket seat beside him as he drove the grown-over two-track. The girl looked very serious as she often did when she was chewing on serious thoughts. "Bampy," she said. "I'm changing your name."

"You are? Why?"

"Bampy's a name kids use and I'm not such a kid anymore."

"You're what now, thirty-four?"

"Bampy!"

Shigun was giggling madly, as he often did.

"That's true, neither of you are such kids anymore. Do I get to hear my new name?"

"Grady," she said solemnly.

He laughed. "That *is* my name."

"Well, now it is to me, too."

"*Us*," Shigun chimed in.

"Are kids supposed to call their fathers and grandfathers by their given names?" he asked them in a serious voice.

"Well," Maridly said, her eyes twinkling. "We could just keep it at Bampy."

She knew how he hated the stupid name. "Grady's perfect."

"So, Grady," Maridly asked. "Where are we going?"

"She means, what's our destination?" Shigun added.

"The Magic Kingdom," Service told them as they drove westward from Marquette.

"The one in Florida or the one in California?" she asked. "And why are we taking the truck?"

"The one in Champion," he answered, "We're taking the truck because the roads are bad."

"There's a Magic Kingdom in Champion?" Shigun asked. "That's in the U.P."

"You're one very sharp cookie."

"He's not a cookie, he's not even a muffin, he's a boy," Maridly said.

"Ah . . . you're both a coupla goofball *Muffins*!"

"You're a *Muffin* too!" Maridly said with a squeal that sounded like radio squelch.

"There is indeed magic in Champion, Michigan," Grady told them, "Right here in our own U.P."

"The U.P. is ours?" Shigun said, astonished. "All of it?"

"Not yet, but I'm thinking about buying the whole thing and kicking everybody out."

Shigun said, "I don't want my friends to go."

"Okay," Service said, "For you, your friends can stay."

"And Maridly's," Shigun added quickly.

"Absolutely, her friends too."

"You wouldn't kid us, would you, Grady?" his granddaughter asked.

"No, honey. Fathers and grandfathers aren't allowed to kid their sons and granddaughters."

"I'm not legally your granddaughter, and Shigun's not legally your son, and you tease us *all* the time!" Maridly said.

His son had never married the girl's mother, but he *was* her grandfather. "That was back in the old days when I was Bampy. Now I'm Grady and I don't do that stuff anymore."

"You are Grady," Maridly said. "And you're the best Bampy a girl could ever have! You are."

Service kept easing down the two-track trying to see the thickly overcast and greasy gray sky. Brush scraped the sides of his personal Ford, and the sky definitely not looking like it was getting ready to spit out a miracle, but Karl said it would happen fast, and if anybody would know, KB was the man.

"This doesn't look anything like magic," Maridly ventured quietly as they pulled into a clearing. "It looks like a pile of gray rocks."

"*This* is *it*?" Shigun asked skeptically, looking around.

"Keep the faith, troops. It's both," Grady said. "magical *and* a pile of gray rocks."

The kids laughed at him, and looked disappointed, their eyes squeezed down to slits, their little jaws firmly set.

He parked the truck and they got out and the kids scampered over to him and each took one of his hands.

Maridly asked, "Where's the magic, Grady?"

"All around us," he answered.

Both kids turned slowly, looking around. "I'm not seeing it," Shigun announced.

"We'd better have lunch and just wait. Mutts or muffins, are you two hungry?"

"We're not mutts," Shigun said.

"No, *you're* a muffin," Maridly said.

Again the kids laughed like this was the funniest line ever uttered. "Mutts or muffins, are you two hungry?"

"Always," Maridly answered, "Got Grady chili?"

"Yep, and saffron cookies from the Wood'n Spoon in Mohawk."

The kids applauded. "We *love* saffron cookies!"

Grady warmed chili over a small burner set on his tailgate, and scanned the area and sky while he stirred mindlessly. When the chili was done, he ladled portions into thermos cups and gave them spoons.

"Do you think it's all right to eat your cookie before you eat your chili?" Maridly wanted to know.

"Probably not until you're all grown up."

She looked pained. "How long will that be?" she wanted to know.

"I don't know," he said, "maybe next year, or ten years, you know it's not *that* long."

"Ten years is *way* more than we've been alive," Shigun pointed out. "And that's a very long time."

"You know what?" Service said, "that's a very fine point you make. How about we say you guys are all grown up right . . . *now*?"

Both looked up at him. "Really?" Shigun said.

Service nodded. Both kids put their cups on the tailgate and grabbed their cookies and attacked them.

"Got red-hot railroad peppers for the chili?" Maridly asked as she chewed her cookie.

"My red-hot railroad peppers?"

"The ones you chop up teensy-weensy and sprinkle on everything and then Tuesday always says, 'See how smoking killed your tastebuds.' *Those* railroad peppers?"

"You bet I have them but you have to sprinkle them on lightly. If you touch them and then rub your eyes, it will make you cry. You like your chili hot?"

She made a face at him. "Melt a dinosaur's butt," she said.

Shigun laughed so hard he spit out his cookie, and dribbled saliva down his chin.

Neither kid was picky in their eating habits, and Maridly was like her namesake, Grady's late love and girlfriend Maridly Nantz, whose appetite had been legendary.

He watched the girl sprinkle peppers on the chili and saw she had remarkable hand-eye coordination, did almost everything with grace and a minimum of effort. He wondered what she would do when she grew up, not that he wanted to hurry the process, because it was already moving too fast, and he didn't get to see her that often. He wanted very much to be around for these kids growing up, and had every intention of doing so, but in this job you never knew. Like someone in the security and self-defense business once said glibly, "The day picks you."

Chili and saffron cookies consumed, they washed their hands with what Shigun called "handitizer" and Grady looked up at the sky and down at his watch. Ten minutes to two. Running out of time. If this thing was going to happen, it would be soon, or not at all. First time he'd seen it, he'd been with his old man, and a much-younger Limpy, and it had left him speechless. "Let's take a little walk," he told them and they took his hands again.

"The lunch was good, but the magic's not much," Maridly said as they walked.

"Let's head over to the edge of the hill," he told them.

Shigun said, "Edge of a hill, like a cliff?"

"Just a small one," Grady answered, "but we have to be careful. The footing can be bad."

"I'm like a mountain goat," Maridly announced. "No worries, Grady."

When they neared the edge he made sure to keep them back, but he didn't make a big to-do about safety. Still overcast. He lifted his binoculars off his chest and scanned the greening marsh below.

He felt the sun before he saw it, and then there it was, bright and hot for this time of year.

Maridly shrieked, "It's *Magic*!" as the sun struck the hill and turned the ground to twinkling white diamond fire as specular hematite began winking thousands of tiny points of light. As the kids cheered and sang some ditty he'd never heard, he kept his binos sweeping the marsh and when he passed over a dark lump, he stopped moving and reversed direction and adjusted focus.

Maridly squealed. "The Magic Kingdom! You brought us to our own Magic Kingdom, Grady!"

He felt warm inside.

The kids yelled "It's a miracle!"

And Grady Service, his binos now finally focused on the lump on the swamp ground below them said, "Son . . . of . . . a . . . bitch!"

The kids scowled. Maridly told him, "You mustn't say naughty words. *Why* did you say that word, Grady?"

"There's a moose down there," Service said.

"Can we look?" the girl asked.

"No, honey, it's dead."

"Can we go gut it, Grady?" Maridly asked.

God, how things came back to you. Last year he had taken them to his deer blind and shot a buck and they both had been so fascinated by the gutting they wanted him to name every organ in the dead animal. Neither of them seemed the slightest bit fazed by the sight or smell of warm blood and viscera. It had been a great moment.

"We can't gut this one, guys."

"But you said it's dead," Shigun pointed out.

"It's not supposed to be dead," he said.

His precocious granddaughter said, "Everything dies, Grady. It's how life works. My daddy died and I never even got to *meet* him. That makes me real sad, but Mum says that's just how life is sometimes. I wish I had memories of my daddy."

Daddy was Grady's late son, murdered along with Nantz, his girlfriend. "I wish you did too, honey." He wished they both did.

"How'd the moose die?" Shigun asked.

Moose hunting was illegal in Michigan, and this one had been shot. "Some jerk poached it." The head and antlers were gone, and, he guessed, not all that long ago.

“Can we eat it?” Shigun asked. “It shouldn’t be wasted.”

“You’re right about that, bud, but we have to call a biologist to come out and look at it and tell us how and when it died.”

“Will *he* gut it?” Maridly asked.

“I don’t know, honey. Maybe.”

“Good, I hope he does,” she said. “I feel sorry for Mister Moose.”

So did he. She had said the very same thing after he shot the buck last year. When she had her first taste of fresh venison, she had held up her fork and announced, “Sorry, Mr. Deer, thanks for your food.”

He had laughed then. Now he felt like crying.

“Can we see?” she asked.

Let them or not? “We have to leave it for the biologist for now,” he told them, and handed Maridly the binos and helped her pinpoint the dead animal.

He noticed she was grimacing. “I don’t see any—sonovabitch! Somebody cut off Mr. Moose’s head!”

“You’re not supposed to use naughty words like that,” he said.

“You say them, and Mr. Moose doesn’t have his head. Why?”

“I think somebody wanted the antlers,” Service told them.

“Sonovabitch,” Shigun said, echoing Maridly. “Are you going to bust his ass, Grady?”

Grady shook his head. “When I find him, hon.” If he found him.

“Know what, Grady?” Maridly said.

“What?”

“This is our U.P. Magic Kingdom and that means you’ll find the bad man and bust him. The Good Guys always win in the Magic Kingdom.”

“They do, do they?”

“Damn right,” she said, and grabbed his hand and squeezed it hard. “I love you, Bampy.”

“What happened to Grady?”

“Sometimes a girl needs her Bampy.”

“Did a wolf get it?” Shigun asked.

Grady looked at his son. “Something worse than a wolf, kid.”

“What’s worse than a wolf?” the boy wanted to know.

“Us,” Grady said. “People.”

CHAPTER 6

Near Champion

MARQUETTE COUNTY

This way lies the game.

—William Shakespeare, *Henry VI, Part III*

Grady dropped the kids with Tuesday in Harvey, turned around, and returned directly to the moose-kill site.

He had tried and failed to find a Marquette County officer. They were all on pass or occupied with other things, so he called the new probationary conservation officer in Houghton County and asked him to drift over to Champion. Not exactly Hoyle, but neither was killing moose.

The new PCO's name was causing a distant buzz in Service's brain, but registering nothing useful. The new officer stood maybe five-eight and with five-pound weights in his pockets might tip the scales at 160, but he had a barracuda's eyes and a come-hither smile preachers sometimes ascribed to the devil.

Bapcat was one of two new officers in Houghton and Keweenaw Counties, both out of the same DNR academy class, and one look at the kid's eyes and smile and Service knew he would be good, and this even before he figured out who he really was.

"This isn't my county," the new officer greeted Service.

"I'm Service. Hop into my truck, shut up, and listen," Grady told him. "Word is you were with the SEAL teams almost ten years."

"I know who you are, and word is that you were a jarhead. We got oil and water here?"

"Not on my part," Service said. "I've always thought rust-pickers were pretty amusing. Why'd you leave the Navy and SEALs?"

"Had enough kicking in doors at night and scaring the shit out of families."

"You think that sorta shit's wrong?" Service asked.

"For the place and politics where we got sent, no way, but it got into my mind over time that if I was going to be a law upholder, I'd rather do it in my country under oath and badge, and a functioning legal system. I never much liked the vigilante gig."

"That what it was?"

"More often than not."

"How'd you like our training school?"

"The physical part wasn't all that demanding, but the mental part, the cop mind, that took some adjustment."

"But you were number one in your class."

"Only because I worked my butt off for it."

"You like being number one, the big winner?"

"Just like you, I hear. Are we two battle dogs sniffing each other's asses?"

Service grinned. "I'm not even here. I don't exist."

Bapcat stared at him. "What?"

"I'm undercover and just wanted to meet you. Do you know anything about the new Keweenaw officer?"

"Something," Bapcat said.

"I guess something fits the category of anything," Service said.

"She was my main competition at school. She's about the size and bulk of a popcorn fart with the brain and heart of an aircraft carrier."

"Seriously."

"Patty Something's the real thing."

Had he heard right?

Bapcat smiled. "Yup, her actual name is really Something."

"That's a new one on me. You know we do some of our best work at night?" Grady asked.

"I heard that. How many times have COs gotten the address wrong?"

"So far? Never, but it's always possible, I suppose, if you don't nail all your details."

"Where I was, we were right about half the time, and I am talking about some very long-ass stretches in the game. This did not sit well with the teams, and it remained a problem when I detached and separated," Bapcat replied.

"We don't move in until we're *ready*," Service said, "and those who have to go in, always make the final decision. We're not anonymous chess pieces being jerked around by shiny brass collars and Lansing politicians."

"That's why I'm here," Bapcat said, "to play my game in the context of our game, and not their game. I hate suits with snoots in the federal money trough, so am I supposed to be with you for a while?"

"You're not supposed to be with me at all," Service said. "I'm oot and aboot for a while."

"Deep undercover?"

"Just oot and aboot is how we like to put it. You always talk so much and so candidly?"

"I'm fixing that right now. Done talking."

"While we're together I have only three rules. First, never fart in my truck. Ever. Second, never call me dude."

"That's two," Bapcat observed.

"The third rule's whatever I think ought to be a rule at the moment I need it."

"Kinda chickenshit egocentric view of the Grady Service world," the new officer said.

"Rule Three, never use big words like 'egocentric' and for the record, I happen to like chickenshit rules when I'm the one making them."

"You gonna ask me if I shot people over there?"

"Runway behind you. Yesterday's in the shit pile. All we get now is today and tomorrow."

"Never figured you for a philosopher."

"You figured right, kid."

"Don't call me kid, dude."

Grady looked at the other man and smirked. "I think we'll get along just fine, rust-picker. What did the academy teach you about moose cases?"

"That they are big freaking deals and that dead ones stink. That what this is about, a moose case?"

"No, numb-nuts, you think it's a *zebra*? Of course, it's a moose. In Marquette County."

"Not my turf," Bapcat said.

Service grabbed the new officer's sleeve, and turned him sideways: "Look at your patch. It says Michigan, not 'that ain't my county.' And why the hell do you think I mentioned moose if the case wasn't a moose?"

"I have no idea what rule we're on now."

"Does it matter? I ask about a moose, there's a nine in ten chance we have some business with a moose."

"We?"

"I meant you. I just said we to make you feel better."

"You don't have to look out for my feelings. Will knowing the case involves a moose lessen the stench?"

"Not one iota."

"So now you get to use fancy words, and I don't?"

"Life's a bitch ain't it, rust-picker."

"Call me Jordy or J.L."

"This moose lands in your lap, Jordy, and you're lucky. Most officers will never catch a moose case." Then it sank in. "Bapcat, *that* Bapcat, the way-back Keweenaw officer?"

"Great-great-grandson."

"That a burden?"

"Time will tell. It seems like someone always brings him up."

"He was a *great* officer."

"I never knew the man."

"You look just like pictures of him." Why had he not noticed this right away?

"Yah, I've heard that one too. But my great-great was adopted."

"Wow," Service said. "I still see the spitting image."

"About the moose?" Bapcat said.

"What moose?" Service said.

"Our moose case."

"I don't have a moose case. *You* do."

"What exactly am I supposed to do?"

"Investigate, make the case, solve it, and hammer the asshole who did it. That's why the people of this great state pay your ass so much money."

"Suggestions, hints, tips?"

"Yah, don't fuck up."

"Because it would make you look bad?"

"No, numb-nuts, because it's your first case and you can't win them all if you don't win the first one. And because fucking up will make *you* look bad."

"You're a maniac," Bapcat told the detective.

"Ding-dong, now that's some *big* news. That's your tip."

"What the hell are you talking about?"

"Ding dongs, maniacs. It takes a real knucklehead to poach an elk, wolf, eagle, bear or moose in this state, because even the dumbest violators out there know we go ballistic over such cases and the one thing maniacs without badges fear most are maniacs *with* badges."

"Are you saying there are no rules in cases like this?"

"No, I'm saying we want the wingnuts to *think* that's how it is."

Bapcat looked at Grady. "That is actually a useful tip—I think."

"You think all former Marines are poster children for the home of the brave."

"All of them I've known are poster children for some kind of home, and I make it a point to never think at all about former Marines."

"There are no former Marines," Service said. "Once a Marine, always a Marine, but I'm glad to hear a former canvas-climber's opinion. Most Navy guys make it a point to never think at all."

Bapcat laughed. "You haven't heard that the Navy's progressed past sailcloth and masted schooners?"

"Glad to hear that because most former or ex-Navy guys I know make it a point to never think, period."

"Do we have a corpus delicti?" the PCO asked.

"Damn right. See that creepy little fucker over there by that gray rock pile?"

"He one of ours?"

"Kind of. His name is Allerdyce."

"Oh fuck," Bapcat said.

Service laughed. "Now I see how you got to be number one."

"Is he like *with* us . . . officially?"

"He doesn't even exist officially on this deal."

"This is like totally weirding me out," Bapcat said.

"You have no idea, yet. But don't worry. He doesn't bite—much."

"So I go with him, and not with you?"

"You go with him and God's good grace—like all the rest of humankind."

"You tip the weird scale pretty hard by yourself."

Grady flashed his best professional smile. "Done talking, get out of my truck."

Service put down his window and held out a cigar to the kid. "Good time to shut off your olfactory lobes. This stinker will help."

"Thanks but I'll smoke it for pleasure. I was born without those lobes."

"Lucky you. This is the right calling for you."

"That's the same thing SEAL leadership told me."

"Were they wrong?"

"Not for a long while."

"Good. This is a great way of life, Bapcat, with a good paying job thrown in."

"*Semper Fi*," Bapcat said and began walking toward Limpy Allerdyce.

Grady Service was tickled beyond words. He couldn't wait to hear what Limpy would say when he found out who Bapcat was.

CHAPTER 7

Harvey

MARQUETTE COUNTY

I do in friendship counsel thee to leave this place.
—William Shakespeare, *As You Like It*

They were making their usual breakfasts, each doing their own thing, the conversation usually nil. Grady was hand-piling Dodos (Cheerios) on his instant oatmeal (two packets, adding no-sugar-added peaches), and wondering what sort of juneberry crop would come in July, if any, and Tuesday rubbed his arm lightly. "You awake?"

"Twilight zony, but steadily gaining altitude. What?"

"Remember that murder case you passed to the county?"

"Vaguely." This had been quite a few years ago. "The dentist who allegedly helped his son bury a woman in the U.P.? Way long ago. Nobody could find a body or even a named missing person to match the claim. That case?"

"Freedo thinks he's got something."

Joe "Freedo" Feldt was a Marquette County homicide detective, a quiet, effective cop who made no waves ever, except where there was a case he took on, and a solution he was convinced was right. Under those circumstances he was the definition of stubborn, and a Tasmanian devil in the interests of justice being served. Over the years Feldt had managed to solve quite a number of very cold cases.

"Really?"

"Could be," Tuesday said. "He wants to meet with me tomorrow, show me what's he's got. Too bad you'll be gone again. This whole UC thing is getting *real* old. Bub."

He didn't disagree. He was in and out of the situation, mostly to uphold his undercover identity. "Maybe I'd better show you my stuff before he shows you his stuff."

"That was last night," she said, smiling. "You crack me up. Act your age."

"What age might that be?"

"Nobody can count that high," she fired back, and he laughed.

Friday shook her head. "Honestly, Grady, I can't remember how old you are. You're like that obnoxious bunny with drums that used to be on the TV, and by the way, and for the record, I hate it when you go undercover, especially a case that drags on like this. It scares the hell out of me. Undercover work is for younger officers."

"And just last night you were praising my youthful vigor, and besides, no case goes on forever."

"Unless it kills you."

"That's not fair," he said.

"That's my point," she came back. "No undercover job can last forever, no matter how insignificant it looks at the starting line, so don't be blowing smoke up my skirt."

"You're not *wearing* a skirt," he said.

"Knock off the chip and lip. You know damn well what I'm saying about undercover work and younger officers."

"I think my age makes perfect sense in this case. Who uses old farts for UC?"

"Sometimes I'm not sure what dimension you're living in," she told him.

"It's the same world you're in," he told her.

"You only live in my world part-time and that's not enough for me, or for Shigun, or for Maridly. And when you're here part-time it's often not even a major part."

"My world *is* you, Shigun, and Maridly," Service said.

"And your dog Newf, and Allerdyce, and Treebone, and Shark, and . . . "

"Hey, your point's made. I can walk and chew crud."

"Gum or cud," she corrected him.

"I never touch the crap, it sticks to my teeth."

"You have no teeth. They all got knocked out one night—when you were undercover?"

"I no longer recall, but I will concede the possibility and every point if you must insist."

"This isn't tennis, Service. It's our life and we're living it apart."

"I hear you," he said.

"No, you hear the sounds, but not what's in the sounds. I'm going to stay on this point until you wise up and hang it up."

"What would you and the boy do with me underfoot all day?"

She sniggered. "We will have no trouble sorting that out."

"I have a case to solve."

"And then you'll hang it up?"

"I never *said* that." He'd never really thought it either and, so far, the mere thought of retirement disoriented him. Retire? Why? What would be the point? "What's Freedo got that he feels the need to share?"

"You know the man: forthcoming isn't in his operating genetic code, but I've gleaned some information from other sources."

"Not Freedo?"

"Only partly and indirectly from him."

Service loved this about Tuesday. She was a great investigator, creative, relentless, dogged, and when it came to crime and criminals she was genuinely cold-blooded and processed what she had while shutting off her personal beliefs and prejudices other than her absolute belief in justice and fairness.

Tuesday looked at him. "This is all tenty-tenty, yes?"

"Tenty-tenty?" he asked.

"Meaning extremely tentative and paper thin."

Grady nodded. "Okay, tenty-tenty it is. Go."

Tuesday said, "Couple of Tech students up in the Keweenaw were exploring an old mine adit that led to a shaft and one of them fell about twenty feet and got busted up pretty good and couldn't climb out on his own, or even with his buddy's help, so they called 9-1-1. One of your officers was closest and first on scene and rappelled down the steep stope so she could get over to the kid. I can't remember what's called what in hard-rock mines."

"Which one of our officers?"

"PCO Something. Fresh out of recruit school."

"And she was out alone?"

"Her partner's got the flu. You want to hear this or play mealy-mouthed prosecutor for adherence to department policy?"

Service bowed his head. "I'm all ears."

"She gets the victim his help and while she's down there, she starts looking around and she sees skeletons. Want to know what kind?"

"Cave bears?"

"Wrong."

"I'm all ears now. I can't believe cave bears was wrong. I really like cave bears. So what kind of skeletons?"

"Human, seven so far."

"Good grief."

"Good grief, and holy shit, indeed, and *molto* flukey. One is female, still had some hair and a gold bracelet on her wrist. The bracelet has an inscription, TLOML, and a date."

"DOB?"

"One possibility," she said.

"Freedo's cold case?"

"He's holding that option open. But based on where your informant said they buried the body, this is not likely that same case, right?"

"If it isn't Freedo's cold case, it's maybe someone's open, hot and current case."

"That's what I'm thinking."

"Which county?"

"Keweenaw."

"Where?" he asked.

"Don't have the precise loke yet. When the kid had the accident, the cops put a silencer on the whole deal, lest the skeletons news leak."

"Could be the old bones of miners."

"Could be, but not the woman. And the clothing fragments were vintage by any measure."

He looked at her. "What the hell more can Freedo tell you? You seem to know everything already."

"Isn't that a detective's job?"

"It's kind of creepy," he said.

"Detectives are a blend of nihilism, skepticism and Lahrism?"

"What the hell is Lahrism?"

"Bert Lahr. *If I only had a heart—for courage.*"

"You've got plenty of all that, and sexy too."

"For an old broad?"

"For any broad. Sexy doesn't carry an age limit. You think this cold case will ever get solved?"

"Not by me it won't, but my guts have always told me that there was a lot more to the claim than some anonymous dentist helping his son out of a misguided sense of familial solidarity."

"Guts don't think," Grady said.

"All body parts can think," she said. "Take last night."

"I'll happily take all the last nights we can," he told her.

"Which is why you need to hang it up, Bucko."

"Not ready yet."

"Will you ever be ready?"

"What do you think?" he asked her.

"Like I said before, I think undercover work is for the young."

"You're putting a stick to my happy?"

"You're only happy when your ass is hanging out the window of something going two hundred miles an hour in the dark, and drugged-up violators are trying to run you off a cliff."

"That's never happened," he said.

She smirked. "Yet. I can see the gleam in your eyes, Old Man."

CHAPTER 8

Camp ROCK

KEWEENAW COUNTY

Honour is mere scutcheon: And so ends my catechism.
—William Shakespeare, *Henry IV, Part I*

Abel Tooler was six and a half feet tall and sometimes was paired with Service in training with his newfound ROCK comrades. Tooler was a quiet man with the eyes of a zombie, in astonishing ultra-ripped physical condition and, as they began to work at their training tasks, Tooler pushed his older partner to extremes Service had not pushed himself to in years.

In strength drills involving the lifting and moving of two-hundred-pound boulders, Tooler asked, "Need a break?"

Service said, "No breaks, let's double our rate. We're too pokey."

Tooler looked at his partner as if he were demented. "You're a hard-headed old man," Tooler said.

Old? What was it about people and loose language?

"When was the last time on an actual real mission you had to lift two hundred pounds of dead weight?" Service asked his younger partner. The question was designed only to buy time, not elicit an answer. This boulder-moving crap was killing him.

"Every mission for me, and not ever for others," Tooler said.

What the hell was the man talking about? He wanted to ask, but knew better than to press for details or a deeper explanation, at least not yet. It seemed sometimes that all the lips in this outfit were sealed with Gorilla glue. Their silence and inverted ways made the National Security Agency look like a gossip factory.

The ROCKs were neither friendly nor unfriendly, which he supposed benefited their presumed newly acquired status of deceased and reborn. They were not the least bit social, never complained, had no senses of humor he could detect, and showed no hint of anything he could call esprit de corps or morale, a quality every fighting unit had to possess if they expected to prevail and have results.

In his day, war-fighters tended to be individualists who willingly operated in and as teams in order to be effective units. Individualist operators, absent social glue, were not the sort of bricks one wanted for a foundation.

"Guys here don't talk much," Service commented as he struggled to wrestle another boulder.

"Work time, training time, worship time, social time, everybody's got their own schedule and keep to themselves," Tooler said as he too tried to pick up a boulder, but lost his grip and it fell and hopped about three feet down a short, steep slope. Grady dropped his boulder with the others they had moved, came back to Tooler, and grabbed the rock the other man had dropped.

"Don't," Tooler said. "It's mine."

"Your name isn't chiseled anywhere on it," Service told him, lifted the boulder, and stumbled over to the drop area. "You drop it, your teammate picks it up, that's how teams work," Service said quietly.

"Who the heck were you with before this-here, the Foreign Legion or the Gray Panthers?"

"You keep dogging my age," Service joked. "I may have to show you what real dogging is."

"You could try," Tooler said ominously.

"Now's good for me," Service said. "Now good for you, Abel?"

"Training is training," the younger man said. "We can't be messing it up with personal stuff."

"Or fun," Service said.

Tooler stared at the older man. "You think *this* is fun?"

"I think kicking your ass would be fun? What's life without some dust-ups?"

Tooler gave him the sort of look some reserved for harebrains and fools. "Don't think I'm afraid of you," he said, and sighed.

"I'd never insult you with words, friend, just action. You want me to grab another boulder for you? You're looking sort of peaked today."

"I don't need no help from nobody," Tooler said.

"You mean you don't want my help. Maybe you're slowing down and at your limit and don't want to admit it. We all have limits."

"Limits ain't allowed."

"Too much talk here. This is serious training," Toller declared.

"Only one of us is training seriously. The other one's starting to drag his ass, and he knows it and hates knowing it, and can't get his head around taking some help."

"I've *got* this," Tooler insisted. "I do."

And with that, Grady Service knew he was into Tooler's head. "So you say, but I just moved a third boulder for you, and my three as well. The behinder you go, the behinder you get."

"I ain't *behind*. Ain't nobody counting this shit."

"Shit? I thought this was serious training."

Tooler put his massive hands on his hips. "You think you're Superman?"

"Superman was nothing but a creep in pretty pajamas, and an illegal immigrant. You think I'm an alien, Abel? Do I look alien? No, of course I don't. I look just like you, proud and white and Christian."

"But a lot older," Tooler retorted.

"I'll give you that. See, I'm not Superman and neither are you."

"Trainees ain't supposed to talk."

Service took hold of Tooler's fourth boulder, but the younger man pushed him aside. "Mine."

"Must be your break's over."

"That weren't no break."

"The boulder count says different."

"You're one strange motherfucker," Tooler said, hoisting the boulder and moving it.

Service smiled.

"Why you grinning like that, Old Man?"

"First, that's the only off-color thing you said since I met you. I was starting to think you're some kind of android fueled up on artificial intelligence. Second, what kind of army worth a shit doesn't throw around motherfucker with every other word?"

Tooler half grinned. "We're all human."

"Good to know," Service said. Clearly these men were all damaged goods in some way. "How long we got to move these rocks?"

"Till whistle sounds, same as always."

"We're like Pavlov's dogs."

"Who?"

"Ivan Pavlov, a Russian scientist who studied dogs and learned that his dog linked a bell to eating, so if Pavlov hit the bell, the dog started salivating, whether it got food then or not."

"We ain't drooling."

"Yet," Service said. "You ever think that this is some sort of elaborate game we're playing?"

"Ain't nothing here feels like no game to me."

"The best and worst games are those that don't look like or feel like games," Service said, "especially given how much *we pay* to do this crap. But to be honest with ourselves, it is one great trick to get us to give them big bucks and then have to wear these cheap-ass costumes. We look like silly damn mustard seeds."

"It's an honor to be a ROCK," Tooler implored.

"Really? Maybe sometime you would be so kind as to show me how we measure this honor thing."

"You make my brain tired," Tooler told Service.

"That's because you aren't keeping up with the boulders," Service said, grabbing another from Tooler's pile, moving it, and forcing himself to smile while he wondered if something inside would break if they had to keep doing this make-work crap.

Tooler said, "Don't do that no more, okay?"

"The more appropriate response would be 'Thanks, Partner,'" Service said.

"Our only partner is Jesus," Abel Tooler said.

"You think he thinks that too?" Service asked.

Tooler sighed and stared at him.

Service knew he might've pushed too far. "You think Jesus told knock-knock jokes?"

"You got you one very weird brain," Tooler said.

"Too many concussions," Service explained.

"I get *that* shit," Tooler said.

• • •

He'd pushed hard on Tooler's buttons without much of a response he could use. In working undercover, your goal was to push upward until you found your object, in this case, alleged bald eagle feathers, but Tooler was in most ways a very hard read, and given the pushes during their training session he was afraid he'd honked off the man and he regretted this. Tooler was an okay guy, not a thinker, merely a follower, and when you were behind the curtain there was no point making enemies, especially when everyone you met undercover was an enemy or foe by definition.

The ROCKs who visited The Fortress slept in a single barracks room with twenty bunk beds, capacity of forty, but Service had never seen more than six or eight men in the bunk room, and these quarters were separate from the colonel and his body-men and a couple of others with dubious ranks and duties.

After chow Service found Abel Tooler sitting alone on a stump outside the mess hall cabin, smoking. The colonel/commander allegedly never smoked, toked, or drank, but did not forbid such pursuits by his men, and from what Service had seen so far, this all-male outfit leaned sharply toward asceticism.

Service walked over to Tooler. "Sorry about getting into your shit today. The outfits I've been in, we always pushed each other all the time, nothing personal, for the betterment of the unit. I was out of line."

Tooler looked up with tired eyes. "I've been down them roads too," he said.

"We good?" Service asked.

The man shrugged. "It don't mean nothing."

An old troop term from Vietnam, but this guy was not nearly old enough for that war. Where had he picked up that lingo? "Last time I heard those words the next words out were, 'We gotta get out of this place if it's the last thing we ever do.' Turned out for a lot of guys, getting out of there meant getting dead, and it *was* the last thing they ever did."

"Was a song by somebody, right?" Tooler said, for the first time showing a little glimmer of life in his voice and manner. Tooler held out a pack of Marlboro Light 100s to Service, who took one, lit up, and sat on a chunk of firewood.

"The Animals," Service said. "A great group."

"You was a volunteer?"

Service nodded. "Marine."

"Heard that whole deal sucked."

"For some more than others."

"You?"

"Couldn't bitch. I volunteered. You volunteer, you get on board, right?"

"Like here and this," Tooler said. "We're all volunteers in this outfit."

"*Are* we volunteers, or *recruits*?" Service asked.

Tooler stared at the ground. "What's the difference, volunteer or recruit? We have a shared mission."

"Really? To share a mission the guys have to, every one of them, know what it is," Service said. "Or are we in some kind of test-the-new-guy period before they lay out the real shit?"

"Some one-timers can get confused," mass-of-muscle Tooler said.

"You a one-timer?" Service asked. This term was a new one.

"Ain't none of us knows that," Tooler told him. "And ain't that some shit! The old man can talk team and mission, but if what he's sayin' don't match up with doing. . . . "

"Are you telling me every one of us here for training is here for a one-time job?"

"That's scuttlebutt from some of the men."

Service took brief refuge in this fact. This group, like every military group, lived at some level on scuttlebutt versus official pronouncements, and this could create some troublesome reality gaps. "Scuttlebutt ever say what kind of one-time jobs?"

Tooler shook his head, took a drag on a cigarette. "You one strong sumbitch for an old man."

"That a compliment?"

"I ain't all that sure yet," Tooler said and laughed out loud, and Service laughed with him.

"Truth, man," Service said. "That was mostly show today. I didn't want my age to brand me as the weak one. Whenever a man gets tagged with that, you know how shit flows, and it ain't uphill."

"I get it," Tooler said. "What you do for work when you ain't here?"

"I count birds."

"You *what*?"

"Count birds. You got a problem with birds?"

"What kind of birds?"

"Whatever the outfit payin' me wants me to count."

"Like Heckles and Jeckles, and Tweety Bird and such?"

Heckle, Jeckle, and Tweety Bird? Good grief. "Pretty much."

"That's cool," Tooler said and smiled.

"How about you when you're not here?"

"Transport."

Transportation? "That's a big field. What exactly?"

"I deliver school busses or RVs from companies make them in Indiana to wholesalers, mostly in the Midwest, but I've been all the way down to El Paso and Key West, and up to Seattle too."

"One-way drops? You fly home?"

"Public bus."

"That sucks."

"Cheap though and my choice. They pay me real good to make deliveries, why burn through your shit just getting home? Planes ain't cheap."

"A practical and frugal man."

"Raised that way," Tooler said.

"Sounds like a pretty good gig, delivering stuff."

"After a while routine gets boring. But you get used to it, I don't even notice it no more."

"Like here and this?" Service said.

Tooler lit another cigarette and handed the pack to Service again. "I ain't got used to nothing here yet."

"You had much contact with the colonel?" Service asked.

"I think it's too vague for me. You ever hear that kind of talk from the colonel himself?"

"The colonel don't talk to the likes of me. He talks mainly to Perms."

"Perms?"

"Them guys he brought all the way in already."

"Like guys who've done a mission for the outfit?" Service ventured.

"I don't know. All I know is I heard he bring on some Perms on account they got special skills. Did you talk to him?"

"Do I look like the kind he'd talk to?"

Tooler frowned. "I just don't know what that man wants or expects."

"What are we *doing* here?" Service asked his compatriot. "We can't train 24/7 and we can't train properly unless our mission is clear and we know how our role fits the big picture, right?"

"I hear you," Tooler said. "I really do, man. The only thing I know for sure I don't know nothing, but I heard this Perm one day say something to another guy about the Sank."

"Which is?"

"No idea, but it seems to hot them up and then I realized that I maybe heard something wasn't supposed to hear, so they walked away quick, and didn't have nothing to do with me after that."

"Piss you off?"

"More like creeped me out, like I had the leprosy or something."

Risk time. "How about if I hear anything about the Sank, I tell you what I heard, and you do the same for me? Over time maybe we can find the light together."

"I ain't no damn spy," Tooler said forcefully.

"This isn't spying. We're trying to become good ROCKs are we not?"

"I guess."

Time to shift gears again and Service took one of the cigarettes and lit it. "I owe you a pack, brother?"

"Ain't no big deal," Tooler said.

"You on the time-pay plan with your K and C?"

"Hell no," Tooler said. "I have always sucked at paying bills. I got me together a lump, but it was like really hard. I sold almost everything I owned, divorced my old lady, got half her shit too, and I sold that. Then I drove buses till I couldn't see straight, and saved up."

"Kids?"

"Don't got no kids, and don't want none. How you do your K and C?"

"Robbed a bank."

Tooler started to chuckle, but stopped. "Truly?"

"Fuckin' eh. Banks have money. And I don't. Think Robin Hood."

"Robin Who?"

"Guy who robbed sheriffs in England."

"Never knew sheriffs had money like banks."

"Robin Hood was long ago, in a place far, far away."

Tooler's face lit up. "Far, far away, like *Star Wars*, man! They doin' a sequel on the Robin dude? I seen all them *Star Wars* movies."

"Not that I heard."

"Too bad, man. They did, I'd go. Robin Hood?"

"Yeah, Hood, like on sweatshirt. It ain't his real name. It's like his post-dead name, like us."

"Way cool," Tooler said. "He believe in Jesus too, this Hood?"

"Probably. He went on Crusades."

"What that is, Crusade?"

"Bunch of Christian guys get together like a posse and head for the Holy Land to kick Arab asses."

"The Christian guys got rockets and tanks and choppers and drones and such shit?"

"No, this was a long time back when they fought with spears and bows and arrows and swords, and such. They used horses like tanks."

"Man, you know some sweet shit. You go to school long time?"

"Longer than I wanted to."

"I always wanted to go to school more, but our old lady she traveled all the time, and dragged us with her."

"Her job?"

"Not like you and me know a job. She was all the time changing husbands."

"That must've been hard on you."

Tooler looked nonplussed. "Didn't make me no never-mind. You have an old man you knew?"

"Not really. He was a lush."

"That's some hard shit," Tooler said. "My old lady, too. Killed her ass finally, your old man too?"

"Him too."

"We be pods, you and me, Old Bro."

Pods indeed. "We better break this up before one of the Perms gets thinking we're planning a coup."

Tooler laughed. "Me? Not no way."

Service thought the younger man's voice a bit strained. "What you think all this means?"

"I ain't all that sure yet, but after dropping all my savings into it, I ain't leavin', no matter what," Tooler said.

The Sank? What the hell was that? This *place* was getting weirder and creepier by the minute.

CHAPTER 9

Copper Island

KEWEENAW COUNTY

> Such welcome and unwelcome things at once, Tis hard to reconcile.
>
> —William Shakespeare, *Hamlet*

Absent clothes, Limpy Allerdyce looked like a hairless pug, all wrinkles and folds, set off by his eternal ain't-I-cute-and-who-can't-wait-to-pet-me look.

Service had to rub his eyes to make sure he was seeing what he appeared to be seeing, Limpy trussed with duct tape in the camper's only chair, made of wooden spindles and not sturdy by any measure. It came with the camper, a sort of trademark of the dealer in Marquette who sold Back-Home RVs and employed, "Ain't a little wooden chair like we grew up with, a perfect touch of home?" "God save us from all salesmen," Friday liked to say.

Allerdyce looked entirely too content. Service read the situation in a split second, before Worm, standing behind the door, stepped into the light to proudly announce, "Worm she got It, by God she did."

Predictably, she was *au naturel*, and if anything, her figure was even more memorable. "I think Worm get got," he told her.

"Worm don't get got she don't want get got," she replied in her ever-disturbing third person gibberish.

"Dat dere girlie's a synanthrope," Allerdyce said, with a vague hint of his near demonical cackle. The old violator seemed to be enjoying this! Whatever *this* was.

"Impressive word for the likes of one trussed in tape," Service told him.

"Tell girlie His name," Limpy implored. "Tell Her Him a Him not no It."

Service looked at his house guard. "Why did Worm feel the need to wrap that . . . thing, in tape?"

"Was snoop-around, and Worm catched him good."

Service looked down at the old man. "You feelin' a chill? *Were* you snooping around here?"

"Already 'splained this. Don't like dis deal youse put goin'."

"That's not your business," Service told him.

"Youse is *my bidnet*," Allerdyce said gruffly.

"Him *Her* business, Not Old Man It's business," Worm said to make her view known.

"Ain't Her bidnet," Allerdyce said. "Girlie!"

Worm looked at Service, and said brusquely, "Worm say what Worm's business. Him Boss want Her Make Old Man, It go poof-poof, bye-bye?"

Grady couldn't help smiling. "Been a whole lot of people tried to make that thing disappear, yet It still be."

"Sits," Worm corrected him. "Worm did good," she added.

"Worm get got," the detective told her again.

"Mister Tell Worm why Mister think that," she insisted.

"Your old, trussed, hairless pug is Allerdyce, whom, I think is a lot like Worm, but old enough to be your great-great-great-great—"

"Knock offen dat great-great, Sonny. Limpy ain't old. Limpy just cured real sweet and nice."

"Butchers cure only dead meat," Service said.

"Worm think Her hear nothing makes sense."

"Get used to it," Service said. "You hang around that thing too much, nothing will ever make sense. How's Worm think she got the get on it?"

"Watch It two day. It good in woods, Worm have to give It that, but It not Worm-good. Worm let it see Her, and when It settle down to watch her It went sleep. and make Worm grab It real fast before could run or fight." She gave Allerdyce a severe look of disapproval. "It don't look like much, Worm thinks."

Service said, "Let's make some coffee," and he looked at Worm. "Time we add to your education. That thing there is already loose. I don't know how, but if he wants to stand up right now and grab you, he can do so. You only think you caught him unawares. You walked into a trap."

Her consternation showed. "What unawares means?"

"By surprise. You thought you were surprising It, but it was It who got you to make the grab."

She shook her head. "No fight. Worm surprise big! No problem."

"Her like dat Tarzan jamoke, raised up by gorillerapes, but bein' human bean, she can't do widout da likes of us pipples."

"Tarzan, isn't, wasn't and never will be real," Service lectured the old man. "How about you get out of that stupid chair and put on some clothes? We're sick of looking at you."

"Girlie dere tooken Limpy's duds and he don't got none now," the old man said.

"Give clothes back to It," Service told her. "You *do* have them, right?"

"Worm got. Too small keep for Worm."

"This man is friend, not enemy."

"Worm catch snoop-around."

"That is undoubtedly true and in that regard both of you are very much alike, but he was snooping because he was worried about me."

"Worm worry 'bout Mister too," she said with pout.

"You still think something bad will happen to me?" Service asked her.

She grimaced. "Think Mister try Welsh Worm on what Him Her owe."

"Worm's been cheated before?"

"*Foo*, Worm not Him tell."

"Fair enough, but just get the man's clothes. I need food and time to think, not waste time playing capture-the-flag with you two oddballs."

"Worm not oddball," she said. "She pearl in rough."

Limpy stood up and all the tape fell to the floor. "Dat how gottatalk to Sonny-boy," Limpy said to Worm.

Her mouth was open. Service said, "See Worm get got. It Allerdyce let Worm take It."

"Mister wrong," she protested.

"Maybe so, but there stands Captain America in all Its glory. Get his damn clothing, and while you're at it, put on some clothes yourself."

"Mister no like look Worm."

"Limpy like look Worm," Allerdyce said.

"It shut up or no get clothes," Worm told him.

To Service. "Him bad man?"

"Bad to some, worse to others, not bad at all to a few."

Worm rummaged in a drawer, and threw a pile of clothes on the floor in front of the old violator. "Worm say It put on now!"

"Normally Limpy don't take no orders from no wymyns, but in dis case, anyt'ing youse want, girlie." Allerdyce began dressing.

Service raised an eyebrow at her. "You get dressed too."

"Worm no like clothes."

"Pretend it's winter."

"But this not winter."

"Get dressed anyway, end of discussion."

She left in a huff and slammed the door.

"How far is her hide from here?" Service asked his partner.

"Less den mile, speck. She hide damn pretty good, Girlie do. Move t'rough woods like owl, can't hardly hear her."

"You let her grab you."

"Figger less scrap dat way, and when I seen 'er in raw I t'ink it better I get closed-up, make sure I ain't seein' stuff ain't dere. Besides, never like beat no crap outten bootiful wymyn."

Nor any woman. Despite rumors, and occasional hints from Allerdyce himself, Service had no evidence that Limpy had ever hurt a woman, including one who had once tried to poison him.

"She real good in da woods," Allerdyce confided. "Could be deadly, she wants to."

High praise, given the source.

"Girlie was one tell Limpy she synanthrope," Allerdyce said.

Grady found it uncomfortable to be in the presence of two strange individuals with questionable motives both of whom sometimes talked of themselves in the third person.

"She tell me she gettin' dat word fum Big Book Is Two Books Sleeps Words."

"You know what she's referring to?" Service asked.

Allerdyce shook his head.

Worm came back inside wearing all green and looking very much like a conservation officer, and the sight made Service blink hard several times.

Limpy greeted her, "Hey girlie what we got eats?"

"Cut out own guts and chew," she said and leered at him.

Service said, "Big Book Two Books Sleeps Words, let me guess. Somewhere you found an Oxford English Dictionary."

"Got glass can turn sun speck to fire."

"Close-looker," Allerdyce said.

"Where did Worm get an OED?" Service wanted to know.

"Her had long time, mebbe somebody drop somewhere and Her pick Him up."

"Fell off the back of a truck?" Service muttered. "Maybe the owner didn't even know he lost it?"

"Her thinks Mister right. OED Hers now."

Allerdyce sidled close and whispered. "Dis girl doin' youse?"

"No, you old fool. I hired her as my camper lookout and I do not fish off company piers."

"She ain't *in* no company and how Missus Tuesday feel 'bout dis?"

"She doesn't know about this, and she's not Missus."

"Worm no like Him-It make bzzbzzbzz."

"Limpy don't neither. Let's hear some sweet girlie talk."

"Worm don't know sweet girlie talk."

"A loss for all manskind," Allerdyce said.

"Her place more secure than this?" Service asked Limpy.

"Wunt take much. Dis stinks. She got her real good spot."

"She got food?"

The girl objected. "Nobody go Worm's place, but Worm. Don't nobody know where Worm's place be."

"I know where," Limpy said, and cackled maniacally.

Worm laughed at him.

Service said, "Believe him if he can take us to it?"

She gave both men a derisive scowl and a dramatic wave of a huge hand.

Grady sensed her unease. Allerdyce had that effect on everyone. Even him.

• • •

The place was an old mine adit she had discovered, an adit being one of the mine's horizontal tunnels used for venting and safe escape, but was closed up when the mine went defunct. But now time, the elements, and erosion apparently had created a partial opening, which she'd found, widened, and re-hid.

About sixty feet in there was an opening from above that let a blade of sunlight down, not adequate for easy seeing, but just enough to take some of the freaky dark edges away. Whatever else Worm might be, she was obviously enterprising and could take care of herself. When he saw her OED, he could tell it had been used as regularly as Bibles in pioneer times.

When Allerdyce led them directly to the opening, Worm looked crestfallen, but Service patted her back supportively. "No matter how good we think we are at something, there is always someone who is better than us."

"It better than you?" she asked.

"At some things and in some ways," he admitted. "I don't take it personally. I try to learn from him."

"Worm not like how It look at her."

"That," Service told her, "how he looks at Worm, she should take *very* personally."

"Worm maybe not understand what Worm feel."

"I don't want to hear about Worm's feelings."

"Worm think boss not such boss in all things."

Worm would be right. They brought several days of food from his camper. For a cookfire, she had a tiny rocket stove.

"Something else Worm conveniently found in the woods?" Service asked.

She grinned. "Worm know how to be lucky, mebbe. And how keep eyes open all times. Allerdyce, It fool Worm?"

"He fools everyone he wants to fool," Service said. "It's his gift."

"Worm can learn from It?"

Service guessed that would lead to trouble, but he wasn't sure whose trouble, Allerdyce's or his. "From now on when I come up for air, can we come here instead of to my camper?" he asked the lanky girl.

"Him pay?"

"Sure, how much?"

"What boss Him think is okay for Worm? Then, Mister come here much, maybe?"

"No way to know," he told her, which was true. The ROCK schedule was erratic at best.

"Dis t'ing youse doin' almost over?" Allerdyce asked.

"I have no idea," Service said, and it was also the truth. The ROCK thing was so far a strange sort of wheel-spinning exercise, and looking like it might stay that way. How long would Captain McKower accept that? Not long, he guessed. And how was she going to react to learn not only of Allerdyce's involvement, but at the behest of the FBI and probably the ATF too?

CHAPTER 10

Marquette

MARQUETTE COUNTY

What do you read, my Lord—Words, words, words.
—William Shakespeare, *Hamlet*

"What *is* Coldbeg's problem?" Service complained. "Can't you get me out of these stupid meetings!"

"I've learned a few things. He's not as young as he looks, so he's a little ouchy about his career prospects. He was an FBI director's chosen rising star, but when that director bailed out under a cloud, Coldbeg got ticketed to Marquette by his boss's previous critics."

"Marquette becoming what Montana was under Hoover?" he said.

She just slowly shook her head, and said quietly, "Hoover played dictator for half a century. I expect it will take another half-century to undo that bastard's work. And even without a dictator in the top chair there, the career lesser lights always have the ability to mete out their own forms of political justice."

"It's a snake-pit," he said.

"And every damn one of them poisonous," she added.

"The thing is," Service told her, "the field agents have never struck me as political."

"It's the old Lansing snake-pit metaphor," McKower said. "Any time an organization has a head office, the same organization invariably becomes to those not in the head office, the asshole office, which is usually not very far from the head politically and anatomically."

Service smiled. "You still have a way with words."

"Some of it I learned from you. How's Friday?"

"Deep in her cold case."

"She can't be happy about that."

"Actually, she thinks there might be a whisper of a lead."

"She told you that? Miss Professional Lockjaw?"

The captain smiled. "She is the consummate pro. How's Shigun?"

"Still sweet—and a funny little pup."

"Enjoy it while you can," she said. "My own girls refer to me as the evil stepmother. How do children ever grow up to be normal people and good citizens?"

"Define normal," he said, and leaned toward her. "Can you explain why these yayhoos are risking my ass and cover by calling me to meetings *here*?"

"I've had exactly that discussion with Coldbeg and he got pissed at me questioning his authority. I told him I would never question his authority, only his stupid decisions which risk my people."

"Why did he want this meeting today?" Service asked.

She stared at her detective, "You think you're the only one out in the cold?"

"Sometimes I think I don't know what I know or don't know anymore," he told her. "Drives me nuts at times."

"No eagle feathers?"

"Not even a tickle so far, and the truth is, it's hard to get these people to talk. They are a very tight-lipped crowd."

"So why are you still there, and why are we still in this case, or whatever it is?"

"You sent me there, remember?"

"I did not *intend* for it to be open-ended. We have a lot of cases pending where your attention and experience would be helpful."

"Undercover detective business is invariably open-ended," he said. "We spend one hell of a lot of energy just scratching surfaces, but this time all I see so far is a bunch of toy soldiers. Can't call them bad or good, just odd fish and it's not against the law to be odd. And so far, I really don't get the feds' interest."

She smiled. "If it were against the law to be odd, I'm afraid we'd *both* be criminals. So why the hell are we there?"

"*We* aren't," he reminded her. "*I* am."

"*Any* sniffs of criminal intent in there?"

"Sniffs, sure. Strange drooly drivel about the war against Christians, but no details. It's kind of like being a Catholic. Everything always seems to point not to now, but to some imprecise, unstated, unknowable time in the future and some other location not of an earthly domain."

"Cult?" she asked.

"These militia outfits usually have some or even all the earmarks of cults, but this one doesn't seem to have its act together and they put a lot of emphasis on getting money from members."

"What do you make of that?" she asked.

"I don't yet. It just looks and feels pretty odd, like the lead banjo in the banjo marching band doesn't have its strings tuned quite right, or his are right, but the rest aren't in tune with him, and I don't know if that's an accident, or intended."

"What about the place itself?"

"Isolated but close enough to civilization. Well selected ground to defend, so there seems to be some quasi-competent military intelligence at work, but when men who are not soldiers put on soldier costumes and play soldiers with real weapons, there's always a hint of something criminal in the wind, even if you can't quite catch the exact scent. It's like a fart that flicks past you, like a fox just cut across your trail and you can smell where it was, but can't see it."

"I worry about you being undercover."

"Me too," he said. "It is always a crapshoot."

"How does Tuesday handle it?"

"Use your imagination."

"That doesn't take much."

"There you go."

"You see anything in the ROCKs that concerns you—since you're not getting any feather leads?"

"Vibrations, some of them seem nasty, but I can't read anything clearly, either because they want it that way, or because that's my own prejudice, but so far it's just vibrations."

"We don't make cases on vibrations."

He grinned.

"What?"

"You remember our PPP case?"

She chuckled. "I sometimes wonder if that really happened to us."

"It was your case," he reminded her. "Gal called the RAP line to report her husband because he had taken her vibrator to use on all the deer he was shooting at night. She just wanted her vibrator back."

McKower said, "She was late forties and very polite. I met her in the next county and she told me her husband had shot at least twenty does that fall, all of them at night."

"No bucks?" Service asked.

"'Can't eat no horns,' she said."

"I asked her, 'So you eat the deer he shoots?'"

"'Are you kidding me? Never,' she tells me, 'that idiot uses the meat to trade for sex with professional women.' I had no idea how to respond to that one. Drew a complete blank, but she was kind enough to fill in the picture. A couple of years before that she kept complaining about all his all-night hunting and he'd gone out and bought her a two-hundred-dollar vibrator, brand-name Purple People Pleaser, and it turned out she liked that 'way more better' than him, so he stole it from her and used it on deer, which she called his 'sickness,' and 'why should she have to sleep with him when her Three P was a better husband than he could ever be? And furthermore, her Three P didn't need her to cook for it or clean the bathrooms or wash dirty skivvies.'"

"Every contact, you just never know what's going to come out of people's mouths," she said. "If all you have are vague feelings from this ROCK outfit why are you still in there?"

"Every time we get a major case, it's always seems like six months of getting-to-know-you."

"Are you?"

"Getting to know them? The better question seems to be are they getting to know *me*? That's the normal progression for these abnormal operations."

"You want out?" she asked.

"I always want out of undercover, but not before I assure myself there's nothing there, or decide it's a bridge too far, or think I learned enough to get at them through another avenue."

"This outfit?"

He shrugged. "Honestly? Beats me. So far." He caught her studying him. "What?"

"Let's go see what our federal colleagues have in mind."

"Feds like to tango too," he said.

"I heard that, especially those in the federal political class. You still voting for Zolton Ferency for governor?"

"Every single election."

"He was a Democrat."

"Bullshit, he was Don Quixote. He didn't care whose windmill he jousted, and if the windmill was crooked, he was all in against that sucker."

"I suspect you think the Lone Ranger was God."

"He wasn't?"

"How's the Lone Ranger's sidekick these days?"

He knew this was a shot across his bow over Allerdyce. "Real quiet. He's given up being a wood tick or skulking red devil, take your pick."

"You know how I feel about that creature. Tell me he is *not* involved in this case with you?"

"He's certainly not inside with me."

"I find that very highly unreassuring."

"I always follow orders, Cap'n, but think about this. If one has a case with eagle feathers, who better to ask than Tonto?"

"You just can't help living on the edge," she said.

"I was a hockey player. What do you expect? If you're not on your edges, you're on the ice on your butt, and not in the game."

"Jesus Crookfoot, Grady."

"Relax, Lis, we will always understand each other and these jobs we do. We got this."

"The nerve-basket that is my gut says differently."

"Then don't listen to the damn thing. Where is this meeting, anyway?"

• • •

They met in the FBI's conference room in downtown Marquette and were greeted by cold, hard masks.

The regional ATF man looked like he'd rather be taking out trash.

Coldbeg had the personal charm of a fridge-chilled carp and was known around the local law enforcement community as Coldback.

Service sat back and watched McKower, who clearly was straining to understand interagency politics. Why he was in these task force meetings continued to elude him. He'd done interagency work in the past and undercover always stayed buried. He doubted the Feebs would risk one of their own tribe this way.

Not one person in the room brought any information to share and Coldbeg asked the only question, which involved Service's estimate of the number of bodies actually under the ROCK umbrella. "Not easy to answer," he told the group. "There's a bunk-room could hold forty, but I've never seen more than six or eight guys in there, and there's another level of cadre who must reside in some other part of camp."

"What are you *doing* with your time in there?" Coldbeg challenged him.

"Make-work, same as you Feebs, we pile up heavy rocks we take from one place, and then, once they're over there, we start lugging them back to where we started. They are keeping us busy and in the dark."

"How difficult can it be to move rocks?" Coldbeg asked.

"They're two-hundred-pounders, you should try it. And you are required to move them by yourself. No team-lifting."

Having no personality and seeing no need to behave in any other manner, Coldbeg said with neither prelude nor foreplay thirty seconds later: "We've lost an inside asset for Operation Fractal Splinter."

Grady felt the captain's boot tap his boot under the table, a signal for him to keep his yap zipped.

Two Fish and Wildlife agents, missing from previous task force meetings, were mysteriously present today and the ATF man looked over at McKower and lifted his chin as if a large wind were about to blow into the room. The Fish and Wildlife agents—who covered the U.P. as part of a larger geographical portfolio, boundaries of which they never fully specified—immediately lit up over this new information.

The newcomers were unknown to Service, and introduced themselves as Covin and Stepanishin, the latter a female.

Covin, a Georgia boy, stared at Coldbeg, "Lost an inside asset, what the fuck does that mean? We thought our inside asset was the game warden here."

Covin's partner Stepanishin pointed at Service. "Isn't he our undercover? Are you telling us there were *two* assets inside?"

"I told you what I told you," Coldbeg said, "end of discussion."

"There's been no discussion," McKower pointed out.

"Operational security," Coldbeg said.

The captain said derisively, "*What* operational security? My man is inside and you risk blowing his cover by bringing him here for these Mickey Mouse meetings, what *is* your problem, Special Agent?"

"You lack requisite clearances," the FBI man said.

"This is bullshit, jackwad," Stepanishin said, "you keep us in the dark and think that's operational security? Bullshit."

"This is a procedural matter," Coldbeg said, "and there is no need for public displays of professional discourtesy."

"What do you mean you 'lost' an asset?" McKower asked.

"We are not at liberty to discuss the matter."

"You mean you aren't going to," Covin said, "and were it up to me, I'd have your nuts separated surgically and sewn to your pinhead. *What* other inside asset, pinhead?"

No response. Coldbeg didn't rattle. Was he insensate?

"We had hoped," Coldbeg eventually said, "that this task force could be of assistance in clarifying some rather disturbing gaps in our knowledge base."

Stepanishin said, "Like you dudes running an asset you didn't bother to tell us about, *that* sort of disturbing gap in our collective knowledge base?"

"I understand the source of our angst," Coldbeg told her.

"Seems to me you don't understand anything," Stepanishin yelped.

"Guys, we're getting nowhere with these attitudes," Coldbeg complained.

"*Guys*?" Stepanishin and Captain McKower said in unison.

McKower leaned forward. "Tell us who is lost and how, if you know, and how this person dovetails with my detective's work and role, and our *so-called* collective effort."

Service knew her temper was full-on and fraying.

Coldbeg looked at Service. "The asset was inside the ROCKs as Chirac. Familiar?"

"Uh, Special Agent, did you not understand that everyone in that outfit is officially dead and now with a new name and identity?"

"That point was not lost on me."

"I've met maybe a dozen guys so far and sent out the names to you, per my instructions. Chirac rings no bells. Do you have a photo?"

"I suppose that could be arranged," Coldbeg said.

McKower again, now on her feet and adjusting her gunbelt, a sure sign she was ready for a fight. "You suppose . . . you *suppose*! You've called us all here because of a lost asset, and you didn't think to provide a photo for us to use in trying to identify this person? Are you not paying attention to the kind of work we are involved in?"

Covin said, "Undercover cases tend to rattle brains and bones back in Washington."

"And balls too," Stepanishin added, "assuming there were any there to start with."

"You people are not leading this task force," Coldbeg scolded.

"Neither are you, fuckwit," this from Stepanishin.

Covin said, "The only reason you came into this case is because it looked to us like it was going to go into some shitholes outside our mandate and remits."

McKower lurched. "Fish and Wildlife had this case *first*?"

Covin looked at her, "You didn't know? Eagle feathers and some possible international parts trade, classic CITES stuff."

"The feathers and parts trade we knew about. But we didn't know it started in your hands," she said.

"How long until we see the photograph?" Service asked. "My cover is as a professional bird counter and while this gives me some flexibility, I can't be running back and forth on somebody's whims, and frankly, I should never have been here in the first place."

"How can we get the photo to you?" Coldbeg asked.

"Unless you have it here and now, you can't. Captain, can you explain to our *colleague* what it means to be undercover?"

"This entire task force is questionable. Operation Fractal Splinter, we were not even aware this task force had a name," she said.

"The task forces don't have names, only operations do," Coldbeg said officiously. Service thought his captain would jump over the table at the man, but she remained calm. "How about twenty-four hours to produce a photo for us to look at?" She looked at Grady. "Twenty-four doable?"

Service said. "Will have to be."

"You have twenty-four, otherwise we are pulling out of all this."

"Your governor may take exception," Coldbeg warned her.

"I know her personally *and* really well, and I doubt that very much. She's not one to needlessly risk police officers' lives."

"This is not normal," Coldbeg complained.

"Finally, we agree," McKower said and tapped Service's shoulder. "Saddle up, we're out of here." She looked at the Fish and Wildlife people. "Not happy we didn't know of your involvement. When we run an op, everyone involved in every aspect is aware of man-down procedures."

"States have different mandates," Coldbeg tried to argue.

"I've always believed that human lives are valued equally by all of us, no matter our jurisdiction."

"Goddamn them," McKower said as they barged toward the stairs.

"Them?" Service said.

"Anybody and everybody who isn't us," she said.

"They're all us in the bigger picture," he told her.

"Bigger picture, my ass," she said. "No photo by tomorrow, you, me, and us are out of this goat rodeo."

"Let's not be too hasty, Lis. What's the first rule of UC?"

"Protect your people. Get them out alive."

"Bullshit. The first rule is to listen dispassionately to all input data and make decisions based on that, not your heartstrings."

"You don't want out?"

"Of course, but I don't want to make that decision based on whether the FBI can get us a photo in twenty-four hours."

"You are not normal," she said.

"That damn word again," Grady said, and laughed at her, and that in turn made her laugh.

"What's that Tina Turner line from *Thunderdome*?" McKower said. "Ain't we a pair, raggedy man?" And then she started laughing again.

CHAPTER 11

Camp ROCK

KEWEENAW COUNTY

> I alone, alone do me oppose against the pope and count his friends my foes.
>
> —William Shakespeare, *King John*

The colonel's skin resembled that of unshelled pistachios, and Grady wondered if Harlikin had some medical condition that made him look simultaneously creepy and sickly.

As at their previous meeting, the colonel had a body-man close by, but this was a new face, albeit with the same wrestler's build and impassive countenance. How many body-men did the colonel have, and why more than one? The whole idea of a body-man was security and presumably the more people you let in close, the higher your risk. Very odd. Fear for sure, but of what? Attack? Germs? Was Harlikin paranoid, or did he have a valid reason for fear?

"Your latest bird count stint was shorter than we expected," the colonel greeted him.

"Most bird counting outfits don't have a lot of financial backing; they run on bare-bones budgets, and sometimes, when they set a count for a certain period, they also set a number for the target species, and when that number is reached, the count stops, no matter where the count is in the time sequence."

"Yet they can afford to pay people like you to do the work."

"They'd prefer volunteers, but professional counters can produce reliable data, and depending on the study or goals of the sponsoring group, data are a lot more valuable than the money paid to gather them."

"Spoken like a scientist," the colonel remarked.

"Me? Not hardly," Service said with a grin. "There are a lot of birds I count for which I don't even know their Latin names."

"That sounds both unscientific and unprofessional to my ears," the colonel said.

Service shrugged. "I don't have to be able to build a VW to know what one is. I get paid for the results I deliver."

"Other counters must also deliver reliable numbers," the ROCK commander said.

"Not all counters or counts are the same, and those who employ me tell me my *sitzfleisch* is what gets me hired."

"You speak German?" the colonel asked.

Service chuckled. "I can barely speak English, but I know what *sitzfleisch* is because someone explained it to me. It's the ability to sit on your butt and concentrate for long periods of time and to stay focused on what you're doing."

The colonel joined his bony fingers in front of him. "I intend no insult here, but I wish to have a demonstration of your bird-counting skills."

What was *this* about? "You want to take a walk in the woods with me and have me tell you what we're looking at, or hearing?"

"I prefer something more controlled," the colonel said. "I've managed to secure a testing instrument from Audubon."

"Visual or oral?"

"You have a preference?" the colonel asked.

"I can do either or both. It all depends on the targets, the time of year, and the watcher location. When I'm going somewhere I've not been before, I generally have to do some homework and refresh my memory, or install new information for birds I haven't previously dealt with."

"How much do they pay you for this work?" Harlikin asked.

"That's none of your business, Colonel. How much do you take from the money you gather from us? I paid my K and C like everyone else, but I haven't signed a personal financial disclosure with you—and I don't intend to. Seriously, how much *do* you make off this thing we do or are supposed to be doing? You know to the penny how much you pay me, but nobody knows what you get paid."

"You are not an easily intimidated individual," the smirking colonel said.

"Are you?" Service answered.

"I try not to be," Harlikin allowed.

Grady decided to test the man's emotions. "Having your own body-man makes life a hair easier than walking on your own two feet." Service thought he detected a slight pause, as if he'd caught Harlikin off balance. Interesting. Was the colonel touchy about his unmanly personal security arrangements? "Nobody's calling you a pussy for hiring help," Service said to reassure the man. "The men get that."

"You men talk about my security?" the colonel wanted to know.

"I don't, but I listen to what others say. Are we going to do this bird test or not?"

A second body-man, also a new face, brought earphones and a video monitor. The colonel said simply, "Put on the headphones and identify anything you see or hear."

"That's all?"

"We are told that the very best professional bird counters rarely exceed 60 percent in this exercise. Are you among the best?"

"I guess we'll find out," Service allowed. Did he intentionally make errors in this test, to keep his score in the reasonable and expected range, or should he nail it all to clearly establish he knew what the hell he was doing? He held up the palm of a hand. "American birds, right? No African crap or stuff like that?"

"Africans a problem for you?"

"I just don't count birds other than ours. I know some of ours hit the Bahamas, or Mexico, or some even dive deep into South America every year, but I don't know all the birds that hang out in those places."

"Are all counters the same as you?"

"I don't know all of them, and there are counters all around the world."

"Do American counters go to other countries to count birds?"

"Some do, yes."

"You?"

"I'm American, and I like it right here in my own country."

"Because we're a more blessed place than others?"

"Are you saying we're *not*, Colonel?"

"That is something perhaps for us to discuss down the road," Colonel Harlikin said and pointed at the video monitor and said, "Commence."

The first song he heard was a veery, followed in close succession by a wood thrush and a rose-breasted grosbeak, and then there came a broadwing hawk flying directly at him, but out at a distance where the bird was sort of bent in a thermal, which caused the tips of its wings to momentarily look pointed, and then in the distance a loon, and some white pelicans, a bald eagle, three merlins and a smaller kestrel, a northern harrier he called a marsh hawk before correcting himself, a northern flicker he called a yellowhammer and a dollar butt, and quickly corrected himself again as the parade of sounds and sights continued and he sat in place thirty straight minutes.

Eventually the colonel raised his hand. "That's enough."

One of the body-men took away the headphones and monitor, and minutes later handed the colonel a blue sticky note. The commander looked over at Service. "Impressive: 97 percent versus experts rarely exceeding 60 percent. That's rather astonishing."

"Which ones did I miss?" Service asked, knowing full well which ones.

"Does lack of perfection bother you?"

"The way I see it, only God is perfect, or gets to claim so."

"Claim? You think God isn't perfect?"

"I honestly don't know, Colonel. Supposedly he made us in his image and look what a mess we are."

Harlikin grinned. "Do you think said lack of perfection among humanity suggests a plan in how He made us what we are?"

"Be pretty dumb to think otherwise, Colonel. I'm just a regular guy. I see what I see, and try to say what I think."

"A commendable trait, which can be quite troublesome for some individuals," the colonel observed.

"Only if that man lacks discretion and common sense or, or doesn't know when to mimic a closed clam."

"You interest me, Mister John Eben Batanovich. Are you ethnically Russian?"

"Nossir. I'm red-blooded American, same as you and the other men here."

The colonel smiled. "I had a hunch about you early on, Mr. Batanovich, aka Wyndham Vold. I have gone to considerable expense to find out who you are, and as sometimes happens, I was quite surprised with the results."

What was Harlikin talking about? Had the feds fucked up his cover story and fake identity, had he, or was his imagination on overload?

"You are, or seem to be, exactly who you told us you were and that alone is somewhat concerning. Most people we recruit are trying to hide something, or from something—from themselves, or from others, it doesn't matter which, but there's always some degree of holdback, which I'm sorry to report we did not find with you, and not having found what we invariably find, we are faced, if you will, with a sort of perfection in candor where such perfection is unlikely. Thus my quandary. Is ROCK Batanovich too good to be true? I'm sure you can understand the position this puts us into."

"I don't see a problem," Service told him. "You said improbably, not impossibly. Me, I'm a longtime believer in the quacks-like-a-duck school."

Harlikin looked tortured. "You came across so simple, and uncomplicated, yet I see now this is at odds with what my instincts insist I pay attention to."

Service shrugged. "Okay then, Colonel. If the test is over, will there be anything else?"

"You anxious to be shed of my company, son?"

"I wouldn't put it that way, Colonel. I can see you're a busy man and I know that when I'm busy with important stuff, I hate anybody eating my time."

"Even your boss?" Harlikin asked.

Service paused a long while before answering. He wanted this inflection to be *just* right. "*Especially* bosses," he said.

Harlikin grinned. "Which is to your profit. You loathe superiors and any people looking over your shoulder, especially individuals lacking your skills but trying to impose their lower skills on you. Am I describing you?"

"That was me at times," Service said. "Now I've been reborn and I'm trying to get it right this time around."

"You have trained with ROCK Tooler?"

"I trained with an individual who claimed that name."

"Do you know what a Perm is?"

"I heard the term tossed around, but not a definition."

"Perms are official parts of the First Monarchy."

"We're a democracy in this country, Colonel. I thought we dumped monarchies back when we kicked England's ass, and I already paid up and thought that was what made me part of the outfit."

The colonel smiled benignly, and said, "As a Perm you become a legal part of the movement. The level you're at now merely gives you the opportunity to be chosen and I am now informing you that you have."

"How much will that cost me?"

"For some of the elect, nothing at all. But for most of us twice the original K and C."

Service made a lemon face. "*Fifty* grand?"

"It's a pittance for a guaranteed place beside God."

"Tooler get to the Perm step too?"

"Tooler did not measure up," the colonel said. "Is that your evaluation of the man, too?"

"Nossir, I think Tooler's a *real good* man. He's strong, tough, honest, got endurance, everything."

"Interesting," Harlikin said. "He said the same thing about you this morning."

"Good," Grady said. "Then he *did* make it."

"No, he was eliminated this morning."

"May I ask why, sir?"

"Never ask. Can mere men ask God why and expect an answer?"

"Could always ask, but I guess we couldn't expect no answers."

"Good. It's the same here."

"Does this mean I'm in?"

"As soon as you produce the requisite K& C for next phase."

"Fifty thousand is not an insubstantial amount of money, Colonel."

"One lump and no payment plans from now on," Harlikin said. "Got a plan to come up with it?"

Grady looked right at the colonel. "Truth is, sir, I could come up with enough to buy you."

Harlikin showed no surprise, and touched his heart. "I do believe you mean that sincerely, Birdman."

"And what does the colonel's instinct tell him about that?"

"You'll be the first to know, ROCK Batanovich. Bring the money, and then we'll talk. Dismissed."

"Training tomorrow, sir?"

"No, as of today we are commencing a two-week stand-down."

"But I just got *back*."

"We are bigger than one man," the colonel said.

"Everybody is in stand-down?"

"Report back in two weeks unless you get a different order."

"Is there a problem, Colonel?"

Harlikin said, "Life itself is defined as a continuous challenge, and I would never deign to refute that, but nothing is a problem if one learns how to look at it in the right way. You can go now."

As Service got up to leave, the colonel asked, "Did you ever have to grab someone when you were in uniform?"

"Grab?"

"Remove them from circulation, for interrogation or to take them off the field of play?"

"We did that with bullets. It was a lot less trouble and expense in the long haul."

"How did you feel about such work?"

"I like to hit what I shoot at."

"I hope to see you in two weeks," Harlikin said, got up, and left the room with his body-man as a shadow pasted to him.

A two-week stand-down? What kind of chickenshit, amateur outfit was this? Tooler hadn't measured up, but *he* had? Was this sudden break about the missing FBI asset, routine, standard operational procedure for this group, or something else? No way to know yet, or to guess, and this ambiguity was so typical of undercover missions, shit happening you could never anticipate, and with no explanations to help your clarity.

What a pain in the ass, but the time away might be good. Would be good. He could use it to his advantage. Could and would. *Sitzfleisch* indeed.

CHAPTER 12

Copper Island

KEWEENAW COUNTY

Like to a chaos, or an unlick'd bear.
—William Shakespeare, *Henry VI, Part III*

What the hell was he supposed to do now? Two weeks off was good, or could be, but what to do after he alerted McKower and the Operation Fractal Splinter team? Special Agent Coldbeg had the nominal team lead, but he had come to the team via Michigan's governor and his own DNR senior management, and McKower had been added recently, and still he had no idea what that wrinkle meant. The whole damn thing felt unwieldy and ill defined, a disaster in the making and the more he was away from the ROCKs the further he felt he was slipping away from where he needed to be. And who the hell came up with the names for government operations? It was like trying to name four hundred kinds of ice cream, or describing the latest vintage of fine wine, a great deal more creative license than practical reality. No doubt a computer did such tasks these days.

He had no worries about McKower covering his six, but the rest of them? And even knowing this, she was the latest captain of the DNR's investigative ship and shouldn't she have her butt on that ship's bridge with an eye for where her fleet was heading, not trying to run the damn engine room of a single ship while she directed the fleet?

He had to admit, however, that having her close helped in some ways to make him feel more secure; in the past he had been on some undercover jobs where he felt no such support or security. This time was an improvement, and yet not. Why was this kind of work never straightforward?

Unexpectedly cut loose for two weeks, he had to try to figure out how to best use such a gift of time. But first things first. He punched in McKower's number as he stood atop the mountain above Worm's hide.

"Captain McKower, Investigations."

"Grady."

"What's wrong?" she asked immediately.

"Why do you assume something's wrong?"

"You just went back under. Usually you're inside for a while."

"The rules changed this morning. Harlikin has the whole circus on hiatus for the next two weeks."

"Why?"

"No clue. It's not a place that favors explanations, but I'm wondering if the loss of the FBI's asset has something to do with it?"

"No details?"

"Zippo and zilch."

"And your read is that the lost asset was some sort of catalyst?"

"I'm not sure that's my official read, Lis. All I know is that the colonel ran us all out of Dodge. And all of them in there show a tendency toward group lockjaw."

"Two weeks?"

"Yes ma'am and I got that straight from the colonel's mouth."

"No instructions for what you should do during this time?"

"Nope, at least not to me. Is the colonel telling others to do certain things? No way for me to know that. All I heard was like beat it, dude, and don't let the door hit you in the ass."

"Coldbeg know this yet?"

"I thought it would be better coming from you to him, but now that I'm out I've had a chance to think about it, and what I can tell you for sure is that I'm impressed at how quickly and efficiently Harlikin's operation shed its people. Now that I'm out of there and looking back, it feels to me now like that crowd has run this drill before."

"Cult leaders like to keep their people guessing," she said. "You think this thing is a cult?"

"Any closed and tight organization is culty," he said, "even a small church in a country village, with a minority of the villagers as members. Individually or collectively, we humans seem to always find a way to boil everything down to us versus them. But Harlikin as a leader is the antithesis of awe-inspiring."

"You should tell Special Agent Coldbeg about this new wrinkle."

"I'd rather eat my own eyes with a fork. I'd prefer you handle that front for now. The man is supposed to be in charge, but it doesn't feel like he's in charge of anything, including his own emotions. You and the governor ordered me into this goat rodeo, so I figure it should be your job to liaise with the feds."

"All right, I'll talk to Coldbeg, but how about you brief the Fish and Wildlife people?"

"Which ones? We saw Covin and Stepanishin at the last task force, but nobody at the earlier task force meeting. The regular guys we work with seem to be AWOL, and based on the FBI / Fish and Wildlife animosity we saw, I wonder now if Fish and Wildlife ever had anything at all to do with our getting involved? We also have ATF in the room, and I'm not exactly sure why, and it seems to me that if eagle feathers is the rationale for being there, then this is first and foremost a US Fish and Wildlife case. Coldbeg needs to know that the group's on mass furlough, but I don't want to talk to the man. If he's the leader, let's let him lead, or at least let him think he's leading."

"You always assume the worst," she said.

"He hasn't told us a damn thing about the so-called missing asset, and still no photo, right? I may have seen the asset at the camp. I'd think Coldbeg—or someone—would want to know at least that. Have you heard anything since the last task force meeting?"

"Nothing but silence," she said. "Agencies are supposed to cooperate in good faith," she lamented.

"That sometimes doesn't even happen at the state level," he reminded her.

"All right," McKower said. "I'll talk to Coldbeg, but what's your next move?"

"Thinking I may run home and arrange for more cash to move up to the organization's second level."

Silence from the captain. Then, "*More* cash?"

"It boils down to a gnarly sort of entry fee, which they call the K and C, short for Kit and Caboodle. It took twenty-five grand to get inside and now they want fifty more in cash to move up to what they call the Perm level."

"This is the first I'm hearing about *money*, Detective. Whose *budget* did it come from?"

"Is that so critical?" Why did he mention money? Stupid! He'd purposely not told her about the money because she was tight with department funds and pissed and moaned like it was her own. He could afford to handle the money from his own resources, and get it reimbursed later.

"I don't know," she said. "Is it?"

"Seems a real small detail to me."

"You want to tell me where said money came from?" she asked again.

"From me," he answered.

She laughed. "Are you crazy? You've put your personal money into a public and government operation? Public interest lawyers will jump all over that with hobnail boots—and should."

"It cuts red tape, so we can move faster."

"Where is your common sense, Grady? You can't afford it! And even if you could, it sends the wrong message if it becomes public knowledge."

"Screw the optics. I just want to get this case resolved, and the way the group has this set up, no money means no access, no entry, no information, no operation, and if we don't have someone inside, there's no reason for a task force. I briefed you on this, Lis." Which he had, only he had held back the financial angle.

"You may think you did, but I can assure you that you did *not*. This is the first I'm hearing of any monetary component, and I am not liking it, not at all. The FBI or Fish and Wildlife or even the DNR should be financing this, not you. What's this next fifty grand for?"

"I don't really know, Lis. The ROCKs are buttoned up tight and their leader-dog is quietly bat-shit crazy in that I-know-all-the-shit-there-is-to-know way."

"This Harlikin calls himself a colonel. Is he actual former military?"

"I should think the task force would be all over that. It's not the sort of thing I can easily or openly push from inside without looking like I'm trying to push some sort of coup," Service said. "But, my gut says this guy is strictly a toy soldier. And, he's very, very cautious. Just before he gave us the break-camp order, he put me through a bird identification test."

"Was he testing your cover story?" she asked. "Why?"

"We have to assume that was what he was doing, but there's no way to settle on why. And I don't know If I'm a special case or this is SOP for all his people. Maybe the missing asset is mixed up in it and Harlikin's feeling some paranoia about the mustard seeds around him. I just don't know."

"Mustard seeds?"

"That's what the uniforms look like—to me."

"How did you do on the test?" she asked. "He must have been astonished."

McKower knew how well he knew birds and other wildlife. "The test carried a sort of ceiling of 60 percent and I threw the man a 97."

"Let me guess, you purposely missed the 3 percent."

"Perfection is never in the best interests on a UC gig."

"You're a maniac and the older you get, the worse you get, Grady. Does Tuesday know how reckless you are with money?"

"She doesn't care." In fact, she had no clue that he was wealthy, and by and large he gave her no reason to think differently. "Maniac? What kind of chickenshit shot is that?"

"You know it's true," the captain said. "So what's next?"

"As I said, home to Tuesday and the kid and get some more cash."

"Did we not just have this discussion? Any money you use must come from the government and be properly accounted for."

"Fine," he said, not meaning it. "Listen, Lis, I have no idea what this outfit is really up to, but the colonel invokes the name of God all the time."

"Maybe God wants you on hiatus for two weeks," she said.

"Harlikin told me, 'Two weeks *unless* contacted and instructed otherwise.'"

"Contacted how?" she asked.

"Dedicated burners. Our use only, and we turn them in for disposal."

"The outfit at least sounds somewhat organized."

"It may very well be," he said.

"You don't agree?"

"Cautious and organized aren't synonyms," he told her. "I don't know enough yet to have opinions."

"And no feathers, I suppose?"

"Shall I laugh out loud? Nary an Indian war bonnet nor a fluffer's fan in sight."

"Fluffers?" she said. "*Really*, Grady?"

"Made the point, didn't I? I'm going to head home and mostly ride this thing out and wait for my callback."

"I'll get to work on money allocation for you," she said. "How do they want it?"

"Cash, non-sequential bills."

"Good grief. They sound like kidnappers."

"Aren't all cults that—to some extent?"

"Tell Tuesday hey," McKower told him.

"You got it, Lis."

"Your mind is twisted, my friend. He who uses fluffering as an illustrative point is operating on a different frequency."

He was pleased she hadn't asked about Allerdyce. The captain saw no role for the old violator, but he did, as did Coldbeg and the FBI. If violators knew nothing else, they knew patience and how to look and watch, and most importantly the good ones knew how to see what they were watching. However, Worm seemed to have some promise, but no training, which left her as an unknown and untested quantity—who had already been fooled and bested once by the old man. He considered calling her back and telling her about Allerdyce, but decided against it. In time she'd know, or she wouldn't and he would deal with consequences then.

CHAPTER 13

Worm's Hide

KEWEENAW COUNTY

A kind of excellent and dumb discourse.
—William Shakespeare, *The Tempest*

But he didn't go home, and couldn't. Not yet. Tuesday would be tied up in her cold case and the ROCKs finally had piqued his interest. It felt good to hike into Worm's hole in the hills. Fifty grand more for a shmoo like Harlikin that would bring his part alone up to seventy-five. Was every ROCK putting up this kind of cash? How? And, why? Were the ROCKs truly some sort of whackadoodle patriotic religious militia, or something entirely different? A scam built on the foolishness of wannabe soldiers? Or maybe they just want to leave their old selves and identities behind, become someone else in a new life, and they see this as an opportunity to overcome inertia.

Something surely stunk here, especially with God being used as a heavenly seal of approval with no use-by date, or some other raison d'être he could not yet see clearly, or maybe were both applicable?

"Mister got the hinks," Worm announced as she suddenly spoke up from the darkness.

"I'm not hinked," Service told her.

"Worm know hinks when Her sees hinks. Him gottem them hinks real oh-oh big hinks." She was clothed, which surprised him, but her eyes were wide as a deer's in oncoming headlights.

"Worm earned a medical degree while I was gone?" he asked sarcastically. "Stop talking in third person, or people will think you're crazy."

He heard her restlessly moving around and then she said: "Her see two, not three. Where Him Mister see third Him? Hinks no good, her thinks. Makes Mister act *stoopid*."

"Oh good, your medical degree includes a specialty in psychiatry. You've been a busy girl."

"Sarcasm make no effect on Worm."

"This could turn out to be a life-gift, the inability to feel the teeth of sarcasm, but it suggests other emotional responses may also be missing in action."

"Now who plays psychiatrist?"

Was her language improving—in small ways? "I hear you knocking, but you can't come in," Service said. "I am fine, end of transmission, and end probe into Planet Service."

"This means?"

"I'm done talking." Maybe he *was* a little hinky. The mass withdrawal from Camp ROCK had been bizarre, yet orderly, reason for the group action unknown, and there was nobody he could see to talk about a possible explanation. Back when he was a Marine, he always had others close by to help keep touch with reality, but in this outfit Marine-type camaraderie was not encouraged. How did Harlikin envision a military unit where it was every man for himself? But if bugging out was SOP in this outfit, Harlikin had for sure achieved that much, and the word to boogie given, the whole mustard seed bunch smoothly and efficiently transitioned quickly into bug-out mode. It was like the aftermath of the once vaunted neutron bomb, where, after the blast no people would be left, only what few facilities there were. A head-shaker, the Mustard Seeds were.

"Mister, Him back soon, Worm thinks," the feral girl-woman had greeted him. Her being dressed suggested Allerdyce was not far away and this showed her good sense. "Limpy here?"

"Old Man, It out," she said. "Worm need talk."

"Think of me as here," Service said, "but not here. I'm thinking."

"Him cannot be not here, Worm thinks. Must be one, or other, not both."

"Consider this a good practice exercise for your imagination."

"Hmm," she said.

"Where *is* Allerdyce?" he asked again.

"Said. It Old Man here, not here."

He liked this girl.

"Worm learn," she said, "When Her got good teacher."

"Why you back?" Allerdyce asked, materializing like some sort of magical transporter had plunked him behind Service.

"The outfit closed shop for two weeks."

"Yah, sure, I seen da rats jumpin offen dat ship."

"How many you count?" Service asked.

"Me, I seen six, but youse wunt one a dem."

"The six come out together?"

"Dey all come oot alone. What goin' on?"

"Don't know, but I need to figure it out. So far reading this outfit is like trying to get instructions for building a rocket off a can of chicken soup. You hear anything?"

"One jamoke say somepin' aboot dat colonel and his damn military VRBO."

What did this mean? Vacation Rentals By Owners? Was Harlikin renting the camp and training facilities to *other* groups? If so, why?

"You have any idea what that means?"

The old man shook his bobblehead. "Nope. Youse?"

"Not sure, but I think I'll need your help to find out."

"We sit on da place?"

"Not me, you."

"What is 'sit on?'" Worm asked. "Mister and It Old Man make strange talk, Worm thinks."

Service explained. "It means to watch something in order to help us try to understand it."

"Like Worm sit on Him's place? Like word in Big Book, surveillance?"

"Bingo."

"Is game old peoples play," she said. "The golden years, Gray Panthers, AARP."

"I like da Bingos," Allerdyce volunteered.

"She rests her case," Service told the old violator.

"Dat an insult?" Allerdyce asked, the corners of his mouth curled down.

"Sarcasm," Worm said.

"If youse so smart, girlie, why dose jamokes shut down dere camp?"

"Jamokes?" she said.

"It means anyone who isn't us," Service said. "It's a kind of slang term from another age."

"Another age, like Roaring Twenties in Big Books?"

"I was thinking more like the Pleistocene," Service said and the lovely feral girl burst out laughing.

"What so funny, girlie?" Limpy wanted to know.

"Pleistocene," she said in a singsong voice, "in adjectival form means relating to, or denoting the first epoch of the Quaternary period, between the Pliocene and Holocene epochs."

"All dose big words don't mean nuttin'," Allerdyce grumbled in his chippy-chirpy voice.

"Means you're old," Service said.

Worm amplified: "Big Books say Pleistocene 2.58 million years to ten or eleven thousand, seven hundred years ago. That *very* long time ago!"

Service stared at her. Had he just heard correctly? "Have you *memorized* the Oxford English Dictionary?"

"Two books and close-lookers," Worm confirmed. "Is like long, confused story."

Service had felt something in this kid that was special, but so far hadn't been able to put his finger on it. She barely had any schooling, and often talked like E.T., but her mind seemed to be impressive. If she was game, maybe there was a way to bring her back into the village. Her woodcraft was clearly superior. Her social skills were questionable and what was she thinking about as a future, if anything? Could she even comprehend a future further out than tomorrow?

"Okay girlie, grab youse's gear, saddle up, we gots to put her goin'," Limpy told her.

"Wait a minute," Service said. "I said *you* would sit on it, not her. She's not trained."

"Dis be girlie's OJT," Allerdyce said. "Same way I learned in da way back. She good, youse know, dis girlie, oot in da woods."

"Worm have name," the girl said.

Allerdyce scrunched his face. "Worm ain't no name for wymyns, nor pipples. Worm is trout-bait."

"Worm likes Worm."

"Youse stubborn," Allerdyce declared.

Worm nudged Service. "Stubborn good, Worm thinks. What Mister think?"

"Sometimes yes, sometimes no."

She looked confused. "Like here but not here, this sometimes yes, sometimes no?"

"Think of them as twins," Service said. "One never goes anywhere without the other one being real close."

"Is times Worm think Mister got no brain in head. I go with It, Old Man?"

"I don't like the idea at all," Service said.

"Worm think Mister not boss of her."

"So I should stop paying you?"

"Haven't started," she reminded him.

She was a load of volatile mercury in a human body. "Go, the both of you." He turned to Limpy. "Surveillance only, no direct action, you hear me?"

Allerdyce grinned and nodded stupidly.

The old violator was hopelessly mired in his own ways, but he was a survivor, and if anyone could ferret out what someone was up to, it most likely would be Limpy. "I hope I am not going to regret this decision," Service said, already sensing he might. Using Allerdyce was always a gamble. And who knew what might happen by adding Worm to the formula?

Five minutes later he was alone. Had he just thrown the dice to test fate, or set a plan in action? He had no idea, but done was done. They would watch Camp ROCK and *he* was going home.

CHAPTER 14

Harvey

MARQUETTE COUNTY

Speak what we feel, not what we ought to say.
—William Shakespeare, *King Lear*

They each had their own space in the house for at-home work, his space cluttered with piles of out-of-season clothes and ammo boxes and plastic pop bottles, a few mementos from across his years in the woods, two pairs of old, worn-out boots he couldn't dump because of his strange emotional ties to things that had served him well, his massive gun safe, an upright freezer and a chest model, both for preserving case evidence, which all officers had some form of at home and on their own dime. The state provided evidence freezers and lockers at various state DNR offices, but most conservation officers lived long distances from such centers, and consequently, at some point in their careers, bought freezers. Some officers had tried to argue that the state should pay for these, given how much fuel would be wasted running back and forth to a DNR center, but such arguments with the official state mechanism didn't even warrant formal recognition that a question had been raised, and officers continued to buy freezers with their own dough, and grudgingly accept this as how it was, and this allowed them to focus themselves on more important matters.

By contrast, Tuesday Friday's office looked almost sterile, nothing out of place except when she was working on a case and everything back in its place as soon as it was closed.

Only when she was in max horny mode did Friday's tight control of organization briefly lose its grip, and at such times she would leave a trail of clothes as they beelined to wherever they were headed for their nookie-cookie (her term, not his). Their son, Shigun, would find his mom's clothes flung here and there, and every time this happened, he made a beeline to Grady to ask why Mama's clothes were all over the floor in the hallway.

"Address such questions to your mother," Grady would inform the boy.

"You don't know the answer?" Shigun would ask.

"I know my answer, but it's her's that counts more than mine because it's her clothes you're asking about, get it, Big Man?"

"Yep," the kid would say, and scuttle away to find his mother who invariably would tell him, "Ask Dad, it's his fault this happens."

When Tuesday worked at home, which she loathed doing, she would grouse incessantly to Service, "Personal time should be personal time. State troopering is not the way of life you game wardens seem to thrive on."

But when she did work at home, she went at it intensely and pretty much shut out the rest of the world for the duration of whatever work task had her attention.

Today, however, he found her standing beside one of the wooden stools by the island in their kitchen, staring at a cup of coffee, its contents cold, judging by the lack of steam rising. He dumped the contents, poured her a new one, and set it down.

His presence had not seemed to register with her. "No work at the office?" he said.

She turned and looked at him. "*You're* home."

"Should I chase off the pool man?" he answered.

"We don't have a pool," she said.

"A technicality," he clarified.

"Why *are* you home?" she asked.

"I asked first."

"No you didn't."

"When you say, 'you're home,' there is an implied question mark and the understanding that the asker wishes to know the reason for aforesaid presence."

"The hell it does," she said. "It's that damn cold case," she added sourly.

"Thought you might have found the key to the treasure chest."

"It may very well be a key to something, but so far we're not at all certain what that something might be, if anything."

"Want to talk about it?"

She flashed a mock scowl. "So you can be confused too?"

"Confusion seems to be my most recent address," he said.

"What *are* you doing here?" she asked, and then and only then was he fairly certain she had joined the reality of the present from wherever her mind had been. For how long she would be here was a different issue. Tuesday was a great detective, a born puzzle-buster and problem-solver, and she *loathed* leaving anything undone.

"I live here," he said, "or one version of several mes does."

"We all have several versions of ourselves," Tuesday said, "or more."

"A golden tidbit from the head-shrinkers' deep end of the pool."

"We all change," she told him.

"Not me," Grady said.

"Even you," she corrected him.

"Okay, maybe, but not for long," he said.

"True enough. At your core you somehow remain the same near-stable maniac as in your alleged youth."

"You never knew me when I was young."

"I said alleged, and thank all the gods for that," she said. "Could be, we'd have never gotten out of bed."

"You're assuming we'd have bothered with a bed, and who cares anyway?"

"The world writ large does not hold couples like us in high regard," she said.

"No?"

"We remind them of what they don't have, never had, never will have, and have not one iota of understanding for. Our kind of physicality stirs the social pot."

"Cooks up some envy, does it?"

"People fear what they don't understand and when they don't understand it, they tend to demonize it."

"You're calling us sex demons?"

"You, *not* me. I'm just bewitched. I'm the victim in this."

"Are bewitched and bedeviled the same thing?"

"In our case, you betcha, Bub."

"The life of outcasts," he said, grinning.

"Only because we're cops," Tuesday said. "We see sides of life most people can't imagine, or can, and don't want to think about. You ever think about what it is we really do?"

"We try to keep people inside the fences called laws."

"Even those fences we don't think should be fences," she said.

"We don't build the fences," he reminded her. "We just patrol them."

"You still haven't said why you're home," she pointed out.

"My loopy toy colonel put all ops in deep freeze for two weeks, and dispersed the force."

"Reasons given?"

"Nope."

"Meaning you have a two-week break?"

"Looks like, but I've got plenty to keep me busy," he told her, lest she hand him a leg-long honey-do list.

"What's with Freedo and the seven skeletons?"

"Not all that damn much, yet. Lansing sent additional forensic help, but you know how slowly help can be in getting from below the bridge to we rustics above the bridge."

"They even here yet?"

"Some bets are on tomorrow."

"Your tone suggests that's not your bet."

"I never bet on anything I have no control over."

"Have you seen the remains?"

"I have and I'm surprised we don't have TV-6 at our doorstep already."

"Sounds like your people are airtight in keeping secrets."

"Ours are, but Lansing's coming in."

"Ever the nightmare scenario."

"Have you met the new COs over there?" she asked him.

"Met the guy, Bapcat. I passed the moose case to him."

"I met and liked both of them," she told him. "They seem to be those rare new kids with all their shit together right from the get-go."

"What's her name again?"

"Something, Patty Something."

"Bapcat's no kid. He was a SEAL for ten years."

"You think he'll find this job too tame?"

"Time will tell. You and Freedo talk to the Tech kids who led to the skeletons?"

"Not me. Freedo. Nice boys, he calls them, with a prospecting bug."

"Shocking," Service said. "Tech kids with the hots for old mines and poor rock piles. I'd like to talk to them," he added.

"Why?"

"Pick their brains about mines and stuff up that way."

"They're just students."

"If Techies, presumably with high IQs and serious minds."

"Freedo wants them kept behind the wall for now, but you can have your visit as soon as he loosens up. Or, are you asking me to push it?"

He smiled. "No, it was just idle thinking on my part. I'm right in the middle of this deal and feel like my ship is still at sea with land nowhere in sight." The Keweenaw is a honeycomb of old mines and tunnels, most of which are blocked off and well known in certain circles, especially among prospectors. But there's also old shaft and adit openings being found and the finders, who want to be first in, keep quiet until they can explore and remove their finds. "You guys get any good evidence off the seven remains? It is still seven, yes?"

"No comment, other than things may be looking up."

Her signal meant more than seven sets of remains. "Sounds like you're into the human equivalent of an elephant burial ground."

"No comment, yet."

"Meaning not ruled out?"

She nodded almost imperceptibly. "Jesus," he said. "When news of more than seven bodies breaks, all hell might break loose with it. There could even be national attention. That kind of attention can really help ID a missing person," he told her.

"True, but Freedo's worst nightmare is the media spotlight on an in-progress cold case." She added, "He fears that such attention invites the Feebs to shoulder their way in."

"The Feebs' pockets and resources are deeper than the counties' and states'," Grady reminded her.

"But it's *our* case," she said in a tone that told him she had locked arms with Freedo. She smiled. "Will you be here for dinner tonight?"

"Not sure. I may try to meet Patty Something."

"She is a yes, sir, yes, ma'am kind of girl and it's not an act."

"Good to know."

"She's the type to call bullshit to some of your games and tricks."

"I don't do games."

"I call bullshit," Tuesday Friday said.

"But I might do a trick," he said. "Where's our kid?"

"With Maridly and her mom, back after nine tonight."

"Hmm," he said. "And dinner here's when?"

She looped her arm through his. "Right after you show me that trick you were talking about," she said, and took off down the hall, her clothes flying as she went, and he was right behind her, both of them laughing like naughty kids.

CHAPTER 15

Allouez

KEWEENAW COUNTY

Let's further think of this.

—William Shakespeare, *Hamlet*

"Something? Service here."

"Detective Friday said I might be getting a bump from you, but I didn't expect it so soon."

"Shit happens," he explained.

"I heard you're a man of few words," she said, "and so far that's just five of them. What can I do for you, sir?"

"The case," he said. "And don't call me sir."

"I have several cases," she said.

"Bones in the hole."

"*That* case."

"Can we meet and have a chat?"

"You on duty?"

"You're not?"

"I'm on pass days, the next two."

"You find a place to live yet?"

"Bumbletown Hill."

"Near the tower?"

"You sure know the U.P."

"Not as much as I'd like, but that spot I know. Who you renting from?"

"Nobody. I own it," she said. "My folks had the place for the last fifty years, and I'm buying it from them. Can see the towers from my front room. How soon do you want to meet?"

"Sometime today?"

"You know Slim's?" she asked.

"Every game warden who works any time at all in the Keweenaw knows Slim's. Word has it there are new owners."

"But same good service, food and amazing bakery," she said. "How about lunch there tomorrow?"

"Too damn public. I'm on a case right now, undercover. You know the Cee Vee Cee Vee?

"Sure," she said and laughed out loud, and Service liked the fullness of it. "You *do* know your way around," she said.

Cee Vee Cee Vee stood for The Cliff's View Cliff View, a location on top of the ridge some called the Cliffs, which looked down on the bar on US 41 called the Cliff View.

"I know it," she said. "Where are you now?"

"Three counties away but I can be there in three hours. I'll be in civvies and in an unmarked black Ford 150."

"Isn't three hours pushing it?" she asked.

"It's not pushing me. Pushing you?"

Another laugh. "I'm still trying to find my way around this place. The peninsula bends northeast, so I'm never sure if east is north or north is east."

His turn to laugh. He'd had the same experience batting and bunting around the Keweenaw many years ago, and then had gotten turned around more times than he cared to admit, even to himself. He still seemed to have the inner compass he'd been born with, but there were days when he wondered if that inner compass was wobbling and precessing, and if so, why. But failures were few and rare, and he was still getting around just fine, so the old rule was invoked, if it ain't broke, don't fix it. "I've played that song myself," he shared with her.

"It can be frustrating," she said.

"Not a permanent condition. It just feels that way," he said. "See you in three hours?"

"Yes, sir, up on the cliff."

Service supposed he should bump her sergeant, but he had no idea who that was at the moment. New sergeants and lieutenants seemed to rotate through areas and districts continuously, and he had stopped trying to keep track. But he called her back. "Something, Service. If you want to let your sarge know we're meeting, it's okay by me."

"No need," she said. "It will be on my daily."

"Right, the daily," he said, and hung up. He had forgotten about reports which uniformed officers had to file electronically daily and periodically during the day, like a personal tracker, which allowed management to reconstruct their movements and time usage.

So far, detectives were not required to do such time-wasters, but he assumed this might change one day, and he wondered what it was about Lansing that made for what looked like massive mistrust of field officers? Hourly accounting of officer time use was an unadulterated waste, and an insult besides.

• • •

It had been years since he'd been on the ridgeline that once supported the famous Cliff Mine, from which about a zillion pounds of almost pure native copper had been dug out of the Keweenaw's rocky ground. As the Ford climbed the hill, he felt a little flutter of the heart at his first direction decision point, but a second later his memory told him he'd guessed correctly and he relaxed.

His latest vehicle was a Ford F-150 taken by the Troops off a bank robber in Monroe, who'd shot off the big toe of his own left foot in his too-hasty getaway attempt. The pain had become so intense so quickly that the man had just sat in his truck with his hands up, weeping, and waiting for officers to cuff him and get him to an emergency room. The arrest came less than seven minutes after the alarm in the bank was triggered, and later the court had condemned the vehicle, which the DNR properties people then picked up at one of the state's periodic auctions of confiscated and condemned equipment. It was not a great truck, but it was functional, which was all he needed. He was not the first employee to use it, and after so many years with a badge, he hardly noticed his wheels, except when the ride let him down. No doubt he would not be the last state employee to use the truck. When he was done with this case, he would be done with the Ford.

Something's state truck was nowhere in sight. Either she was late, or had already learned how to stash her ride. Or maybe she had been called to something or somewhere with a higher priority. This happened all the time to game wardens, who might schedule a meeting then be hours late because reality and unexpected situations overtook control of their own time.

Service parked, got out of the truck, and walked to the cliff's edge where he looked down to his left to see the bar. He lit a cigarette, reminding himself as he lit up that he had promised Tuesday repeatedly that he would quit and sometimes he had, for months, and even once for years, but he always drifted back to the nastiness when he was bored, or ramping up for action.

"How many citizens of our state even know we have views like this?" a voice behind him asked, startling him.

He turned and stared. She was a shade over six-foot, rangy in build, and her skin the color of coffee beans.

She snickered. "I'm guessing by the look on your face nobody told you I was Black. Is that a problem for you?"

"Not me. You brought it up."

"You were thinking, 'she's Black.' A woman knows these things, especially a Black woman."

"I heard you had superior skills, but nobody mentioned mind-reading."

"All *Black* women have to be able to read minds. It's standard-issue equipment," she said, grinning. "What's up, Detective?"

"Grady," he said, extending his hand.

"Patty," she said, accepting.

She had a confident, firm grip. "You have an unusual sense of humor," Service told her.

"Nothing funny in being named for Patty Cakes, or having a mother with tits like Tina Turner, and me with the chest of Muhammad Ali."

"Correction," Service said. "Not an unusual sense of humor, it's downright weird." Her *mother's tits*? "We've only just met and you're talking tits to an old white dude?"

"Shock has it uses. I've heard you're a frequent practitioner, and by the way, your friend Treebone says 'Semper Fi.'"

Luticious Treebone was Grady's oldest and best friend. They had served together in the Marines in Vietnam, started out together in the Michigan State Police, and transferred together to DNR law enforcement, but Treebone had later, at his wife's urging, transferred again, this time to the Detroit Metro Police where he retired as a lieutenant. Service bought his friend a remote hunting camp in Chippewa County as a surprise retirement gift.

Something said, "He says to tell you that you work too damn much."

"He always says that."

"He always means it," she said.

"How do you know Tree?"

"My older sister went to school with his daughters, and Kalina and my mom are longtime friends. My mom's a lawyer, too."

"Defense?" he asked.

"Assistant Prosecutor, Wayne County. She's a pit bull in high heels."

"Her daughter a pitty too?"

Something flashed her teeth. "When circumstances dictate."

"Jab your bowels, finding those skeletons?"

"Man," was all she said. She pursed her lips tightly and closed her eyes.

"Would do that to anyone," Service said. "You seen your two students since then?"

"Once, at a donut shop halfway up Quincy Hill."

"*They* shook up?"

"I can't read them," she said. "The Troops took the case, and then the Feebs tried to elbow them off it." This was Friday's case now? No wonder her back was up. Her case, but she was letting Freedo in on his cold case. One of her hunches, maybe? Hard to know. "When did you hear that the Feebs were trying to muscle in?"

"On my way to meet you, why?"

"Who told you?"

"Detective Friday. She said to tell you not to worry about her, she *has* this."

"Did she sound pissed?"

"She sounded highly professional and cool. She told me if you're thinking about talking to the two college students you should expedite in the event the Feebs do get control and clamp muzzles on potential witnesses, yada-yada."

Meaning jurisdiction was still up in the air, another political football with no air in it.

"You think the feds could sequester witnesses?" Something asked.

"They'd first have to define a case. What Friday's doing is connected to a really old cold case out of Marquette County. Can you get hold of the two students?"

"I can try."

"Let's give them a bump and see if they'll talk to us."

"It's a possible homicide, what's our angle in? Are we case rustlers here?"

"They're fair game. Trespassing and after state minerals, which are natural resources."

"You could say the same about air," she pointed out.

"I have when I've needed to," Service admitted. "It's not the road that matters, it's where the road leads you."

"Cool," she said. "Donut shop on Quincy Hill okay with you?"

"I prefer somewhere not so public," he said.

"Are you UC on a case near to here?"

"Something like that."

She thought briefly. "Central has a visitor center. People from the Keweenaw County Historical Society gave me keys to all their properties."

He knew Central, which was pretty much off the beaten track. "Try for a meet tonight after the visitor center closes?"

"Can try, but they're college boys and you know how goofy that set can be."

"Tech kids generally tend to be serious students."

"Not these two, I think," she told him. "These guys are like mercury . . . will flow to wherever there's a space or opportunity."

"Ages?"

"Mesnard George is a master's student, twenty-three. The other one, Nankervus, is a sophomore and a hockey player."

"Grad students and sophomores didn't hang out together in my day," Service told her.

"Did you guys have to wear your academic gowns off campus in your day?"

He pointed a finger at her. "Back off the age bit, Something. Think of me not as vintage, not old."

"Didn't know there were vintages in two-buck chuck," she shot back and they both laughed.

"These guys have rocker's plague," the newly minted CO told him. "I have a touch of it too," she said.

Service smiled. "A disorder not uncommon among the indigenous peoples hereabouts. I have it too," he confessed. "I never really thought of myself as a rock-picker until I was fishing one day for brook trout, and the rocks along the edges looked more interesting than the trout."

"I *get* that," she told him. "I'll call the boys. You want to share one of those cigarettes?"

"*You* smoke?"

"Only when I know I can get away with it."

He gave her two and she walked away fiddling with her phone, and he looked down at the view from atop the cliff and smiled. Many, many years ago, he and an old girlfriend had come up here to be alone and were undressed and about to fool around when he smelled smoke and had to get dressed and get on his radio to call in a possible fire, then go see if he could locate it. She got dressed and tagged along in the passenger seat with a pouty look until the fire had been located and put down and then she demanded he take her home to Kearsarge, and her final words to him were: "This pilot light's out for you, man."

He'd never seen her again but heard along the way she had relocated to Arizona and there married a nationally syndicated television evangelist called Boots Young, now a US senator from Arizona.

Something came back. "They say not until the day after tomorrow noonish at the Pilgrim River Tubes. Do you know where that is, and is that timing okay?"

"I know the spot. The timing will have to do," he said.

"You can crash at my place if you don't want to make the long drive home and come right back again."

"Thanks," he said, "but I have another place to crash over this way."

"I scare you off?" she asked.

"If you know Tree, I'm sure he's already set you straight on that count."

"I didn't mean to crash as in crash together in the same bed."

"Not taken that way either. Another time, maybe?" he said, and cringed.

"That a double entendre?"

"Not from a game warden. When I've got something to say I try to make it plain and to the point."

CHAPTER 16

Owl's Pit (North of Central)

KEWEENAW COUNTY

> I am ready to distrust mine eyes, And wrangle with my reason.
>
> —William Shakespeare, *Twelfth Night*

Moments after PCO Something left him, Service's personal cell phone chirped, and what he heard made him suck in a deep breath.

"Sonny, Sonny," Allerdyce squawked. "Youse need get 'ere quick-like!"

The old poacher rarely showed emotions, but his voice now was rich in fear, or was it panic? Whatever it was it put Service's hairs on end, and his own emotional control swung immediately to frigid resolve and a readiness for violence. "Where are you?"

"Youse know dat summer crickle da pipples call da Owl's Pit?"

Service closed his eyes and tried to scan the maps in his head. "On Central Road, just over the top, to the west, maybe a quarter-mile?"

"Dat's it. Hurry, up top da cliff part, up high!"

"Others involved?"

"T'ree," the old man answered. "Where youse at now?"

"Cee-vee, Cee-vee, not that far." Six miles, tops.

"Dat's good. Step on 'er," Limpy said and broke off.

• • •

Owl's Pit was a steep, rocky defile most late summers and autumns, but in spring through early summer, it was an interesting little brook with gin-clear water, all sorts of sheltering woody debris, beautiful long pools some four feet deep, and not a fish of any species anywhere, the rill entirely sterile for no apparent reason, and unstudied by state fish biologists, who had more watershed systems assigned than they could ever properly manage. Typical U.P. metaphor: all promise, no return; all appearances, little substance.

Above Owl's Pit was a nasty unnamed cliff known to few and feared by all who did know because the area was not easily reached and the ground littered with loose conglomerate, which made steady footing a dicey proposition, and if you were near the edge it was just less than a hundred feet straight down.

Service didn't know this area as well as he knew some, but he had seen the cliff from above in a Cessna on jack-lighting patrols and had pressed the terrain picture into his memory bank. Next time in the area, he had made his way into it on foot, looked around, and decided it was too damn dangerous, despite an interesting overview. Even Limpy was wary: "Dat crickle and cliffy dey's for demm fools!"

Only one person he knew of had ever died on the cliff, but this had been enough for the state to post danger signs, and the thickness of the undergrowth and poor, rocky footing kept foot traffic to a minimum. There was no way to get any vehicle closer than a quarter-mile away.

Allerdyce had not specified his exact location other than on top, but the pitch of the man's voice suggested he was near the precipice itself.

Service hid his truck in a thick patch of alders that surrounded a small lily-pad pond and took off on foot, making his way quickly but methodically, watching where he placed each step, not running headlong like he usually did or using the Marine recon shuffle, which he often used to carry him long distances. At the start, footing was relatively easy, but the higher he climbed and the closer he got to the top and lip, the worse it got.

Disaster, he knew, was always close to life. Limpy had been with him one night when they heard dispatch call for help with a fire at a camp and he and the old man had been closer than any other law units and raced to it, and there found an old camp engulfed in fire and an old Finlander sprawled on the ground below the steps of his back porch. Something had bitten the man on the inside of his leg and nicked his femoral and he had bled out where he landed, presumably escaping the fire.

Turned out the old man lived with an old dog, a white-faced rottweiler, whose body was found in the room above the steps where the man lay. The fire inspector had a hell of a time reconstructing the events, but finally concluded the old man had probably tried to pull the dog out of the fire, and the animal, in panic, had nipped at his master and caught the inside of his leg.

Both died under totally bizarre circumstances.

From then on Service always reminded himself everything he did could turn sour at any moment, and while it never stopped him from going in harm's way, it slowed him down some, and this alone bothered him because before the old man and dog night he had had only two speeds: stop and go like hell.

Closing on the location, he shortened his steps and paused to listen, knowing he was unlikely to ever hear Allerdyce, who rarely raised his voice above an audible whisper when he was in the woods. But there might be other voices or clues. The old man had said there were three people involved.

Of his penchant for a low voice and silent movement, Limpy would preach, "She make dese places in quiet for da critters. Pipples got honor Her work," her never being identified by name, but assumed by Service to be Mother Nature, which made him want to laugh. Limpy Allerdyce might demand respect for natural silence, but there was not a speck of romantic impulse in this: Silence was the rule for all nonhuman creatures of and in the woods, except perhaps for periodic mating rituals, or when they were alarmed or trying to join others of their kind. Silence let Allerdyce pretend to become prey so he could kill more efficiently as a predator, and had done so for decades, all over the Upper Peninsula.

Approaching the precipice, Service took longer and longer pauses and eventually, looking slightly north and west toward the cliff edge, he saw an odd hue of yellow-green, the same mustardy color Colonel Harlikin's odd-ball soldiers wore. *Good grief.* What had the old man stumbled into this time, and was there something here that could threaten his own cover? They were a good crow-fly of eight miles from Camp ROCK, and Harlikin had dismissed his troops. With Allerdyce, life was one long, ever unfolding what-the-hell.

Minutes later Service found himself slightly below Limpy and two men he'd never seen before, both in ROCK yellow. The two men were seated back-to-back on boulders six feet apart and close to the edge. Limpy sat ten feet back from the cliff, grinning stupidly, a shotgun balanced on a knee. *Shit*! Whose shotgun? The man was a felon banned from firearms.

Both strangers had dry blood caked on their faces, but one seemed to still be leaking slightly from a forehead wound.

There was no need to signal Limpy that he had arrived. The old man could always sense such things, but Service cautiously moved closer in case what seemed to be, wasn't, and he came up on Limpy's left, staying well back from the cliff's edge.

"Welcome to da party, Sonnyboy!" the old man chirped.

"Funny, I didn't hear any singing or sounds of celebration," the detective said, studying the pair of strangers. He couldn't recall having seen either man before. Both were clean-shaven, with mostly brown hair and hints of gray, volunteers, both with military short haircuts, like fake grass on fake putting greens on mini-golf courses. Both had dry blood caked on their faces and in their hair, the one on Service's left looking like he was leaking steadily, his shirt wet and dark, a shiny vermillion. "By the looks of you two," Service told the men, "it's been a lousy party."

"Dese fellas 'ere was gonna t'row nudder feller offen da top up ere," Limpy announced.

"We've done nothing wrong," the least injured of the pair declared forcefully.

"Youse an youse's mate dere opened up yappers and me an' da girlie heard ever't'ing got said," Allerdyce announced.

"Won't mean a thing in court," one of the men in mustard duds said.

Where was Worm, aka girlie? Service wondered.

"What courts youse t'ink dat is?" Allerdyce said. "Oot ere all got Limpy's Law, and I'm d'jutch."

"What the hell is a *Limpy*?" the bloodier of the two inquired.

Service had already heard enough to know these two were not native Yoopers, which squared with Colonel Harlikin's reputed notions and preferences for recruiting from other parts of the country. "Limpy is your worst nightmare," Service told the men, and glanced over at Limpy. "Where's the involuntary flyer?"

"Da Worm she tooken 'im to da safe place."

"You know where that is?"

"Speck can find when time come."

"That insane old man and a giant naked woman attacked us without provocation," the less bloody one complained. "What is going on up *here*, and what is wrong with *you* . . . people?"

Service said, "Like you just said. They're quite insane, and you may be real lucky I happened to come along."

"And who the hell are *you supposed to be*?" the bloodier one said venomously, "the Lone Fucking Ranger?"

"I'm the person who can guarantee you two won't become involuntary flyers yourselves, provided you're both cooperative. Everybody who lives out this way knows better than to venture too close to cliff edges, especially here. This is a *very* dangerous place."

"It's public property," the same man insisted, and then he whined and whinnied like a frightened horse.

"Were you men to die up here, the point of public versus privately owned will be rendered moot."

"We have a right to be here," the man insisted in a weak voice.

"Says who?" Service came back.

"We're soldiers," the less bloodied one said. "For Jesus," he added.

Limpy cackled. "Youse look like cheap tarts somebody got bored wit' and tossed youses over da side."

Service decided to call them Dry Guy and Wet Guy.

"We have a right to be heard," Dry Guy, the taller of the two said.

"Impressive spunk," Service told them. "Given that you both got your asses kicked by a naked woman and an old man barely strong enough to pick up a small dog. Don't you gents feel even the slightest shame, and when exactly did Jesus start sending His soldiers to strong-arm women and old men?"

"*She* is not human," Dry Guy said with a moan. "That female . . . creature . . . is Lilith!"

Who? "The character in the Frasier sitcom?" Service asked.

"Not dat!" Allerdyce cackled, "Lilith was dat Adam guy's first wifey."

All three men stared at the old poacher. "What?" Service said.

"Real haywire bitch was dat Lilith girlie. Wunt let Adam got on top 'er and den she say da name of Gott and fly away, and she been pain in Gott's butt ever since, eh, an' now Lilith mostly mess wit' new kittles just been dropped out borned."

In all the years Service had known the man, he had never heard Limpy spew such trivia, and he had no idea what to say.

But Wet Guy did. "That story is *not* in the Bible!"

Allerdyce waved his shotgun in the man's approximate direction and the man instinctively raised his bloodied hands as if flesh and bone would deflect a 12-gauge slug.

"Ain't in dere, onnaccount da censor-cuttin 'er out an' kept Lilith outten da Good Book, so dey tell how Gott make second goofy wife, Evie for Adam, an' her comin' along really mixin' up da rabbit food bowl. Youses read Isiah in da Old Testicle she dere, not much, true, but she dere for sure, Lilith. Guy back den tell dis story wildcats meetin' hiney-eeners goat demons talkin' trash wit' each udders, an' dere da guy writin' dat junk he plop down bitch Lilith an' she still want be on top wit everyone, even goats an' t'ings, and cause she allas want on top, Gott punish 'er, tell 'er no sleep for youse, toots, not fornever-never."

Grady almost laughed out loud. Where did Allerdyce come across such outrageous information?

Dry Guy and Wet Guy tried to rally, the former saying, "Better to roll stones with a wise man than drink wine with a fool, carry on no nonsense with a sensible man, and reveal not thy wit to a senseless one."

Allerdyce chuckled and said dismissively, "Dat's da Book a Tobit, stuff 'bout dis Ahiker guy pinched for da crime he claim he ain't done. Dat story an' hull bunch udder stuff in Oldy Dimes and dat Ahiker he dere in the Old Testicle onny once mebbe, but he dere for sure, just like dat Lilith she dere too."

Oh my, the things swirling in Allerdyce's mind.

When Service first arrived, Limpy's voice was frigid with homicidal cold, but the old man now was clearly settling down and where all his ranting came from Service would not even venture ten free guesses, but he knew Limpy well enough to not dismiss out of hand what the man saw. If Limpy insisted Lilith and the other fellow were in the Old Testament, there was a more than an even chance they were.

"I didn't climb all the way up here for a theology lesson," Service declared, "or to referee a senseless argument." He pulled out his badge and held it close enough for both men to see, and having done that, said, "Now what in the hell is going on?"

"We were assaulted," Wet One whinged.

Service nodded to Limpy who, quick-as-a-bobcat, hopped off his rock perch and whacked the man in the head, the blow causing renewed blood flow.

The plainclothes detective announced, "That was neither an assault nor an attack. What it was, was what we call a memory-helper. You two had another man up here with you," he added forcefully. "What were you three up to?"

"I want my lawyer," Dry Guy whined.

"Don't know youse's lawyer,"Allerdyce said. "Don't want to neither. Ain't no bidnet for mout'pice up 'ere. Up ere we want onny 'ear trut.' Youse lie, youses fly, an' if youses fly, youses die, and dat's all dere is to dis. Onny law up ere is me. I t'ink youse need udder law, I mebbe given youse over to Sonnyboy dere."

"But he's the one with the gold badge," Dry Guy complained.

Allerdyce smiled. "He don't get use dat badge official till I tell I'm okey-doke. Right now, my onny job decides if youses go fly from way up high." The old man looked over at Service. "How high up we?"

"Ninety-three feet, I think. Just a hair further than home plate to first base." Service looked at the two men in yellow. "Again, and for the last time, gents, spit 'er out. Why were you three up here?"

Finally they talked, reluctantly.

"When did banishment become vanishment, like dead?" Service asked them. "One's a felony and the other probably no crime at all, depending on circumstances."

"Banish means like make vanish?" Wet One said.

Where and when had these two gone to school? "Banish means to order someone to leave a certain set of circumstances on the banishing group's authority to issue such an order. Vanish means to disappear from sight or existence—as in completely gone."

"Right, like that," Wet Guy said. "We were told to make 'im go away permanent-like."

"Someone gave you that order?" Service asked.

"We were told it was the colonel's order."

"Were you told what specific rules the man broke?"

"Colonel gives orders, not splainations," Wet Guy declared.

"You should have asked because if you two intended to throw someone off this cliff, that is one of many felony charges we could bring."

"But ain't nothing done happened," Dry Guy insisted. "Old Man and crazy girl jumped us. Ain't nothing happened, and we ain't done nothing wrong."

"When you try to rob a bank and you don't get it done, you still tried to rob a bank."

"That don't seem fair," Dry Guy muttered.

Wet Guy looked at his partner. "Now that we didn't get this done, colonel he gonna put BFL order out on us. Colonel don't tolerate no failures."

"If you get the right lawyer and can wiggle out of charges from today, you can always go back to your colonel and try to explain what happened."

"ROCKs don't explain nor make no excuses," Wet Guy said.

"There still can be a way out for you guys. What's that third guy's name?"

"Tooler, we was told," Dry Guy told them, "but ROCK names don't mean shit. We all got new ones."

"Really?" Service said, acting surprised. "Why's that?"

"Because we're all legally dead," Wet One explained.

Service chewed that for a few seconds. "Which means if your colonel has you killed, it won't matter because you're already legally dead."

"Dey don't *smell* so dead," Allerdyce said.

They characterized Tooler as a fuck-up, which Service knew to be untrue, so someone must've told them that. Tooler was also called a violator of the Rules of God, and the laws of the Regiment of Christian Knights. Tooler had been sentenced by the colonel to banishment for life, which one of them called BFL.

"Listen men," Service said, "if you haven't actually banish-vanished anyone, even though your colonel ordered you to, there's light, okay? You tried and failed and prosecutors will insist you pay for that. Homicide in the first degree is the Big Loser's Big Prize in a court of law, but with your testimony, the state will have the colonel for issuing such orders for conspiracy and he'll be the one to pay the full price."

"He'll find us," Dry Guy said.

"How youse know dat?" Allerdyce asked.

"He's God's warrior," Dry Guy said. "The colonel told us that."

"What if dis colonel guy jus' beek bag hot air?"

"He's not," Dry Guy insisted.

Service explained, "But you're here facing charges and he's not and *he's* the one who sent you. Does he get to walk just because he was the boss?"

"Lousy boss," Allerdyce added happily. "Look how 'e screwed youse two."

"Why does the colonel think he can give such orders?"

"The First Monarchy," Wet Guy said.

"The what?"

"Get rid of deep state scoundrels and replace the whole crooked lot with a king and everything will get better," the man said earnestly.

"He's going to be king of the whole country?" Service asked them.

"Just Michigan to begin with," Wet One said. "Your governor's a bitch."

"None of that can happen under the state's constitution," Service pointed out.

"How do you know God doesn't have his own Constitution and that he'll send that down to us the way he sent down the Ten Commandments to Moses?" Wet Guy challenged Service.

"Shouldn't he send that to his troops *before* they act?"

"God don't have to make excuses," Dry One said.

Was this man thinking God and Colonel Harlikin were one and the same? He didn't remember hearing any of this stuff about a king or a First Monarchy while he'd been at Camp ROCK.

"How exactly does the colonel think this plan will work?"

"People will rise up and God will appoint him governor until he can change things around to make himself King for God."

Service saw that even Limpy was stifling a scoffing laugh.

"The ROCKs will be the ones to take this action?" Service asked the pair.

"We don't know that. A lot of units are comin' through camp to train."

"The groups are linked?" Service said.

"In our hearts if not in our different organizations," Dry Guy said.

"What groups?" Service asked.

"We heard of three. Michigan Mission Men, Minnesota Freedom Guard, and the Wolverine Watchmen, they seem to be out of Wisconsin?" Dry Guy said.

"And you all believe the same things?"

Wet Guy spoke up: "low to no taxes, small, skeletal government, freedom to carry arms anywhere anytime, never letting nobody never tell us how to live our lives or help us when we don't need no help."

"So you ever pray to God for help?"

"Sure," Dry Guy said.

"So it's okay for God to help, but not ask the government."

"God don't take our money to help other yayhoos that don't deserve no help," Wet Guy explained.

Service wanted to ask them how much help God actually delivered, versus the government, but kept his mouth shut. "Stay with these guys," Service told his partner. "Stay until uniforms arrive to take custody, and make sure the patrol guys know you were never here, except as a good Samaritan asked by a cop to lend a hand."

Limpy nodded. "Okay, Sonny."

"If these two give you any trouble, do anything you have to, but nothing extreme." Service drew his forefinger across his throat. "None of that, okay?"

"Gotcha, Sonny."

The colonel had shut down ops for two weeks and instead of a sleepy hiatus, everything felt like it was flopping around and threatening to blow up. The colonel wanted to take over the state? How ludicrous! This he had to check out and share with other agencies. Did Harlikin actually think he could pull off something like that?"

As he hiked toward his truck Service called Allerdyce on his cell. "Ask your pals if they know anything about eagle feathers."

"Golden or bald, mature or kittles?"

"Just find out."

• • •

McKower was all ears and all business on the phone, heard what he had to report, hung up, and called him back five minutes later. "The governor now knows. We have Troops coming to take custody of your prisoners. They'll be temporarily housed in Marquette. Meet the Troops at the sheriff's office in Eagle River and don't let the Troops take them inside. Keep them moving to Marquette. What's your next step?"

"Find the guy they were going to vanish and hear his story. This pair today I've never seen before, but the third man I've trained with."

"You know him, then."

"Training with and knowing are different dogs."

"Can we work with this man?"

His hunch was yes, to some extent, but it was just a hunch. "I don't know yet, but I should quickly get a pretty solid read."

"Where's Number Three now?" the captain asked.

"Safe."

"Who's with him?"

"Don't worry, it's covered."

"Covered by whom?" she pressed.

"Stop micromanaging," Grady countered, and heard her grumble.

"All right, I'll get out of your hair. Go make your hand-off. These two are in protective custody of the state, by verbal order of our governor and our AG. All the paper on this will get done and sorted out down the road, and coordinated out of Marquette."

"You going to tell Coldbeg?" Service asked.

"I'm going to think about that for a reasonable amount of time. You think this deal is real?" his friend and captain asked.

"The two in custody seem to think so. Both of them are scared shitless of Colonel Harlikin."

"Assume that same posture, Grady. You sound all jazzed up like when you were twenty," she added.

"You didn't know me then."

"Thank the gods for that small favor. You're not, you know."

"Not what?"

"Not twenty."

"Would you buy twenty-five?"

She chuckled. "Hell, we've all been buying you as twenty-five for twenty-five years!"

She was going to lay an egg when she found out Allerdyce was in this, and as for Worm, where the hell had she gone and how would he explain Worm to his captain? Or anyone, for that matter.

• • •

Service called the Michigan State Police to find out who was coming to retrieve and transport the prisoners, and then called the assigned Troops to change their instructions. Why even go into Eagle River if it could be avoided? This done, he called Limpy and told him to bring the prisoners to him. When they got there, Service loaded the pair in his truck, left Allerdyce where he was, and took the prisoners over the mountain to Eagle Harbor Road, then west to Copper Falls Park, and there he made the prisoner hand-off, and the Troops never even had to drive through Eagle River.

Hand-off complete, Service doubled back south on Central Road, and collected Allerdyce. "Dat went quick-fast," the old man said.

Service nodded. "Where the hell are Worm and Tooler?"

"Allerdyce 'pose to know ever't'ing?"

"He'd better know *this* thing, and he'd better be *right*!"

CHAPTER 17

Stone House

KEWEENAW COUNTY

> As slippery as the Gordian knot was hard!
>
> —William Shakespeare, *Cymbeline*

"I'm waiting for directions," Service told Allerdyce.

"Got t'ink, Sonnyboy," the old man muttered.

"Did you talk to her before she took away Mr. Tooler?"

"Not in no spoked words," Limpy said.

"So now you're a telepath?" Service said sarcastically. "I've been meeting a lot of your kind recently."

"I told girlie go safe place, she given me da nod, grabbed holt da guy and dey was gone slickety-lick."

"What you're saying is that you don't *know* where they are."

Allerdyce glared at the younger man. "Trying not say dat, dat way, but youse keep pushin', pushin', pushin'!"

Service pulled the truck to the side of the road. "You know, or you don't know? Which is it?"

"Dis ain't pick or da salt pepper t'ing. Dere lot stuff t'ink aboot, noodle. Got smokes?"

Service handed him a pack and a lighter. "Anything else to put your mind at ease, povitica, or a nice espresso?"

"Povitica dere jus for Christmas sweets, and Limpy don't drink no wop coffee."

"We're on a timeline here," Service told his partner, which was not entirely true, but sometimes you had to push the old man to make something . . . anything happen, and other times Limpy was an energy storm.

The old man sat with his chin poked upward, like he was trying to stretch his scrawny muscles' neck tendons, and after a second cigarette, he looked over at Service and said, incredulously, "Okay, why we sittin' ere, Sonnyboy?"

"Am I supposed to use my own telepathic powers to discern directions from your brain waves?"

Allerdyce chuckled and made the chittering sounds of an anxious chipmunk. "Some times youse talk weird, Sonny. Jus' keep on sout' ere, take Central Road up top over to old path to schoolhouse and stop right dere."

"There's an old schoolhouse up here?"

"Jus' old foundlenations," Allerdyce said, "but dat ain't where we goin. Dere's dese old two tracks turn into trails across da hills ere, was built back Roseybelt's time when da CCC guys was buildin' trails an' such crosst da steepy hills, and dey made some little tad stone huts where pipples rest, get outten snow or da rain, and crap."

"The schoolhouse is reduced to a foundation, but these huts still stand?"

"Last Limpy seen."

"The place got a name?"

"Stone House."

"But it's huts, not a house?"

"I din't name it, Sonnyboy."

"But this is where Worm is?"

"We gone find out."

"Is this place difficult to find?"

"Not if know where look, eh?" Then Limpy looked over at Service. "We almost dere, Sonnyboy?"

"I have no idea. I thought you were navigating."

"No, I just showin' da way, see down da hill dere's a trail open? Stop 'ere!"

• • •

"Amazing," Service said after they hiked more than a mile west, and finally across a high boulder field to an almost-scenic stone building, not quite a ruin, not an impregnable bastion. It was definitely not a showplace for *North Country Living*. "She's here?" Service asked his guide-dog.

"Dis where I bring 'im was me had to bring 'im. Youse want go first, Sonny?"

"And spoil your grand entry?"

"Dis girlie worry me plenty," Limpy said.

Which made two of them. She seemed wildly self-sufficient, and yet oddly needy.

"Worm think Mister never get here," she greeted them.

Service saw Abel Tooler sitting on a hunk of log by an old stone fireplace in which there was no fire. "You all right?" Service asked the man.

"Batanovich?"

"In the flesh, Abel."

"I'm like confused," the big man said.

"As are we all. Why were those apes after you?"

"All they said was the colonel had decided."

"Decided what?"

"They never said."

"But maybe you guessed?"

"They took me up on that cliff and were going to throw me off. It don't take no rocket science figure out what they were up to."

"Her and Him find Tooler man there, Her take Tooler, old Him take other two."

"Them I know what they were doing," Tooler said. "What are you doing *here*? Who the heck *are* these . . . people?" Tooler asked, glancing at Allerdyce and Worm.

"All that matters is that you're safe."

Tooler looked at Allerdyce. "Where are the other guys?"

Allerdyce answered with a grin.

"You throw them off the cliff?"

"He sent them flying, but not over the cliff," Service said, intervening. "They are out of the way now and no longer a threat to you. Never mind details right now. Did either of them ever say what mission the colonel has in mind for the ROCKs?"

"Mostly they didn't say anything, but at one point I heard them talking about how the colonel believes the actions of Jesus had more impact than his words, and how you have to really wake up people before they'll listen to you. The colonel said you have to do something big to make bigger stuff happen."

"Specifics?"

"None, but they were complaining about the state's governor, how she's like that Roman dude who nailed Jesus?"

"Punches Pirate," Allerdyce said. "Was da governor back den, over dere Jesusland, real hard-ass jamoke didn't tooken no shit offen nobody."

Allerdycean biblical history, Service thought, and shook his head. Michigan's governor and Pontius Pilate? The combo made his head spin.

"Why all talk-talk?" Worm wanted to know. "Make Worm's head sore."

Service showed Tooler his gold badge.

The man stared and looked up, "You're like what, a game warden?"

"Close enough," Service said.

"Game wardens are jokes where I come from," Tooler said.

"Here dere super cops," Allerdyce said.

"You were undercover?" Tooler asked Service.

"Never mind what's behind us, Abel. You think the colonel told these guys to throw you off the cliff?"

"You know how things are there. Don't nobody do nothing, they don't have orders from the colonel."

This seemed true to Service's experience. "But why you?"

"Colonel himself said it was down to you and me and when he asked me who I thought he should pick, I told him to pick you and he said, 'I like an honest man with a clear mind. It is him and not you, but thank you for your candor and for your contributions to our mutual cause.'"

"And then you were brought out here?"

"Next morning."

"You didn't boogie when he dispersed the rest of us?"

"Got message to stay, meet the colonel."

"The two who brought you here. Ever see them before?"

"First time was the night after I met with the colonel. They brought women and we had a party."

"Women, in Camp ROCK?"

"No, they led me out of the camp by an underground trail and then we walked to a vehicle they had stashed in the woods and drove that to some little town. Is there a Copper City?"

Service nodded. "Not that far. You were in a town?"

"No, out in the woods."

"The girls were there?"

"Not at first. One of the guys fetched them but I don't know from where. They were both pretty high when they sailed in."

"Local girls?"

"No idea where from, or who," Tooler said, "But they were real friendly girls, kind of hookers but not hookers?"

"You paid them?"

"The two guys said the party was on the colonel and the girls were volunteers. I didn't pay nothing. That ain't my way."

"But the colonel *did*. How's that jibe with Jesus and his teachings?"

"I wasn't thinking about none of that. When a colonel says party-down, I party-down."

The classic good soldier, following orders. "You heard the colonel order troops to party-down *after* he cleared the camp?"

"I only know what the two guys told me," Tooler admitted.

"Did the colonel party-down too?" Service asked.

"He wasn't there," Tooler said, "but the guys were and they told me party hardy, soldier, so I did. Late next day they woke me up, said come with them."

"They tell you where?"

Tooler shook his head. "Not real talkers, them two."

"What did they say when you climbed up to the top of the cliff?"

"They said I wasn't chosen."

"That's all?"

"Like I said, not big talkers."

"They took you up there to kill you, Abel? That's what you think?"

"Now," the man said. "I didn't when we first got up there, but then they got to pushing and fooling around and making jokes about flying for Jesus, and other shit. And when they grabbed me, I shook them off and when they pushed, I pushed back. That's when your friends showed up to help." Tooler looked at Limpy. "Thanks. Never got a chance to thank you before. You saved my life."

"Worm there too," she said. "Worm get no thanks?"

"I meant *both* of you," Tooler told her.

"You look at It, Old Man only say thanks," Worm said.

"I'm really sorry," Tooler said, making eye contact with her.

"Worm think mebbe Worm should have let them throw Him over top."

"I'm sorry you feel that way, Miss. I'm still really shook up. First time anything like this ever happened to me. I'm really glad you done what you done."

"Miss got name," she said.

"Miss Worm?" Tooler tried. "I like your name."

"Worm like too. Some days."

Tooler turned to Service. "You're the cop, what happens next? You think they'll keep after me?"

"Those two won't," Service said. "They're now out of action."

Tooler asked, "Will he send others?"

"Not until he learns his first team failed, and even then I'm not sure what he'll do. You never saw those two until that day?"

"That's right."

"Roughly speaking, how many people did you meet in the camp, total over the whatever number of times you were there?"

"Counting the colonel, those two and his body-man and you? Dozen and a half, tops. Am I under arrest?"

"No, but we think protective custody makes sense—better to be cautious, eh?"

"When the colonel finds out his men didn't take me out, he may send others, but if they can't find me, they can't hurt me, right?"

"That's the theory."

"So where am I going?"

"The three of us won't know. You ever see all those jars of ticks the colonel keeps?"

"Creeped me out, man. I asked him what they were for and all he said was 'absolution,' and what the heck does *that* mean?"

"No clue, I'm glad we were able to grab you."

"How did you know I needed help?"

"I didn't," Service said. "They did."

"Been a long time since anything made any sense to me," Tooler allowed.

Service was mulling what he had heard: "absolution"—as in holy water? Was the colonel batshit crazy or a mind-fucker, a game-player? At this juncture either was possible—and both.

Worm nudged him and he followed her outside. "Others come?" she asked.

"Not tonight, but sometime maybe, we just don't know, but we're going to act like they are. Is there food here?"

"No, this is run-to place, not stay-safe hide place."

"I have MREs in my truck. Can you make a fire?"
"What is MRE?"
"Food in shiny foil."
She laughed. "Eat shiny foil?"
"Not me, but you can if you want."
"Worm do what Worm want."

CHAPTER 18

Pilgrim River Tubes

HOUGHTON COUNTY

The scene begins to cloud.

—William Shakespeare, *Love's Labour's Lost*

When Service called Tuesday to let her know Patty had arranged to talk to the Tech students, she made arrangements for a sitter for Shigun and drove over to the meeting place so she could be part of it, and she immediately took over, telling the students, "Relax, you guys seem uneasy, and there's no need to be that way with us."

Mesnard George said, "The FBI thinks we have something to do with those skeletons in that cave."

Service thought, why's he calling it a cave, and not what it is, an old mine shaft. He *knows* what a mine is.

"Do you?" PCO Something asked out of the blue and both men lurched at the question.

Great ask on the rookie's part. In an interview where you aren't yet sure of loyalties, veracity, or anything else, you best keep a subject on his heels.

"No ma'am," Nankervus said after a momentary delay. "Absolutely not."

Mesnard George looked at PCO Something. "I never seen those bones until *you* flashed your light on them. I just about *crapped*! Me and Nannygoat been down lots of holes, but never one with a skeleton. Does the FBI think like we killed them people and dumped them there?"

"Do they?" this question again from the PCO. "And did you?"

"Hey!" Nankervus said. "Nuh-uh and NFW, I don't even try to kill no guys on the ice, eh?"

"Nannygoat?" Friday asked.

"Nannygoat is what everybody calls him, or just Goat for short," Mesnard George said. "He's stubborn as hell, especially on the ice, and they call me Gecko on account I look so weird—you know, like my little head and such?"

"You don't look weird to me," Something volunteered.

Friday began to drive the questioning. "I doubt the FBI think you guys killed anyone, but they want to milk you for as much raw information and evidence as they can, and the best way to do that is to keep you on your heels."

"Like she did?" Goat said, with a nod at Something.

Gecko said, "The FBI guys creeped out the both of us with their stupid questions."

"Did the FBI actually *accuse* you of killing those people?" Friday asked.

"More like they made us feel squirmy," the Goat said. "But it was like our guilt was a foregone conclusion, no discussion allowed or coming."

"Did they read you your rights?"

"Like we could have an attorney, and all that junk?" Goat said.

"Miranda rights."

"Why we need a lawyer if we haven't done anything illegal?" Gecko asked.

"Like breaking into a privately owned mineshaft, that sort of illegality?" the PCO pointed out.

"Half the people in the Copper Country crawl around the poor rock piles and into old mine shafts and adits," Goat told her. "And tourists do it too. Maybe it's a tad-bit trespassing, but hundreds of people do it, maybe more, so what's the big deal suddenly?"

"Seven sets of human remains is what's the big deal," Something reminded the young man.

"Did they give you any indication *why* they think you killed those people?" Friday asked.

"No ma'am," Nankervus said.

"Well, we don't believe you are killers," Friday said calmly and softly, "so relax and answer our questions and help us understand some things, okay? Help us and then you can get on with your day."

The Goat looked up at the Gecko and both of them nodded. "We'll try," the Goat said.

Hockey player as the leader-spokesperson? Service wondered. His instinct said no, and he wasn't sure why.

"Mister Burdon Leaf," Goat Nankervus said and looked to his taller partner for confirmation and Gecko nodded.

Was Nankervus the leader here, and the Goat only their front-man? Odd. Mesnard George was a grad student, Nankervus only a sophomore.

"Leaf?" Friday asked.

"Got him a rock shop over to Dollar Bay," Goat said.

Friday looked at Patty. "Dollar Bay, Leaf, you know the name or the man?"

"I don't, but I just got here. Where's his shop?" she asked Nankervus.

"Watertank Road, off the M-26."

The PCO shook her head. "Been down that way, but don't remember any shop."

"His sign's inside. He ain't put it up yet," Goat explained. "The building's cinderblock and painted a shade of blue."

The PCO grinned. "*That* building I recall."

Friday asked, "What does Mr. Leaf have to do with you guys?"

Goat again, after a subtle glance at his giant partner, "We sort of prospect for him?"

"Sort of prospect for what?" Friday asked.

"Float-copper pieces, some datolite, sometimes silver, the usual junk."

"Silver?" Something asked. "It's only here in small quantities."

"Leaf thinks differently."

Gecko this time. "It shows up in some copper mines, usually mingled with or fused into copper, but now and then pure veins have been found in the Keweenaw."

"Were you two looking for a vein of silver in the mine where PCO Something had to rescue you?"

"Not that time," Goat said. "That was our first time down there and we were just trying to get a feel for the place, you know, like when you're on the road for a game and early that day you take a skate on the enemy's ice to see what it is you'll be dealing with?"

There was some logic to what the sophomore player said, but in Service's mind, this sort of thing was more characteristic of low-level pro teams than collegiate outfits. "You thought there a silver mine in that place where you fell?" he asked Gecko.

"We don't know. There must've been quite the mining down there once. We saw extensive timber support systems down below."

"Was it a silver mine?" Service asked again, this time looking up at Gecko, who towered overhead.

"Mr. Leaf wasn't sure," Gecko answered. "He told us there had been some pretty remarkable and fairly large half-breeds found down there so he was speculating on the chances of a vein in the area."

"Does this mine have a name?" Service asked.

"Mr. Leaf's still researching that. There have been a lot of unnamed mines in the Keweenaw. He can't afford to pay us to research and explore and prospect for him, so he does one part, and we do the other. He tells us where to go and what to look for and that's what we do."

"Are you Leaf's employees?" Patty Something asked.

"Not officially," Nankervus answered. "We're more like freelancers."

"Or contract guys," the Goat added.

"But he *does* pay you?" this from Friday.

"Some cash now and then, but when we make a strike, he'll either buy it from us outright, or split the take with us."

"What ratio?" Service asked.

"Sixty-forty, him," Goat said.

"Sweet numbers, all in his favor," Something observed. "You two take all the *physical* risk. What's *his* risk?"

"Money," Goat said forcefully. "And he's paying all the medical bills for Gecko's arm."

"Damn generous in these days for a small business that doesn't even have its sign up yet," Detective Friday said.

"You guys find anything but bones in that cave?" Service asked.

"*She* found the bones, not me or us," Gecko said quickly, pointing at PCO Something. "You should have seen her down there, like Spidey Girl. She rappelled down that face like she does it for a living." Gecko's admiration seemed legitimate.

"Officer Something showed you the bones down there?"

Gecko nodded once, vigorously.

"You guys talk about them?" Friday asked.

Gecko shook his head with equal vigor, "I told her, man, get me the fuck out of here!" The boy's face flushed. "Sorry I said that word, Officer."

The PCO laughed, and Friday asked the two, "Have you guys met with Mr. Leaf since the incident?"

"We ain't never met him in person," Goat said. "He just calls on the cell phone he gave us."

Friday stepped close to the giant grad student, forcing him to take a step back.

Service smiled inwardly. She was invading his personal space to keep him off-balance. Had she also concluded he was lead dog here?

"Why did Mr. Leaf send you down *that* shaft," Friday asked.

"We already said," Goat told her. "We were exploring first, to get the layout down pat, y'know?"

"Kind of test run, is that what you're saying?" she asked.

"Sort of like that, yeah."

"You're not answering the question," the State Police homicide detective said. "What did he tell you to get you interested in doing the job for him? You did other prospecting jobs for him?"

"This was the first job," Gecko said, stepping in for his partner. "Mr. Leaf said he had some reliable information that there was a good bit of half-breed in hand-size chunks down on the level where I hit when I fell. I believe the first thing he wanted us to do was verify his source was not misleading him. Prospecting always includes a lot of gaslighting and mind-games."

"Are the skeletons still there?" Goat asked.

"They've been removed to the crime lab and the shaft is now officially closed with crime scene tape, and it will remain that way until the Michigan State Police decide they've milked the site for all the evidence it has to offer."

"How do you know there's evidence?" Goat asked.

"Odds, and Locard's Exchange Principle," Friday said. "The Frenchman ran the world's first forensics lab, in Lyon, France, and he believed that every human contact leaves a trace, and that, given the plasticity and atomistic nature of the world, a criminal cannot avoid leaving some trace of their presence, and taking something away with them. Studies since then, over many years, show that the average major crime site possesses at least ten useful forensic clues."

"*Ten*?" Gecko said and looked at his partner with what Service read as alarm in his eyes.

Service wondered what the hell they had here.

"How many skeletons were down there?" Gecko asked after taking a deep breath.

"You didn't count them?" Friday asked, again swooping in from right field.

"No way, I just wanted out of there. Plus my arm really really hurt. Didn't *you* count them?" the boy asked Something. "You're the cop."

"Of course I counted them," she said. "We were just wondering how much you had your wits about you."

"I said my arm hurt like hell," he said.

"You told me it was numb," Something said.

"Which it was when you first got there, and then it started to hurt."

"You never mentioned any pain at the time."

"Because I'm not a crybaby."

"Except for wanting me to get you the fuck out of there," she reminded him.

"That was different. I never saw a dead person before."

"Not even a mummy in a museum when you were a kid?"

"We didn't have any museums in my hometown," Gecko told them. "And, you don't think of mummies as people if they're in museums," he added.

"Where is your hometown?" Service asked.

"French Lick, Indiana."

"Larry Bird's hometown."

"Larry who?" Gecko said, and looked dumbfounded.

"Larry Bird and Earvin Magic Johnson and their epic basketball battles."

"I don't play or follow basketball," Gecko told the group.

"How many people in your hometown?" Service asked.

"I don't know. Maybe a couple thousand?"

And he didn't know who Larry Bird was? Curious.

"So how many bodies were down there?" Goat asked.

"Who said there were any bodies?" Friday asked him.

"She did," Gecko answered, pointing to the PCO. "She just asked me how many bodies I saw. We been over this."

"I said skeletons," Friday corrected him.

"Stiffs are stiffs," Goat said forcefully. "Bodies, skeletons, dead is dead, who cares about that?"

"*Homicide* detectives care," Friday told him.

"So how many?" Goat asked.

"Confidential information," Friday told the boys. "Sorry, we can't share."

"That's unfair," this from Goat.

"How many times did you guys talk to this Mister Leaf?" Friday asked them.

"We told you," Goat said.

"Just the once?" Friday said.

Gecko nodded.

"He called before your accident, right?" she inquired.

Goat said, "Right."

Friday said, "Then how did you guys know he's taking care of Mr. George's medical bills?"

"He left a text message," Gecko said. "We missed the call and he left the message. That ain't the same as talking on the phone."

"You'd think he'd show a little more interest," PCO Something said.

"Why would this guy pay your medical expenses when you're not his employees and he has no formal fiduciary connection to you?" Grady asked. "That never struck you two as a hair on the odd side?"

"Maybe a little," Mesnard George allowed.

"Won't your student medical insurance cover an accident like this?" Service asked.

"It should," Gecko said, "but there are always leftovers and gaps."

Friday pushed close again. "You know this how, about leftover expenses?" Friday asked.

"Five years in school at Colorado College, lots of prospecting out there, but under the student policies at CC, you were on your own if you got dinged up. Mining was considered an inherently hostile environment, and above the risk comfort of student medical insurance policies."

"But your policy took care of injuries out there?" Friday asked.

"Most of it," Gecko told her.

"But it won't do that here?"

"I haven't asked specifically."

"Why is *that*?" she demanded.

"I wasn't expecting to get hurt, I guess."

"Did Leaf ask you two if you had medical insurance before he asked you to work for him?"

Goat and Gecko looked at each other and Service wondered what that mental mind-meld concerned.

"I guess he did, sort of," Goat said for them.

"So his offer doesn't look so generous in that light," Friday pointed out.

"Guess not," Goat allowed. "Put that way."

"Listen boys," Service said, "When it comes to money, always look at *everything* as coolly as you can."

"We try to," Gecko said.

"How did the FBI leave this thing with you two?" Friday asked.

"The agents say we're confined to classes," Gecko said.

"And the ice rink," Nankervus added.

"When's your next meeting with the FBI?" Friday asked.

Goat told her, "The agents never said. Does that mean there won't be one?"

"It means only they didn't say anything," Friday told them. "The FBI has its own way of doing things. If they ask you to do something, do it. If it doesn't sound right, or, if you're confused, you can call me." She handed each a copy of her MSP business card. "Which special agent did you guys talk to?" she asked.

"Guy named Cold-something was one of them, we're not sure where he's from," Nankervus told her.

"Coldbeg?" Friday said.

"Yes, and Swaytkall," Gecko added.

"Where's Swaytkall say he was out of?" Service asked. This was a new name to him.

"Milwaukee, I think," Gecko said. "He was pretty laid back, not like the local guy."

Service thought. Didn't Nankervus, the Goat, just say he didn't know where Coldbeg was from? And Tuesday hadn't said either. So how did Gecko know he was "the local guy?" Friday was glancing at him and he was trying to read her. Was it the Milwaukee office mention that jabbed her? Very unusual to have a Milwaukee Feeb here, unless Marquette and Milwaukee were both on the same case. But what case would that be? How much were the Feebs hiding from state and local agencies? Not your business, he reminded himself. Homicide was Tuesday's trade and she was damn good at all that went with it.

"You boys gonna be in Dutch for missing class today?" PCO Something asked.

"Dutch?" Nankervus asked with a perplexed look.

"Means trouble," Something amended.

"I get it," Goat said. "Students are incidental to this prof at best."

"You guys get a lot of work this way?" Friday asked. "Some guy calling you out of the blue?"

"No, but it happens," Goat said. "He told us that a lot of people watch him and try to horn in on his projects, so he keeps to phones. But he told us where his building was and we went over there and had a look. The Rock Shop sign was inside, on the floor. The building's being renovated."

"Did you talk to the renovators?" Something asked.

"No, we went after work hours," Goat said.

"Trespassing, *again*?" Something pointed out.

"We didn't take nothing," Goat said defensively.

"You don't have to take something to be guilty of trespass," Something explained. "Did you guys take something from the place where Gecko broke his wing?"

"We ain't took nothing from nobody nowhere," Goat insisted. "The building he's redoing is junk-ass. It dates back to like eighteen something."

"Not a word to Leaf about the FBI or what you saw?" Friday asked Mesnard George.

Both men shook their heads.

Friday looked at each of them. "You guys going to go back down that same shaft and look for those silver half-breeds?"

Gecko said, "If he asks again, we'll have to think about it, but I'm not going anywhere until this cast comes off."

"I ain't never going down *that* hole," Goat said emphatically. "Not with all that crap was in there last time. What if there's more of them in that hole?"

"More of *them*?" Friday said.

"You know, stiffs," Goat said with a nervous smile.

"When did skeletons become stiffs?" Something pressed.

"Skeletons aren't deceased?" Gecko challenged her. "Are we about done here?"

Friday looked at her compatriots and they were silent. "You guys can go, but don't get caught violating any FBI orders."

When the boys were gone to rejoin their clueless professor, Friday elbowed Service. “Boy do I remember this place!” she whispered.

“Who were you with?” he reacted.

She tried to shoot an elbow into his ribs, but he pivoted away. “Jerk,” she said.

PCO Something said, “Do you two need time alone?”

Friday laughed out loud.

“Are you two always so flirty?” Patty asked, and laughed.

“Hey,” Service said. “Focus! Observations?”

Tuesday said, “I can’t believe the FBI is looking seriously at those two for anything.”

The PCO nodded agreement.

“How does this guy Leaf fit in with these kids?” Service asked. “Something doesn’t feel right.”

“What, and based on what?” Friday asked.

“I don’t know. A gut thing. You don’t feel it? A guy speculating on ores with college kids and doing everything by phone?”

“I feel something maybe, but not full-on. There are ways to check their claim on phone calls,” Friday pointed out.

“With warrants and probable cause,” Something pointed out.

The other two ignored the new officer. “You care if we check out this Leaf guy?” Service asked Friday.

“It’s a homicide case for me and your natural resources angle would be *what*?”

“The man is talking to these two kids about harvesting the state’s natural resources.”

“I’ve got no problem with that,” Friday said. “If the mineral rights belong to the state, and aren’t privately held.”

“My impression is that the chances of private mineral holdings up here are pretty rare,” Service pointed out. Friday looked at Patty Something. “Your dad was a geology prof. The pile of hidden half-breed ring true to you?”

“What the heck *is* half-breed?” the new officer asked. “My dad never talked work or rocks at home.”

“Silver mixed with copper,” Service told her.

“How do they get like that?”

"It's science: Universes expanding, black holes sucking, who the hells knows, or cares?" he said.

"You want to know how silver and copper get together, don't ask me," he said. "GTS."

"Google doesn't have *all* the answers," Patty pointed out.

"People act like it does," Service said.

"*Some* people," she corrected him.

"Fine," he said. "I stand corrected."

"Write this down," Friday said, "Grady Service just accepted correction. There won't be many more moments like this."

"You want company checking out Burdon Leaf?" the new officer asked.

"I already said *we*," he told her.

"But you didn't ask."

"Would you help?"

"Love to, sure."

Friday shook her head and turned to leave. "You kids have fun, I have to get back to work in Marquette."

"More duels?"

"Continuing clean-up from the last one," Friday said.

"Duels?" the PCO asked.

"You do *not* want to know," Friday told her and made a calling gesture with her hand and fingers. "Please?"

"I might be too decrepit to dial," Service said.

"You're obviously too senile to recall dial phones died decades ago."

"No kidding?" he said.

"If the Leaf gent ends up pointing to more bodies or homicides, call sooner, not later," Friday told them.

"Yes'um," Service said, adding, "Sir, Ma'am, Sir."

Friday looked at Patty Something. "Bear in mind at all times that your partner can be a colossal jerk."

"But you love him anyway?"

"It's a damn sad statement, isn't it."

"I hear you, sister."

"I'm sick of hearing it," Service told them. "Whose side are you on, PCO?"

"Really?" Friday said. "You actually *asked* her that?"

CHAPTER 19

Dollar Bay

HOUGHTON COUNTY

> Knavery's plain face is never seen till used.
>
> —William Shakespeare, *Othello*

A red truck marked Red Jacket Glass was parked in front of a blue cinder-block building, the color neither navy nor ultramarine, but more of a listless Prussian blue, and oddly foreboding. Inside, the COs found a man with a graying goatee. He was in coveralls decorated with gaudy patches of fruits and flowers and, as soon as the man spotted Patty Something's badge, he thumbed a shoulder strap and announced, "My wife's idea of styling, *not* mine." Then he laughed.

"Styling's certainly one word for those," she said with a smile. "We're looking for Mister Burdon Leaf, the building owner."

The glass man pulled a red kerchief from his pocket and wiped his forehead. "You must have the wrong address. This place belongs to Joe Sklarus of Traprock Electric. I never heard of Leaf. I'm here to put in new windows for Joe."

Service saw an old, large, faded rock shop sign leaning against a wall and nudged his partner. "We were told Leaf is opening a rock shop," Something told the man.

The glass man looked puzzled, then amused. "That old sign? Yah, was a rock shop here mebbe six hundred years back. I was just a kid then."

"You've aged well," the PCO told him and the man smiled.

Service looked at where the sign was and saw that there was no way anyone could see it from outside the building. The Tech kids had to have come inside, and he wondered if they had *broken* in.

Service saw Patty's easy way with the glass man and guessed she could mix with anyone, and being a young, tall, good-looking black woman up here was nothing like the job in some counties BTB, especially near larger cities.

"You must be one of our two new game wardens," the man said. "Word's out we're getting two newbies. Where are you transferring from?"

Service closed his eyes. People in the U.P. could name their local game warden before their sheriff, mayor, or the state's governor. And a lot of them could tell you the game warden's daily schedule because they paid attention to such things in ways most citizens from below the bridge would not understand.

"I'm fresh from the academy," she said.

"Heard that's a tough road. True?"

"Tough enough," she said. "My partner was a Navy SEAL for ten years before he went through the academy. We graduated together."

"What did you do before this?" the man asked.

"Box," she said, and the man's jaw dropped.

Patty laughed. "It was amateur."

"Like Olympic stuff?"

"Actually, I was an alternate on the last Olympic team. Close but no cigar, right?"

"How many fights have you had?"

"Never counted them," she said.

"Your record any good?"

"Good enough for the Olympic Committee."

"Jinx Paanko is my handle," the man said. "I think I recognize your name, Something. There was a Tech professor had a place up on Bumbletown Hill like forever. I'm sure his name was Something."

"My dad," she said.

"Where is he now?"

"We lost him last year," she said.

"I'm real sorry to hear that," he said, and stared at her for a minute. "I always heard that the prof had a daughter but I don't remember you ever going to school here."

"They sent me to Detroit for schooling."

"Cranbrook or one of those good private schools?"

"No, Detroit Public Schools, Cass Tech."

To this the man had nothing to say, and reached clumsily for a segue. "How is your mum?"

Service watched the interaction as he studied their surroundings. Rock shops tended to have a lot of shelving and display cases. This space had none of that, and no apparent special lighting.

"She's doing all right so far. She's almost as hard-headed as he was. She's selling me the house in Bumbletown. She's in a condo in Hancock."

"Nice," Paanko said. "Winter up on Bumbletown can get on the owly side, but people there stick together."

Patty said, "Guess we'll get out of your hair, Mr. Paanko."

"Jinx, please." He took off his baseball cap and rubbed his bald head.

"I'm Patty." She scribbled something on a business card and handed it to the man. "My personal cell is on the back. If you ever need me, please call."

"My shop's up to Laurium," Paanko said. "Just around the corner from Toni's. All cops are welcome anytime and there's always a coffee pot going. Both county sheriffs are friends, and a lot of their deps hang out."

"I'll remember that when my caffeine levels sink too low, and I'll be sure to stop by."

"You can't miss it," he said. "I live right upstairs."

Something said, "Have you heard anything about anyone opening a new rock shop anywhere in the area, Jinx?"

"No but if I hear any scuttlebutt, I'll call." He waggled her card at her, and smiled. "Rocks are eternal and so are people chasing them, but only a few rockers are foolish enough to try to make a living off the infernal things."

"Thanks, and even if you think something's only a rumor, please call," the PCO said.

"You one of those game wardens who crashes into a new territory like Attila the Hun?" Paanko asked.

PCO Something grinned. "I've not met Mr. Hun, so I can't compare styles, but I'm pretty straightforward. Rules are rules and they apply to everyone."

"Can't disagree," Paanko said and looked past her at Service. "Who's the big galoot with you?"

"My grandfather," she said. "He's why my skin's not darker."

"Okay then," Paanko said. "I hear anything about rock shops, I'll call," and he dug one of his own cards out of his coveralls and held it out. "That's me. You ever want to see a real old and historic Yooper deer camp, gimme a call and I'll show you one. It's—way out near High Rock Bay and been there almost a hundred years. I got tursts crawlin' all over the property all year long."

"We'll put your camp on our patrol itinerary. Are there other camps out that way?"

"Yah sure, all of 'em in way-far-middle of nowhere. Mine's got hundred sixty acres in three chunks."

Something began to walk away, but turned back. "How often have you been here working?"

"Three, four days a week, but will be done once I get all this old glass outten here, and get new product installed," he said, and added, "I don't know where Joe Sklarus come up with the money, but he's going to move his electric business down here."

"You see anybody hanging around who seems out of context, let me know that too, okay?"

"Sure," Paanko said and followed Something and Service out to his black Ford. "Where's your badged truck?" the man asked. All DNR law enforcement trucks had large gold badges painted on their doors, and some Yoopers called them badge buggies.

"In the shop for some work. Grandpa here's my chauffeur for a couple of days."

"The state allows that?"

"What the State doesn't know, can't hurt the State," Something said in a conspiratorial tone.

"I hear that," Paanko said and paused. "Ya know, there is one weird thing I seen, two or three times, but I didn't really think much about it until youse asked about people hanging around."

"What's that?" the PCO asked.

"There's this guy from the county, the retired magistrate, I think. Seen him this week, and coupla times he was stopped right out front, and stared at this building. I think I seen him last week too. Struck me as goofy, eh?"

"Name?" Something asked.

"Irkka Vorpi, was State Troop and then retired, then he was Houghton County magistrate, and now he's retired from that—and here's something odd, I think he's a rock nut. Makes, sells jewelry, good stuff, not no cheap crap neither."

"Silver jewelry?" the PCO said.

"Yah sure, how did youse know *that*?"

"Lucky guess," she said.

"But only native silver and copper," Paanko said. "Local stuff."

Something thanked the man and got into the truck.

• • •

"Magistrate Vorpi?" she asked when they were moving.

"Met him couple of times, way long time ago. Had a reputation as an 'operator,' you know, the type who's always got some scheme running on the side."

"Rocks?" she asked.

"I don't remember that specifically, but it sounds enough off the wall to fit what I know of him."

"Will we ruffle any feathers if we talk to him?" she asked.

"Depends on how you approach him."

"I meant we," she said.

"And I meant you, solo. I'm still undercover, and though I've only met the man a couple of times, I don't want my face freshly reimprinted on his brain—just in case. Tell him your interest is in the ROCKs and see how he reacts."

"Of course it's rocks," she said. "I was listening."

"No, not just plain old lower case rocks, but all upper case R-O-C-K."

"What is *that*?" she asked.

"Regiment of Christian Knights."

"That's a new one to me."

"Just see how he reacts. As the old county magistrate, he'll know things few others will have been privy to in the county."

"What else can you tell me about Vorpi?" she asked

"Shit all, but Shark will know something. He always does."

"Shark?"

"Yalmer Wetelainen, a friend. I'll introduce you."

"Personally?"

"You bet."

"You aren't afraid of leaving a fresh imprint of your face in this man's brain?"

"No, he's practically one of us."

"Like Allerdyce?"

Service laughed. "Allerdyce isn't like anyone or anything."

"I thought he was your partner and friend."

"He is—both, and he and I go way back, and what he may seem to be now is a far cry from what he once was, or maybe he isn't. With Allerdyce you just can't know for certain."

"And Shark?"

"Flies as true as an arrow can fly. Your partner has already met him."

"He has?"

"Over time you'll get some very good cases from Wetelainen. For long periods you may not hear anything, and then bing-bang-bing he'll hit you with a bunch of good stuff. When Shark calls, listen carefully and act accordingly."

"That sounds like high praise."

"The highest, and if you want help from someone who is superbly good in the woods, he's your man. He can track a snake across concrete, make a fire in thirty seconds with not much more than his imagination, and can double-time over damn near any kind of terrain all day long."

"He sounds relentless."

"That's Shark."

"I frequently hear that same word applied to you," she said.

He acknowledged her with a dismissive grunt. "Service lives south of Houghton right on US 41. Fasten your seatbelt and let's roll."

"It gives me chills when you take charge."

He laughed. "Cap'n McKower says it gives her hemorrhoids."

• • •

"Already met your partner," Wetelainen greeted PCO Something. "Nice to finally have a full complement of game wardens up this way. Been a good long time since we've been fully staffed. Lots of shenanigans going on up here and some local yahoos now think they have a free pass, and that they're immune to the magic wand of the law."

"You two can play nicey-nicey-getting-to-know-you another time," Service said. "What can you tell us about the county's retired magistrate?"

"Irkka?" Shark said. "Can tell you they're about to put him in a rubber room."

"Explain?" Service came back.

"Are youses not scanning the county cop frequency?"

"She is," Service said with a nod to his partner. "Aren't you?" he said to her and she rolled her eyes.

"Which county?" the PCO asked.

"The both of them," Shark said. "Deps from both got the call, but Bapcat was closest, and first on the scene."

"What scene?" Service asked. Wetelainen, like Allerdyce, took his own sweet time to spin out a tale, no matter how minor or major. "Irkka Vorpi?"

"Trying to tell you. Was kid from Tech up Houghton Falls yesterday. He's working for the State Parks crowd this summer, doin' a survey and blueprint for a handicap access boardwalk out to the falls, so the wheelchair folks can get out there."

Vorpi! Service wanted to scream, but knew better. Pressure would make his friend draw out the story even longer. What he said was, "You gonna read all kid's survey numbers or does this story have a point?"

Wetelainen grinned mischievously at his longtime friend. "You *haven't* heard!"

Something looked at the two men, and Service picked up on this and touched her sleeve as a signal to let Shark talk. "Obviously," Service conceded.

Wetelainen flashed a big smile. "I like it when I get the news before Mr. Long Nose," he said proudly.

"We're all aging here," Service said. "All three of us. She was just twelve when we got here. *Now* look at her."

Wetelainen said, "So this kid he sees this fella at the cliff edge with the real rainy face, and kid's afraid the guy's up to something self-destructive. Is a real smart kid, this Tech student. Majoring in civil engineering, and he's got a very cool head, I think. Youse ought tell state hire this kid now or lose him to someone else."

"What about the guy with the real rainy face?" Service prompted.

"Was old Irkka Vorpi, by God. I didn't say that already?"

"Vorpi was the one with the rainy face?" Service said for clarification.

"Youse's guy Bapcat talked him out of jumpin' off," Shark reported.

"Where's Vorpi now?" Service asked.

"They stuck him in Aspirus up to Laurium."

"Not Portage Hospital?"

"No room at the inn. Portage they got two rubber rooms, but both occupied right now."

"Vorpi *told* Bapcat he was going to jump?"

"Said he was thinkin' about it on account of nothing going right for him no more and even God don't much like him."

Mental illness made people really difficult to deal with, and Service had always found such contacts perplexing because the people were unstable and unpredictable.

"God doesn't like him? How well do you know Vorpi, Shark?"

"Fished with him some. Talks the good game, but more jibberjab than puttin' brookies in da creel."

"You ever sense he was unstable?"

"Years back, after he first retired from the MSP his first wife left him and he was down real bad over that for long time, but then he met a nice girl, she was a bunch years younger, but they got married and had them a kid quick-like and couple years back he came home one day, and found her, the kid, and his two black labs gone."

"She left him?" Service said.

"He never did find out where she, the kid, or the labs went off to."

"He flip out then?"

"Heard he started down that road, but he met some sky pilot who got him settled down and he seemed to be doing just fine until this thing out to Houghton Falls. Was damn good thing that Bapcat kid was there."

Patty said, "I can vouch for that. He's unflappable."

"Aspirus in Laurium?" Service asked, wanting to confirm what he had heard.

"I'd guess he's still there," Wetelainen said. "The docs don't seem so quick to let the mentals walk out so soon after a deal like this. Why youse want know about Vorpi?"

"Do you know if he's a rocker?" Service asked.

"Was once *big-time* rock guy," Shark said, and started giggling.

Service let whatever it was that tickled his friend work itself out and finally the man said, "Youse don't think this is *funny*?"

"What exactly is funny about a a man threatening suicide?"

"Rocker going off his bloody rocker, *that's* funny," Shark said and started giggling again.

When he regained control, he looked at the two officers. "You two take life too seriously. Guy wants to jump bad enough, he'll find way to jump, and if so, that's too bad for him, mebbe, but long as he don't land on nobody like a body-bomb, it ain't no big deal. But that crap went down up to Copper Harbor last night, *that* shit was scary!"

The officers looked at each other. Service said, "*What* are you talking about?"

"Turst shop got hit closing up time, youse know da place, one got knick-knacks and such, and some eats, and booze? The clerk she locks front door, goes back to the cooler to do some chores, and when she come back out, there's a stranger puttin' a burrito into microwave, and she blinks and thinks she's sure she locked the door, and she looks past this guy and sees the door's been smashed out, and she never heard a thing, and the guy says real calm-like, 'I don't want to hurt *you*, lady, so how about you calmly walk across the street and call the cops, okay? You can tell them I'll be right here waiting for them.' So she did," Shark concluded.

"It took almost two hours for the cops to talk the wingnut out of the store—but not until the crazy bugger smashed every freezer and cooler door in the place."

Something said, "Let me guess, Bapcat was first there, too."

"Naw, Bapcat wasn't there! Was just some deps and mebbe a trooper or two. You two didn't know about this one *neither*?"

"Did Vorpi ever remarry?" Service asked, by way of getting back to why they were there.

"Nope, guess two strikes was enough for him. What youse think about that Copper Harbor deal?"

Service said, "I think that gent has some issues and he was looking either for help, or suicide by cop."

"Sickindahead is worst thing can happen to a person," Wetelainen said. "Youse gonna go see Vorpi?"

"Maybe," Service said. "How big a rocker was he, big enough to open a shop?"

"Was time he talked that way, but his interest mainly was copper and silver and nothing much else."

"Why silver?" Something asked.

Shark shrugged. "Why does one guy like redheads, and the next guy prefers blondes with red pimples? We're all wired differently."

"You ever think Vorpi's wires were crossed?" Service asked his friend. "And by that, I mean wound too tight, or too loose?"

Shark shrugged and hunched his shoulders. "I don't know the answer, but one time, him and me was up to Copper Harbor fishing those big splake come in late summer and instead of talking fish, all he wanted to talk was some lost silver mine and some crazy crap like that."

"A lost silver mine, around *here*?" Service asked.

"Youse know how that air-castle crowd is about their secret stuff," Wetelainen said.

Actually, he didn't know. "I'll take your word on that. Did he ever mention the name of this secret mine?"

"It wasn't no secret," Shark said. "It just ain't been found again. It's called the Three T Mine."

"You say that like it's real."

"In Irkka's mind it was, and what else counts? Actual mine name is Two-Ton Too."

"Two-Ton Too is same-same as Three T?"

"Yup, and it's awful alliteration," Shark said, "and very fifth-graderly at that, eh, but there you are. A name's a name. Entrepreneurs and speculators in the rock game all seem lean toward fifth grade reasoning, and a world of polar opposites. Yes-no, black-white."

"Your tone of voice suggests skepticism," Service told his friend.

"You still got the good ear. There was supposed to be a mine with a thick vein of native copper, maybe two- or three-foot diameter, and from what I heard, it was not a vein, but like a massive heap of float copper, only it wasn't no copper. Was silver and pure, weighed two tons, story says, and the guy found it named the mine The Two-Ton, and he got the ore out of the ground and then rumors started 'round that there was another vein, as good as the

Two-Ton, and maybe better, and of course, everyone started calling that one the Two-Ton Too."

"The guy who found Two-Ton," Service said. "Did he also find Two-Ton Too?"

"Nope, he died from buzztail bite while diddling a buddy's wife out in western Pennsylvania."

"She get bit too, the wife?" Patty Something asked.

"No, ma'am and she didn't even know he was bit until he went real still . . . uh . . . like . . . in position? The lady told the coroner she hadn't noticed nothing wrong on account everything was nice and snug where was supposed to be nice and snug, and she thought he was just enjoying the moment like she was."

"*Ew*," Patty said softly. "That is *sick*."

"Maybe so," Shark allowed, "but it gives going out with a bang a whole new level of meaning."

"Vorpi was a believer in the second silver mine?" Service asked.

"He was that one time him and me was fishing, but since then, I don't know, and back then he wasn't walkin' around thinking about flying off the top of no cliffs neither. Youse two see him, tell 'im Shark says hey."

"Will do," Service said. Vorpi wigged out at almost the same time as some strange guy in Copper Harbor? The world was taking some screwball turns.

Back in his truck he looked at his partner. "See all the great shit you missed growing up BTB?"

She laughed. "Believe me, Detroit has its own special brand of nut-jobs."

"Like a girl passing up going to rich white kids' private school?"

"For your information, I wasn't given a choice in the matter," she said.

He shrugged, and aimed the truck north again, this time to Laurium.

CHAPTER 20

Allouez

KEWEENAW COUNTY

I like not fair terms and a villain's mind.
—William Shakespeare, *Merchant of Venice*

But Laurium was not to be, at least not yet, and herein Service knew was the usual practical conundrum of any game warden's day. You could plan to do whatever you thought you ought to be doing, but real events could change the plan even before you put her goin'. He was back in the truck only moments when the ROCKs burner phone flashed a text message: REMAIN AS IS, PLUS TWO WKS. It was not signed, but only Colonel Harlikin could use the thing. Remain as is, meaning stay in the hiatus, plus two more weeks? A month? What the hell was going on? Very frustrating, and no way to know being out here, and not back there where he could see and analyze.

This new pull-back was bothersome especially because the colonel had made himself out to be the gung-ho sort. Had Harlikin learned about the botched murder of Abel Tooler, and the arrest of his would-be assassins? Turning off the burner phone, he wondered if the colonel had put devices in the burners, like super chips, or had some sort of specialized apps to let the ROCK leader record and/or track the whereabouts of his own people when they weren't in camp? A chilling possibility! His own knowledge of modern communications technology, he was almost certain, was less than the average second grader these days. He needed help and advice fast.

He tapped in Friday's number, and when she answered he said, "Me here, I need answers to some questions from a commo whiz." He knew that the Michigan State Police employed a number of such technicians.

"There's a young guy, O'Dell, everybody calls him Click-Clack. He's the hottest of the tech guys, and even more impressively, he can explain tech crap in plain English, and never mind if his preferred tongue is Vulcan, and he's also duly certified in Klingon."

Vulcan and Klingon? "Is that a joke?"

"Not to Click-Clack. He holds the KLCP rank of *po'wi*," she said. "That's Klingon for 'expert.'"

"KLCP?"

"Klingon Language Certification Program," she said.

"This shit is real?"

"It is to O'Dell and others like him. I heard such certification is really difficult to achieve. Tests are hard and promotions up their ranks are even harder."

"Did you ever imagine in your wildest dreams a time when we would be treating weirdos like this seriously?"

She hesitated. "Like when Allerdyce is living with us half the time?"

He started to argue, but stopped. Her point was valid, and she was not a fan of Limpy.

"No worries is what it is," she told him. "I never imagined this kind of thing, but I also don't fret about it either. Any word from your toy soldier pals?"

"Got a text this morning. Hiatus for another two weeks."

"Does that strike you as odd?" she asked.

The whole situation struck him as odd, even ludicrous, especially his looking for eagle feathers, and this alone made him wonder if someone had read some piece of intelligence wrong, or if Harlikin was more sophisticated in his thinking, planning, and doing than the impression he made face-to-face.

"I'm wondering if we have a security leak," he told her, thinking he wished he knew more about the "source," the heretofore unknown source or asset the FBI was alleging to have lost, or blown. Even verbs got twisted when you dealt with feds. "What happened to the kumbaya-let's-all-join-arms-and-make-one-big-happy-family-almost-writ-in-blood pacts after 9/11?"

"Unlike real glaciers melting, bureaucratic glaciers can melt only so much before protect-our-silo-thinking reasserts itself," Friday said.

"Less than comforting," he told her.

"Is the extended hiatus for your toy soldier pals bugging you?" she pressed him.

"It makes me wonder what the hell is really going on, and that's just with the ROCKs. The government silo crap has hurt us all before and it will again. In fact it could kill us all, if we let it."

"We can do everything possible as individuals to make sure there are no silos, but finally all law enforcement is tribal and the rules of our home silos sit heavily on our shoulders."

"I hate how clear-eyed you are."

She laughed at him.

"How do I reach Mr. O'Dell?"

"Tell me when and where and I'll make sure he's there. You want me too?"

"That's a separate question," he said. "You slid that in on purpose."

"Damn right," she said, "but it has been on my mind . . . is *always* on my mind."

"Ditto," he told her. "I may have to retire just to get that part of our life back."

"Works for me," she said.

"Click-Clack available tonight?" He knew this was a stretch. The Michigan State Police controlled work time as closely for its people as the DNR for its various forces. Technicians, however, were often excepted as various computer upgrades had to get installed and there were only so many techs to cover fleets of vehicles and chains of state police posts.

"When and where?"

"Tonight, on Bumbletown Hill north of Allouez, at the towers on the bluff. I'll wait on Bumbletown Road and lead him back to a private spot. Tell him I'll be in the black Ford 150." After a moment he added, "Can he drive unmarked?"

"He can and will. He'll be in a minivan which says Technology in Vulcan. Will that work?"

"Spell it."

"Not in a million years with a million tries, nor can I pronounce it. Is this crazy, or what?"

"As a very wise lady once proclaimed, 'it is what it is.'"

"So sad," she said. "I'll bump you only if he can't make the place. You want me to have him bump you when he crosses the bridge to Hancock?"

"A bump from Calumet will suffice," Service said. "This guy the tight-lipped tech type?"

"He's a lot like you. What he hears stays with him, no loose lips."

"Typical Vulcan," he muttered. "Why can't you guys hire normal humans?"

Friday started laughing so hard she had to break contact.

• • •

O'Dell was nothing like he expected. The "unmarked" minivan had its Vulcan written in dull gray, which made it virtually unreadable. The van looked like it had traveled a lot of hard miles. The man himself was built like a Cornish wrestler, short bow legs under a long torso with long spidery arms and giant hands, and he spoke so softly Service had to strain to hear, never mind understand.

They stood outside their vehicles and O'Dell invited him to step into his control room as he opened the side door of the van. When they got inside, Service saw it was filled with video monitors and electronic gear, black boxes stacked on black boxes. Service shook the man's hand and said, "I hope we can do this in plain English. My Vulcan's in the shop for repairs."

O'Dell smiled. "Was just about to send my plain English to the same place, but my gut told me to hold off, that the shopwork can come later. You a Trekkie?"

"Nope, I'm an independent with a record of voting for Earthmen over extraterrestrials."

"Detective Friday didn't tell me you had a sense of humor."

"I don't—by her standards."

"She told me you have some questions about burner phones."

"Not sure they're questions or what."

"Ask away, my time is your time."

"Confucius was a Vulcan?"

"History will one day prove that, and Shakespeare as well."

"Hitler?"

"Clearly a Klingon, real nasty-nasty. What *about* burners?"

"That's exactly my question," Service said.

O'Dell said, "I don't have deep experience with the DNR, but Detective Friday told me you're a detective in the Special Investigations Branch. I know what MSP detectives do and have a rudimentary understanding of the principles of undercover procedures, but as far as your outfit goes, you're an unmarked clay tablet."

"Think of us as hounds on very long, invisible leashes. We've had the basic tutorials on cell phones and tracking: GPS off, phone off, invisible as if Scotty beamed you somewhere else."

O'Dell chuckled. "If only we had transporters, but alas, we don't yet. But that does not mean we are lacking in some very, very cool toys. We have access to much of the technical capabilities of national intel and DOD."

"If it's not something I have and can put my hands on, I pretty much don't need to know about it."

"University of Ignorance is Bliss, eh?"

"More like the college of No News is Good News," Service said.

O'Dell looked at him. "Your phone on?"

"Which phone? I carry a DNR cell, an SPU cell, my personal cell, a phone from a case I'm working and another I use with my own informant network."

"*Impressive.* You have *your own* burner system?"

Service nodded and didn't tell the man that his system amounted to one man: Allerdyce.

"Have you ever wondered if your devices can talk to each other without you knowing?" O'Dell asked.

"Doesn't every normal paranoid adult in the cop world?"

"The fact is, they can, and they do," O'Dell said. "It's human nature to wonder about how far technology can intrude into our personal lives."

"Not to mention superstition," Service added.

"In part, maybe," O'Dell told him. "But in fact, let's focus here. Some cells can and do communicate—if that's how the manufacturer designs and builds them, which some do, some under government contract, both friends and foes, and others build in such capabilities as safety features, to enable them to track their folks in the event of trouble. And, more to the point, to lurk in the cracks between friend and foe."

"The transactionals," Service said.

O'Dell nodded. "Yep, the club of what's in it for me right now and let what's down the road go hang. Where there are cracks or dips or holes or shadows I can slide into so that I might know what various players are up to."

Service mulled this. "What if an undercover is given a burner by the people he is undercover with?"

O'Dell smiled. "'Dangers, doubts, wringing of the conscience,' that's from *Henry the Eighth*. 'You feel your arse dipped in double knavery, thine arse hung out there nak'd.' That Vulcan Shakespeare was a very smart and prescient cookie."

Was this bazonko? "What the hell would Shakespeare know about undercover?"

"Every fiction writer is undercover, Detective. He pretends to be someone other than who he is, and weaves a lie that might eventually surround and point to the truth. Who are actors in costume on stage or screen but undercovers?"

The kid had a point.

"More Shakespeare?"

"More like mock-Spock. Lots of assholes like to make up Vulcan wisdom and hope to profit from it. There are scoundrels everywhere, Detective, even among Vulcans, the most perfect of creatures, albeit not entirely so. Self-interest, it turns out, is not limited to humankind."

"Should one take solace in that?"

"Depends on whether one believes that the same God alleged to have made us, also made the Vulcans."

"You mean Noah?" Service said. "Without him and his clan, the earth would be empty and very, very boring."

"You're an interestingly old fellow, Detective. Tell me your exact concern."

"Same as everyone who does what I do, to maintain my cover security, which means my personal safety and, theoretically, the safety of my family, too."

"I see," O'Dell said. "With such delicate burthens of dildos and fadings art thou faced."

"We seem to be edging toward Vulcan," Service said. "Dildos?"

"In mind," O'Dell explained, "I think the Elizabethans were a model for Vulcans. Dildos and fadings are nonsensical refrains in ballads, with overtones of serendipity, as in your work you're involved in a secret world that can weigh you down and fuck you over in the blinking of an eye."

Who *was* this kid, really? He seemed to have a good sense of the role of an undercover. "My main job, my default position, is always to protect the mission."

"Understood," O'Dell said. "You got a burner from the group you're inside with."

Service nodded.

O'Dell continued, "and you're wondering if they've built some sort of tracking capability into the burner?"

Another nod.

"Your forensic tech people swept the thing, right?" O'Dell asked.

Service smiled. "We have no forensic tech people or even a separate law enforcement tech commo group. Mostly we do our own thing with occasional help from you guys, or sometimes from US Fish and Game, and only rarely from the FBI and ATF."

"I'm not with the state police whiz group, Detective. I'm here on a contract to analyze and evaluate State Police technical capabilities."

"On contract to whom?"

"The governor's office."

This registered somewhere between okay, then, and what the fuck? "But Friday called you and told me you were with the Troops."

"Which I am until my contract is fulfilled."

"And your normal employer is?"

"Myself, my own company. But I was a long time in the technological bowels of various federal agencies."

"Which you're not going to list."

"Need-to-know, Detective. Need I say more?"

"I know that tune," Service said.

"Would you like for me to examine and sweep your burner?"

"I would indeed. How long will this take?"

"About as long as it takes to ply it into my brain, but I should tell you that this kind of thing you fear is damned pricey, tricky to manage, and most small rogue outfits lack the resources and capabilities to employ it."

Service gave the man his burner phone.

"C'mon," O'Dell said, "Let's step into my laboratory."

The man swiveled his chair and lowered a console of instruments and Service swiveled his as well, and ten minutes later O'Dell returned the burner to him. “Clean as your mama’s unseen regions. You can take a nice deep breath now.”

Service took the breath and exhaled slowly, partly as a joke, and partly because his relief was real.

O’Dell looked at him. “Okay, that was your look at what they might be throwing at you, now let’s look at what you might throw at *them*.”

“Like a secret ray gun?”

O’Dell chuckled. “A ray gun’s a fancy laser. I’m talking about a way your people can find you pronto.”

“My people include Friday, my captain, my chief, and I suppose my governor.”

“I talked to the governor after I talked to Friday. She’s on board and ordered me to do anything I can to help you. I think she’s your fan.”

“I’ve only met her once, and briefly.”

“Like all Vulcans, I love Babe Ruth, but I never met the man.”

“Vulcans like Babe Ruth?”

“Vulcans are by and large ectomorphic beings. They admire mesomorphic bulk and grace. Want to hear what I can do for you?”

Service held out his hands. “I’m listening, but the last person who used that sales pitch was a Marine recruiter, and the what was Vietnam.”

“What I’ve got for you, you could have used in that quagmire, as I understand it.”

“Okay, I’m all in,” Grady told him. “This anything like a Vulcan mind-meld?”

O’Dell smiled. “You *are* a secret fan, Detective.”

Forty minutes later Service was fitted with a small, pin-sized device, under the skin behind his left ear.

“Soreness for a couple of hours, no mark will show and it will take only a couple of minutes to retrieve it when the job is done,” O’Dell said. “Live long and prosper.” He gave some sort of oddball Vulcan finger sign.

“For Babe Ruth and the American way,” Service answered.

“That’s the spirit,” O’Dell said. “No worries, Detective. And no nets. Trust the technology.”

“Which famously and invariably fails me.”

“This won’t. My reputation rides on it, *and* my livelihood.

“Screw your reputation and paycheck, it’s *my* ass on the line.”

CHAPTER 21

Allouez

KEWEENAW COUNTY

By false intelligence, or wrong surmise.

—William Shakespeare, *Richard III*

PCO Jordy Bapcat looked out the window of Patty Something's place on Bumbletown Hill and said unenthusiastically, "I really need to do something with that property."

Grady saw that the PCO was staring across the road at a dilapidated, ancient log building blackened by age, and guessed the thing dated to the early twentieth century, or before. It was cool in its being old, but a real eye-sore. "What property?" he asked the new officer.

"That place," Bapcat said. "It's been in my family since my great-great-grandfather bought it off the state in the Twenties. His wife was well-heeled and refused to live in the cabin, but he had a soft spot for it, and kept it as a camp and a get-away. There weren't any other people way up here back in those days."

"Bapcat's not in the plat book," Patty pointed out.

"The plat book says Topofthehill LLC, that's a family business."

"Your family's in the land business, and you're not?" Something said.

"It's not really a *business*. It's more a legal safe harbor for some family land."

Patty said, "That property across the street has got to be worth a fortune."

Bapcat shrugged. "Dough isn't my deal. Protecting resources is."

"Have you ever been inside it?" Service asked.

"What, and disturb the *porcupines*?" he said, and laughed. "My dad once told me there's a tunnel that runs all the way from the top of the cliff down to the valley floor."

"I remember a steel door at the bottom of the cliff," Patty said. "We kids used to play down there when I was visiting."

"Kids probably still try to see what's inside," Bapcat allowed.

"I can't believe *you* don't want to see," Service said.

Bapcat shrugged. "Just don't. Different strokes, I guess."

"A game warden always wants to know what's behind every closed door, or locked gate," Service pointed out.

"Guess I kicked down enough doors already. Are we going to talk cases here or play drivel pool?"

"We're neighbors," Something told her colleague.

"No we're not," Bapcat came back. "I own the land. I don't live on it." He turned to Service. "Your pal Wetelainen is a treasure house of local lore."

"Take-it-to-the-bank-stuff, too. Not *gossipus droolus*. He would have made one hell of a CO, but he's allergic to being on somebody else's payroll—truly a free spirit," Service said, and continued, "I'm guessing he gave you more details on that Korean professor and the guys who forced him to take moose jerky for his fresh brook trout."

Bapcat grinned. "Some."

"He say where on the Elm?"

"Tech property north of Tormala Road."

"And the individuals he ran into?"

"Two jamokes decked out in mustard yellow?"

"Mustard yellow?"

"That's how Professor Kim described them."

"Kim?" Service asked.

"Right, Paul Kim, you know him?"

"Know *of* him. Shark says the man can drop a fly in a Dixie cup at ninety feet."

"Shark fishes with him?"

"He tries not to, because Kim always out-fishes him and Shark does not like to be out-fished by anyone, ever."

Something intervened. "Let us guess. Shark fishes alone most of the time."

"You prescient?" Service asked her.

"No, just a loner, like most COs maybe."

"We never say loner. We prefer, 'self-contained.'"

"Point noted."

"Did you talk to the prof?" Service asked.

"I did, and he offered me moose jerky as a truck snack."

Service felt the hairs on his neck bristle. "The same jerky the Mustard Seeds forced on him?"

"Mustard Seeds?" Bapcat said. "I *like* that. But I didn't ask. I just took the stuff and said thank you and sent some of it off to the Lansing lab for DNA work."

Service rubbed his forehead. "Good job. Is Kim a hunter?"

Bapcat said, "I saw no head mounts, just fish, and I've queried all Canadian provinces, Alaska and Lower Forty-eight states with open or limited moose hunt to find out if Kim ever had a permit from anywhere, but I do know he's never had a hunting license here in Michigan. I have our computer people searching the states, but nothing has come back yet. Sometimes computer people promise a lot more than they or our equipment can deliver."

"Same way as in the Navy?"

"No way. Too many lives on the line for them to be cavalier or to oversell."

"Notice anything different about Kim?" Service asked.

"Other than him being Asian?" Bapcat questioned back. "I did. The man talks with a heavy Yooper twang. It really bugged me at first."

"He grew up in Copper Harbor. Adopted when he was a baby. His parents ran an agate shop in town."

"Kim's Agates and Curios?" Something asked.

"The family business. I think his sister runs it now. The family has a major collection. of huge datolites, some of which eventually will go to A.E. Seaman Mineral museum up to Tech. Kims are superstars in the rock trade, and are known to be very, very secretive."

"Illegal stuff?" Bapcat asked.

"Never heard that, but they're said to know a hell of a lot more than they share publicly."

"There's neither rule nor law against husbanding one's assets," Bapcat pointed out.

"True and it makes such people a potentially rich source under the right circumstances."

"I hear you," Bapcat said.

"Me too," Patty added. "Is datolite their only specialty?"

"The way Shark put it to me, they'll collect and pursue anything *interesting*."

"That's a wide door," Bapcat pointed out.

"Silver?" Patty asked. "Would not be a bit surprised," Service said. "Now listen up, you two. I need to brief you on the case I'm working undercover. There may come a time when I need help and backup pronto."

"Where?" Something asked.

"There's a 240 in South Houghton Township, right on the border of the Sherman Township Natural Area. Bruneau Creek runs through the north end of the parcel."

"That's way out there," Something said.

"Been doing your homework. Not so much verticality as sheer rough ass, rocky terrain. Keep doing your homework. It's your job to know the land here better than everyone. The better you know it, the better you can take care of it."

"What's in that 240?" Bapcat asked.

"HQ, barracks and training ground for an outfit called the Regiments of Christian Knights, ROCKs in short."

"Religious outfit?"

"Yes, and a well-armed militia."

"One with a potential bite?" Bapcat inquired.

"How much of a bite is yet to be determined."

"Let me guess," Something said. "The ROCKs wear mustard yellow uniforms."

"How did you figure that?"

"I was watching your eyes when you were talking to Jordy and they seemed to light up when he mentioned the yellow outfits."

"Remind me to never, *ever* play poker with you."

"No worries," she said with a giggle. "I'm too frugal to risk money in games of chance."

"Yet you risk your life every day in this job," Service pointed out.

"It's not the same thing," she said.

"No? I predict that over time you'll change that tune."

"How do we help you?" Jordy asked.

"I'm not yet ready to lay out all the detail, chapter and verse, so here's the elevator version: If you get a bump on the radio calling for backup and support, drop what you're doing and fly to me."

"How will we know where you are?"

Service picked up a plat book from a table and leafed through it. He showed them the parcel. "That's where I'll be."

The PCOs huddled over the book.

Bapcat said, "There's not a damn thing out there."

"We're all you have?" Something asked Service.

Grady thought of Allerdyce and Worm. "You two will be the only badges starting out."

Bapcat looked at his partner. "Does he always talk like some kind of secret squirrel?"

"You know how legends can be," Something said.

• • •

Grady Service had never been much for romantic dreams, or even dreams in general, but there was one dream he had from time to time over the years and he'd decided it was his mind telling him he'd overlooked something obvious.

The dream was more fragmented, regurgitated memory than what he considered a full-fledged dream, and this one always ended exactly the same way.

It went back to a time when Lisette McKower was a brand new CO and his partner. It was one of her pass days and she was at the wedding of one of her girlfriends as the maid of honor or whatever the best gal was called.

He was north of Rock on a two-track that led to the rock-strewn headwaters of the Rapid River, which eventually dumped into northern Lake Michigan, some twenty miles downstream. Station Twenty in Lansing had relayed a complaint from a woman who reported that her husband, a retired Air Force chief master sergeant, had been threatened and driven off the river by a group of younger men chasing steelhead, cursing him for being in "their hole." The NCO had spent twenty-seven years in uniform and had thousands of flying hours as a boom operator in KC-97, and KC-135 refueling aircraft. He didn't want to report the incident, but when Service showed up, he relented and cooperated.

The retiree gave Service a rough map of where the events had taken place. With the map in hand, he made a beeline for the site. Four against one was bad numbers for an unarmed military retiree, and not so great for himself, but he was fired up, and intended to straighten out these people.

By the time he hiked into the spot, the foursome was drunk and/or high, and loud, each of pretty fair size and despite this, he thought he could manage the situation, but in keeping with departmental directives governing officer safety, he had called the county and requested backup to be in the area—as opposed to officers flying to him.

Seeing how trashed the men were, Service crossed upstream of them and worked his way through heavy tag alders before he stepped out, figuring that if they were in the mood for making trouble they would have to cross the fast flowing water to get to him and in their impaired state on that kind of sharp and uneven rock, making it across was dubious at best.

Because the four men appeared to be trashed, neither his badge nor the river were impediments and they came at him almost immediately in pairs. He calmly put finish to the first pair, then drove the other two into temporary retreat while he cuffed the first pair. Then he heard a siren, and then saw a green DNR truck burst out of the woods onto the scene, and out the truck door came new CO Lisette McKower, her eyes wild and jaw set, her face red, folds of a pink dress draped over one arm, a pistol in her other hand, her gun-belt slung over her shoulder like a makeshift bandolier, her legs in stirruped green duty pants and her feet in bright red high heels as she charged across the rocky shore into the water and crossed directly toward the yet-free pair and Service was yelling, "Whoa! Whoa! Situation under control! *Copy!?*"

"Copy," she said, breathing like a big bull in a small ring, snorting, her nostrils flaring like an enraged wild beast.

When she finally backed off her adrenaline high, he gave her a cigarette and she took one puff and began a coughing fit.

"Thanks," he told her, "Great job."

Charging headlong into certain trouble was an earmark of an officer with a great future, and now McKower was captain of detectives and retained the same vigor and attitude she'd started her career with.

"One question?" he said as they smoked and the prisoners carped and whined to each other.

"Sure," she said, coughing.

He looked down at her bright red high-heeled shoes. "Did I miss a memo on uniforms?"

She looked, laughed, and said, "Oh shit." Then, "I've got to get *back* there. I heard your call for backup just before the vows! I've got to *go*!"

"You don't think they went on without you?"

"Not a chance," she told him. "They'll wait."

"I'll take two of these fools and you take the other two."

She looked at him. "Are we in Delta or Marquette?"

"Geez," she said. "Escanaba's a long haul."

"So's Marquette, but Rock's close and that's the wedding site, right? The sooner we get this bunch loaded the sooner we can deposit them, the sooner you can get back to celebrating."

McKower stood up and glared at the steel-headers. "Do you ass-wipes like weddings?"

"Oh man," one of them said with a moan.

Service laughed and got it. "You jerks better behave, or I will turn her full loose on you, and you do *not* want that." He looked at her. "You do have boots in your truck, right?"

"Of course," she said.

"Next time, don't let your adrenaline override your common sense and details."

"I hear you," she said, looked at one of her shoes, and frowned. "Dammit, you jerks made me break a heel!"

She looked up at Service. "I *hate* it when that happens!"

"We didn't do nothin'!" the four-man chorus wailed as one.

"Shut up!" the officers returned song.

Details. He had always dreamed of McKower's red heels when something not yet evident was eating at the back of his mind.

Red shoes, why this recurring dream memory? What part was significant? The fact of details being overlooked? Something that should be obvious? What were red shoes other than not regulation? Bright color. *Blue building*, his inner voice whispered. The college kids swore they'd not gone inside the blue building, which had to be a lie, but why? There was no way they could have seen the old rock shop sign unless they had been inside the building.

Service crawled off Something's couch and padded to the PCO's bedroom. The door was wide open. "Patty," he said softly.

"Unh?" came the response. Then, "Wha?"

"You awake?"

"Service?"

"In person, fresh from a gig on your couch."

"What *time* is it?" she asked.

"No idea," he said.

"You want in here?" she asked, her voice dropping.

"No, I want you to get up. I'll make the coffee."

"Seriously, Grady. What *time* is it?"

"I don't know."

"I'd rather you in here asleep than me out there awake. Go back to your couch, *please*."

"Wake up," he insisted. "Something's not right with those college boys."

"What codge boys?" she mumbled.

"Clear all your cobwebs, PCO. Put your footsies over the bed-side and flat on the floor."

"Don't got flats feets," she mumbled.

"And to think how worried I was about *that*," he said. "I'm going to make coffee," he said and left her to find her way out of the sleep sack.

When she joined him, her eyes were slits. She wore green gym shorts, and fuzzy gray mules that flapped like flippers when she walked.

"In all your sartorial glory," he told her and handed her a cup of coffee.

"Up yours," she came back. "Really, what's the time?"

"There's no clock in here," he pointed out.

"I keep meaning to get one on pass days, but they never seem to unroll *as* pass days."

He said, "Do you ever think on your pass days that while you're screwing off, bad guys are violating left and right?"

She grimaced. "I do, and how do you turn off that thinking?"

"You don't. You have to ignore it."

"I can't do that."

"It will happen over time. The fact that you feel this tells you you're in the right work, that you give a shit. That's what every cop has to feel before anything else."

"Is there anything *in* this coffee?" she asked, staring at the cup in her hand. "What *about* those college kids?"

"Gecko and Goat," Service said.

"What *about* them?"

"Something about their story."

"They didn't really have much of a story," she said, stifling a big yawn.

"They said they'd never met the guy who hired them."

"I remember."

"Remember when you couldn't remember a rock shop on Watertank Road?" he asked.

"Uh huh."

"Goat told us the sign wasn't up yet and the building was painted blue."

"I remember," she said, "and I told him I had seen *that* building."

"Goat also claimed they had never met the Leaf guy in person."

"Remember that, too."

Grady asked quietly, "If the college boys had never met Leaf, how did they know the sign wasn't up yet?"

She shrugged. "Not awake." She drank more coffee.

"We're missing something simple," he said, and added, "Cops have antennae, although reception varies. We need to run down these kids and talk to Irkka Vorpi."

"The retired magistrate in Aspirus, right?"

"Hooray, you're starting to wake up."

"You know him?" she asked.

"Met briefly a couple of times years ago, I never *knew* him, but Shark does, and Shark says Vorpi was interested in the Three T Mine."

"You're going too fast for me."

"I'm probably going too fast for me too, but sometimes everything piles up and you just have to spit it out in order to start sorting it out."

"We have to get to those kids again, and to Vorpi. Listen carefully. Gecko, the tall one, I asked him how he felt about Larry Bird."

"So?'

"He said he never heard of Bird *or* Magic Johnson."

"Three-quarters of the world probably share that with him."

"Gecko is from French Lick, remember? That was Bird's *hometown.* I challenged him on this and he brushed me off, told me French Lick has two thousand people and he can't be expected to know them all."

Her hand went to her face.

"How many kids in Cass Tech?" the detective asked her.

"More than two thousand."

"You knew them all?"

"Course not, but everybody knew the star jocks and star students."

"Exactly," he said. "Those kids *had* to have broken into that shop. That's how they knew the sign wasn't up. And Gecko is lying about being from French Lick. Why? Let's call Houghton County and verify Vorpi is in Aspirus. Privacy laws may not let them disclose such info to mere game wardens."

"Will that annoy you?" she asked.

"No, but it adds drag to one's fly, and drag makes trout wary."

"Your metaphoric world is fascinating," she said. "And very confusing."

"The thing is," he said, "you need to get all the drag out of your line and keep it out by making a big mend at the start, and smaller mends as the drift goes on."

"I hate sewing," she said.

He looked at her. "Not that kind of mending. Have you ever fly-fished?"

"Nope."

"We are going to fix that. Fly fishing will help you be a better person."

"Isn't Vorpi a fly fisher?"

"Think how off the wall he'd be if he weren't one."

She stared at him. "You're serious."

"As a fart in a diver's suit."

"Do you have to think up stuff like that?"

"No, I have an unhealthy memory for fifth-grade filth and humor."

She finally looked at her phone. "Oh it's zero four hundred."

"Want me to make breakfast?" he asked.

"Feel free. I'm going back to bed."

"But the bad guys are running amok out there," he said.

She rolled her eyes, grinned, shook her head, said, "Let 'em," and flipper-flapped her way back toward her bedroom.

Thirty seconds later she was back. "Why did you have to say *that*?"

"Because it's true."

"There's no point calling the sheriff's office until daylight," she said.

"Agreed. Pancakes or eggs?"

"Neither. I need *sleep*," she said, turned around and left, and seconds later she was back again. "Do we two-on-one each kid, or one-on-one, swap, do the other one, and compare notes?"

"You make notes about your swapping?" he asked, deadpan.

"Friday told me you exhaust her."

"Toast or biscuits?"

"You are bound and determined to make me eat breakfast."

"Most important meal of the day."

"Two eggs side by each, downside up easy, and a pair of rye toast, dark. There're some ham slices in the fridge. One of those please, and lots of onions," Patty said.

Service grinned. "That'll make the bad guys quake in their boots."

"I don't plan to kiss them. Can we stop talking now?"

"Sure," he said. "Were you really a *boxer*?" he asked.

CHAPTER 22

Laurium

HOUGHTON COUNTY

> This cold night will turn us all to fools and mad men.
>
> —William Shakespeare, *King Lear*

Service parked in the Aspirus east lot (which doubled at times as a medevac chopper LZ) and with Something walked around the building to the entrance on the west end. Grady couldn't remember the last time he'd seen Irkka Vorpi, but back then the man had been confident and physically imposing. What faced him now in the Aspirus Health room was a bone-bag with sagging yellow skin and an eel's eyes.

"Been a long time, I.V.," Service greeted the man, I.V. having once been Vorpi's preference for a nickname.

The old magistrate blinked slowly several times. "The game warden?"

"Grady Service."

"I remember your name. Youse a long way from home, eh?"

"New job these days and all of us cover a lot of ground. It's not like the old days."

"The old days were better for some of us then the now-days," Vorpi said in a papery voice.

Service made a point of looking around the room. "I don't see any rubber walls," he told the man.

Vorpi managed a life-worn smile. "Walls are walls, eh. Nowadays it means close surveillance, not physical restraint, though the result's the same, and if youse get a little rambunctious, they lower the boom."

"Mere medical orderlies can take down a former Troop?"

"I think they give their new lot bouncer tests before they hire them," Vorpi said. "I don't want no trouble here—or anywhere."

"What *do* you want, I.V.?" Service asked. "We heard that our new kid Bapcat found you out by Houghton Falls."

"Bapcat? I guess I didn't catch his name, but I was impressed, even through my fog. Calm as ice the lad says to me, 'You really wanna jump, I'll hold your coat, and phone, and stuff.'"

"'You tellin' me not to jump?' I asked 'im."

"Kid says, 'Nope. It's your life. Spend it how you want. I'm just an onlooker here.'"

"*Did* you want to jump?" Service asked.

"That's not a question so easily answered. Not sure I have the answer for myself, but I admit I was giving the idea some consideration when your officer showed up."

"Well, I'm glad you didn't take that step."

"You ever been there?" Vorpi asked.

He'd been to some places like that, Service told him. "Probably, we all do at some point."

"And you're still around," Vorpi observed.

"So far, so good," Service said.

"You know, when you hit bottom, you think, okay this is really shitty and all, but this is the worst it can get, and I'm still alive and I can deal with this, whatever it is, and *then* something *worse* falls on your head, and pushes you *even* further down."

"Maybe sometimes we bite off more than we can chew," Service suggested.

Vorpi nodded. "And that bite can be self-immolation, remember those monks in Nam dousing themselves in gas and lighting it?"

Service remembered photos, had never personally witnessed such an event. "I do."

"They were extreme," Vorpi said. "Immolate just means sacrifice, not self-fucking destruction, but I guess that's how it plays out for some."

"Like tiptoeing off a 110-foot waterfall?" Service pointed out. "Where's the sacrifice in that? What's the purpose? If you're a cop and some asshole is shooting up a school, or bar, or church or corner grocery, you hustle your butt in there to take out the shooter as quickly as possible, but going in, you're fully aware in the back of your mind, the shooter may get you first, and still you go, because ultimately *someone* has to do it. To me this is the definition of sacrifice, your life for something better at least for others. That better thing. I don't know *what* that is."

Vorpi sighed. "Wish I knew, but I don't."

"Ask you about another subject?" Service said.

Another sigh for an answer from the retired magistrate.

"You used to be a rock collector, am I remembering correctly?"

"I was," Vorpi said. "Long time back."

"Word's out locally that you're going to open a new rock shop."

"I don't think so," Vorpi said.

"Who do you think might be saying stuff like that?"

"Got no idea," Vorpi said.

"You used to make silver jewelry, or is my memory bad?"

"Your memory's fine and I did make silver jewelry until my second wife pulled the ripcord on us. Lost my enthusiasm after that."

"I heard you made some real fine pieces."

"I guess I managed to sell one or two."

"I've always wondered if a man in that business found it essential to maintain a stockpile of silver."

"Some do, some don't," Vorpi said.

"You one who did?" Service asked.

"What the hell are you trying to get at?" Vorpi suddenly lashed out.

"We've been told you've been seen hanging around a certain property in Dollar Bay."

Vorpi made a face. "What that means, 'hanging around'?"

"Have you been there or not, I.V.?" Service asked pointedly.

"Where in Dollar Bay? It ain't Detroit, but it ain't no punk-ass Helltown neither."

"Watertank, off M-126."

Vorpi grinned crookedly. "Da Blueberry?"

"Come again?" Service said with a glance to Patty Something.

"Building on Watertank painted sick blue. The locals call it Da Blueberry or Da Bloob."

"Have you been *there* recently?" Service continued.

"Not inside I ain't."

"Are you saying you've been around the outside of the place?"

Vorpi's lips pressed back. "Could be. What's *this* about?"

"The Three T Mine," Patty said, her first words since they entered the room. "Two-Ton Too," she added.

Vorpi looked at Service. "What's her *kind* doing in green?"

"Her kind's in trooper blue too," Service reminded the man.

"What about my *kind*?" Something asked Vorpi.

"We've not been introduced," the retired Troop said.

"I'm Patty Something," she said. "*Conservation Officer* Something. You don't like my plumbing or my skin color?" she asked, stepping toward him.

"Not looking for no fight with some croissant with a chip on her shoulder."

"*Croissant*?" she said and Service pulled her behind him.

"You never answered the officer's question about the mine," Service reminded the man.

"I thought *you* were interviewing me," Vorpi contended.

"What about the Three T Mine?" Service asked.

"It's those damn kids, isn't it?" a suddenly exasperated Vorpi said. "Of all the nerve!"

"What kids?" Service asked. They'd struck a nerve—finally.

"The long, tall drink of water and his bone-cracker chum from over to Tech."

"They have names, these two?" Something asked.

"Tall one's Gecko, the hockey player goes by Goat."

"What about actual names?" Service pressed.

"Last names George and Nankervus," Vorpi said. "Coupla pushy young punks they are."

"How'd you meet them?"

"I never did. They'd called me out of the blue on the damn phone."

"Looking for?" Patty asked.

For the first time Vorpi looked at Something. "What do rockers always want?" he came back. "Information, treasure maps, the usual bullshit they think will make them rich."

"Why'd they call you?" Service asked.

"I'd say for the same damn reason you're here," Vorpi said. "I used to work silver and I had a pretty fair stockpile at one time."

"Had?"

"Unloaded it over time after Wife Two hit the dusty trail."

"Did you hire these kids to prospect for you?"

"Hell no, why would I do *that*?"

Service said calmly, "Seems pretty odd them barging in out of the blue and you no longer with any silver interests."

"I thought the same thing," Vorpi said. "It did not make me happy."

"Did you help them in any way, cooperate?"

"What the hell does help mean? I was blackmailed. One doesn't cooperate with such assholes."

"You never met them?"

"No, but I seen 'em when they broke into the Blueberry."

"Why'd they do that?"

"They think they can open a rock shop, which the Blueberry had been a very long time ago. They figure if they can score a substantial amount of silver ore, it would provide start-up capital."

"They told you that?"

"Some they told me outright, some I gleaned. You're a cop, you know how to listen, same as me."

"Blackmailed you, how?"

"Told me they know where Wife Two is now and she might be willing to come back under certain conditions."

"I hear no blackmail in that," Patty said.

"I had just started seeing another woman, and these jerks asked me how I'd like it if they had a chat with my new lady about Wife Two and how she run off because she didn't like how I took care of her—you know, in bed?"

Something jabbed Service in the back as a signal to keep quiet and let the man stew a bit in his own juices, and then Patty said, "real jerks for sure."

Vorpi nodded heavily, "Yes, Officer, they are."

"So you decided it would be easier to help them than have them mess up your relationship?" she asked. "Was it you who told them to go into the mineshaft?"

The former state policeman and magistrate stared at her. "I heard, some Black cop went down there and pulled the tall one up. Was that you?"

"Yessir, I was down there. Why were they?"

"That spot's got a nice sharp hundred-foot vertical, which legend says so too does the Three T. It was to be a warmup exercise."

"You believe there *is* a Three T?" Service asked.

"Not saying I do, or don't, but the rumor's been solid and consistent since I was a kid up here, so I haven't written it off."

"You know Joe Sklarus of Traprock Electric now owns the Blueberry?"

"I know Joe, and I heard rumors that he was the new owner, and it made me wonder where the hell he got the dough to buy a building. His business is in shit shape and he's got a nasty habit."

"As in a drug habit?"

"Saw the man in court many times when I was magistrate. Hardly had a pot to piss in, then or now."

"Are you saying Sklarus *isn't* the Blueberry's owner?"

"What I'm saying is I don't get how he could possibly buy it with his own resources—unless some lunatic infused him with cash. I'm damn sure no local bank would back him."

"Where is Sklarus's business located?" Service asked.

"He runs it out of a house-trailer out on the Copper City–Gay Road. There's five or six acres, part in Keweenaw, part in Houghton County."

"What sort of property?"

"Scrub brush and rocks, nothing but crapland," Vorpi said.

"Who is Burdon Leaf?" PCO Something asked.

Vorpi laughed. "Is that a joke?"

"Nossir, that's the name we heard you were using," the new officer told him.

"Why the hell would I do *that*?" he asked.

"*You* tell us, I.V.," Service said sharply.

Vorpi shrugged and grinned. "He's not a real person. The name is one some rockers use to keep a deep-pocket buyer's identity secret hidden."

"Why would they do that?" Service asked.

Vorpi shrugged again. "Rockers seldom know why they do anything, other than they want something in a big way." Suddenly the patient laughed. "Know what I once heard? I heard the Blueberry was going to become a recruiting office."

"*Military* recruiting?" Service came back. "Pretty out of the way for that."

"Only kind of recruiting I know of and it didn't make sense to me either."

"We're going to get out of your hair, I.V. We may be in touch again."

"Do me a favor and kick these kids' asses hard. They're mean little fuckers."

"One of them is seven-foot-four," Service pointed out.

"More of him to be mean is all," Vorpi said. "They're shit-birds, the both of them."

CHAPTER 23

Kearsarge

HOUGHTON COUNTY

All is oblique.

—William Shakespeare, *Timon of Athens*

They were returning to Bumbletown Hill and Something's residence to fetch her truck when Service got a call on his personal cell. "And it came to pass," Tuesday Friday greeted him.

"If this is the *Book of Mormon* calling," he retorted, 'You've got 998 more uses of that phrase to go."

"My message is much briefer than the *Book of Mormon*, Detective. The Crime Lab Team wanted a cadaver dog to have a sniff at the site where the skeletons were found. I arranged for Lucy Sweet to bring her boy Angelo."

"And it came to pass?" Service said.

"Angelo found another one."

"Another skeleton?"

"No, there is usually some fleshy matter around skeletons and bones, and that's how these dogs find old cemeteries and all that, but in this instance, Angelo took the team downward from the main body of evidence."

"As in lower down, vertically?"

"Precisely sixty-two feet deeper, and this one mostly still in the meat-bearing phase."

"Fresh?"

"Fresh enough. Having seen this I'm now thinking that all those skeletons found above this were intended for deep deposit. The most recent remains have already been identified as Brewster J. Yearwood."

"No bells ringing," Service told her.

"Late of the FBI, special agent allegedly gone deep undercover—like someone we know—and isn't *that* just a dandy coincidence?"

"Don't tell me. Yearwood is the missing asset from my case?"

"We do *not know* that," she said. "You need to get out of there, Grady."

His instincts were similar, but he had reservations about dropping out of any case. He hated to lose, and pulling out was quitting, which he equated to losing. "We don't know if Sane Zane and his mouth breathers have anything to do with this special agent's death. Your lab people get a cause of death yet?"

"Yeah, impact. Somebody apparently threw the poor guy eighty feet down, more or less. Broke everything but his piggy bank."

"Signs of torture, resistance, anything?"

"Nada so far. Tell the DNR the case they gave you is a case too damn far."

"The governor endorsed my participation."

Friday laughed sarcastically. "She doesn't even know you!"

"Granted, but she is the governor and our boss, both yours and mine. Have Coldbeg and Cap'n McKower been notified?"

"Only the Feeb, and then Coldbeg immediately froze all further notifications and traffic regarding same."

"He can't *do* that."

"But he has."

"Can you call McKower on the Q.T.?" he asked.

"I can't, but *you* can. As the state's dick on this one, my hands are tied."

"Lis will go ballistic over this," Service said. "She hates internecine warfare between governmental agencies."

"Not sure Coldbeg is as much at war as just plain befuddled, and afraid. I don't think he knows what to do next, and that being so, nothing is what he will opt for. He's gonna wrap his arms around himself in a big old poor-is-me self-hug, sit on the damn thing, and sweat it out, waiting for another shoe to drop."

"A very mixed metaphor," Service said. "This is classic Francis Kelsey Syndrome."

"Beg your pardon?"

"I had to work with an FDA inspector on a case once, and he told me the history of the FDA and thalidomide, how the agency doctor monitoring the clinical development of the drug by the sponsoring company got a medal for keeping the drug off the US market, when in fact she never did a damn thing, and never said no. All she did was delay *any* agency decision, and keep asking for more and more information until such time as other countries who had approved the drug began reporting fetal deformities and only then did FDA say no to the drug, and Kelsey got a medal."

"Lesson being, the real gold is in delay, not decision," Friday said.

"Give that beautiful lady a kewpie doll," he said. "Does the deceased agent have a family?"

"Coldbeg isn't saying."

"Asshole," he said. "Is there a time of death yet?"

"Without precision, but there's a preliminary."

"A guesstimate or a preliminary?"

"Technically it's a prelim, but I got this only because I pushed so hard—so it may be significantly off the final number."

"Granted, and taking that caveat under advisement, what's the TOD?"

"It's within a day or two of that task force meeting you had in Marquette."

"Jesus. All Coldbeg told us was that he'd lost an inside asset from Operation Fractal Splinter."

"He's all heart, the special agent."

"Has he confirmed yet that the deceased is indeed the missing inside asset?" Service asked her.

"He's not given the slightest indication of telling anyone anything about the deceased and has attempted to put a full freeze on the state lab, et cetera. Do you think this hiatus your bad guy put you guys into is about Special Agent Yearwood?"

"Can't rule it out, can we?" he said. "But we need to know, and I especially need to know. Why is Coldbeg reacting this way?"

"Grady, to be fair, there may be other factors at work here, things nobody else knows."

"Such as?" he said.

"This may be the first man he's ever lost in the line of duty. I mean he's been in the U.P., not DC, or NYC or LA."

"Grant you that," he said. "But what's your gut telling you, Tuesday?"

"My gut says this is the undercover asset, but I've been wrong before."

"I'm calling McKower," he said.

"Don't let her get all riled up," Friday warned him. "Don't let her blow up the whole thing. If this case goes public, even the fact of there being an FBI-led task force, all sorts of shit will hit the media fan. Dare I ask where you are now?"

"Flitting around like a lightning bug on fire. Bunked one night at Something's."

"Please tell me you didn't snore her out of her own place."

"I don't snore," he said.

Friday started to say something, but stopped. "Know what, Bub? Been so long since I slept with you, I can't even *remember* what your snoring sounds like."

"A C-119 with untuned, failing engines, crashing into an airshow crowd was your most colorful word rendition of the sound."

"Now I remember. Don't do that to Patty."

CHAPTER 24

Allouez

KEWEENAW COUNTY

The affair cries haste, And speed must answer it.
—William Shakespeare, *Othello*

Chas Marschke had the kind of intense, optimistic personality you couldn't break with a two-person jackhammer. "Got a writing instrument?" Chas greeted Service on the detective's personal cell phone. Marschke ran a small, powerful wealth management firm in New York City, and had connections through all levels of American government and private industry, both inside and outside the United States. Why Chas had such contacts Service didn't really know—or care. What he knew was that man had integrity, and took care of him, and these were what mattered.

"Poised to scribble," Service said.

"Long story short, or long story long?"

"Long story long as long on paper?"

"Long story electronically, same as paper," Marschke said.

"Make it long story short and mail me the long version."

"You've got it. Here's the elevator version. Remember the earlier track-downs to Arizona, Colorado, and Kansas?"

"I do."

"All these have led us further afield to Lima, Peru, and Mexico City, and to a company called LFJ, which trades in played-out mines of precious or strategic metals. They identify a property, do extensive testing, and if they can verify harvestable potential, they look for a developer-buyer, and take a finder's fee and a percentage of gross income off the asset."

"You're telling me they're a broker and they're linked to the states previously reported and now to Peru and Mexico outside the US?"

"Eventually," Marschke explained. "The route is rather circuitous and it seems there are probably some other connected companies in New Mexico,

Idaho, Wyoming, Nevada, and Montana. There could be something in Arkansas as well, but we're investigating that right now."

"All this connects to my interests how?" Service asked.

"Only you can answer that. All we can do is provide raw data."

"My main, no, my *only* interest is getting everything I can on Hista Zane Harlikin."

Marschke seemed to hesitate. "That's probably who and what I'm talking about," the numbers man said.

"All I've heard so far is a litany of companies, states, and countries," Service said.

Marschke said immediately, "Bartlett Gabbart III is the presumed current owner and sole shareholder of LFJ."

"And I am supposed to be interested in Mr. Gabbart Third, and if so, why?"

"Mr. Gabbart Third's legal name is Histah Zane Harlikin."

"Aha. The man goes by two names."

"There could be more. Harlikin is a self-promoted colonel of a quasi-militia outfit called Regiments of Christian Knights, or ROCKs, and this you are aware of, yes?"

"I am. Is there a formal filing somewhere for tax purposes showing plural regiments, and if so, where other than in Michigan?"

"We're not sure yet, but it's possible the ROCK outfit is either a part of something larger, or it is the umbrella for a number of like-minded, smaller organizations."

"But Gabbart Third and Harlikin are the same man?"

"Undeniably."

"And Gabbart Third alias Harlikin runs the company LFJ?"

"He seems to be a very, very silent owner, buried very deep in paper and electronic filings."

"Is he off the books?" What the hell was Chas trying to tell him?

"We suspect he *thinks* he's off the books, and assumes he's therefore entirely incommunicado," Marschke explained, "but such off-grid invisibility is simply not possible for someone with wealth and assets."

"Who *actually* runs LFJ?" Service asked.

"It was the firm's founder Fawn Dawn Loire, but she disappeared in 2009 and Gabbart's sort of run the show since then—but from afar."

"Who runs things day-to-day?"

"We don't know that, but we're looking."

"Gabbart Third works for the company's founder?"

"In a sense. He was married to her."

His wife? "And she disappeared?"

"The *Federales* first thought she was caught up in a kidnap-for-profit snatch of a wealthy gringo, but no ransom demand ever came, and nobody ever saw Lady Loire again, which, by the way, was how people in her burgeoning little empire referred to her. Bottom line: The Mexicans rarely solve MP cases, especially if the right-size gratuities don't find their way into the correct political and bureaucratic pockets and purses."

"Ah," Service said. "Crime fighting at its zenith using graft to fuel justice, a novel approach. Are we concluding she was not grabbed for ransom? Do we even know that she *was* grabbed, or did the lady perhaps simply decide to go walkabout? What is the theory now?"

"None we can determine. The Mexicans couldn't solve the author of a turd hanging from a man's ass, even if he pointed to it and said, 'Hey, that's mine, Amigo!' I am, of course, weighing a dive into the Mexicans, but they and that will carry a price."

"Am I to understand that Gabbart Third aka Harlikin is running LFJ from afar, and his wifey, the founder, has gone MIA and nobody knows squat?"

"Maybe he is, maybe he's not. We're trying to figure that out."

"You want to assign a percent certitude to her having been grabbed?"

"Upwards of 90 percent, that she didn't go walkabout. Whether she was grabbed for ransom, or something worse, that's not certain at all."

"Impressively high."

"My people aren't perfect, but they are some of the very best in the business. Where do you want us to go from here?"

"I want everything you can give me personally on Gabbart Third slash Harlikin—and more details on Lady Loire. Why did Harlikin change his name and when? Where does his wife hail from, and where did she work before LFJ? Flesh out the couple for me—as a couple, as much detail as possible, his and her habits, records. I need to know who they are."

"There is a bit more," Marschke said. "Way under 50 percent on this next bit."

"Go."

"LFJ stands for Leasing For Jesus."

"Whacka-whacka, why does my mind keep playing *that* tune?"

"Because it sound weird as all get-out, but we're actually talking about what appears to be a rather successful company run on a very logical and reasonable, albeit niche, business model."

Regiments of Christian Knights, and Leasing For Jesus, was there a connection, and if so, what? "Okay, what else?"

"Loire was the woman's legal family name, and her stage name in Vegas when she was star of an oddball act called Stripping For Jesus, or S4J. She was said to be a looker on the extremely top-heavy side."

"The founder of LFJ was a stripper?"

"Not just a stripper, but a legend in her own right. My people tell me she also made some very limited distribution films and used her natural gift for showmanship to make a fortune, with which she then created a chain of fine silver jewelry shops for wealthy Christian ladies, a chain of forty stores at one point, aiming eventually for a stable of two hundred outlets. A very ambitious lady is our Lady Loire."

"Did the chain ever get that big?"

"No. After she went MIA, things seem to have changed in the home office."

"The home office for LFJ was in Mexico?"

"Maybe yes, maybe no," Marschke explained. "Mexico seems to host a holding company which contains a grab-bag of all her other companies and investments. But that's only a guess being ventured by the Mexicans. Another source has told us that Lady Loire possesses a substantial libido, which she has the decency or cunning to not slake on the home field or office, so to speak."

"What kind of investments?" Grady asked.

"Real estate, tech start-ups, some valuable metals."

"Which metals?" he asked.

"The usual rainbow of hope: platinum, gold, and silver of course, but some strategic metals such as lithium for our future battery-operated world."

The thought of batteries powering life clawed as nastily at Service as did modern smartphone technology, and related fools' toys and other time-wasters. "Did she and the hubby spend a lot of time in Mexico?"

"This could be a point of contention. For a couple of years they were rarely together, and rarely did either of them venture solo anywhere into Mexico. Lady Loire, we believe, owned or leased a place up your way, in Presque Isle, Wisconsin. That sound familiar?"

He knew where it was—literally just over the U.P. border near Watersmeet in Gogebic County. "So they were going their sweet and separate ways, and this was thought fine and cool by all?"

"God held them together, or at least that's the story they told employees, reporters, and financial analysts."

"Did they get into the mechanics of how God accomplished this?"

"Not that anyone has found interesting enough to report on," Marschke said, "but you should know that our sources have been told by sources close to the couple that their love and relationship was solid and special, and seemed real to those who witnessed it up close."

"Chas, where the hell did she disappear from, and when? Does anyone have any evidence that she was even *in* Mexico City when she went missing?"

"Sorry Grady. We're not yet ready to make that call. More votes to be counted," Marschke joked.

"Are any American cop shops involved? Texas for example, feds, anyone?"

"We don't know."

Service said, "Somebody, somewhere, has to have found her disappearance at least interesting, if not suspicious."

"I'm sure someone has and does," Marschke said, "but if so, they are in the run-silent, run-deep mode."

Could this have been the real genesis of Operation Fractal Splinter? There were militias all over the damn country, run on every imaginable platform from anti-Commie to anti-extraterrestrial and a lot of them swore religious affiliations, albeit not within mainline denominations and churches and, at the same time, traded in guns and other weapons. So why the FBI's focus on the ROCKs? What made them so special? It couldn't be their alleged trading in eagle feathers. That was too narrow and skinny water even for the feds, who preferred thick, almost unstirred stews for their ops, not thin, brothy gruels.

"Maybe we should be stirring some pots ourselves, and do some heavy checking north of the Rio Grande," Service suggested. "I assume you can lay out a plan to launch boats into relevant waters."

"We'll look into it."

"Don't start until I flash the green light," Service said, and made a mental note to think through this approach before launching it. "Again, Chas, try to verify if she was abducted in Mexico. This is critical information for what we do next, and how we do it. And wherever she disappeared from, who was last to see her, and how long between the last sighting and a MP report with cops?"

"We'll get after it," Chas said. "Back at you soon, Grady."

The timing in all this was a pain in the ass. Harlikin could recall all ROCKs at any moment, and then Chas would not be able to reach him. McKower needed to know all this and he called his personal wealth manager and friend back and gave him the captain's number and told him, "Pretend you're talking to me when you talk to her and I mean talk as if you're talking to me."

"I'm not good at pretending," Marschke said.

"Baloney," Service said, chiding him. "Anyone who investigates things the way you do has to be an actor, to be able to pretend like they're not pretending when they are pretending. Most of us are uneasy about this part of our work, Chas, and only sociopaths get truly comfortable with it," Service said, and then added, "Tell your troops to dig hard for all details. No detail is too minor, or unimportant. Get DOB, schooling, attendance records, report cards, everything you can on Lady Loire."

"Yessir, back at you soon as we can," Marschke said, and broke away.

Service lit a cigarette and got out of his pickup to think. Gabbart Third was Harlikin? Or was it the other way around? And which was before and after he/they married the former stripper turned Christian entrepreneur and business mogul? Stripping For Jesus? And the Regiments of Christian Knights related, and if so, how? Where the hell were the alleged eagle feathers? Had said feathers ever existed, and, if so, where was the evidence? Was it Coldbeg or Fish and Wildlife who brought in that angle? How did Gecko and Goat miss the body below? *Hell*, how had the local and state police crime technicians missed it? It should have been decomposing and stinking, especially in those closed confines.

And what the hell was with Irkka Vorpi, blaming the Tech students for bullying and blackmailing him? And, if true, what the hell was *their* game? The boys definitely needed another round of questioning, separately, and not by him. Something and Bapcat could handle this part.

What was Harlikin doing right now, and where exactly were Abel Tooler and his assailants? He had no use for militias, never had. They were, at their best, highly trained toy soldiers, actors, albeit often armed with deadly toys of mass destruction. Tim McVeigh of the Michigan Militia had blown up the Alfred P. Murrah Federal Building in Oklahoma City, and another whack-job group in southern Illinois, he seemed to remember, had murdered Mormon founder Joseph Smith and his brother. Militias might be clown shows, but their toys were lethal, and even clowns could quickly become violent mobs.

But militias were not his concern, nor his colleagues', yet, but many of the state's COs had had some odd contacts and run-ins with members of such outfits around the state while they were out fishing, hunting, or running around pretending to be soldiers.

What to do next? Was Harlikin preparing to make a recall soon, or was he using this time to pull up stakes and melt into the ether?

How had crime techs missed the body in the mine? He called Tuesday Friday. "We talk twice in one day? Huzzah, Honeybunch! This has to be a record," she said.

"Don't call me Honeybunch, and nobody but cartoons say 'Huzzah.'"

"You prefer OO-rah or OO-ray?"

"I prefer sanity and calm in the demeanor of the lady on the other end of the line. And I hate Caller ID."

"Then deactivate it," she said, but added quickly, "You don't know how to do it, do you?"

"*It* I know how to do just fine," he answered. "The phone is another issue."

"What can *you* do with that phone?"

"Make calls, read map APPs, drop markers, I'm a veritable whiz."

"You're a technological putz is what you are. What is it you want? I'm busy."

"We arrested those two ROCKs," he told her.

"Right. On what charges?"

"Another ROCK alleges they tried to throw him off the top of Owl Creek Falls."

"Now *that* could hurt," she said. "Fight over a woman or money?"

"Boss's orders," he told her.

"Damn," Friday said. "You believe the allegation?"

"Looks like it's true. It came from my ROCK training partner."

"Amazing, and you were going to tell me this when?"

"I'm telling you now is when, but there's no homicide, only the attempt."

"Which you stopped. Am I guessing correctly here?"

"What's it matter who stopped it?" he asked, not wanting her to know about Limpy's role.

"Has it occurred to your reptilian brain that someone who unsuccessfully attempts homicide may previously have succeeded *elsewhere*?"

"Where are said suspects now?" he asked.

"Marquette County had them," she said, "but the MSP picked them up and transported them."

"And the alleged target?" he asked.

"We secured him," Friday said.

"I may need to talk to him again."

"Can be arranged, I think. Just give me a bump and some time. Does Lis know any of this yet?" Tuesday asked.

"Not really."

"Were I you, I'd call her right quick, Bub—*before* she hears it from another source."

• • •

Service knew Friday was right, hung up, and called McKower. He heard her suck in a breath when he began to relate all that had happened and all he had learned so far, but she settled quickly and asked sensible and supportive questions. "Want me to ring the bell of other states and federal agencies?"

"When that seems to be the way to go, but not until we have more information and can use it like a rifle, not a shotgun."

"Stay safe," she said.

"You too."

Phone calls done for the moment, he sat brooding in his truck. This job used to be about putting your boots in the dirt, mud, and snow and walking until your legs started to turn to rubber. Now it seemed to be about talking on damn radios and telephones until your brain turned to Jell-O. Why was he putting himself through this shit?

"Fuck," he shouted out loud, this concluding his thinking.

A voice from the transceiver behind his ear said, "We *heard* that."

Big Brother was everywhere, even in a recording telling you to fasten your damn seatbelt, even after you just loosened it to jump out of your truck and chase some asshole fleeing into the woods.

CHAPTER 25

Worm's Hide

KEWEENAW COUNTY

I am out of breath; confusion's near; I cannot speak.
—William Shakespeare, *As You Like It*

How in a "case" seeming to go nowhere fast could there be so damn little actually *happening*, and so damn much to do? And why was there even a case? Eagle feathers, his ass. Service wanted to put Something and Bapcat onto Gecko and the Goat, but right now he was feeling overwhelmed by silence from Allerdyce and Worm, that combination alone making his stomach twist. The offload of information from Chas made his mind spin. Lady Loire, Gabbart Third and Harlikin. S4J, LFJ, and ROCKs? The thought of his unlikely watchers high-hawking Harlikin's property gave him some sense of security equal to unspecified fear that something could, at any moment, go dreadfully wrong.

Experience and priority reminded him to personally check on his watchers before mobilizing his PCOs. *Colleagues*? Good grief: They were mere children beside his hoary head. The world was upside down and inside out!

What was that song Tree was always singing back in the day? "We gotta get out of this place. . . . " The more things changed, the more they remained the same, no shit. That was a grand and sorry goat rodeo that war, and now there was this. Would it never end?

His first surprise as he approached Worm's Hide was to be greeted by his dog Newf, a 130-pound Presa Canario, a Canary Island mastiff, with a head the size of a bear, spewing buckets of slobber. She was old now, still a beautiful girl, with her dappled gray muzzle seeming to whiten more almost every day. "Hey girl," he greeted her and she banged into his leg and he had to brace himself against her enthusiastic mass. How did *she* get here, and why, the questions being answerable by only one possible person.

The dog suddenly reeled and galloped into the brush that hid the cave entrance, and a voice said with a growl, "Where's dat old fart of youse's, girlie?"

Limpy Allerdyce. How that dog loved the old violator, who came out grinning.

"Figgered 'bout time youse showed up. We just gone cook some grub," the old man announced.

They went inside and Allerdyce pointed to a camp chair. Worm was already there, in another chair, her legs crossed demurely. Interestingly, she was fully dressed in summer-weight camo pants and short-sleeve shirt, her feet in expensive canvas boots, her skin glowing its rich tan. The dog sighed, circled multiple times, and collapsed loudly between the two camp chairs, positioning herself equidistantly between Grady and Worm.

"Thought you two were on watch duty?" Service said.

"Nuttin' 'appens dere dis time day," Allerdyce said, from the little stove where he was cooking.

"Ever, really? Your tea leaves tell you that or have you switched to reading chicken bones this year?"

Allerdyce looked back at Worm. "He makin' da stupid jokes, girlie. Pay 'im no never-mind."

"Why is my dog *here*?" Service asked.

"Worm likes Newf," the feral girl said and Newf's heavy tail slapped the stone floor a couple of times.

The dog obviously reciprocated the affection. "So, nothing's going on there and you two are playing house in a cave, and that's it?"

"Ain't nuttin' 'appens since we seen Wilt Da Stilt," Allerdyce said.

This took him by surprise. "Wilt the Stilt, as in Chamberlain?" Service said.

"Yah, dat sumbitch allatime brag he screwt ten t'ousand wymyns back in da day," Allerdyce said, admiration thick in his voice.

"Ten thousand?" Worm said. "How this is possible? How does person have so much time to meet so many . . . ?"

"You know who Wilt Chamberlain is?" Service asked her.

"Old Man, It tells Worm, yes."

Allerdyce was still It, not quite a Him yet, but her language sounded smoother. "Did It think to include the fact that Wilt's been dead, like forever, and that he was black as toast, which is not the flesh color favored over there in ROCK camp?"

"He come back from the dead as white boy," Allerdyce declared with certainty.

Service grimaced. "Wilt came back to life as a white man. Is he still tall?"

"Taller," Allerdyce said. "But white, not Black."

"I'm pretty sure if Wilt came back and saw he was white, he'd look for some way to resume being dead."

"Explain," Worm said. "Worm, She is confused."

"You're with Allerdyce. He creates confusion, spawns it everywhere he goes. Wilt Chamberlain did not come back to life from the dead. And even if he had, he would not have come back as a white man, or to be in the company of so many white people, excepting perhaps receptive females, and had the same sartorial presentation as you often do and by the way, I *like* today's ensemble."

"Old Man, It find these for me," she said. "Worm wishes to learn this word *smart-orial*."

"*Sartorial*," Service corrected. "It means someone who is very selective about their clothing."

"Worm is selective," she said.

"Worm rarely wears clothes," Service reminded her.

"But when Her does, she is selective. Worm wants to look 'sharp.' Old Man, It teach her this word, 'sharp.'"

Service knew these two, neither of them anchored in a reality anyone except them could understand, could easily drive him quicksilver batty.

"Worm has smart device," the woman announced.

"Good for Worm. It's nice to see her wriggling into the twenty-first century where she can suffer along with the rest of us."

"Worm thinks Service making joke to her."

"If so, he's in the same boat with her."

"Boat is smart device?" she asked, her eyes hard slits.

"Sorry, there are figures of speech and metaphors where one says one thing when they mean another."

"Worms calls this a lie."

"And it is," Service said, "sort of, sometimes, except when it's not." *This kid!*

Worm held out her smartphone and showed him a picture.

"Fuck!" Service said.

"Now?" Worm said. "Her and Him, here?" She turned to Allerdyce. "Go away, Old Man!"

"I know this guy," Service said, ignoring Worm's misread.

"Youse know da Great Wilt Da Stilt?" Allerdyce asked in an air of awe.

"This person isn't Wilt," Service said, showing the old man the phone screen. "Wilt is Black. This person is white as a cue ball."

Allerdyce giggled. "Tole youse he come back white. Even got da pitchers proves it."

Good grief. "Wilt was Black and seven-foot. This guy is white, and seven-four. Apples and oranges," he chastised the old man.

"Worm love oranges and apples, but like other thing more better."

"What other thing?" Service said.

"Her hear Service, Him say 'fuck.' She tell Old Man 'It go away!' Now Him want talk apples and oranges. Worm feel very confused."

"Why youse got pick nits wit' girlie?" Allerdyce demanded.

"When was this guy here?" Service asked, holding up the phone photo.

"Which guy?" Allerdyce asked.

"There was more than one here?" Service asked. Would he ever get a straight story from Allerdyce?

"How many jamokes we counted, girlie?" Limpy asked the girl.

"Her remembers only things Worm need remember," Worm said dismissively.

Service looked at her. "People coming and going on that property *is* one of those need-to-remember-things."

"Ask It," she said, with a nod to Allerdyce.

"There were others?"

"They all wrote down," the old man said, grinning. "We know our bidnet."

Their bidnet? Good grief. "May I see the alleged list?"

"Why di'n't you just say so?" the old violator said.

"I just did."

"Coulda ast before."

"I didn't know there *was* a list *before*."

"Geez oh Pete," Allerdyce said. "Of course dere's a list."

"Got camera's too," Worm added.

Service looked at her. "You mean smartphone pictures?"

"Say one thing, mean another," she parroted, and grinned triumphantly.

"Are you having fun?" Service asked her.

"Worm, Her always has the funs, but some funs more funs than other funs."

This he could believe, even if he could not understand how in the world she came to be who she was. "Make sure Her always has the funs," he told her.

"Not a problem," she said.

"Who taught you to say *that*?"

"It, Old Man," she said, nodding at Limpy.

"That old man," Service told her, "is the last person you want to rely on for language help and advice. Or funs. Anytime he tells you something, check with me before you use it."

"Geez oh Pete," she said.

"That phrase, for instance," Service said.

"Him don't like Pete?"

"I don't even *know* Pete. *Nobody* knows Pete."

"Old Man, It knows Pete," she said. "It say all time, Geez oh Pete."

"He doesn't mean a person named Pete."

"Pete not person? What Pete is?"

"Just words," Service said in exasperation, and feeling sorry for her.

"If just words, why Him so upset? Him make Him's sick-apple face." She laughed.

Then he laughed. "Let me see these alleged cameras."

"Just got da one," Allerdyce said, and showed him a disk, which the old man slid into the camera and plugged it in so they could see.

Grady scrolled through the stills and saw twelve different individuals, including Gecko and Goat of MTU and what the hell were they doing here, especially since the FBI had them confined to classes and the MacInnis Student Ice Arena on campus. All the individuals in the photos were in pairs, except the Tech kids, who appeared separately. What the hell was going on?

"When was White Wilt here?" Service asked Allerdyce.

"Come yesterday," Worm answered.

"Came and went?" Service asked.

"Just come, still over dere we t'ink," Allerdyce answered.

Service pointed to Goat Nankervus. "And this one?"

"Come late day before," he said with a glance at Worm, who nodded her assent.

Who *were* these college boys? What was he *missing* in this? "Both *still* there?" he asked his watchers.

"Dey bot' still dere, we t'ink."

"How do you know? Have you put eyes on them?"

"Cause we ain't seen 'em leave yet is why," Allerdyce said.

"That doesn't mean they're still there," Service repeated. "This place is a huge chunk of property, and they can enter and exit from anywhere."

"No, Sonny. Dey come to t'rough da entrance, same place youse go in and come out."

Allerdyce had been surveilling *him*?

"Not worry, Sonny. Like I said before, nuttin' never 'appen dis time day," Allerdyce said, seeing Grady's skepticism.

"Why It call Him, son?" Worm asked. "It Him's papa?"

"Technically and biologically no," Service said, but he also knew that in recent years the old man had been more of a father to him than his own father had ever been. Focus, he told himself.

"Okay, we'll assume you're right and the two men are over there."

"We say dey dere, dey're dere," Allerdyce said and Worm added, "Her think them there."

"What about the other ten individuals?" Service asked.

"Dey gone same day come in," Allerdyce answered.

"But not Wilt and the other guy?"

"Nope, dey still over dere, dose two, but dey not come as two, dey come in as two ones," the old man told him, and again Worm nodded.

"Got that nailed down. They came separately, not as a pair. Have you seen either man since they got there?"

"No, youse want us slip over dere, take look-see?" Allerdyce asked, his voice thick with hope.

"That is the very *last* thing I want," Service said.

"Youse don't care what dey do over dere, white Wilt and udder jamoke?"

"I don't, not really." Not true of course, but figuring how Gecko and Goat fit in was his problem to deal with.

"Why Him say *not* really, does Him mean *really* Worm wonders?"

"Usually," Service said.

She grimaced. "Usually mean not always so what this means other times when not really is really?"

"Be easier, me and da girlie sleep over dere closer to dose guys."

Worm said, "We got get back. This is leaving time."

"Leaving time?" Service asked.

"Dose pipples all come in 'bout same times and leave out 'bout same times," Allerdyce explained.

"White Wilt and the other one included?" Service inquired.

"No, dey come different times, but same place, eh?"

This was all too strange and he couldn't think clearly enough to figure where to steer his thinking.

"What we do now?" Allerdyce asked. "Sonny? Girlie dere right, dis da leaving time an' we need go look."

"Service, Him come too?" Worm asked.

"No thanks. I've got a lot of other things to take care of." And now a dozen new come-and-gos, including Gecko and Goat, and they definitely needed to be talked to, but not by him in case he bumped into them inside Camp ROCK and had they already seen him inside? This didn't sit well with him, and suddenly nothing came to him as a plan and he knew he needed help to clarify his thinking, or lack thereof.

He called Tuesday, and she answered promptly and listened as he spun his woes: "The two Tech kids we met at the Tubes? They are now with Colonel Harlikin, or at least they're probably on his property."

"Why?" she asked.

"Guess how many jellybeans in the ten-gallon jug," he said. "I have no clue."

"You're still not recalled?"

"Nope, but ten others—twelve if you count the two college kids, have been called in, and sent right back out again."

"Meaning?" she asked.

"Your basic bupkis. This guy Harlikin is either cagey as hell or seriously, terminally disorganized."

"And you're feeling the urge to get back inside to see what's going on," she told him.

"Part of me is, part of me wants no part of it," he admitted. "Especially if those kids are still there, which they appear to be."

"All of me doesn't want you back in there. This whole deal keeps giving me the major creepy crawlies. Shit," she said. "Another call. Talk to you later."

She broke contact and the phone sounded. It was Bapcat this time. "Heard some shit went down."

"What're you talking about?"

"Vorpi's dead."

"What? When?"

"Sometime after you and Something were there."

"Nobody told me. Who called you, Sheriff Born?"

"Uh-huh."

"Why you?"

"We're cousins," Bapcat said.

"Seriously?"

"I've got relatives all over the Keweenaw and the rest of the U.P. Our family has been quite the breeding factory. Where are you?"

Service said, "I'm trying to make my way to Patty's. Do me a favor. Go over to Aspirus and check security cameras."

"County's probably already impounded all of them—evidence."

"Lean on your cousin for a favor."

"Why?"

"Humor me. I'll explain later."

"Okay."

"Check it out and meet us at the Bumbletown Towers as soon as you can, copy?"

"See you there," Bapcat said. "Quick-as." This was game warden humor. You could start your day thinking you were going to do Task A, and current events would sweep over you and it might be three weeks later before you could try to do Task A again. There were days when the frantic nature of the work could make you crazy. And days where by the end you had no idea what the hell Task A had been in the first place.

CHAPTER 26

Allouez

KEWEENAW COUNTY

So foul a sky clears not without a storm.

—William Shakespeare, *King John*

He was at the bottom of Bumbletown Hill when Allerdyce bumped him on his smartphone. The phone said UNKNOWN CALLER, but since it was coming in on a line known only to the old man, Service knew who it was, and answered with a terse, "What?"

"Dat shorter jamoke come same day as dat White Wilt guy, he just come oot. Worm seen 'im."

"And White Wilt?"

"No joy," Allerdyce said with a cackle. They had one night watched a World War II movie and the pilots looking for enemy aircraft repeatedly called "no joy" and this had made the old man laugh for reasons known only to his twisted mind, and ever since then it popped up in his vocabulary and conversations. "We ain't seen tide nor tear of dat guy."

Service grimaced. The old violator's hold, and take on, English was tenuous. "You mean hide nor hair?"

"What I just said, Sonny." The old man sounded a little exasperated. Like many politicians, the lifelong violator never explained or apologized, and instead continued to plunge ahead. "You want me and da girlie go inside dere, take da close look?"

"You would be trespassing."

"Not da way we do it, Sonny. Dey never know we even been in dere."

"Stay *off* that property!"

"Still t'ink we ought try," Allerdyce complained.

"Stay out and stay off, do you *hear*?"

"Awrye," the old man said. "Youse comin' back over ere soon?"

"I don't know what's next from here."

"Okay den, Sonny. Worm and me is holdin' down da fork."

Fort, Service thought, and grimaced again. "When exactly did the shorter guy leave?"

"Was first t'ing dis mornin."

"And you're just telling me now."

"Da sun was just start cuttin' t'rough da trees."

"I know what morning is."

"Check damn phone, Sonny. We been trying call youse since den, but youse don't like no phones smarter den youse, so youse don't pay no damn attention. We did our job, Sonny. Now youse need do yours!"

Service laughed to himself. The old man was right. "Okay, thanks. I'll see you two when I see you, and keep your hands off that girl."

"Girlie got mind she own," Allerdyce came back.

Meaning a mind of her own and he was right about that. "You are sometimes a wise old man," Service told him.

"Wise don't unhook old part," Allerdyce retorted. "Just make one wish it did, eh?"

Service pulled up the two-track to the rendezvous point and saw Bapcat's truck already in place, so he parked behind the new CO. This way, Something could pull in the opposite way and park driver-to-driver. He would stand outside between the young officers' trucks for their meeting.

Something arrived shortly thereafter while Service was fetching coffee he'd picked up from Barnaby's Bluntsnake Bake-A-Cakery Kafe in Copper City. He also pulled out a small loaf of Toni's povitica from his truck's food cache and sliced the bread with his yellow-handled K-Bar pocket knife.

Service handed them each large slices of the savory Croatian bread and gave them steaming coffees from one of his thermoses. Something held a second cup while he poured it and sipped it to make sure it was warm before handing it back to him and he immediately took a big swallow.

"You don't fear obscure, lethal African cooties?" she asked, smiling.

"I stopped fearing cooties from girls when I was three or four."

"Ever the trendsetter," Bapcat quipped.

"At the age of three or four could explain a whole lot about you," Patty said.

"A whole lot of what?" he asked.

"Stories told about your charm and a lot of women's undergarments."

He took another slug of coffee. "Damn, that's still *hot*, and, for the record, there have not been a *lot* of women in the way you mean it."

"That reaction also says a whole lot about you," Something added. "You tend to ignore your own reality."

"Kalina has a very large mouth," he griped, guessing the source.

"And a pachyderm's steel-trap memory," the young officer said. "She remembers everyone and everything."

"You want to see the tapes?" Bapcat asked.

"Here? How do we do that?"

"No, we have to go back to Aspirus. They wouldn't let me copy anything or carry out the originals without a warrant, chain of custody, and all that good stuff."

"I thought the sheriff was your cousin."

"He *is*, but his deps *aren't*."

"OK, I don't really want to go there, but I do want to see. Have you looked at them?"

"Briefly, but nothing jumped out. Should something have?"

"I don't know. Maybe, maybe not. Tapes show inside and outside?"

"Four cameras, but Laurium isn't London if that's your question."

"What the hell does London have to do with Aspirus in Laurium?"

"London is like totally wired with vid-feeds, even most of their public loos. You know London?" Bapcat asked Service.

"Obviously you do?"

"We did a lot of R&R there over the years. Fly from Kabul or Baghdad, raise some hell, or sleep for a solid week, and fly back into the shit. Where'd you guys go in your war?"

"Lots of choices, none of them London. We had thirteen-month tours."

"Where'd you go?"

"Bangkok."

"Same as Tree," Patty said.

"We went together."

"He never said that part," she added.

"The kind of work we did kept us on short leashes."

"What kind of a mission?" Bapcat asked.

"The kind that no longer matters and, as it turned out, probably didn't then either."

"That's also how Tree puts it," Patty said. "Were you guys brainwashed?"

"All soldiers are brainwashed," Bapcat interjected. "They have to be, otherwise, nobody would ever be so stupid as to go to war."

"Bleak," Patty said.

"And dead-on," Service said. "Let's go have us a group look-see, but first give Patty and me a quick briefing," he told the former SEAL.

"Irkka Vorpi tried to fly this morning."

"This morning, not last night?"

"It was full daylight," Bapcat said.

"Nobody saw him?"

"Apparently not."

Something said, "Dispatch said nothing."

"Sheriff's orders," Bapcat said. "People need the hospital and he didn't want a panic."

"Who called you?" Service asked again.

"Sheriff Born."

"Your cousin."

"Like I said. There's a slew of them."

"Did anyone see Vorpi make the flight?"

"Not that I've heard, but I didn't try to talk to anyone. I figure this is the cop house's deal, not ours."

"Technically true," Service said. "But Patty and I just talked to the man and it seems odd that he decided to fly shortly thereafter."

"Maybe you two have that effect on people?"

"That's not funny," Patty objected.

"Wasn't meant to be," Bapcat said. "I served with guys who seemed to naturally attract or find more trouble than anyone else."

"Shit magnets," Service said. "We have them too."

"You one of them?" Bapcat asked.

"On occasion. History says your ancestor certainly was in that club. Did you see Vorpi's body?"

"Briefly."

"And?"

"Not sure. It just didn't look right to me, but what do I know?"

"How many dead bodies have you seen?" Service asked.

"Hundreds, easily, but usually there isn't much left to actually see and viewing turns out to be more of an exercise in imagination than sight."

Service looked at Something. "You?"

"Dead bodies, not many at all, but this is part of the job, right?"

"In the Troops a new officer has to do a number of tasks early in his career. For one, he has to notify someone of another person's death. And he has to recover and process a death and a body."

"Makes sense to me," Jordy said. "Wish we'd have been organized that way, but we weren't. You get a long way down the killing road before you get to see the results of what it is you're training to do. It makes a lot of guys take a big step back."

"You?" Service said.

Bapcat shrugged. "Anchors away and all that shit."

"Why don't you two double up in one truck and I'll drive separately and meet you at the hospital. Where's the body kept?"

"The morgue's not that far from the north loading dock," Bapcat said.

"Let's rendezvous there," Service told them, got into his truck and drove away, and as he drove he called Allerdyce, who answered. "Youse's dime, start talking."

"Been a long time since phone call was a dime, Old Man. What time exactly did the other guy leave Camp ROCK this morning?"

"Youse want da numbers?"

"That's what exact time means."

"Minute," Allerdyce said and mumbled something to someone, no doubt Worm, and came back on and told Service the precise time.

"You're certain about this?"

"Does your doggie slobber?"

In Limpyland's Limpyspeak, this was no doubt intended to confirm his simple question. Why did he hang around with the old misanthrope? Sadly, some questions never had reasonable answers.

CHAPTER 27

Laurium

HOUGHTON COUNTY

> For when the players are all dead, there need none to be blamed.
>
> —William Shakespeare, *A Midsummer Night's Dream*

Bapcat led Service and Something to the room with the body, which had been bagged in black rubber.

"He broken up pretty badly?" Service asked the young officer.

"Not really. His neck's broken."

"From landing on his head?"

"See for yourself. It didn't look that way to me. I saw no real mass trauma on the head, but I'm not a pathologist."

"Let's unzip the bag," Service said. "Isn't there a dep around here somewhere?"

"I asked on the way in. They're apparently calling it suicide, and ergo, no dep," Bapcat reported.

Something undid the bag. Vorpi was on his back, chest up, his head turned more than 90 degrees to the right and sort of hanging, his eyes open.

Service looked around, found a box of rubber gloves, and pulled on a pair. Something did the same thing. "Let's get the head up into normal position," Service said, which the other officer did.

There was matted hair and some blood, but Service didn't see massive external trauma of the kind he'd expect from a body hurtling down from a building onto a hardtop surface. "Maybe the docs see something we don't," Service told his partners. "Which doc looked at him?"

"Don't know," Bapcat said, "but my guess is someone from emergency."

"You'd think an ER doc would pick up on what's broken or not broken."

"Depending on the kind of shift he's coming off," Something pointed out. "This isn't exactly a big-city slaughterhouse, but Yoopers sometimes manage to manufacture their own unique mayhem."

"I'll go find a doc," Bapcat said, and left them.

"Dead people don't seem to make you edgy or nervous," Service told Something.

"Not yet, but neither do I want to do this every day."

"None of us want that," Service said.

The emergency room physician with Bapcat looked to be fourteen tops and his pimp mustache made him look ludicrous. "There a problem here?" the doctor asked with apparent aggravation.

"That's our question to you," Service told the man. "We think the man's head is pretty much intact and that seems odd, given what happened."

"That's your considered medical opinion?" the physician said sarcastically.

Service answered, "Nope, it's only the common sense eye of your average fifth grader. Guy jumps from building, forty plus feet up and lands on his head, breaking his neck—but there's hardly any visible trauma to the head."

"We don't always see the real damage from this kind of thing."

"We don't mean to offend," Something told the doctor.

"I'm not offended. You don't think I'm asking myself the same question, but the job here this morning was a certification of death, and an educated guess at the cause. The fact is that this gentleman is quite dead and his neck is broken, and now it's up to pathology to take the case the rest of the way." The young doctor suddenly looked at them. "Why am I talking to three woods conservation officers about a dead human? He didn't fall out of a tree, you know."

"He was a potential witness in a case," Bapcat offered.

"This man won't be witnessing anything. If there's nothing more, I have patients waiting."

"Your shift ending soon?" Patty asked.

The doc rolled his eyes and sighed. "Just starting," he lamented, and left them.

"Let's look at tapes," Service told the youngsters.

"Do you know something we don't know?" Patty asked.

"Nope, just that it's a cop's job to see to and verify every detail. If you're a beat cop in the city and you're supposed to wiggle every doorknob to make sure the doors of all businesses and government offices are locked, then you rattle every damn doorknob. The reality is: I do know shitloads that you two don't know, and never will know, and even with your brief time in this job, you can say the exact same to and of me. We're individuals."

"Thank you, Giant Yoda," Bapcat said. "When did you get so damn tall? Last movie I saw you in you were the size of a stinkhorn, and about as ugly."

One trip through the tapes gave them nothing, but Service insisted on a second look.

"We going to do this all day?" Something asked. "Suicides belong to the county, not us. What *are* we looking for?"

And at that very moment Service had a notion. "Look at the truck," Service said, pointing. "Red Jacket Glass."

Patty said, "Jinx Paanko, right?"

"His truck doesn't prove he was here," Service pointed out. Jinx Paanko was a towhead, and the man standing by the glass truck had long dark hair in a ponytail, but had his back turned to the camera, and why there was only one shot of him would never be adequately explained. Something in his brain said Goat Nankervus, but his eyes couldn't immediately confirm this. "Can we get some stills on this individual and blow them up, show them to hospital staff on duty last night and this morning?"

Service had a hunch and a concern. "Jordy, how about jumping in your truck and blasting over to Paanko's place? It's just a few blocks."

Bapcat called thirteen minutes later. "I just talked to a neighbor. Paanko owns only the one truck and the neighbor saw it when he went to bed last night at eleven. It was parked where it usually is, in front of the business. I tried to call Paanko, and banged on his door and got no response from his apartment above the business."

Service said, "Let us guess. You kicked in the door."

"You gotta go with what gets you to the dance. I called 9-1-1. Paanko's deceased."

"In his apartment?" Service asked, holding the phone out so Something could hear and talk too.

"He's on the bathroom floor. His neck looks broken to me, same as Vorpi's. But Jinx did not do a swan dive from forty feet. I think this is a homicide, but it's the sheriff's call, not ours."

"Hustle back to us after you make the hand-off to deps."

When Bapcat returned, they looked again at Vorpi's remains and Bapcat said, "This neck looks to me the same as Paanko's. I think *two* homicides. Can we go now and be game wardens again?"

"Hang for a while," Service said, and punched in Friday's number.

"We can't go on meeting like this," she greeted him.

"What about the dead FBI guy?"

"What about him?"

"What's he look like?"

"He looks *dead*."

"You told me his cause of death was impact, yes?"

"Your selective male memory serves you well when you choose. Impact as cause of death was the M.E.'s call," she related.

"What's his head look like?"

"He fell eighty damn feet onto hard rocks, what do you think it looks like?"

"I'm asking you."

"It looked like a smashed pumpkin."

"And his neck?"

"Let's see, a vertical drop eighty feet on the head, which is attached to the neck and spinal cord, what do you think? His neck was broken."

"What if his neck was broken before the fall?"

This drew a pregnant pause. "What the hell is going on?"

"We've got two bodies in Laurium. One flew down off a forty-foot building and has minimal head trauma, the other died in his bathroom and his neck seems broken and it looks to Jordy Bapcat like the neck-break is very similar break to the flyer's."

"A woods cop's take on cause of death?"

"Dammit, Tuesday, he was a SEAL for ten years. He's seen more bodies than all of us combined."

"Why are you guys even looking at this?"

"Both dead men were involved in a case."

"What way?"

"We don't know," he admitted.

"And now you never will," she told him. "Have you told the docs your theory?"

"Not exactly. The prelim call on the flyer is suicide."

"Same guy who was in that hospital for having tried to fly a few days back, right?"

"I know, but there's something here, I just know it."

"Does the M.E. concur on the suicide call?" she asked.

"Haven't talked to him."

"Has the M.E. *seen* the second body?"

"His people should have it by now."

"Both have broken necks?"

"Second one appears to have broken his in his bathroom."

"Slip and slide, you can easily die," she chirped. "Bathrooms are inherently dangerous."

"I know how easily necks can break, but this doesn't look like a simple fall."

"And out of your two, which may not be homicides at all, you ask me about the FBI body in the mine, is that your logic stream?"

"Pretty much."

"You, my love, are a piece of work. The FBI took command of their guy's remains."

"Was there an autopsy?"

"Presumably."

"Any way to see the report?"

"Not legally, and I say that knowing full well that you do not see extra-legal access as amoral, unethical, or illegal."

"Is that yes, we can see a copy?"

"That is: are you sick in the noggin?"

"Remember Goat?" he asked her.

"Right, the hockey player. I didn't really care for him."

"It's possible he's involved in this." Strictly a hunch here.

"Possible in what way?"

"We have a photo that may show him beside a truck that belongs to the other dead man."

"That's not what one calls open-and-shut. Big holes in your thinking, never mind the chain of evidence. How good are the photos?"

"We're having them enhanced."

"Did anyone actually see the kid near the site of the alleged crime at the time the alleged crime is believed to have taken place?"

"Not exactly, but we have witnesses to when the kid left another place about sixty minutes before this first death happened."

She said, "Those aren't nails for a case either."

"The point is, he had time to get here and do both kills."

"Why would he? What the hell is his motive?"

"For one thing, he and Gecko were allegedly blackmailing the flyer."

"Hmm," she said. "That is at least intriguing. Do you have the interview recorded?"

"No."

"But we *do*," Patty said to Service's phone. "They taught us to record everything when we were at the academy."

Service looked at her and grinned stupidly. "Really?"

She nodded. Service told Friday, "I guess we do have a recording."

"Keep it safe and let's get a transcript made, ASAP. Do you remember when we talked to that kid what he said about the mine where his buddy Gecko had to be rescued?"

"Mostly."

"The part where he said he was never going in that mine or any other mine ever again, remember that?"

He did. "Uh huh."

"Okay," she said. "Did either of these two poor men die in a mine?"

"No."

"Do you have any evidence of your college kid even being in another mine since we last saw him, either a witness, or a photo, something real and concrete?"

"No." Where was she trying to go with these questions?

"Then you have nothing with which to make for a case on the Feeb in the mine."

"There's the autopsy report."

"That's hope, not evidence. And we don't know what it says. Where is your theoretical witness right now?"

"In the wind," Service had to admit.

"Search underway?"

"Not exactly," he said.

"Charges contemplated, and if so, may I ask *what* charges?" Friday said.

"Both college boys showed up at Harlikin's camp."

This seemed to knock her back. "Why?"

"Don't know."

"You'd better find out, Bub. And, by the way, you sound uncomfortable."

"That matches how I feel."

"No recall for you yet?"

"No, but Harlikin's recalling others and kicking them loose the same day."

"Sounds like he's looking for something," she said.

"My read too." Exactly *what* was at this point still unreadable.

"If the sheriff and M.E. over there judge they have a homicide instead of a suicide, ask them to put me in the loop. Meanwhile, I will try to get something on the FBI casualty. No promises!"

"Sure, good, okay."

"Don't sure, good, okay me," Friday said, and hung up.

"I don't think that's Paanko by Paanko's truck," Patty told him when he was off the phone with Friday.

"Agree," Service told her. "Want to venture a guess who it might be?"

"I have one crazy idea."

"Spit it out."

"The Tech hockey player, Goat."

"You heard me talking to Friday."

She shook her head. "I was totally focused on the camera images."

"Why Goat?"

"Body posture," she said. "He alternately thrusts out one hip, and then the other—like his feet forgot they weren't on skates."

"Remind me to *never* play poker with you either. I think it's him too."

"By his walk?"

"I'm not sure what's catching my buzz, but I do know that Allerdyce saw him leave the camp this morning, in enough time to get here for Vorpi's last flight."

"But why kill the subject you're blackmailing?" Something asked.

"I hate the intrusion of reality," Bapcat grumped.

"Embrace it," Service said. "It interferes all the damn time."

"What was the kid doing at the place where you're undercover?" Bapcat asked.

"Excellent question," Service said, then, quickly, "How about you two lock onto the sheriff's people, and track action and progress with these two deaths?"

"I signed up to be a game warden," Bapcat said again.

"You are, but some of our cases tilt in unexpected directions."

"Good God."

"If God was good, we wouldn't have so many assholes on the loose."

"I hope we're wrong about this," Something said.

"My notion, not yours. You bear no guilt."

"You're my partner and we share the whole deal."

"We're not wrong about this. I just don't get all the angles yet."

And then he told her about the ROCKs and the Tech kid being there and leaving, and he began to wonder out loud if there was time for Nankervus to have done this, given his departure time from Fortress ROCK.

"You're undercover with *that* outfit?" she asked.

"So far," he said. And he saw her staring at a wall and guessed she was thinking about how she would do undercover. Every cop thought about it, sooner or later.

Was he crazy with this notion? And if it was Nankervus, who the hell was he and why do this to Paanko and/or Vorpi, and was there in any of this, a connection to Harlikin? "Nasty," he said out loud.

Patty Something stared at him. "What?" she asked.

"Damn near everything," the relationship with Friday included. Why the hell would she want to marry the likes of him?

CHAPTER 28

Allouez

KEWEENAW COUNTY

All's True that is mistrusted.

William Shakespeare, *The Winter's Tale*

Bapcat and Something were tied up all day with the Paanko and Vorpi deaths, so much so that their sergeant drove his duty truck all the way up from the Baraga office to find out why his officers were tied up in matters that weren't the DNR's concern.

The sergeant's name was Masterman, but those reporting to him called him Taliban because of his antisocial, by-the-book, no-exceptions-brooked ways, and what some of his reports considered questionable management practices. The trip came about after Something called the sergeant, and it had been Service who suggested she do so.

"Just throw him a small bone," he'd advised, "something he can grab hold of."

"Such as?" she asked.

"Tell him your regular partner seems to be regularly AWOL."

"That will piss off my partner."

"*What* partner? You've yet to work with the man. He's never there for you. Besides, he's a big boy. He'll just shake his head and keep on keeping on."

Sensing her reluctance, he explained. "Your partner's on the float-down to retirement. My guess is that when there is the slightest friction from above, he may pull his plug and go early."

"So then we'll have to work with *Taliban*?" she said, not hiding her concern, or was it irritation?

"Beats nobody," Service said, "and Patty?"

"Sir?"

"Taliban's been a damn good CO over his career. You guys may not like his style, but tough shit. Learn from the man. He's got plenty to teach to those who want to learn."

"Yours are the first positive words I've ever heard about the sarge."

"You never asked and you and Jordy both need to keep in mind that, relatively speaking, we are a very small state organization. We are also an elite force, and in small, elite units you always have specialized bitching and several grapevines that crosswire and duel with each other. Don't write off anyone until they give you a reason to do so—and by that I *don't* mean hurt feelings."

"You're full of advice today," she said.

"I hate doing this shit. I just want to get on with my job."

"Helping other COs isn't your job?" she asked incredulously.

She had a point. He sighed, and said, "I stand corrected. Sorry I was a jerk."

"Only the end bit," she said. "Until then, you were great." She added, "Those photos of the individual with Paanko's truck, I'm sure it's that kid Nankervus, from Tech, the one called the Goat. Jordy had the same reaction as me. Maybe we're both wrong, but two tentative IDs are not nothing."

Service likewise thought it was Nankervus. "To hell with the Tech kids for now. You two keep your minds on Vorpi and Paanko. Let the Sheriff's Department deal with the stuff they're trained to deal with."

"We're right on the edge of something," she said.

"Here are the facts I see," Service said. "There are two dead men. Vorpi fell off a building. Paanko broke his neck in his bathroom."

"There's more to it than that," she tried to argue. "You *saw* Vorpi's body."

Service gave her a look. "So you two have a shared hunch, good for you. Leave that crap alone for now. Vorpi flew," he told her. "That's *all* our evidence says as of now."

"Jordy and I feel differently."

"You may consider feelings your own personal facts, but that doesn't make them evidence-related facts that can pass the tests of evidence. Vorpi fell," he repeated.

"Or jumped," she said.

"Yes, or he was pushed," he told her, "or . . . "

"There's another *or*?"

"Or, someone killed him, and *then* threw him off the building. But all of that is speculative, and not evidence-based. Right now all we know is that the man fell."

"But there's the Riddle of the Mostly Unbroken Skull," she said.

"Riddle, yes, scientific base, not so much," Service said. "If we're right, science will at some point establish that. Riddle of the Mostly Unbroken Skull, I like that. It sounds like a Sherlock Holmes tale. The scientific reality may be that the skull is broken, but it is not funky enough to conclude that it should be more severely smashed in order to prove gravity broke his neck. Right now the medicos have a different take on the facts than we do."

"Then we agree, you, Jordy and me?" she said.

"Of course, but we have to maintain order here, work the process, and let the system play itself out."

"You have a reputation for fighting, or at least resisting the system."

"I do," he agreed, "But you have to pick the right time to fight, and the right fights. We don't have all the facts yet. Shit happens and it takes time to sort it out," he told her.

"Let me share this with you," Service told her. "I had this case: A woman in some apparent distress called her sister-in-law who reported the caller was making strange grunting sounds and calling for help. I was nearest, heard the call, and took it."

He continued, "I found her at the bottom of the stairs in her garage, blood everywhere, and a huge knot on her head. There was the handle of a coffee mug buried deep in her upper arm, where it cut her brachial artery, and she bled out before I could even get there. She was in her forties and looked to be in good shape, but the autopsy showed she was probably suffering a cerebral event as she went into the garage, only God knows why, got dizzy, fell down the eight stairs, knocked herself out, and in the process of landing, the dropped coffee cup broke, and the handle got driven into her upper arm. In some of the things we see, we have to let science replace what we think we're looking at."

"Where will you be today?" she asked him.

"In the wind again," as he had been for weeks. "My case has put me in a state of limbo."

"Not a pleasant place to be," she said.

"Tell me," he said sarcastically. "I may need a bunk tonight."

"You know where the key is," she told him, having shown him the first time he had been to her place. "Stay safe," she added.

"You too," he said, and ended the call. Gecko was still alleged by Allerdyce to be somewhere in Camp ROCK and he had no idea why that kid, *or* his pal, had been there, and separately, or why Goat had been there and left. He knew the time the Goat left the camp, and this was important, but did the Goat have enough time to get to Aspirus *and* Paanko's place, *and* be picked up in the video feed? To be sure, he needed to create a hard timeline and try to approximate various time scenarios. Something *seemed* to be going on, but what was not clear at all. And what if Paanko and Vorpi had nothing to do with each other?

He called the university and asked to be put through to the athletic director, whom he'd never met. A door-guard administrative assistant tried to block his inquiry, but he brusquely told her he would be there in less than an hour if the AD did not talk to him on the phone.

Seconds later, the AD was on the line. "What can we do for you, Detective?"

"My name is Service. You have a kid on your hockey team by the name of Nankervus. He's from Sudbury."

"I was the varsity hockey coach before taking this position, Detective, and I can assure you that we have no player, or student in any capacity in our program by that name. And we currently have no players from Sudbury."

"Some call him The Goat," Service tried.

"I think someone has made you the goat of some prank or joke. You know how college students can be . . . " and the AD paused. "Wait, Detective *Service*?"

"Yes, Service."

"The hockey player Service?"

"Once upon a time," he answered. "A long time ago. I doubt I can even stand up on skates now—and that's if I knew where my skates were, which I don't."

"We've got plenty of skates," the AD told him. "Anything else we can do for you?"

"Is there a seven-foot-four player on your basketball team?"

"We only *wish*," the man said, laughing. "We rarely get true Bigs at our level, much less Super Sevens."

"Bigs, Super Sevens?" Service said.

"I take it you don't follow basketball," the AD said. "Bigs are six-ten plus and Super Sevens are those players way above seven feet."

The truth was he didn't follow any sports at any level, and had not done so in a very long time.

"It true that the DNR has a hockey team?" the AD asked.

"The Law Enforcement Division, not the DNR itself. They're called the Fighting Fish Cops," Service told him. "They play exhibitions for charities and other noble causes."

"We should put your boys against our boys," the AD said, "y'know, for a good cause?"

"Some of our boys are girls," Service said.

"Even better."

"They're not nice, sweet girls. They carry pistols all the time, even when they're off-duty. They don't play nice with others."

"I see," the man said. "It was just a thought."

Service thanked the AD and called the office of the university's president. After a brief skirmish over privacy laws and warrants, and such, the man passed him to the school's dean of students.

A woman in the job, with a firm confident voice, business-like. "We're trying to determine if the university has a graduate student enrolled by the name of Mesnard George, of French Lick, Indiana," he began.

"Bird's hometown," the dean said.

"Bird?" Service said.

"Larry Bird, remember him *and* Magic?" the woman said.

Good grief, even this dean knew about Larry Bird, so why didn't Mesnard George? It was ludicrous. "Do you or do you not have such a student? He's seven feet four inches tall."

"I'm sure you're aware that there are state, federal, and university laws and privacy regulations, and I can't confirm anything for you unless you produce a proper warrant."

Bottom line at that stop: no joy. Grady Service stood outside his truck, took a sip of lukewarm coffee, lit a cigarette, took one pull on it, and noisily spit it out. It tasted like shit.

Mesnard George, aka Gecko, and now aka White Wilt (thanks to Allerdyce) and Nankervus, aka the Goat, and why did they not have a first name for the Goat? Maybe they were students, maybe not. Maybe blackmailers too, maybe not. Clearly I.V. had not been in his right mind in his final days. No way to confirm they were or weren't students without a warrant, and that was not going to happen at this point. Perhaps more puzzling, what were they doing at Harlikin's camp? Were they Mustard Seeds, and, if so, what did that have to do with their rock store plan, if anything? Or the Three T Mine?

Service pressed the heel of his hand to his face and a woman on in-line roller skates zoomed over to him and yelled, "Havin' a hard time, are we, hon?"

"One of those days," he mumbled.

"I used to have that problem but now I just skate away from them," she said as she performed a tight circle in front of him.

"The problems don't follow you?" he asked.

"They wouldn't dare!" she yelped happily, and went click-clicking down the street.

"I love blind optimists," he said out loud.

Who would gain by Vorpi's and/or Paanko's deaths? The blackmailers would certainly gain; they'd have nobody to accuse them. Did anybody else gain? Not that he could think of. Not yet. Talk about optimism. He laughed out loud at himself.

He was getting into his truck when his cell phone fired.

"Chas here," Marschke said. "Is this an inconvenient time? I can call back."

"What have you got, Chas?"

"Consternations bordering on frustration," Service's financial guru said.

"Lady Loire, aka Star of Stripping For Jesus, has *never* been officially reported missing, at least not anywhere we can discern, and her name doesn't come up on the NamUs system." Service knew that NamUs was organized to assist families and investigators in matching long-term missing persons with unidentified remains to resolve cases.

"Very disappointing," Marschke told him. In a year in this country there are up to six hundred thousand missing persons reported, and of that, at any given time in the year, there can be a hundred thousand unaccounted for. Many are found just fine, but some stay missing pretty much forever either because they are deceased, or they don't want to be found, and have proved adept at disappearing. At any given time, we also have around ten to twelve thousand sets of unidentified human remains in the system, so NamUs endeavors to focus on those as a starting point.

"Okay she's not showing up. What else?"

"It's confusing. She's not officially missing, but she was at one time reported gone and this was back in 2009, and you know how such climates and cultures can allegedly cause strange behaviors in official paperwork. Some insist it is a localized form of magic wherein certain reports and paperwork appear to grow feet, and go walkabout."

"Are the Mexicans holding open her case?"

"*Qué caso, señor*?" Marschke said with a laugh. "However, from the Ship of More Promising News comes this: I can now report with some confidence that Lady Loire, MIA was born Fawn Dawn Loire in St. Ruth's Hospital, Kansas City, Kansas. Newborn Loire's mother died giving birth to her only daughter, who came into this world with a full head of popcorn-blonde hair—and a full triangle of pubic hair, also popcorn-blonde, a match both north and south. Someone contemporary, never to be identified, scribbled on the baby's clinicals, "Poor child, doomed from the start."

"What the hell does that mean?" Service asked.

"As best my people can determine, there is a superstition among a certain element of folks in that great Kansas metropolis who believe that a baby born with a full patch of pubic fur will end life badly. Sometimes the most foolish superstitions seem confirmed by the most random happenstance."

"Loire was born in 1970 and disappeared in 2009, meaning she was thirty-nine at the time," Service said.

"Yes, and apparently she was rather fond of saying that she was then at her absolute sexual peak and sporting horns around the clock."

"Sounds like something a husband would not like hearing being bandied about. Was she discreet in said proclamations?"

"Not in the least. She told all within earshot and there was said to be times in business meetings when she did hour-long soliloquies on her sexual appetite and needs, and her talents as well, which she characterized as world-class, and when Lady Loire would go on in this manner, those in the room would gaze surreptitiously at Gabbart Third for any sort of confirmation of her claims, which he would eventually reluctantly accede to."

"Trouble in River City," Service said.

"Nobody likes being made a fool, which rhymes with tool," Chas said.

"Bad chemistry," Service said, which could point to motives. "But homicides aren't my line, Chas, which is to say I care little for how one is dispatched, even if by violent means. My interest in said events ignites only when the effects of said act can have an effect on things I'm charged with looking after."

"A wholly reasonable and focused job description," Chas said. "So, our lady is born of humble means in K.C., and her papa, devastated by his wifey's passing, cannot find equal value in the life gained versus that lost and thus infant FD Loire with angel hair is sent to be taken care of by an auntie who becomes the baby's permanent guardian in San Antonio, Texas, where our Kansas girl grows into a hale and hardy Texas girl, third academically in her class of several hundred at Thomas Jefferson High School. During her time in school she is not known for her burgeoning sexuality, but only for her raw brainpower and she is declared a whiz in higher maths. This the sort of thing you're looking for, Grady?"

"Probably. I'm still listening and making notes. She must be eighteen by then?"

"Barely seventeen at graduation, so she was emotionally and physically young. She blasted through four years of high school in a mere three, and from there she was off to that oasis of light and oxygen that is Austin, surrounded by the great dark shadows of heathen, conservative Texicana. Six months later she is stripping for Jesus, and presumably anyone else with the price of admission, which 'weren't cheap' one old Texas boy told us."

"Did she enroll at a university?"

"She did, and pre-law was the silo of her choice, but she was a no-show for too many classes and consequently given the old administrative heave-ho. By then she had paid cash for a townhouse near campus and was living the life of a high-earning working girl."

"Problems with drugs or anything like that indicated or suggested?"

"In the broadest construal of addiction yes, but her magnet, it appears, was money. Loved having it. Loved spending it."

"She bought a townhouse?"

"She was barely eighteen when she bought it. Lady Loire did specialized bookwork for certain businesses by day—various specialties in the so-called flesh trade—and artfully and profitably took off her clothes for pay at night."

Service was intrigued and always had been by the peculiar twists in fate and choices in every human life. Lady Loire seemed a very interesting character. "Would we now classify her as a businesswoman rather than a student?"

"Yes and no. She eventually returned to college, albeit part-time and selectively, and continued to build her financial worth. At some point she attained a degree of financial grace and flexibility that allowed her to jump to Lost Wages Las Vegas."

"Were all her business interests flesh-related?" Service asked.

"Sort of, but where such involvement can lead to disaster for most, Lady Loire is the exception. SFJ made her a superstar and with that fame and the resultant income, she formed LFJ, Leases For Jesus, a very queer business, but with a very good business plan in a well-defined niche. Her company buys mineral rights outright, and leases them to others for development. The apparent great strength of LFJ is exploration rather than exploitation. Lady Loire became an amateur prospector in her Lost Wages days, and her primary interest then and continued to be so-called bling-rock, gold, platinum, silver, as well as certain scarce strategic minerals."

"When's Gabbart Third come into the picture?" Service asked.

"Seems to have entered her life from places and in circumstances unknown around 1997. They married a couple of years later."

"That would be 1999?"

"By my math and their marriage license, yes, 1999, and here's a curious fact: They got hitched on April 1 of that year. Lady Loire appears to hold some fascination for April Fool's Day."

"It was her birthday," Service said, remembering what Chas had told him earlier.

"And her marriage day, and the day she went missing on the same date as well. Very strange coincidences."

"All coincidence is odd, Chas, and, in my work, such events can mislead and lead one down false trails and rabbit holes. What else is there?"

"That seems to be all for now. However, and I hesitate to broach this, given the thin strand it is supported by, but we have some reason to believe that Lady Loire was in Wisconsin, specifically Milwaukee when she went missing."

"Do we know with certainty she was in Milwaukee, April 1, 2009?"

"No, we do not, but we have seen copies of a memo from LFJ pointing to business meetings in Wisconsin, perhaps Milwaukee, perhaps elsewhere, on or around that date."

"Traveling with whom?"

"That iron is in the fire, boss, and should be out soon and cool enough to handle."

"Call me as soon as you know," Service told his friend. "You told me earlier you think she owns or leased a place in Presque Isle. Any evidence she was up that way?"

"Got somebody snooping around up there as we speak," Chas said.

Milwaukee, Wisconsin? Odd. And more or less adjacent to the U.P., as geographical proximity went. Neighbors almost. After all her dealings all around the country and Mexico, and Peru, now Wisconsin? The old ditty of childhood danced in his brain like an earworm, "my name he's Yon Yonson, I liffs in Visconsin, an' virk in da loombermill dere." If he ever had occasion to meet a flesh and bone John Johnson, he'd vowed as a kid to punch him in the nose—on principle, for all those other kids who'd been saddled their whole lives with the damn ditty. And what the hell was he doing getting over-amped about Yon Yonson, when he was up to his ass in his own problems, not the least being, the games his own brain was playing? This thing needed to remain focused and not allowed to precess like a cheap China-made compass. Why was he thinking compasses? Because compasses give direction and right now he had zippo.

CHAPTER 29

Allouez

KEWEENAW COUNTY

The wildest hath not such heart as you.
William Shakespeare, *A Midsummer Night's Dream*

Grady Service found himself swimming at loose ends, all of them trying to grab at him and pull him under so they could drown him professionally. Gecko and Goat both showed up at the toy soldier play house, but the Goat boogied. He was torn. Tech officials wouldn't confirm the pair's enrollment, and he and Friday and Something had interviewed the boys while they were supposed to be in a class near Painesdale, *supposed* being the operative word. If they weren't students, why and how were they auditing official university classes? He knew of no-pay drop-in auditing available to retirees, veterans, and the elderly, but not for younger folk. The two were said to be rock nuts. Was this their main connection or was there something else?

Patty Something walked into the kitchen, looked at him, poured more coffee in his cup, then filled her own. She was wearing a red sweatshirt emblazoned with "Rockers Rock—Or Die."

"What's that crap supposed to *mean*?" Service said.

"You want a beautiful, lyrical, large description to make your heart pump faster, or the Three D version?"

"That being?"

"Down-Dirty-Ditty."

He laughed. "That wins."

"It just means do what you do best and love most, or suffer the consequences."

He smiled. "The literary skills of you later generations leave much to be desired."

"This from a man whose generation's idea of literature was *MAD Magazine* and funny books?"

"*Classic Comics*," he corrected her. "Not plain old funny books."

"That distinction certainly convinces me," she said. "You look pretty frazzled."

"Maybe I miss my dog."

"But does your dog miss you, *that* is the question."

"Leave me alone, I'm trying to think," he told her.

"I can hear the gears rubbing, *and* your pain. Have you ever heard two heads are better than one?"

"Not if one of them is like twelve and the other one's like crowding a hundred."

"If your thinking equals your math, you may be in deep trouble."

"They teaching ESP at the academy these days?"

"No, they teach Blassel."

"What the hell is that?"

"B-L-A-A-S-L, Body Language As A Second Language. We call it Blassel."

"I'd call it bullshit," he said.

"Not at all. The FBI and other federal agencies have been using it in their academies for a long time. We're the first state natural resources law enforcement division to give it a try."

"Maybe a push off a cliff would be better," he suggested.

"It can help us read when others are conflicted or having problems. I thought about singing an old Negro spiritual when I walked in here and saw your head hanging low, but I thought it might make you cry with despair."

"I don't cry."

"Never?"

"Hardly ever," he said. Which was true. He had no objection to crying or tears, but his own tear ducts seemed to be mostly glued shut and he had no idea why, or cared.

"I cry," Patty said.

"You're a girl."

Her eyes hardened. "And you're what, a boulder? Every stone weeps. When spring sun warms winter-cooled rocks, and the snowpack goes down, the rocks sweat moisture," she said.

"You're a romantic," he told her. "And here I had you down as a *realist*. We should call you Stonewall."

"Who?"

"Stonewall Jackson, Lee's main man. Stonewall's men loved him to death, literally, in fact they shot him and killed him one night as he was coming back into his camp."

"Where do you find your facts?"

"Depending on the audience, I make them up."

"And that works?"

"The trick is in the telling, and rarely in the story itself."

"A Houghton County homicide detective showed up in Laurium today," she said. "Jordy and I told her about the injuries and she locked onto that like a laser."

"Limey Pykkonen," he said. "Right?"

"You know her?"

"She's damn good, and she's married to Shark Wetelainen. What was her take on the injuries?"

"Preliminary, she thinks both men were killed by a blow to the back of the neck, or some kind of pressured twisting motion. And we told her about the other body, the FBI asset you told us about. She said she'd heard a rumor of something, but it was unconfirmed until we told her. She's going to call Tuesday to talk to her, but bottom line, she's thinking there are definitely two homicides here, not one and a suicide. Do you think we could have three murders?"

"The other body was found eighty-two feet down that old mine shaft where you rescued Gecko. Based on physics and facts, it doesn't seem to me that this last guy was a master spelunker who had a tragic accident. But a homicide? Facts will decide that."

"Which is still not in our purview," she said.

"When we find a body, we turn it over to others to deal with."

"Unless it's a snowmobile, boat, or ATV fatality," she pointed out.

He sighed. "Most deaths on those devices are accidents, not homicides." There was a place in Alger County where a private citizen made cedar coffins for snowmobile victims. When and why this had become a *thing* over on the east side of the U.P. had always eluded him, but he and another detective had stopped there once and seen and smelled thirty freshly made white-cedar coffins and his mind had never been able to shed the image, or the scent.

Patty's talk of snowmobile mishaps led him to think about that room filled with coffins and as that image flooded his mind, he closed his eyes and the picture changed to rows of thin boxes, perhaps a foot wide, grooved, and in each groove a stone core sample that looked like it was from a mining operation in the state. The samples were pure rock and about the diameter of an old 35mm film canister.

"They teach you academy sharpies about the State's Rock Library?" he asked her.

"Not so much taught, as briefly mentioned."

"They say who runs it now?"

"I'll have to check my notes."

"You have notes from your academy classes and they're so organized you can actually *find* stuff in them?"

"Why else would you take notes?"

"That's rhetorical, right?" he said. He jotted notes in small notebooks, but most were from cases over many decades and dumped into boxes and wooden footlockers. "Didn't figure you for a paper-pusher," he said.

"I don't push paper. I employ and utilize the information it contains."

"And a wordsmith too. You'd better be careful or they'll promote you and plunk your butt behind a desk in downtown Lansing."

"What's wrong with that?"

"Everything. The best office you will ever have is in your patrol truck, and the most fun you'll ever have will be out in the woods. There's no fresh air in Lansing offices."

She laughed and handed a notebook to him: Her note read: "Rock Library: slated to move to old K.I. Sawyer AFB. Current manager: Faith O'Mary."

There was a telephone number, an e-mail address, and a regular street address on Cherry Creek Road, south of Marquette by the old state fish hatchery. "You should see those old warehouses in Marquette," he told her. "They're like something out of *Indiana Jones*: kinda cool, kinda spooky, kinda sad even."

"Books?"

"Almost all ore samples have to be submitted as cores. When you own or lease mineral rights and do *any* exploration, you have to be registered with the state, and provide drilling core samples as the state instructs. The library has a sample from every registered mine in the history of the state, in fact, let's call her right now."

"It's not state office business hours," Something reminded him.

"We're game wardens. We don't have state business hours. This isn't a job, it's a way of life."

"HR at the academy pounded us hard about accounting for and keeping our programmed hours."

"Screw HR, their way of life is eight to four and cocktails afterward. If they had their way, they'd have you walk away from a dead body if you were out of hours. I knew a deputy and a trooper in Iron County one time who worked seventy-two consecutive hours on an assault that eventually turned into a triple murder in two states. You think someone called them out for going over on their hours?"

"That's harsh," she said.

"It's also reality: Those people live in an office environment, not in the woods and out in the elements. They have no clue about what we do. Let *them* wrestle all night with a bunch of armed, drunken wingnuts and then have one of their kind bugging an officer about how they assigned their hours."

"We don't have O'Mary's home phone," Something told him.

"Friday will have it," he told her. "She and I merged all our numbers years ago."

"Was that fun, merging?" Something said, grinning.

"Worst merging I ever experienced was fantastic," he told her.

"Why, I believe there may be some signs of life left in that old man," she said.

He looked at her and shook his head. "I'm not as old as I look." Or as young as he wanted to feel, but this he kept to himself. He pointed at her. "Shut up and do something constructive."

"Age is just a number, right?" she said.

"Right, until you hit a hundred, and then it *might* be relevant—but to what I can't imagine," he added and they both laughed.

"Listen," he told her. "If you can still do a job and want to do it, why stop doing it?"

"Sounds like a TED talk on self-talk."

He didn't ask her who TED was and speed-dialed Friday. "Still swimming in dead bodies?" he greeted her.

"More every day and you people seem bent on becoming one of my main suppliers."

"You people? You're not glad to hear my voice?"

"One cannot hug a voice, nor can a voice hug its son."

"I'm at Patty's. We need a phone number for Faith O'Mary."

"The new rock librarian?"

"You know her?"

"No, but I've heard good things about her."

"Do we have her home phone?"

"Nope, but give me five minutes and I will use my super powers and text it to you."

"You want to call her, or should I ask her to call you two?"

"Great if she called us like ASAP," Service said.

"I'm naked," she said.

"You're just saying that to drive me crazy."

"Yes, I'm saying that to drive you crazy, and I am also gloriously stark, raving naked and drinking a beer. Now if I may, I'll get the rock librarian to call you and you can dream about me sitting here in all my natural glory."

"You do have some real fine glory to think about," he said.

She hung up laughing.

"Do all old people talk like that to each other?" Something asked.

"Let Tuesday hear you call her old and you will be a greasy spot on cement."

"You two are like superbly peculiar."

"Every couple is that way, young lady."

"Even my folks?"

"No exceptions. We differ only in the tunes we sing."

"I find that scary," she said.

Fifteen minutes later his work phone rang. "Hallo," a voice said, "Faith O'Mary here. Detective Service asked for a bump. I find that slang so *cute*."

"Thanks," Service said, "I'm with Officer Something and we're going to put you on our squawker."

O'Mary said. "Grady Service, right?"

"Right," he said.

"You knew my predecessor."

"I did," he said.

"Did you sleep with her?"

"What?"

"I asked if you slept with my predecessor."

"That's none of your business."

"I'll consider that a yes. Men always tell you it's none of your business when the answer is yes. Why do you think that is?"

Was this woman nuts? "No, I didn't sleep with her. Is that more definitive?"

"Actually, Officer, I find such sudden capitulation rather disappointing. My predecessor was very highly selective in who she took to bed."

"Are you okay?" Service asked the woman. What in the world was this?

"Me?" O'Mary said. "I'm so peachy keen, me and my gummies brightly sheen, recreationally speaking, and it's early in the evening, not even close to peaking."

Service looked at the younger officer who pushed a note to him. "THC in her food. She's high."

Service rolled his eyes. "What flavor?"

"Raunchybeery."

"That's a new one," he said.

"Cause I just made it up. Gummies stimulate my imagination and you know what James Joyce used to say."

"I guess I forgot."

"Imagination is just working over old memories, pretty weird, eh? Know what?"

"What?"

"Joyce had beady little rat-eyes, the little Irish prick. Gummies goose my libido," O'Mary added.

"How about we call you tomorrow at your office, Faith?"

"Pff!" the woman said. "Got a pencil in hand, Service, Grady, and I'm ready to scribble. Hope I can read my notes in the morning! Sometimes gummies turn my handwriting into hieroglyphical chicken-scratchings, and it's not easy to differentiate."

"Really," Service said. "This can wait. We're sorry to disturb you at home."

"Don't be such a pussy!" O'Mary taunted. "Hi-ho hoppy hip, let 'er rip, skip. I *really* like rhymes. You too?"

"A rhyme in time," he said, and Something slid another note to him, which he read out loud, "Drop a dime into a mine, oops that doesn't quite rhyme."

"Pfff!" O'Mary said. "Internal rhymes and close rhymes all count. What is it you want?"

"You'll be at the warehouse in the morning, right?"

"Do bears do you-know-what-you-know-where and in doing so get little poopies in their hairsies? Really dealy I can take down your information, and I will be able to read it, and then address it to the best of my ability, I ain't no hillbillity, not to worry, Murray. I am ready and steady for beddy, Teddy, I'm your kid, Syd."

Grady rolled his eyes, read off a list of mine names, and asked her to read them back to him, which she did flawlessly with no sign of gummy fog.

"I shalt call thee back—and thy front too!" O'Mary said. "Are you certain you didn't sleep with my predecessor, Detective Service? Would be just like that chick to sleep with a dick."

"Good night, Faith," Service said and before he could end the call, the rock librarian said, "Ten fricking four, haul your big old ass out my door."

"Gracious me," Patty Something said. "There's some time out of our lives we will never get back!"

"We'll call her again tomorrow."

"What exactly are you after?"

"Something to give us some direction."

"You forgot Two-Ton Too in the list you gave her."

"We want facts, not myths."

"Who can separate fact from myth from conspiracy theory these days. Just look at social media."

Service felt his phone buzz, and he hit the receive button.

"You did *want* to sleep with her, I knew it in my bones—even if you didn't consummate," the rock librarian said.

"Sorry, Faith, we have another name for that list we just gave you."

"Good, I still have a pencil in my hand and I was just looking at it and asking myself, what's *that* doing *there*?"

"Can you see your list?"

"Damn sight right," O'Mary said.

"Write this: Three T, or Two-Ton Too. Read it back, please."

"Three T, or Two-Ton Too."

"Great. Give us a bump when your ship makes landfall."

"You're funny," O'Mary said. "My predecessor only slept with funny men."

"I wasn't one of them," he said.

"Oh damn, Sam."

CHAPTER 30

Allouez

KEWEENAW COUNTY

As imagination bodies forth The forms of things unknown.
—William Shakespeare, *A Midsummer Night's Dream*

Service was beset by inertia, as one becalmed in the Sargasso Sea, when time evaporated and one with it, and tempted, oh god, so tempted to jump into his unmarked and just drive away and wait for Harlikin's callback, but that wasn't smart. Better to stay the course here, drink Patty Something's coffee, track what all the others were doing or not doing, saying and not saying, lost in his own thoughts and more than a little whining about his circumstances, and lack of action, or inspired direction.

His personal cell burbled again and he momentarily thought about crossing the street and chucking it off the grainy stone hill. There was no solitude anymore, no downtime, no uninterrupted time to think and work out problems and puzzles, nowhere to chill your brain and emotions and relish the pure liberty of not being bugged by the world buzzing around the self, his world it seemed, overwhelmed by telephones, intellectually toxic toys most humans thought of as happy-face tools that let them never have to be alone or confront themselves. They were toys, miserable toys, no less, no more and all around the world personal bank accounts dropped daily, call by call, as people wasted their time in jabberwockyland.

"*What?!*" he snarled into the phone when he activated the call.

"Worm is making calling to Him Service."

Geez, even Worm was already trapped by the toy. "This is Service. Is this you, Worm?" She was as feral as an old wolf and already and inexplicably attached to a cell phone. How sad a thought. The damn things were evil.

"Yes, this is Worm making calling Her says."

Her third-person referencing sometimes put him at a dead stop, and at other times made him want to laugh at her clumsy formality. Go gently, he reminded himself. She's emotionally just a kid.

"Worm is to say Her has seen hookey player come back. What is this hookey, Her asks?"

"Hockey, not hookey. It's a game," Service told her.

"What is game?" the girl asked.

"Mostly a waste of time," he said tersely. "Like sleep." But one kids were encouraged to engage in as kids, so they could grow up, to *what*? Waste more time in games? Many tens of millions did.

"Worm likes sleep much, but Old Man It here so close, make Worm have wet skin. Bad things can catch Worm when Worm is sleeping. Worm wakes up often, never sleeps long like Old Man, It."

Feral as a wolf, there in a nutshell from her own mouth, restless sleep to maintain guard and personal safety. Dogs did it, wolves did it, actually all canids, and too few humans. "There is a double edge in quid pro quo," he told her.

"What language to Worm Him Service speaks?"

"English. When you sleep you risk bad things by choice so that your body receives new energy."

"Worm always have new energy."

Because she's more wolf than human, no doubt, and therefore had far more energy than the average human. Exactly what she was or could be, or wanted to be if there was such a thing, was far from certain. This was Allerdyce's phone, the one he had given the old violator.

"Where *is* the old man?" he asked her.

"It, Old Man, tell Worm, 'call Sonny, honey, tell him we seen da hookey player and we on da trail.' Why It say *we* when It leave Worm, and only It go and Worm must use this . . . *thing*?"

It had been years since he tried to carefully decipher Limpy-speak and Limpy-think. "It means he's tracking the hockey player."

"Worm can do tracks good. Her go now, join It?"

He didn't want either of them in faux colonel Sane Zane Harlikin's toy soldier kingdom in the scrub-country. "You, Worm, stay put. Where are you?"

"Last place Service see Worm," she said. "Him Service come here too?"

"Not yet. Worm needs to stay where she is and wait."

"What if Old Man, It not come back?"

It would serve Allerdyce right. He'd told him to stay the hell out of the guts of the game and off the playing field, but Limpy had not listened, and it dawned on him only now that Limpy was incapable of foregoing an action he saw as needed. Service told her, "It, Old Man, will be fine." He always had been, mostly. But Allerdyce who did not walk on water like Jesus, did walk and talk a lot like the late Harry Houdini. Throw the old man into a barrel of bobcats and he'd come out wearing a new bobcat fur coat. "He'll be okay," Service repeated, and wondered if the reassurance were for her or himself.

"Old Man, It just a man, Worm thinks."

"Old Man *is* just a man," Service said, "and Worm she is just a special girl."

"Ah, Worm see this good now."

"Was the hockey player alone?" he asked her.

"Yes, alone Him, no White Wilt, yes?"

Right, White Wilt, there was the Allerdyce influence again, imposing his own language. Some notions she seemed to capture easily and immediately. And yet was she expressing herself a bit more smoothly now?

"Hookey player and White Wilt are good guys wear White hats? Worm asks?"

As in a wolf's world, so too in Worm's: Things were friend or foe, food or not food, good or bad, black or white, a life devoid of gradation. "We don't yet know," he told her. "Let's wait for the old man. He might help us figure that out."

"Service Him shit Worm not?"

He had to get her apart from Allerdyce, and soon, otherwise he suspected she might become another Limpy, and was that right? Should he allow it, or not? Using her, he thought, for his own purposes, not prurient, but in the interest of the case, as he had always done, rightfully or wrongfully. Was this his right? Had it ever been? Why had he so seldom questioned his younger self, the one now looking more and more separate?

Worm's woodcraft, whatever its source, how hard-earned and however it had come to her, was on par with himself, and probably Allerdyce too, a hard realization, this bit. "Service shits Worm not," he confirmed. At least not on purpose, he reminded himself, or maybe by accident. "Okay?"

"Worm say okay."

"Where did the hockey player show up, same place where all the others come and go?"

"Not same place this place, this over little ridge south by creek Old Man calls 'da bleeder.'"

"Feeder," he corrected her, "a little trickle from springs that flows into a bigger one."

"Worm wonder if people are feeder people."

Her mind was sharp as knapped black obsidian. "They can be," he told her. And those were the ones who served as feeders that blindly followed the orders of misdirected, or truly bad people. This last part he didn't tell her.

"Worm is feeder?"

"Worm is a bigger stream all her own."

"Worm feels smile inside."

"Smiles inside are good. Wait for Allerdyce."

"How It find Worm? She have smart-talk box."

"Worm shouldn't worry. Allerdyce doesn't need technology to find Her."

Service heard a muffled giggle. "Something funny over there?" he asked.

"Worm Her think It, Old Man, more like Worm than other human people."

She might be right about that, depressing as that thought was, but he had no time now to figure out how to help this strange girl enter the mainstream. "Worm just hang tight and wait, okay?"

"Youse betcha," she came back. "Worm Her want see Him Service."

"Be there soon as I can," he told her, not sure if he meant it, not sure if he dared.

"Worm worry It, Old Man, mebbe kill hookey player."

Grady hoped not, but had already had a similar chilling thought. With Allerdyce all bets could be off depending on the circumstances. If Captain McKower knew he was using this unorthodox pair she would likely go full ballistic, and he couldn't blame her. At the moment he was questioning his own sanity, and his judgment. When was Harlikin going to recall him, and why were others being called back, and not him? And what if there was never going to be a recall for him, that Harlikin had his money and that was the end, a silly scam for cash from imbeciles, and emotional cripples?

"Have others come back to the regular entry place, not where you saw the hockey player?" he asked her.

"Every day we see some go in."

"And stay?"

"Worm Her think some yes, some no. Her not sure."

"How many a day?"

"Worm think four fingers, five mebbe."

"Okay, stay where you are, please."

"Youse betcha, Sonny," she said.

He cringed. How long until Allerdyce owned this woman and her choices would be gone?

He had a headache when he broke contact, and knew he desperately needed to hear Friday's voice, her compass, and he also knew he was still trying to figure out how, or if to tell her about nature girl Worm who went about in the nude.

• • •

"Grady Service," she answered, reading his Caller ID. "Do you *ever* sleep? Do you know what time it is?"

"It's the middle of the damn day. Why would I be sleeping or even thinking about sleeping?"

"You need to come home, Grady. We can't stand having you on the permanent float."

"Is that what this is, floating?"

"Feels like it to me," she said, "and to Shigun. This morning at breakfast, he asks, 'Is Papa a ghost?' I almost laughed out loud and then when I thought about it, I damn near bawled. This poor kid is trying to figure out why you're never around like other dads, you know, normal people?"

"My world doesn't see a lot of normal people," he said. "Especially in recent months. How's your cold case?"

"We just got DNA, she said—on the female remains."

"An I.D., too?"

"Her last name is Loire, initials F and D."

Service felt a stab in his heart. "Fawn Dawn Loire," he told her and heard her gulp air.

"How can you possibly know *that*? Jesus, Grady, you *knew* the dead woman?"

"I didn't know her. I never met her, but ironically I know the name. She's Sane Zane Harlikin's missing wife."

"The Harlikin from your case, your ROCK commander?"

"The one and same. Apparently, she's been missing since 2009."

"Why apparently?"

"Because nobody has ever reported her missing, except perhaps one time in Mexico City, and that of course means nothing because gringos go missing in Mexico City all the damn time. We have a developing lead suggesting she was last in Milwaukee, on company business."

"And nobody reported her absence?"

"Not a peep. Harlikin wasn't Harlikin then, or at least I don't think he was. Then his name was Bartlett Gabbart III, or maybe Gabbart Third became Harlikin, that part's still sort of misty right now."

"Jesus, Grady, how the hell do you know all this? And *why*?"

"It will take some time to explain to you." And a lot more, and he knew he owed it to her. Shigun, his son, wondered if his dad was a ghost? Good grief.

"What kind of wild-ass spirits are ragging your ass and life, Service?"

"Phooey!" he said. "I don't believe in that crap."

"You should," she came back. "You are spooky at times."

"And that's a good thing, right?"

"No, it's distinctly *not* a good thing," she said. "I can't believe I'm hearing this *shit*. We just got DNA and an I.D. thirty minutes ago. What the hell else do you have on her that I should have, since, as I understand it, this case belongs to Freedo and me, not the damn DNR, FBI or anyone else. She's *not* your case, Grady."

"I don't want the damn case. But she was born April 1, 1964, and married April 1, 1999, and went missing on her birthday, April 1, 2009."

"How long have you known those dates?"

"I'm not sure. Couple of days? I think I lose track sometimes, and everything seems kind of foggy some days."

"Sometimes? This isn't normal, Grady. It's not healthy. Do you remember a gold wedding band found on the woman's skeleton in the mine? It was inscribed LOML, 4-1-99."

Shit. Love Of My Life. How had he missed *that* connection to Lady Loire's wedding? "Guess I dropped the puck," he admitted.

"I think you need to get your skate blades sharpened. And tighten your chinstrap, Bub. You seem to be flopping all over the ice these days."

"Get my skates sharpened. Is that some sort of secret language for getting our horns trimmed? Did I tell you that Fawn Dawn Loire went by the business name of Lady Loire?"

"*Jesus*," Friday said and ended the call.

"We are not in a happy place," he said out loud to himself, and then he reminded himself how much he loathed psychobabble self-talk, and bubblegum philosophy. Because Gecko fell and got hurt, Patty Something found Lady Loire's remains, then unknown, and because Patty found her remains with others, the remains of a missing FBI special agent were also found, and now Gecko and Goat were in or in and out of Camp ROCK and why? And where the hell was Allerdyce and what was he seeing, and when the hell was he coming back to Worm, and oh God, his coming back to that girl was one of the foulest notions he could possibly imagine.

CHAPTER 31

Allouez

KEWEENAW COUNTY

How chances mock, And changes fill the cup of alteration
With divers liquors!

—William Shakespeare, *Henry IV, Part II*

Service wanted desperately to head home and spend time with Friday and Shigun, but instead found himself still anchored atop Bumbletown Hill. At home in Marquette he would be two hours or more from Harlikin's property. Here the travel time was reduced to the time needed to walk in a few miles from his camper in the woods over to Camp ROCK. He had to stay here. Not an easy decision.

Patty was on patrol, doing only God knew what, and it was good she was still out. He needed more time to think and get ready to re-enter the Fortress ROCK world. Be it by recall, or assault, one thing was clear: Either way he was going back and soon, very soon.

Still hard to believe he'd been pushed into this case over eagle feathers, which were sacred to Indian tribes, but just another commodity to other folks, like holy water to Catholics, he supposed, and what was the big deal, a ten-thousand-dollar fine per feather you were not authorized to possess? Talk about steep. Until only recently a hornophile in Michigan could shoot a twenty-point buck and not pay that much in fines and costs, or get jail time either. But raptor feathers? Sweet Jesus, this justice system had some damn ugly and bizarre wrinkles and crinkles, things he had no power to change, and therefore he tried not to fret over the unchangeables. You had just so much energy and you had to conserve the big surges for those fights and challenges that mattered most.

While the ROCK case may have begun with a tip or rumor on feathers, he had no idea which, or even if, the op had taken on a different weight, and he found himself faced with the whole concept of civilian paramilitary militias, which he found loathsome in concept and outside the constitution in their existence, but this was his take, and policing militias was neither his job nor in the roundhouse of his expertise, but who the hell organized these zany outfits, and why were they seeming to change character, not just the usual blowhard patriotic spout and vitriol, but really what the hell did they think they could do that police and the US military could not? And why were eight-ball politicians nowadays seeming to give nods to these creep-wads? This seemed less and less the country he came back to from war, never mind the country he thought he went to war *for*. He did not like some of the directions he now felt pressing down.

What he had learned over the years in having some contact with militia members was scratch a militia and chances were you'd find a gun dealer making money off his recruits, and never mind the outfit's rhetoric, political or otherwise. Or in Harlikin's case, religious rhetoric? The First Monarchy? What the hell did that even *mean*? This was the first religious militia he'd encountered, but he'd heard about others, most of which seemed to pay lip service to Christianity.

Harlikin didn't seem to fit any stereotypical militia mold. Clearly the man was trying to milk and bilk his soldiers for cash, but was there something more nefarious than that, something dark and secret he didn't yet know of? Like a missing and now confirmed dead wife. How would Harlikin take that news?

The ROCK philosophy of taking only reborn humans, those using the system to die and come back in a new name, was downright clever, and Harlikin's reasoning that the government was less than attentive to the dead was probably a pretty sound read on certain levels of law enforcement mind-set. So what did Harlikin ultimately want to achieve, overthrow the government, carve off a piece of geography for him and his kind, perhaps even secede? Was the man *serious*? Did he think the Mustard Seeds could actually do this? Crazy!

One thing was certain, guns and religion were truly an odd couple.

What level of involvement, if any, had Harlikin had in Lady Loire's company, Leasing for Jesus? Talk about a strange business? Most states, or federal governments, controlled mineral rights. The ability to even buy such things seemed to him to be rare, and how could you run a business off that model? Scarcity made value, he got that, but the scarcity was valuable only if the mineral rights you owned went with an actual supply of minerals others would want for commercial exploitation. Precious metals, Chas Marschke had told him, was the business pushed by Lady Loire, the founder and now late CEO.

It seemed safe to assume that if LFJ was here in Michigan, even if, so far, there was no evidence of that, it would be ostensibly because its exploration people had found something of value. If true, when had this happened? On Lady Loire's watch or on Harlikin's? Did it matter ultimately?

Undercover police work was a lot of things to a lot of law enforcement agencies, but to those individuals who willingly went down such rabbit holes, it felt more and more with each case like some sort of Russian roulette and only a matter of time until the odds caught up. Whatever else it might be, undercover work was scary all the time, every time, and maybe McKower was right, that he should bail. God, his kid was wondering if he were a ghost so what gave him the selfish right to risk making that become a reality? Enough was enough, and the longer you did this crap, how did you measure up to what was essentially unmeasurable?

When his phone startled him again, he laughed at his own reaction. The real fuel of the world seemed to be not fossil fuels, but interruptions. The phone screen said PRIVATE CALLER. *Now* what?

"Where you at?" Shark Wetelainen asked gruffly.

"Something's house."

"Huh," Shark said.

"Don't give me your 'huh' shit."

"What?"

"Turn off your dirty-thoughts switch."

"I don't got me one of them. The wife don't allow it."

Grady laughed out loud. Shark's wife, Limey Pykkonnen, was captain of their ship. "What do you want?" he asked his friend.

"You got a great attitude going," Shark said.

Service immediately apologized. "Sorry my frustrations are showing."

"I get same way when brook trout refuse to play nice," Shark said. Brook trout fishing was a near-religion for his friend.

"You calling to talk brook trout?" Grady asked.

"Nope, I know how to deal with ornery fish. You and me talked about Mesnard George, Da Gecko kid, yah?"

Had they? "I guess, but I don't remember that."

"You don't remember the Korean professor from Tech run into two guys in Yellow playing sojer-boys?"

That he remembered. "Okay, I'm back on the beam again. What's Gecko got to do with the professor? We got the moose sticks from the prof. Jordy's having DNA profiles run to see if there's a match on one shot in Marquette County."

"I seen Prof yesterday out to da Elm, and he was real talky-talky which usually he ain't, and he told me the George kid was one of da toy sojer boys in da yellow kit and he said he felt sorry for da long tall drink a water on account nothing fit 'im. Prof said kid look downright goofy."

Service closed his eyes. "Are you telling me Gecko was on the river that day in a militia uniform?"

"Yah, I taught youse knew?"

"The professor never told me that."

"Funny all he wanted do was talk wit' me about that kid. Says he got 'im inna class called Michigan Mining History and Architectural Principles or something along dose lines."

So Mesnard George *was* a student. Did this materially alter anything?

Shark had a habit of taking a long time to get to the crux of what he had to say. He was a man who talked as slowly as he fished, and he fished ploddingly on his fastest day. "What's the point here, Shark?"

"Prof says kid's hung up over some goofy mine story."

"Let me guess: The Three T or Two-Ton Too."

"Geez, that's pretty good. Yah, that thing."

"The Prof knows the story?"

"Says so."

"You got his number?"

"You betcha."

It was time to hear this story from someone who should know about the Three T, especially if the prof taught mining history. "Waiting to write."

Shark said, "With smartphone can type right in, don't need no paper or pencil."

"Shut up and give me the number," which the man did. "You know where the professor lives?"

"Yah sure, he's got an old house looks out over Houghton from way high up Quincy Hill."

"Okay to call him?"

"Yah sure, tell 'im Shark give you 'is number."

"Thanks friend."

"No problem. Limpy witchyouse?"

"Nope."

"Tell old fart hey when youse see 'im."

"You've got it. Say hi to Limey."

"You betcha," Shark said.

Grady punched in Jordy Bapcat's number.

"Yo," the young officer greeted him.

"You get DNA results back on your moose meat?"

"It's like a total cone of silence, which is really weird. We were seeing results in Afghanistan in twenty-four to forty-eight hours."

"Maybe Afghan DNA is simpler."

Jordy laughed heartily. "Those assholes are *the* most screwed up cats ever! I think they practice ESP, but only with each other. They always made out to not understand anything we told 'em."

"State Police Lab doing the DNA?"

"I wish, because it's an animal, they shipped it to an outfit in the Chicago area."

"Get their number and jangle their asses."

"Define jangle."

"Tell them you'll kick down their doors if they don't get on the stick most ricky-tick."

"I can do that?"

"You've done it before."

"That was a different place, time and context. And it was humans, not moose."

"Listen up, PCO Bapcat, whenever you find some assholes killing for galls, or paw pads, or moose, or wolves, or elk, you are going to find a whole shitload more. This kind of kill is a marker for a 'Holy Cow Case.'"

"That's official terminology, 'Holy Cow Case?'"

"Make the call, Jordy. Land in their shit with both boots."

"I don't report to you," Bapcat pointed out.

"Call Captain McKower and see what she suggests."

"*Me*, call a *captain*? No way, dude. You're putting me in a hard place."

"This job is by definition a hard place and you won't get many shots at Holy Cows. Get used to it, or find another job."

After Bapcat, Service called the Tech professor, who answered, "Paul Kim."

"Professor, Detective Grady Service, DNR."

"How may I help, Detective?" Paul Kim responded.

"Cup of coffee, maybe?"

"I was just about to make a pot. When are you thinking?"

"An hour from now be all right?"

"See you then." Kim then gave him his address. "The house is painted apple green, my wife's idea, not mine. There's a gravel alley just above the back of the house, and some steps down into the garden through a gate. Easier to park back there than out on the street."

And no doubt less visible to his neighbors as well. ATB and across the U.P., a home visit by a game warden was the sort of thing neighbors took note of, and almost always set tongues wagging. Locals knew where you parked your truck, knew when you left home for patrol, and returned home, often told each other what part of a county you were in, and it was sometimes as if the game warden's whereabouts were the central concern of the U.P.'s small towns. But he was driving the unmarked truck and in civvies today, which meant where he parked had no meaning for the community-at-large.

CHAPTER 32

Hancock

HOUGHTON COUNTY

Two truths are told, as happy prologues to the swelling act.
—William Shakespeare, *Macbeth*

Shark's fishing pal lived on Sunshine Street in a large wood frame home painted wild-frog green. It overlooked the Portage Ship Canal and the city of Houghton on the canal's south bank, both Houghton and Hancock being rather vertical and terraced like ancient mountain towns in parts of Europe. The Hancock side sat higher and steeper than the Houghton side of the canal, and Hancock's Mount Ripley Ski Hill was located just east of the man's green house.

Service checked his phones were off and walked down the steps to a small backyard and to the back door of the house. When he reached to knock, the door swung open and a smiling man motioned him in. "My office away from my office," the man told him, and held out his hand. "Paul Kim. You're Detective Service?"

"Yes, DNR."

"That work must have some interesting moments. Our mutual friend calls you a 'shit magnet' in a tone that suggests a high compliment."

"Depends on the circles you're in," Service said, looking around. Bookcases everywhere, books stacked man-high along walls. There were a half-dozen spectacular-size fiberglass brook trout mounts on the walls. The professor explained, "all from the Grand River up in Ontario on Superior's North Shore, or from Labrador." Every trout there had to have gone six to eight pounds when caught and had spectacularly gaudy fall breeding colors.

The truth of it was that his real shit magnet days pretty much ended when he became a detective, not that the people he dealt with undercover were less loathsome, but they were not encountered by chance and serendipity. In an undercover role you came into cases from a different angle, which sometimes led to political complications, which game wardens loathed. Legal dances to develop cases were one thing, political dances yet another. Unfortunately, over his career, a lot of his cases had pushed numerous sensitive political buttons and the past three years he lived a life more like his old patrol days, freelancing across much of the central and western U.P. unless he was pulled into an undercover assignment, as now, or as he had been more than six months back when this ROCK crap started.

At this point, he wasn't sure how to characterize what he was involved in. Most of an undercover job involved a high degree of cat-and-mouse with your opponent, but not this one, which made it odd and different, and unpredictable, and just the kind of cases the DNR's lawyers grew quite uncomfortable with rather quickly. Lawyers were about keeping clients in low-risk circumstances; undercover cops lived in high-risk conditions and willingly sought them out, some for professional reasons, and some for personal reasons because certain officers were thrill-seeking alpha types, exclusively male in the old days, but now, thanks to McKower, female officers (also alphas) were coming into detective jobs too.

As he continued to examine the surroundings, he saw four photos of very blonde children, none of which showed any Asiatic features, all four looking like Swedes. Professor Kim noticed him and laughed. "I think my wife, Katie, and I defy all odds related to genetics, four blonde girls and not one looks a smidge like their dear old dad. And that's the thing about science, Detective. It makes sense until it doesn't and somebody asks a question not asked before, or not asked in a particular way. Then everybody starts yelling holy moley and we all go back to the drawing board to try to figure out how the new information fits the old, or if it doesn't and that, too, is often reality."

"Sounds a bit like my work," Service said. "Please call me Grady."

The man nodded. "I'm Paul, even to my students, and this informal wrinkle makes all their little heads spin, the antipodal flipside of the formal Asian male stereotype, and then I kill them with reality when I explain that I was born and raised in Marquette, where Mom and Dad had moved from Korea. Appearances can deceive. What can I do you for, Grady?"

"I'm here about Mesnard George, who also goes by the name of Gecko."

"Ah yes, the conundrum. Seems a genuinely fine student, yet running around in that silly costume, which I assume belongs to one of those silly militias the U.P. tends to spawn. He looked like some sort of inept soldier who fell off one of Genghis Khan's Mongol ponies."

"You know the boy?"

"Not well. We've known each other through the college, and then that day he appeared on the Elm. Mr. George is a graduate assistant in the mine engineering group."

"That's your field?"

"Only tangentially. I'm part of the history department and I teach a course focused on the U.P. mining history, which I must brag, is quite popular."

"With all students?"

"Mostly with those with stars in their eyes who hope to find something in my lessons to lead them to some heretofore unknown motherlode."

"That happens?" Service said.

"Not yet, but anything is possible, no matter how improbable, right? Despite known odds, people flock to casinos, too."

"You called Mr. George, 'a conundrum.' What did you mean?"

"Indeed. Until that day I saw him in his mustard yellow duds he regularly dropped by my college office. After those events on the river, I've seen him only once and I think he's trying to avoid me. Embarrassed perhaps? I don't know. The one time we did meet was not over on campus but right in the alley where you're parked."

"What did you two talk about then?"

"Treasure, loot, blarney, vugs, and mythical mines, King Solomon's, the Seven Cities of Cibola, the Lost Dutchman, he was all over the globe emotionally and mentally with all that trash most of us fixate for a time on when we are young and foolish. I call it 'Goonies Syndrome,' a backyard pirate ship filled with treasure and just awaiting discovery."

"In the DNR we have to deal all the time with Walt Disney fantasies," Service said, and shook his head. "We are still dealing with Bambi Syndrome among anti-hunters, and some hunters as well. Reality evades them, maybe because they want it to."

Kim said, "People, especially students with treasure stars twinkling in their eyes, are not uncommon."

"What can you tell me about Two-Ton Too?" Service asked.

Kim smiled. "Ah, Three T, the ghost of the original Two-Ton. Two-Ton produced one very substantial and quite pure two-ton slab of solid silver, and it's said that it's twin, Two-Ton Too, contains an identical twin slab, somewhere upward and further south, perhaps along one of the vertical approaches to the old Air Force radar site.

"What the hell is a *vug*?" Service asked. "You've used that term."

"Sorry. Habit and jargon, right? Vug means a pocket and usually a finite deposit, not a substantial vein which normally leads one deeper and deeper."

"Two-Ton doesn't seem to have left much of a trail or scent," Service said.

"It was never *widely* known, and the operation was kept in a remarkable shroud of secrecy. They took two or more tons of almost pure silver out of a fissure and there was immediate speculation that there was more silver of like quality nearby, north or south was never precisely clear."

"South being federal property, and north being Central Exploration?"

"You have a knack for geography?" Kim said, and then laughed. "Of course you do, being a game warden."

Grady liked Paul Kim. "Wherever it is or isn't, Mesnard George is fixed on that location?"

"He never committed to any location. He only intimated that he knew where it was, or maybe that's just how I interpreted what I thought he was trying to tell me."

"Did the kid claim he'd found Two-Ton Too?"

"He seemed to claim to know where it is, but as happens with such fanatics' fancies, thinking something renders it in effect de facto, a fact. They make no distinction between feelings and facts, between theories and reality, assumptions and conclusions. I told the boy, even if he's right, he needed to do everything on the up and up or he'd land himself in big trouble and that would not help his future in academics or exploration."

"What can he do to make it legal?"

"Secure a lease to the mineral rights from the owner, which up here almost always means the state. There are very few private mineral rights held anywhere in the Keweenaw, or in Ontonagon or Houghton Counties for that matter."

"Why doesn't he just do that?" Service asked.

"Perhaps he has, perhaps he hasn't. Part of the problem with dreamers is, that once they start dealing with officialdom, their secret is in the open and can't be brought back to secret status."

"If Mesnard George gets in touch with you again, please let me know right away, and if you can, please try to find out where he lives." Service handed the man his card and wrote his personal cell number on the back.

"Would be my pleasure. Is this boy in some trouble?"

Service was trying to determine just this. "We don't have an answer to that, but any time you run with a militia, you're never far from trouble."

"Shark says you're an ace with a flyrod."

"I'm kind of rusty these days."

"Pardon me for saying this, but you look like you are within sniffing distance of retirement. That time comes, you, Shark and I should chase some fish."

"Sounds good to me, Paul, but don't hold your breath. I've got no plans to retire soon, or maybe ever."

"Everyone has to retire sooner or later," the professor said.

"I keep hearing that."

Service stood up to leave. "How do you know Mr. George is enrolled? Does his name appear on class lists?"

"Not actively in any of my classes."

"But you see him around the Mine Engineering Department?"

"Not all that often anymore. Like I said he used to visit me, but he's not by nature a social creature."

"Is it possible Mesnard George is not enrolled at all at Tech?"

Professor Kim started to laugh, but caught himself. "Let's get an answer to that right now."

The professor made one phone call, asked the question, and one minute later turned to Service. "Not currently enrolled, nor has he ever been. I'll be damned."

One puzzle piece solved, Service told himself, but was this piece critical or relevant? That he didn't know.

CHAPTER 33

Hancock

HOUGHTON COUNTY

A very ancient and fish-like smell.

—William Shakespeare, *The Tempest*

Grady drove over to a side street just off Quincy Hill, parked just up the steeply slanted street from the original Keweenaw Coop building, and punched in the captain's number.

"Every time I see PRIVATE CALLER on my screen I have to take a deep breath," the captain greeted him. "What's going on? You've been recalled?"

"No. How's Abel Tooler doing?"

"Who?" she asked.

He explained.

"Oh, that fellow."

What was with the tone in her voice? "Everything cool, Lis?"

"Depends on one's definition," she said.

"Tooler's not much of a talker."

"To you, perhaps. Apparently he's a veritable mockingbird around others."

"About his background in the Army?"

"Not that," she said. "Only his current business now," she said with her voice tailing away.

She was jumpy and unsettled, which was not at all like her. Why? "He joined the ROCKs same as the rest of them, and who knows exactly why? They're all bullshitters and dead men," Service told her.

"This is not funny. Colonel Sane Zane Harlikin is a very juicy federal target."

"We know that. The Feebs claimed they had two assets inside," he reminded her. *What* was going through her head now?

"Coldbeg called the person an 'asset,' not a special agent, nor operator, and not an informant for that matter."

"They always use definitions to benefit themselves," Service told his boss. "Let them define it however they want, Lis. The point here is that they claim to have had somebody else inside and nobody told me."

"An asset who is now deceased," she repeated. "Has this fact not yet registered in your *thick* skull?"

It was clear from her attitude that she was barely in control emotionally. Why? This was atypical of her. Normally she had ice-water in her veins. "What the hell is going on, Lis?"

"Our boy Harlikin is tied to all kinds of white supremacist Christian Nationalist groups," she told him. "How the ROCKs fit into the bigger picture, the feds still don't know, but they desperately need to. The Feebs have intelligence sources claiming that a ROCK unit brought a very bad right-wing actor across the Canadian border."

"Geez, Lis, the Minnesotans are bringing across centers and defensemen too."

"Stop blowing me off."

"Then how about you calm down and tell me what you know that I don't. And where is Tooler?"

"Tooler is gone, Grady, and I don't know where, or when, or any details other than an unidentified federal agency took custody of him and his two alleged assailants as well."

"Which agency?" he asked.

"I was told it was the FBI but Coldbeg denies it, and he seems clueless and I suspect the Feebs are fronting for another agency. I have learned that the collection-slash-transfer group included a single FBI special agent and three agents from another agency."

"On *whose* order?" he demanded to know. "The governor?"

"Not her. She's as surprised as the rest of us, and *extremely* unhappy and will soon be applying heavy pressure to certain federal security heads."

"Meanwhile, Tooler remains gone."

"True."

"We'll probably never see him again."

"What point are you trying to make, Grady?"

"I'm not entirely sure, but I have this feeling that we've stumbled into the whale's mouth, and I have no interest in playing Jonah in somebody else's drama."

"You have way more than enough points to walk away and retire, and nobody would blame you."

"Me, *quit* in the middle of something? You know me better than that. What if it was one of our people who was in Tooler's place?"

"Tooler isn't one of ours. He's not even law enforcement."

"How do you *know* that, Lis? You have no clue who the man is, and neither do I. But whoever he is, the feds have him tucked away for reasons only they know. The stench on this thing is growing worse by the day."

"The governor used those very same words."

"And Tooler's assailants?"

"*Alleged* assailants. We think we at least know where they are, which currently is in a federal facility in north Georgia."

"It feels like all doors are about to slam shut," Service told her.

"Why do you always assume the worst?"

"Because I'm undercover and off the radar, and all cesspools eventually smell the same. Did you not notice in our task force meeting that when Coldbeg told us about *his* missing 'asset' he showed virtually no emotion? No sweating, no voice-tone changes, no fidgeting, no darting eyes, nothing. It was like he was announcing last night's bowling scores."

"You have a hypothesis?" McKower asked her detective.

"I don't know a hypothesis from a hypotenuse, but circumstances seem to be telling me we're watching some sort of strange passion play, with play-it-by-ear, say-as-you-go scripting."

"That's a pretty extreme and ambiguous allegation."

"I'm sick of careful language, Lis. This is what free fall feels like, right at that moment before your chute opens or it doesn't."

"You'd know about that."

Which he did. Over the course of his USMC service and DNR career he had jumped out of airplanes into numerous situations, and jumped not always on orders from above, rather, taking such decisions upon himself, which he was not entitled to do, and which sometimes got him into trouble. "Lis," he said, "the thing about free fall is that it always ends, one way or the other. You pull your ripcord and get smacked in the crotch by g-force, or you pull it, and nothing happens and before you can deploy your secondary, you schmuck the earth at twenty-five feet per second per second. The whole deal is over real fast."

"I do not want you going back inside on this assignment, Grady."

"You gave me a week, Captain, and I'm holding you to it."

"There's no way to get Tooler and the other two back here," she said. "You must realize that, and I wish we could, but we can't, and I don't want you going back in there at least until I get someone to tell us what the hell they think is going on. Do you have any ideas?"

"Like explanations, hell no? Gut feelings? Those I have. Can you get inside Special Agent Coldbeg's head?"

"I can try," she said, "but you know how Feebs are. They go armadillo or circle their wagons."

"J. Edgar would be so proud she might go out and buy himself a new frock."

"You are awful," she said, laughing.

"Listen, Cap'n, here's the thing about circling your wagons, no matter how many troops you have inside your perimeter. There's always a hole somewhere, always a way for the enemy to get inside, and here's another reality: Picture all those people inside the circle and which way are they looking?"

She smiled. "Outward."

"Every damn one of them, because they are all in the mindset of being under attack or the threat of an attack from without, so where is their vulnerability?"

"Within," she said.

"Above, below, and within, all of those are vulnerabilities, but few ever think in this way, and not every yahoo outside the wagons is chomping at the bit to lead a Forlorn Hope, either."

She smiled. "It's a long reach back to the Napoleonic Wars."

"No force is ever 100 percent all-in, Lis. No force, ours included. There's a percentage of people inside the circle who resent being there and would prefer to fight it out rather than circle the assets, and would choose impossible offense over defense any day."

"Is this lecture your way of saying the answer is back inside with Harlikin?"

"That much I'm certain of, but what I can't yet see is what the hell his *real* game is. I've thought about this a lot. Pretender colonels and generals of toy soldier-boys like to get out in the field and play big shot alongside their boys, but not Harlikin. He sits tight, inside, with his own personal guards, and doesn't seem to worry about anything but money," he said. "As for the Feebs, they are heebie-jeebied over something we aren't party to, so it seems to me, the only path to an answer is back inside with Harlikin. What it comes down to is that I have to go back in there and you know it, and artificial deadlines are meaningless. You think Eddie will back us?"

Eddie Waco was chief of law enforcement for the DNR. Waco had been a longtime game warden in Missouri when he was hired to lead Michigan's agency. Waco and Service had been partners in a case once upon a time in Missouri.

"What do you think?" she asked.

"Hell, Lis, he won't even blink over this call, but he hates surprises."

"All right, dammit. I'll brief the chief. But please do not go back in there until you at least touch base with me. Can we agree on that?"

"Yes ma'am, Cap'n, sir. When did I ever not follow orders?"

He imagined her still laughing after he broke off the call.

CHAPTER 34

Hancock

HOUGHTON COUNTY

Play out the play.

—William Shakespeare, *Henry IV, Part I*

There was excitement in Shark Wetelainen's voice over the phone. "Youse busy?"

"I've never been good at theatricals, what's goosed you?"

Shark laughed. "Me and the old lady were talking about you, and it seems to us she and you both could use some help from somebody knows the twin counties better than anybody."

Twin counties? This was a new term and notion. "You and Limey are on target. By the way, when did she give you permission to refer to her as your old lady?"

"She ain't quite."

"Mind you, don't piss the lady off," Service said. "I've seen her fight. What did you two come up with?"

"Who said we come up with something? I just said it seems to us youse both need some help."

"We all need help," Service said. "*You* included."

"Limey, she tells me that every day."

"Which makes her right every day."

"Whose side're you on?" Shark said.

"You two are married. I guess I didn't realize there's two sides after you're hitched."

"Which mebbe is why youse haven't married Tuesday yet."

Asshole. "What's the point to this call?"

"There's got be point for friends to talk?"

"Not ordinarily, but you called me and I can hear in your voice a bear who has just found himself a tree full of ripe beechnuts."

"Me?" Wetelainen said, "I got me the perfect poker face."

"That's true, but you don't have a poker voice."

"How long you think that?"

"As long as I've known you. Why do you think I never play in your monthly poker game?"

"Stakes probably aren't high enough for likes of you," Shark muttered.

"I don't gamble," Service said.

"At cards," Shark added quickly. "Ever'ything youse do, except cards, is a gamble. Youse love living out there on the razor-sharp edge."

Geez. "What is this shit, *This Is Your Life*?"

"I loved that program," Shark lamented, "and don't be biting my head off. You and the old lady need to talk to Kenty Kenowyth."

A name from the faded ancient past. Kenty Kenowyth was retired DNR lieutenant Kenesaw Kenowyth, longtime game warden in Houghton and Keweenaw Counties. "He's long gone," Service said.

"Like hell."

Service tried to calculate the man's age but couldn't. "How old is he?"

"Get this: he's one-oh-three."

One hundred and three? "*Get out of here.*"

"I swear, Grady. Talk about one tough old bird? Lives on forty-nine acres Timber Neighbors, Inc. cut out for him fifty years back. He still drives himself around, makes his own wood, and shovels white dirt all winter. It's like the man hit seventy, and never got another day older!"

Kenowyth's living to a ripe old age was a shock. The man had been such a tight-ass, everything-by-the-book-every-time sort of officer, and a sour-puss, that everyone figured he'd go in a hurry once he took off his badge. The gold badge was the only life the man had ever had. "Kenty live alone?"

"Sorta mostly. Got 'im great-granddaughter Chantal lives there too, sometimes. She goes to school at Tech, studies micro-organs."

Great-granddaughter? He'd never known the El-Tee to be married. "Micro-organs?"

"Youse know what I mean. You really think I got no poker voice?"

"Ask your old lady."

"She's still mad at me right now."

"She usually is. Reparable, or no?"

"She'll cool down. She always does, and it's like she always says, temper ain't no tool for fighters or cops."

"Your Limey is a very wise woman."

"Don't I know it, but sometimes I want to figure things out on my own, in my own way, in my own time, like I do with trout."

"I get that," Service said. "How fast can we set up a meeting with Kenty?"

"Just drop in. He'll be glad to see another badge. Youse ever work with him?"

"For a while and mostly at a distance. He retired not that long after I came over from the state police."

"Limey should go too, but she can't real quick. She gotten stuck with some interview with some woman lives out Seven Mile Point Road, got big-ass old house right on the Gray Lady's shore."

"How do I find Kenty?"

"Where youse at now?"

"South of Calumet, moving north."

"Youse not that far. Kenty's place is off Tamarack Waste Water Works Road, on Brewery Creek."

Grady had as thorough a knowledge of U.P. geography as anyone active in the force and he knew this location should pop right up in his brain map, but it didn't and wasn't, and wouldn't. "Tamarack Waste Water Works Road?"

"Youse know where da Allouez Auto is?"

"Yep. Just in from the big curve."

"Take the Bumbletown Road up the hill to Dextron, then right on Dextron and youse'll be going north-like and then she makes honking big ninety to due west and then youse hit Sedar Hill and Dextron, but *don't* take da ninety right onto Sedar. Youse got keep to da left on Dextron south till youse hit Tamarack Waste Water Works Road, then grab a right and look real quick-like on left side for sign with a big ball cut two parts in half."

Service closed his eyes. Right, the locally famous Half-N-Half House. Decades before the house had been built with the county line splitting the house in half and the El-Tee had gotten the land while he was a CO for Houghton County and back then the DNR demanded he live in the county he was assigned to, but the department had been short of badges back then and he spent as much time in Keweenaw as he did in Houghton, so he had the house built in both.

Technically, went the story, 50.1 percent of the house was Houghton and 49.9 in Keweenaw, and his fight with Lansing brass had eventually made the news because there was a local dust-up over which county would collect his taxes and Lansing had shut up and let Kenty work out the problem on his own. Later, after promotions to sergeant and lieutenant, the residence location requirement was no longer an issue. Rank did have its privileges.

The DNR bigwigs in Lansing were never comfortable dealing with the very spare and sour Kenty. He intimidated everyone and there was a clique in Lansing scared shitless he would eventually be named chief, but Kenty never wanted any part of that job (or Lansing) and the point was moot. His officers both loved and feared his ways.

"Okay, I can find that. Does Limey know you're meddling in official police business?"

"Help ain't meddling."

"Whose idea to meet Kenty?"

"Mine, but da old lady likes sometimes some of my ideas."

"Do either of you know the El-Tee?"

"Sure, him and me usta fish brookies."

"In Brewery Creek?"

"I ain't saying where." A true brook trout chaser, secret to all, no exceptions, even spouses.

"Let me summarize. You've had this brilliant idea that can help the both of us, but you haven't told your wife about it because she's told you a million times to stay out of her flippin' work, so you call me and let me make a cold call to her and say, 'Hey Limey, how about you and me go see Kenty Kenowyth?'"

"Flipping brilliant," Shark said. "Be good if you keep my name out of this, eh?"

Service shook his head. His friend was a piece of work. "Okay, I've got this, and how about I go see the man, and leave Limey out of it until I see what he has?"

"You think that's a good idea?" Shark said, "Leaving my wife out of it?"

If the old man didn't run him off his property. "Flipping brilliant," he said. Leaving Limey out of it might take some weight off Shark's narrow shoulders. But there was no doubt in his mind that Shark would soon be on his phone to his wife, and what that portended was far from certain.

CHAPTER 35

Lakeview Area

HOUGHTON-KEWEENAW COUNTY LINE

Time shall unfold what plaited cunning hides.
—William Shakespeare, *King Lear*

Because he drove around so much, and had done so for most of his career, Grady Service made it a point to keep his own mind-map updated. At the very least he liked to know the name of the nearest town or landmark, such as an old post office or mine site. He remembered this area being called Lakeview, which was seated up high on a long series of glacial ridges, with Lake Superior to the north and below him, though it was barely visible between the trees, and in some places, you'd never know the ocean-sized lake was so close. Sometimes there were no logical explanations of how things and places got named.

As he got closer to Kenty Kenowyth's property, Grady wasn't surprised to find Limey Pykkonen in her unmarked, parked on the shoulder of Tamarack Waste Water Works Road. Obviously Shark had called his wifey.

"Surprise," he told her.

She smiled. "For you, not for me. Shark got himself a dose of the guilty conscience and told me he'd talked to you and thought the old man may have some info of use to me as well. I just love it when husbands get guilty consciences," she added.

"This taking you away from anything important?" he asked her.

"Not so much. The California Troops asked me to interview a woman who lives here summers about a neighbor went missing near her home in the hills outside L.A."

"You already talk to her?"

"Raincheck. She insisted that she needed a nap first."

"Elderly?"

"Late forties, max, hi-maintenance type pushing to look and act thirty."

"How *does* thirty act these days?"

"Not how we acted at that age," the Houghton detective said. "I was a beat cop in Grand Rapids when I was thirty, and then I moved to a drug team. I had no social life whatsoever. You?"

"There was an old Nishnawbe grandmother who once answered a question about her past. She said, 'Aw, that's too far back. No one knows the answer to that.'"

Pykkonnen chuckled. "That line work with Tuesday?"

"Never had to use it with her."

"That makes me feel so special," Limey said.

"You *are* special. Look who you married."

"You one of those discretion-is-valor-school types?"

"No idea what you're talking about."

"No woman can ignore a man with common sense."

"No comment," he said.

She asked, "You know Kenowyth?"

"Not well. He retired after I came over from the Troops. Mostly I knew him by his reputation, which was that of a fanatic and stickler for rules. He went by the book and only by the book. He and I bumped heads a couple of times."

"Way Shark and I heard it, you two did not play well together."

"Nobody played well with Kenty," he told her. "It's a genetic thing." Then he laughed. "I suppose I sometimes rubbed him the wrong way."

"But his view prevailed?"

"An El-Tee in his district was, is and ever shall be a virtual potentate. Did he prevail? Sometimes yes and sometimes no. Back then, he was the El-Tee out of Marquette so most of our dealings were through an area sergeant."

"The sergeants ran interference for you?"

"Only when and if they thought I was right. It's not quite like that anymore. Our sergeants used to be first-line, in-the-trucks with their people, supervising coaches and fellow warriors, now they are largely reduced to scope dopes, paper processors, report-writers, and time keepers."

"You sound a very unhappy man."

"Time you spend on your toy computer or toy phone is time you don't spend with your boots in the dirt and snow where the bad guys actually are."

"You're a dinosaur," she told him.

"Bullshit. Dinosaurs are all dead and I'm not."

"You draw a fine distinction," she said.

"Let the dead dinosaurs argue differently," he said. "When Kenty was top cop in Marquette I was out in the field catching guys with loaded guns and ganked deer in back, and I took their weapons, and sometimes their vehicles and stroked their asses on the spot, and if they had an illegal deer, I arrested them, and hauled them to the lockup myself. I didn't write some damn report and wait to see if some snot-nose assistant prosecutor would have the balls to authorize an arrest warrant."

"Ah, the familiar cry of the dinosaur for the good ole days," she said.

"They *were* the good old days in those terms. An officer in the woods has to have freedom to act in order to be effective."

"And your way became the way?"

"Not just my way. Most officers worked the way I did. It just made sense."

"Back then," she said. "Now society is more litigious than ever."

"Not my problem," he told her. "I never lost a case in court."

"The times they are a changing," she said.

"Tell me about it: Lawyers seemed to have taken control in Lansing and we're back to writing reports and submitting them to prosecutors for warrants."

"And you hate it."

"We're going backwards," he said. "Too many prosecutors are now weighing the politics *before* they weigh the law, and a lot of these young prosecutors are city kids who don't know shit-all about the woods, and think DNR violations are minor-league trash, so they pretty much ignore them. Our young officers can make a great case, file a report, and wait months or longer. It's like stroking a fly ball you won't know for months will be caught, missed, or lost in the sun, and never seen again."

"You DNR officers on the other hand have a lot more power than the average cop."

"Not when some prosecutors are *ignorant*, chickenshit, or both. Like I said before, to keep enthusiasm in the woods when you are alone 90 percent of the time, you need to have, and *feel* the absolute freedom to act."

She held up her hands. "Whoa, don't get hot at me. I'm just parroting what others say when you guys aren't around. You want me to take the lead with the El-Tee here?" she asked.

"Not necessary. I always thought him a good man. If I irritated him, there was nothing personal from my end."

"Okey-doke," she said. "You have the lead."

• • •

What Shark had told him was true. The retired lieutenant didn't look a day over seventy, stood ramrod straight, steady of foot, no shaking or tremors, clear skin, and he looked as muscular as he always had. If the man before him was now 103, he looked like a good bet to hit 120 and get his name in some sort of Guinness record book.

The retired lieutenant greeted them with a smile and the words, "Grady Service and Limey Pykkonnen! Now *this* is what I call an interesting pairing. You two here to socialize or do some business?"

Limey said, "We need your help, Lieutenant."

"I've not held that rank for a long damn time. Please call me Kenty. Badges still drink coffee or are you guys now addicted to wheatgerm-oatmilk nose-sprays?"

"Coffee," Limey said and the two followed the man back to his kitchen, which was spic-and-span, nothing in disarray, and hardly looked lived in. Same way the man's office once looked, Service remembered.

The old man played with the coffee pot and put a squealer on the stove and Service saw a green box with instant coffee bags, but no coffee got made or offered and Service wondered what this was about.

Kenowyth gave them empty coffee cups and bade them sit. "DNR and county working a case together?" the old game warden asked.

"Not in the traditional sense," Limey answered. "Grady was working a case, and human remains turned up. That's what brought me into it."

Kenowyth studied Service and smiled warmly. "You've grown quieter in your dotage," the man said, and added, "and before you pull out a warclub, that was meant as a joke. You were a great officer and I assume you still are, or you wouldn't still be packing a badge, and, if you don't mind an old fellow asking another old fellow, why *are* you still carrying a badge?"

"I don't feel like I'm done yet," Service said, realizing his tone was pretty defensive, and he wasn't certain why he felt this.

The retired lieutenant smiled. "You think some kind of sign drops down from the sky when we're done?"

"Did you walk away smiley-faced with an attaboy and a watch instead of a badge and think you were done?"

"I was done politically and that put a finish to all the rest. Took me awhile to adjust, but I like this life I've made, and you *do* have to make it. I like my place too, and my place in the world."

"A lot of officers don't transition that easily," Service told the man.

"I never said it was easy. It wasn't, and as I think I said, it took time to adjust, a lot of hope, and several years for me to get with the program. Pardon my rambling, what can I do to help?"

"We're not quite sure if you can," Service said. "Do you know anything about the Three T Mine?"

The centenarian lieutenant nodded once. "Two-Ton Too? I just may know a tad-bit. What do you want to know?"

"Is it real?"

"I thought so, but like you, I always tended to go my own path on some subjects. There were a lot of people who all thought it a bunch of bee's wax."

"I'm trying to find out from the Rock Library if it's real," Service told the old man.

"That thing is still going is it?"

"Near the old hatchery, but word is out they're moving to new facilities at K.I. Sawyer."

"It's a great resource that library, though in our day we sure didn't make a lot of cases over the state's mineral resources. I guess that's changing."

"Nossir, beyond oil and natural gas and gravels and limestone and such, mineral cases remain rare. You ever use the rock library to make a case?"

"Not directly, but I had what you guys later called a frequent flyer who was mixed up in mines and minerals, including the Three T."

"Care to share?"

"Well the statute of limitations certainly isn't a barrier by now, but remembering sort of rests with my brain's druthers for the given day. Today feels pretty promising. Things decades ago can seem like yesterday, and yesterday can seem like ten years ago, or even like it never happened. Our minds and memories mix up a whole lot of things into a mush or stew, and when we pull something out we like to call it recall when it's probably more made up of bits and pieces, or even stuff we've read or heard elsewhere, than a pure product of our own true memory."

Service understood what the man was saying and didn't want to dwell on the ins and outs of memory and recall. "Who was your frequent flyer?"

"Had a name I'll never forget, Archimedes Rock. Called himself Archie. Was a student at Tech, where he studied minerology, but he just couldn't make himself go to class. Got kicked out several times, and went back several times until finally Tech told him to not bother coming back."

"Pretty extreme," Limey observed. "Colleges don't like to turn down tuition money."

"Archie wasn't a bad kid, but he was a kid in a man's body and he just couldn't figure out how to grow up. Was a shame, really. All sorts of potential in that kid, and he was darn good in the woods too. The boy never fit in with other students and was pretty much a loner and cast-off."

"What did you get him for?" Service asked.

Kenowyth shook his head and grinned. "What *didn't* I get him for? He was a traveling clown show, that kid: fishing and taking without a license, exceeding take limits, loaded weapons in vehicles, illegal fish and deer, and bear, and rabbits, illegal cutting of trees. Unauthorized camping on state land, untended fires, leaving trash piles like personal scat, he was a beaut, our Mister Archimedes Histah Harlikin Rock."

Service coughed. "I thought you said his name was Archie Rock."

"That was the short version. I just give you the full one. Despite trying to do the right things, Archie just couldn't not do stupid. It was funny, and it was real sad too. But I liked him. No mean bones. He just wasn't grown up, and did I tell you about the Air Force?"

"After he flunked out of college?" Service asked.

"I didn't see him for more than four years and then one day I ran into him in the Mohawk Superette and he was wearing Air Force blue, and he looked real good in it too. He'd always had a keen interest in weather, and the Air Force recognized this and made him a meteorologist, promoted him to sergeant and were trying to send him to OCS, but I don't know if that ever worked out."

"No?" Limey said.

"Just like he couldn't make class, he had a hard time showing up for his Air Force work shifts, and he was declared AWOL several times and once a deserter."

"Was he stationed at K.I. Sawyer or Kincheloe?" Service asked. These had been major Strategic Air Command bases in the U.P. in those days. Now both bases were long ago decommissioned.

"No, he was with the radar outfit on Mount Horace Greeley. I think they were part of the BMEWS or DEW system or one of those secret radar chains we shared with Canadians."

Service chewed on this. "The old radar station on our Mount Horace Greeley?"

"That's the one."

"South, across from Central Mine."

Kenty chuckled. "Both are ghost towns now and it's too darn bad. They were once real going concerns. The kin of original Central folk still gather at the old Methodist church over there every year. I used to go, but those I knew are gone now, and I pretty much keep to my place."

Service was lagging several seconds behind what the retired officer was telling him when Kenowyth said, almost in passing, "Archie Rock is Archimedes Histah Harlikin Rock."

What the hell? "Archie's middle names were Histah and Harlikin?"

"Yup, both were on his birth certificate. He once explained to me that Histah meant snake in some foreign tongue, maybe it was from the Tarzan books. Said his mom's name was Jane and his dad read him Tarzan stories when he was a tyke."

"Snake is what Indians usually call their enemies," Service pointed out.

"I think I knew that, or read it somewhere. If it were me and mine, we were the people, the good guys, and everybody else was Other, or in extreme cases, the Snakes."

Grady was determined to keep the El-Tee on track. "So Rock was at the radar station, and he was still out in the woods all the time and still screwing up, but you stopped writing tickets to him?"

"I did. For two reasons. First, he was serving our country, and second, tickets for a military man don't bode well for his career or his service. I lectured him like a preacher and he just grinned and kept on."

"Where does the Three T fit into this?"

The El-Tee lit up. "Swore to me he had found it."

"And you believed him?"

"Like I said, the boy was really good in the woods."

"He say where?"

"Never did, but clearly it was in the Keweenaw and since I never saw him back then anywhere except around the Central Exploration and uphill between there and Horace Greeley, I figured that was the approximate find-site."

"Did you ever look for it?" Limey asked.

"I never did. Probably, deep down I thought he was mostly pushing hope out loud."

"You still think that?"

"Nope. Over the years I've come to think he found it—just as he claimed."

"And registered it with the state?"

"Archie? I doubt it. He just couldn't or wouldn't follow rules."

"Where's Archie now?" Service asked. "Assuming that at some point he separated from the Air Force?"

Kenowyth looked at his counterpart. "I'm not sure he ever got out. I know he got transferred and later someone told me they sent him to OTS in Texas and he then went to some correspondence college while he was on active duty, and managed to collect a college degree, and with that sheepskin in hand, and officer's rank, I heard he was staying in for a career. But that's all hearsay and my memory sure isn't what it once was."

"Was Archie a religious boy?" Service asked.

"You mean Christian churchy religious? Not so much. When he was in the Air Force, he always seemed to have a gal with him, and never the same one. Real lookers, too, and all of them with the same propensity for wearing as few clothes as they could get by with. Have you met my daughter Gemmy-Gemmy?"

"Nossir," Pykkonnen said.

"A sweet soul, that girl, right out of the starting gate. She and my granddaughter Chantal both slept with Archie and I told them both it was a mistake, but the young don't like listening to old folk," Kenty said, his voice thick with emotion. "Gemmy-Gemmy's gone now, but I don't think the two events are linked. Are they?"

Was Kenty's mind wobbling like a bad compass? He'd just jumped from Archie's girlfriends who apparently disliked clothes—to his late daughter and granddaughter.

"How old would Archie be now?" Limey asked.

Service took this question to mean she was sharing his concern for Kenty's recall.

"Arch? Mid-eighties to ninety."

"And Chantal's age?" Service asked.

"Twenty-three, pretty soon," Kenowyth told them. "Or twenty-two. I'm not much good with numbers anymore."

"They sleep together recently?" Limey followed up.

"They try to hide it from me," the old man said, his exasperation showing in a flushed face.

"Where was Archie originally from?" Service asked the retired game warden.

"Somewhere way up in far wastes of northern Minnesota I seem to recall, but don't quote me."

"In your many encounters, did you give him verbal or written warnings?" Service asked.

"Mostly I wrote him tickets while he was at Tech, then written warnings while he was in the Air Force."

"Were the warnings intended to keep him on the straight and narrow after he was in uniform?" the Houghton County detective asked.

"Seemed to. More so than my many citations had. Let me ask, why this interest in the Three T?"

"Nothing definite. Just seeking information for a case we've got," Pykkonen said.

"I had me one beaut of a case once," Kenowyth said. "Was the clap, I think. They used a scientific name for it, but that I don't remember no more. Got it from a girl I met in Tokyo during the Korean War. Hurt like the dickens when I peed, and I peed a lot. Burned like the dickens, it did. I've always peed a lot, but it don't burn like that anymore and that's good!" The man was grinning.

The two cops looked at each other. "Like the detective said, we're just covering details in a case," Service said, pulled out a card, and wrote down his cell phone number. "Just in case you think of anything else, right? Or if you just want some company and to shoot the breeze."

Pykkonnen also gave the old man a card. "If you ever need anything, please call."

Kenowyth walked them to the door. "Truth time now, how'd you two like my coffee? It's my own blend I have made special down in Traverse City."

"It was good," Limey told the man.

"A little airy," Service answered.

Kenowyth pointed a finger at Service. "Yep, that's the whole darn point."

Back at their vehicles, they stood and Service lit a cigarette.

"Wow," he said. "Everything seemed entirely normal one second, and then we were way the hell out in right field and beyond in the next. Now I wonder if *anything in there* he told us has the slightest value."

"Did you hear anything you were looking for?" she asked. "And *what* coffee?"

Service shook his head, and made a pained face. He'd heard something he wasn't looking for and had no idea if it was real or fantasy, or if real, what exactly to do about it.

CHAPTER 36

Hecla

HOUGHTON COUNTY

It lies as coldly in him as fire in a flint.
—William Shakespeare, *Troilus and Cressida*

The stop-n-rob just south of Calumet was not far from the old Osceola Mine location, and the former gas station, known locally as Fast Horse, for reasons Service didn't know or care to know, had a logo that looked like a kangaroo on an acid trip.

He bought a pumpkin cappuccino, which he estimated to a sugar strength of four nines and stood outside Fast Horse sipping the hot drink, and smoking.

Someone with a dark gray, white, and light blue Finlandia Hockey T-shirt said, "Man, them things stink."

The stranger was barefoot and carrying a skateboard under his arm, had stringy, greasy hair braids halfway down his back, and looked to be thirtyish. "So do unwashed bodies, *Man*," Service retorted.

A voice said, "Sad blue, boo-hoo, true-blue, we hear you."

Service looked at the skateboard carrier. "What was that *shit*?"

The man scrinched his face. "You talking to me, Man?"

"That's what I asked *you*, shitball."

"Man," the stranger said. "Why they let your kind loose on the rest of us?" and ducked into the Fast Horse.

"WTF!" Service muttered gruffly under his breath. *Kind*? Thank God he was not wearing a badge.

The voice in his head said softly, "Ease up, Grady. This is just a test. We wanted to let you know we can hear you real good."

"Click-Clack, is that you?" Service asked. He'd nearly forgotten the implant behind his ear.

"Roger, O'Dell here," the voice said, and seemed to be in him and around him.

"Are you guys listening *all* the time?" Service asked.

"Pretty much," O'Dell said. "Where you go, we go."

"That last blue bit almost made me drop my cappuccino *and* my smoke," Service complained. "I thought we worked this out. If I yell blue, you send help."

"That's how it is, but we need to test your ability to receive from time to time, especially since we have no current GPS on you."

"How the hell are you supposed to come to me if you have no GPS?"

"This is just temporary," O'Dell said. "Don't wrinkle your knickers."

Service looked up to see Skateboard watching him and grinning. "Don't worry, Granpa, Scotty will beam you up to the *Enterprise* if you have a problem. Man, you standin' out here talking at yourself like loony-tooney, Man. You gone scare all your great grandkiddies with that shit."

"Go away," Service told the man, "or I'll have you beamed up to the mother ship and made into Vulcan catfood. *Believe me*, man, you do not want *that*!"

"I'd like to see you try, Man," Skateboard said and Service flashed his badge wallet and the man took off, not looking back over his shoulder.

"The Vulcan for cat food is *Aushfa-yem tukh*," O'Dell said. "What was *that* all about?"

"A virus called stupidity. Earthlings, Man, you know what a pain in the ass they can be."

"I hear *that*," O'Dell said. "To repeat officially, we presently lack optional operational function on GPS capture."

"Hey, O'Dell. In real English, not bureaucratese, and not Vulcan, over? Would help for you to grow up, my friend."

"I'm as grown up as I need to be."

"Then you do your job and I'll do mine."

"You're not taking this on board, fellow traveler. We have no functional GPS at the moment."

"Major announcement: I *get* that, I really do. Neither do I. Welcome to the world of the blind."

"You'll have to give us word hint-fixes on your geographic location as you go," O'Dell said.

Hint-fixes? Service heard the seriousness in the man's tone. "You want straight geo coordinates or landmarks?"

"Either, or, and both would be even better."

"I didn't plan on this."

"Neither did we," O'Dell said, "but the good news is we can hear every word you say and if you get close enough, we can hear other voices too."

"How is that possible?"

"You want me to verbalize the schematics for you?"

"No way. What else can this system do?"

"It can be an entertainment system."

Service laughed. "Talk about tits on bulls."

"What I mean is that we can tap you into external sound systems, either to receive or to transmit."

"English, please."

"Say you're in a school or a mall, or a store, with an intercom, internal commo system, we can patch you into that system so you can use it as your own. The bone in your skull becomes your transmitter-amplifier."

"Why would I want to do that?"

"I don't know. Maybe if there's a shooter in the building you can call it out and tell everyone to go quick-hide. I'm just explaining capabilities."

"In the future," Service said, "we need to simplify our commo, you to me, and vice versa. Henceforth, I will say out loud, 'Green Test,' and you—if you are receiving normally and according to your standards—will reply, 'Five Square.'"

"Green Test and Five Square? That's all?"

"Cops favor economy of words in radio traffic, get it?"

"Five Square. Can I say 'roger,' too?"

"Leave it at Five Square."

"Roger, Five Square. Now can we address the GPS malfunction?"

"I thought we just did. I give you geographic coordinates and/or landmarks. Do you want GPS coordinates or map coordinates?"

Pregnant pause. "Hadn't really thought about that difference."

"There is one, and now's your chance."

"What's *your* preference?" O'Dell asked.

"I prefer that your damn GPS will work so I don't have to remember all this crap."

"We're working the problem with our vendor."

Meaning O'Dell couldn't fix the problem himself. Was this implant a mistake? So often it seemed that as soon as you got involved with new technology, that's what drove things, not the mission or your needs.

A second Finlandia Hockey T-shirt showed up, this on a younger man, early twenties. "Hey Pops, I heard there was a Martian or some such shit over here talking to the mother ship."

Service showed him his badge. "I bet your buddy didn't mention what the mother ship is."

"Sorry, Pops. I just like aliens and E.T.s and all that cool shit."

"Go away," Service told the man. "I'm not that cool shit, and don't call me Pops."

The man didn't leave. "Seriously, Man, I don't know where you got that way cool fake badge, but real deps come here all the time, and if they find you talking to yourself, you'll be in the mother ship before the rest of us. Give yourself a break, go elsewhere, and chill."

Service walked across the cement lot to his truck. "Green Test," he said as he finished the drink.

"Five Square," O'Dell answered. "May I ask what that last bit was about?"

"A good Samaritan."

"The guy is right, you know. You have to be careful when you deploy this system, and do you want transcripts?"

"Of what?"

"Basically, your whole life while you have the implant."

"Can I specify excerpts?"

"You bet."

"Do I have to alert you while things are going on?"

"No, later is fine, but you'll need to have a good time-estimate in mind so we can quickly find what you need, otherwise this could be *really* expensive. By the way, who *is* paying the freight here?"

"Send bills to Captain McKower, DNR Law Enforcement, Special Investigations."

"Lansing?"

"Close enough." Her office was in another location, but things addressed to her in Lansing would eventually reach her. The Special Investigations Unit did not like to advertise its whereabouts.

"Great," O'Dell said. "Green Test from you gets Five Square from us. What if our reception's not good?"

"Say 'No Joy.'"

"We say 'no joy' if there's no or poor reception?"

"Close enough."

"And what's the activator code word."

"C'mon, O'Dell, knock off the Vulcan baloney. Any mention of the word *blue* means send the damn cavalry PDQ."

"One small detail," O'Dell said. "Does the cavalry *know* about this?"

They didn't. Only he did. "Let me worry about that."

"But I will need to know which cavalry to call."

"I'll get back to you on that."

"Where are you right now?" O'Dell asked.

"Fast Horse, south of Calumet."

"I *know* that place. Sweet. Man, you've got to try the space-spice cinnamon rolls."

"There's no bakery in this joint," Service said.

O'Dell laughed. "I thought you meant online, man. Fast Horse is a game programming language for culinary virtual and A.I. They got this thing where you think you're eating this cinnamon roll, and oh man . . . "

"Sign me off, Scotty."

"Wait, I may have more questions."

"AMF, O'Dell, make silence be so."

The implant and Click-Clack went click-click.

Second Finlandia approached again. "Hey Dad, whatever you're smoking, can I get me some of that shit?"

Grady gave the young man a cigarette. "Count slowly to seven between each puff. This shit will lift you up like an elevator, and make you smarter than Elon Musk."

The kid lit up, then coughed, and made a face. "Hey Dad, this is just tobacco. It ain't no shit."

"See how smart you are already?" Service said, and got into his truck. He watched the kid slowly puffing and shook his head. Stupidity abounded and what the hell was wrong with him letting these oddballs and losers get to him? The content of routine public contact for police officers was growing more and more peculiar. And his tolerance for it was clearly melting, which was not a good thing professionally or personally.

Rather than rush away, Grady drove west to the old Swedetown location, and parked at a cross-country trailhead, a place where he could be alone and think.

He sat looking at his laptop and six cell phones, not sure what to think or say about the sheer intrusion into a game warden's once very simple life. One of the phones rang and he had to look quickly to figure which one and picked it up. "Service?" a voice said.

"It's your dime."

"How far are you from my place, Grady?"

It was Kenowyth. "Fifteen minutes, max."

"You probably thought maybe I have some screws loose," the retired lieutenant said.

"No sir. But I thought you were maybe a little tired and a bit confused."

"Don't bullshit me, Service. The both of you were thinking I'd drifted off the planet."

"You were a little on the dingy side toward the end," Service told the man frankly. "You even talked about our having coffee we never had."

"Only way I could think to get you and me one on one. DNR business isn't the concern of counties or the darn state."

"We can trust Limey."

"Bullshit. Why put her in a compromising position if the case runs south. Carry your own weight, and only call in your own kind when you need extra heads and muscle. This is the Horse Blanket Way."

Service had not heard the term *Horse Blanket* in many years. It referred back to the early days of the DNR when game wardens wore full-length military war surplus wool greatcoats.

"You're still quick," Kenowyth said. "I ask about my coffee and you called it airy? I like to have laughed out loud! I never served you any coffee, but you and she both acted like I had, so who's screwy?"

The man had a point. "Times have changed, El-Tee. Interagency cooperation is the song of the day."

"Times are always changing, Detective. It's called life. How's that cooperation working out?"

"Sometimes not at all," Service had to admit.

"Silos loathe other silos," the retired officer told him. "Always have, always will. And there endeth the lecture. There's something I thought you ought to know about that parcel where I most frequently ran into Archie when he was in the Air Force: It's for sale."

"Now?"

"Yessir."

"How long?"

"Since you left here is how long," Kenowyth said. "Your asking about Archie leads me to assume that he or one of his kin are in the middle of one of your cases, which must be important, so I decided the obvious."

Service drew a blank. Obvious only to the El-Tee. "Not following, sir."

"Call me Kenty. What this is, is another card for you to play, another angle to dangle."

Geez. "I don't understand, Kenty."

"CK Resources owns the parcel, also called, CKRTCO."

"Still no bells," Service said.

"Chantal Kenowyth Resources Trust Company."

"Your *granddaughter* owns the parcel?"

"Her mother left her a lot of dough and I talked Chantal into buying that land. God's not making any more, you know?"

"I've heard that."

The old man chuckled. "We might could have been good friends, Service. But, we were too much alike, both headstrong as hippos. The land thing's not a rumor, son. Take that one to the bank. You find good land and can afford it, buy it."

Service said. "I think the world thought us to be opposites."

"The world doesn't know shit from Shinola, whatever that means. I never did figure it out."

Kenowyth's daughter owned the property that in her grandfather's experience he thought to be the center of Harlikin's father or grandfather's interest. "Have you been on the property, cruised it, walked it, Kenty?"

"Decades ago."

"You think there's silver there?"

"If there is, it's not a deep-veined in hardrock, it's more like a fissure the Indians used to use to get their copper supplies for trading. The parcel is real hard-going, lots of deep little canyons eastish of the old radar station. Sort of in the direction of the headwaters of Eister Creek."

"How much land?"

"Two forties next to each other almost, but separated by a wedge of government land from the radar station property."

"You acquired this parcel for the trust?"

"With my wifey's approval."

"Asking price?"

"Not the same for everyone. Right buyers, we'd let it go for two thou an acre, 160 in all."

"That's a *bundle*."

"That depends on the land's real value."

"Why didn't Archie buy the property when it was for sale?"

"Because I bought it first for sixteen grand, which back then he couldn't afford."

"Is the fact it's for sale a matter of public record?"

"Do you want it to be?" Kenowyth said.

This angle was something to think about. "How long do I have to decide that?"

"You tell me and I'll see that it happens. I like it that I can vicariously get back in the game on your case. Be like the old days."

"What if someone else wants to buy it?"

"Like who?"

"Me."

"You could swing 160?"

"Probably."

"If you want it, you can have it for the sixteen I paid. Horse Blankets stick together."

"I don't know what to say," Service told the man, which he didn't. This action from Kenowyth sounded rational, but was it, and was Kenty in full command of his senses?

"Kenty, I'm not tracking this whole deal. Why're you doing this? My gut says you know something I don't."

The old man chuckled. "I suspect I know a whole lot you don't know, Grady, and one thing I know is that there's a bunch of chuckleheads in mustard suits running around playing soldier boy up in Section Eight, Township Fifty-Seven north, Range Thirty-One west."

The man's geography was dead-on.

"Who'd you hear that from?"

"Didn't *hear* it. Saw it with my own eyes. I may be one oh three, but I still get around. I saw those fools."

"They're not doing anything illegal," Service told him.

"How do you know that?"

"I'm not at liberty to say, Kenty."

"Course not, and I know better. There's a Harlikin up there, isn't there?"

"You've seen him?"

"No, but a Realtor I know has and she described him to me. Are you aware he's after the parcel we just talked about. You think that's part of his soldier-boy fantasy?"

"I don't know."

"I do. I think he thinks the mine is there. He's after the silver."

"You think he's one of the Rock family you told me about?"

"Don't know for sure, but I'm thinking he could be a grandson."

"I have a picture," Kenowyth said. "Of Archie. Might be useful to you."

It might indeed. "Want me to swing by?"

The old man laughed softly. "I live in the modern world, I'll shoot it to you with a text. You *do* text I presume."

"Till my fingers are bleeding," he lied.

"Modern communications beats blazes out of the primitive radios we had back in the way back."

"True, but there are drawbacks."

"Life's a drawback, Grady. The text is going now."

Service saw the phone light up and make a sound. He opened it, and saw the picture of a young man, who looked like a near-double for the Colonel Harlikin he had met.

"The Harlikin I know is the self-appointed commander of an outfit called Regiments of Christian Knights, the ROCKs."

Kenowyth said. "Maybe this kin is a believer, but if he's like his Grandpa Archie, he has only one true motivator, and that's money."

Service's mind was in wobble mode. "Any two-track or trails, old buildings or ruins near your property?"

"It's Chantal's property, not mine," Kenowyth corrected. "Weren't any structures when I was last there, but the bit you want to concentrate on is tucked almost against the radar station's north cliff wall."

"There's a *cliff* up there?"

"Some call anything with sharp vertical features a cliff. This one isn't *straight* down, but you won't want to try hopping down it either."

"I think you should post the For Sale notice," Service said, not having thought through implications. But if Harlikin was money crazy, and this was where he, like his kin, thought there was a mine, it would be interesting to see if and how he took the bait. Service said, "As soon as you post it, you'll get a call from Mr. Chas Marschke."

"He with the state?"

"He works with me. I'll buy the parcel at the amount you posted."

"I already said you can have it for what I paid."

"But it's Chantal's now, not yours. We'll pay asking, and let's make this happen fast so that by the time you get other offers, you can tell them it's already sold."

"And if they want the name of the buyer?"

"Give it to them."

"Who's Marschke?"

"He operates a land-holding business among other interests."

"All right, then. That's all I've got. Think I'll go make some more coffee."

Service immediately called Marschke and explained the plan.

"Put it in our land trust?" his wealth manager asked. "With the Mosquito Wilderness Parcel?"

"That's the one, but remember we never mention the name of that place you just mentioned."

"Got it, boss. Text confirmation to you soon as the deal is done. And let me say that whatever you are doing I always assume is something that would give most people white knuckles. I could never do your work."

"It hasn't killed me yet, Chas."

"It's the yet part that stabs at me, boss."

CHAPTER 37

North of Mohawk

KEWEENAW COUNTY

> Come what come may, Time and the hour runs through the roughest day.
>
> —William Shakespeare, *Macbeth*

Years ago, his last time down Theiler Road, Service had seen a long-haired black wolf, but this time all he found was himself cursing modern telephone technology for the umpteenth time as two of his phones were exploding simultaneously, his personal cell and his ROCK phone, which he almost missed because of his cranky mood.

He decided to answer his personal phone first, and heard Chas Marschke's voice.

"I didn't text because the explanation on silver is too much for a sentence or two."

"I don't care. Boil it down anyway," Service said. "Stuff's piling up on my plate." What happened to those days when you couldn't find a connection? Now you could barely avoid them.

Not too many years ago he could remember parking his truck in the middle of a road and walking up and down trying to connect or complete a call: Can you hear me now? Can you hear me now? It had been a sick joke and more than once happened in a dangerous situation when you needed backup and didn't want your need going out over police dispatch.

The time he'd seen the wolf he had stopped and the animal had stopped and they had stared at each other until the wolf walked slowly on, fearing no enemy.

Marschke said, "The boil-down's this: Precious metals are led by platinum and gold. Silver's in the family, but not a favored relation except for a few aficionados who have their own reasons, and continue to chase silver. You want more?"

"That's enough." Harlikin seemed an outlier in all ways.

"You still want the land deal we talked about?"

"Absolutely. Text me as soon as you have a verbal handshake. That's legally binding, right?"

"Depends on the individual," Chas Marschke told him.

Kenowyth and his granddaughter, they would be good to their word. "I gave you the names and numbers, right?"

"You texted them! Never thought I'd see a text from Grady Service, and with those big damn fingers."

"I use my pokey-thingey," Service confessed.

"Your what?"

"You know, one of those things with a rubber on the end."

Marschke laughed. "You might rethink that description, boss."

"Thank Tuesday for the term. I learned it from her."

"You know your life has some odd elements and twists to it, right?"

"Reminders daily. A text will serve for the land deal." Then, before breaking contact, he thought about his contact with Kenowyth. "Pencil handy, Chas?"

"There's a Notebook App in my smartphone."

"Will it compose the note for you?"

"Nope, just type it from your voice."

"Then it's not that smart, is it?" Service said, took a deep breath and added: "New name, names to add to our list. Archimedes Histah Harlikin Rock, apparently went by Archie at one point, may at some time studied minerology at Tech, served in the Air Force, first as enlisted, perhaps later as an officer, worked at one point in meteorology."

"Seems like you already know plenty."

"Broad strokes only. I want a deep dive, dates and details, all personal data, present whereabouts, all of it."

"You think Harlikin, colonel of ROCKs was a Rock before there were ROCKs?"

"We'll let the facts tell us what we need to think. My imagination has a tendency to jump into overdrive."

"Anything else while we're in live-voice mode?"

Service laughed, dropped the cell phone and picked up the ROCK burner unit. There was a text. BATANOVICH: RECALL IMMEDIATE RPT DIRECT TO HARLIKIN, COL. ROCK.

He stared at the phone. Who the fuck was Batanovich? What the . . . ? Oh, right, that was him, this lapse the price of being too long out of his most recent UC cover story and role. Before becoming Batanovich, he had been Wyndham Vold. It was both bad and dangerous when you had to stop and think who the hell you were supposed to be at any given time in a particular place, in particular circumstances. Adhering to his cover was one of the main reasons he lived out of his camper as much as he could during undercover jobs. It was easier to stay in the latest role of whoever he was pretending to be.

Per the ROCKs' protocol, he was to neither acknowledge nor respond, and when he reported he would be required to surrender the burner phone to Harlikin.

He touched his implant, even though he knew he didn't need to. "Green test, you there Click-Clack?"

A very feminine voice said, "He lets *you* call him Click-Clack? And here I thought *I* was exclusive to the man."

"Who is this?" Service muttered. How many people were involved in his crap?

"Trooper Tess Trescult, call me Tres Kool, with a K, but there's just O'Dell and me, if you're worried about exposure, loose lips, and all that other paranoid baloney."

"How *many* of the rest of you?"

"Keep your hippers on, Fish Dude. I just said, it's just me and O'Dell, who is a stand-up guy, and my boss, but he's a Luddite in the specific technical glitch now confronting you. But the rest of Tech has our backs."

The rest of Tech? "Again, *what* rest of you?"

"Calm down, there're just two of us for your gig and we'd die before giving up your name, unless of course somebody personally offered me twelve hundred bucks, which is more than my take-home right now."

He thought she was trying to make a joke. "You have a unique sense of humor."

"My mother said the same thing the second time I tried to hang her."

"That's a joke too, right?"

"I don't do jokes. Others say I do, but I don't. What is it you want, Fish Dude? Your whitey-tighties all scrunched up?"

"When's Click-Clack back on duty?"

"When he and his latest squeeze finish their latest scromp-romp. Wanna know what they *do*? We tell each other *everything, him and me*!"

"He really tells you?"

"Hell no, but I've got a fantastic imagination, wanna hear how you and me would get it on?"

"How old are you?"

"Today or tomorrow?"

"Either."

"Twenty-four, both days."

"Do you understand I could be your great-great-grandfather?"

"O blessed skies raining doo doo," she said. "I heard the DNR was hard up for recruits, but man, that makes you like lead guitar in the Funkyland Old-Man Band. Still, might be a kick to give each other a whirl. You do remember how to whirl, yah Fish Dude?"

"Vaguely."

"I could send pictures."

"No thanks, just make sure O'Dell is on the earphones the next few days."

"Whole lotta shaking going on?"

"Could be."

"Way cool. You ever read that Erica Jong, rhymes with Dong, the gal was into zipless fucks and such like that?"

"I know her."

"Personally?"

"No." This gal was a real pill.

"If you can be my great-great-grandfather, how come you're still working? My great-great-grandfather is long gone dead-duckski."

"This isn't the place or time for that discussion, and it's none of your business."

She said, "Still working at your age, and undercover, you must be one very bad MF."

Today he was feeling more old than bad.

"Hey Fish Dude, not to worry, man. Me and Click-Clack got your back, and just so you know, Baby's finally got her shit back together."

"Baby?"

"The gizzy in your head, man."

"Ah yes, my gizzy." Surreal. Everything these days seemed surreal, wavering like a heat mirage on a hot horizon. "Hey, good luck on your next hanging," he told the voice.

"Thanks, Fish Dude. That's like totally sweet. But if you met my mama, you'd want to hang her ass too. She's a total *bee-otch*."

"Done talking now," Service said.

"Fish Dude, before you run off, remember *don't* be touching your neck when you want to talk to us. Touching might give you away. Just talk, copy? This isn't like that *Star Trek* shit and bad guys seeing you touching your junk, they might take out a knife, see what's getting your attention."

"And that would be a very, very bad thing," Service said.

"For you, not for me," she joked. "Confirm your go word."

"Confirm blue, and I'm *really* done now."

His next call went to Tuesday Friday. "I've been recalled."

"Details, tone, feelings, you, others, anything?"

"Addressed specifically to me. Just come on home, E.T."

She didn't laugh. "E.T. was lost, not home."

"E.T.s aren't the brightest creatures," he told her. "Probably rank below Shmoos."

"That's what scares me," she said. "Did you ever manage to get with O'Dell?"

"*He* didn't tell you?"

"O'Dell lives in a parallel world, which may or may not be in our shared universe."

She had that right. "He and Tres Kool with a K."

Friday laughed. "Corporal Tessa Trescult."

"She's twenty-four," Service said.

"She looks sixteen and is she ever *built*."

"She dreams of hanging her mother, and somehow your outfit hired her?"

"Good help is hard to find these days, even crazy good help."

"The Vulcan O'Dell himself is not exactly a great exemplar," he said.

"Just don't you go getting yourself killed by assholes," Friday said.

"Definitely not in the plan book."

"Neither is my finding a new man to love," she said. "Be safe out there." Then. "Dammit!"

"I know, if I get killed, you'll have to dig me up and kill me all over again."

"I really don't understand why so many people think you're losing your grip," Tuesday teased.

"My grip on what?"

"God, you've already forgotten. You are so pathetic, Bub. Listen to me: Things get tighty and untidy, call in the cavalry."

"I will be a far hop for quick help."

"That is a detail I did *not* need to know. You tell Tres Kool and O'Dell your destination?"

"Affirmative. Tres Kool says Baby has my six."

"Then as long as Baby works, you're good to go."

"And if I switch locations?"

"Doesn't matter. Baby knows where you are."

"You ever use Baby?" he asked.

"This isn't the time to talk about such things. I'll be glad when this is over," she told him.

"I'll be glad when I finally figure out what the hell *this* is."

He sat for a moment and found himself sweating, his adrenaline in power-spike mode. It was all piling up in a rush and usually when this happened, his brain automatically slowed it all down and let him methodically sort through every detail. It was like playing hockey at a high level. The higher the level, the greater the skills, but ironically everyone at that level was going full speed and the minds of better players could slow it down to almost frame by frame and look ahead. It was the gift of all great athletes. And great cops.

But today wasn't like that. The damn puck was moving at supersonic speeds and he felt like he was always behind the action, which was a guarantee of losing if you couldn't get yourself back where you needed to be, out in front of the movement.

Recalled by Harlikin: Where were Allerdyce and Worm? Last he knew the old man was still hunting White Wilt's trail, and Worm was sputtering around in the background like a spurned lover or bored housewife.

He buzzed Allerdyce's phone.

"This is Worm's voice of Worm here," Worm answered.

"Grady. Where's Allerdyce?"

"Worm not hear nothing from nobody, or Him, It, Service long time, then Him Service call and want talk Allerdyce. What is Worm, Walt's Bait?"

Walt's Bait was a ubiquitous Canadian company that sold crawlers and red worms all over the U.P. Where had she come up with *that* one? "Where are you two now?"

"Same place," she said. "Watching."

"I'm headed there now."

"You want speak It Old Man?"

"Would much prefer to talk to you, but yes. Is he there, yes or no?"

"Sonny-boy! Just gone call youse." It was Limpy on the line.

"What's going on?"

"Seen trucks dere, in and oot. I t'ink mebbe dat outfit pullin' oot."

"Explain."

"Saw trucks movin' stuff."

"What kind of stuff?"

"Couldn't see dat."

"How many trucks?"

"I seen mebbe one, mebbe two."

"Which was it, one or two?"

"Dere was two I seen."

"Meaning you might have missed more?"

"Can't say what don't know, eh? You know da Brit guys call trucks lorries? Why Brits call trucks womyn's name?"

Allerdyce. "No idea. If it bothers you, Google it."

"I don't do dat Google t'ing. Pipples say the da Google can give one the da leopard-see."

Leprosy? "What pipples?"

"Just pipples know shit is what pipples, youse know."

Obviously Allerdyce had made this up, and why was irrelevant right now. Sometimes on some subjects, Limpy was the Lord of Whackadoodle Dandies.

"You see White Wilt when you were over there? It could make for a dangerous moment if he was confronted by Gecko and Goat at Camp ROCK."

"Seen the little one," Allerdyce said. "He pert good in woods, not easy follow, and I t'ink he look like mebbe he spook easy."

"Is he there?"

"He gone. I seen 'im leave."

"On a truck?"

"On foot, before dose trucks come." The old man added, "All dat jumpin aboot over dere given me some da heapy-jeepies, make my brain itch."

"You think something's wrong?"

"Not think nothin' cause don't know nothin'. Just feelin' is all. You know anyt'ing Sonny?"

"They've called me back to camp."

"Dat puts da big chub-stink on 'er," Limpy said.

"You *eat* smoked chubs."

"Not after sun get 'em all riped-up. When youse got be dere, dat place?"

"ASAP with no specific date, or specific time of day. They know my bird-counting jobs can't be easily terminated and this gives me some time, but I can't push it off indefinitely."

"Dey call back da hull bunch, or just youse?"

"Great question. You're in a better position to answer than I am. Are you seeing ROCKs coming back?"

"No. Just seen dose trucks goin' out, like I told youse. Dat gang don't seem to be gatherin' up. Seems more like dey splittin'."

"I'm sending help, two young COs, Something and Bapcat. When they get there, tell them all you know, but they'll make the calls, okay?"

"Dere green, dose two," Allerdyce told him.

They weren't as green as most new officers, but it probably didn't hurt for Limpy to think them green and back off some on his intensity. "I may call in Harmony, too. *She's* not green." Harmony Wildingfelz was the CO who had replaced him in Mosquito Wilderness Area.

"Dis long way from Mosquito," Allerdyce reminded him.

"I want people around me I have confidence in. You keep an eye on all of them, hear?"

"Where we meet up?" Allerdyce asked.

Service had to close his eyes to pull up a map he could look over. Camp ROCK was along a low ridge in Section 8 in Township 57N, Range 31W.

"Call you right back," Service told the old man. "Do not move from where you are now standing. Understood?"

"I hear," Limpy said.

Service called Patty Something. "I'm recalled and I'm going to need you and Bapcat at Camp ROCK with some other folks. They may appear a bit strange, and they are, but you can rely on them," he told her.

Then he told her exactly where the ROCK outfit was.

She noodled this and said, "I know a guy with a forty in Section 7 near the Gratiot River headwaters. I've got the key to his gate and permission for us to use his property anytime for anything we need."

"You work fast," he told her.

"Not so much," she said. "Rocky Thresh was my dad's oldest friend."

"Bapcat know the place?"

"He's seen it and dropped a pin on it."

"Give him a bump and find out how long for him to get there. How long for you?"

"Thirty minutes max," she reported.

"Good. An old coot named Allerdyce will meet you there and hike you and Jordy to where I want you guys."

"Care to say where that spot is?"

"Too complicated to explain now. Allerdyce will take you there, and remember, the old bastard looks barely alive, but once you step into the bush you'll have a hard time keeping up with him."

"Is this the famous Allerdyce, the equivalent of Bigfoot?"

"Most Yoopers love Bigfoot. They're scared shitless of Limpy."

"I'm on my way," Something said. "Jordy's checking out a wolf complaint in Bootjack. I'll give him a bump and get him moving."

"Tell Jordy to file the wolf complaint in the Bigfoot file."

"There *are* wolves here," she reminded him.

"Right, like how many, four?"

"You're a cynical man."

"Which is a synonym for common sense."

"We'll discuss that sometime over adult beverages."

"I'd rather talk UFOs," he said.

"Too late, Old Guy. UFOs are creatures of the past. Such things now are officially called Unexplained Aerial Phenomena, UAPs."

"Such bullshit," Service lamented.

"At least the government's no longer denying they exist," Something reminded him.

He laughed. "Ah the soothing comfort of naïveté, they're just using new terms to not say shit."

"You sound nervous," she said. "Is that even possible?"

"I'm always nervous," he lied. Usually he was calm before any sort of confrontation and during them as well. "If you're not nervous, you didn't get the message, or you didn't read it."

"Oh, I've got the message, I just have this feeling that you're more than excited."

"Meaning?"

"I don't have a word for it."

"Then keep it to yourself, dammit."

"Grrr," she said.

"Knock off that shit," he told her. "I am good to go, repeat, good to go, I'm, good, I'm fine."

"You know what Shakespeare says," she said.

"Actually I don't. He's been dead like what, a thousand years and anybody that long dead doesn't talk any more, at least not in voices or languages the living can understand. Sorry," he said. "What does Mr. Shakespeare say?"

"There's nothing either good or bad but thinking makes it so."

"So this dead man suggests we all empty our minds the way his dead mind is emptied now?"

"We'll give you a bump when we meet up with Allerdyce," she told him. "Do you think this thing you've been in is coming to a head?"

"You and Shakespeare just told me not to think," he said. "Call me when you and Jordy are with Limpy. He's guiding you in, but you two make the decisions on action. If I need cavalry, I will yell for it. If I yell, knock down everything in front of you to get to me as quickly as you can."

"Roger," Something said. "George-order received and understood."

George was an old informal game warden code for an all-out assault on a target, a term derived from the practice of a longtime CO who barged into everything, using the element of surprise as leverage and an advantage-maker. "You know about George-ing?"

"You think we spent all those months in the academy just learning how to shuffle reports and other make-work paperwork? They taught us some of the fun stuff too."

CHAPTER 38

Copper Island

KEWEENAW COUNTY

One bear will not bite another.

—William Shakespeare, *Troilus and Cressida*

Service had not thought about his camper in how long? He'd positioned it to give him a hard difficult but doable hike to Camp ROCK, and though this might well be his final day in the place, and he could probably park his truck closer to Harlikin's operation, he decided to follow the routine he'd followed since going undercover and hike in from his camper, hoping his legs would hold out. He'd not done his daily weight routine in months, and in recent weeks, he had gotten irregular exercise, spending most of his time sitting in a damn truck, driving around.

It seemed that Colonel Harlikin wanted him back soon, but he didn't intend to go back inside until he had everything arranged as he wanted it on the outside. He would go back when *he* was ready, and not before.

He had positioned the camper early in his UC assignment and as far as he knew, only Worm and Allerdyce knew it existed, and where it was.

The camper wasn't actually his. It was a state asset, something taken off a citizen for some serious infraction and snapped up at auction by the DNR. Even so, he had always tried to treat state-owned property like his own, and he decided to make a quick inspection of the camper while he made his final arrangements and tried to steel himself for his return. Where the hell were the eagle feathers? Did they even exist? Absent those, there was no reason for him to be in there, though now that he was, he had seen that Harlikin's background and probable interest in mines shifted the colonel even further into the DNR's law enforcement purview. A good game warden took care of his shit, and if he was nothing else, Grady Service considered himself a pretty good game warden.

It would, in fact, feel almost normal to sit in his camper and brew some fresh coffee, and take a few moments to pretend he had a normal life.

Having hidden his truck, he hiked to the camper and what he saw made his belly flop. The front door was hanging on the bottom hinge, bent in half like a bow to royalty.

Good grief. Was nothing ever going to go right? The scene before him could be read two ways—human intruders or an animal—and in this case he knew it was the latter, as it bore all the telltales of *Ursus americanus*. This being a black bear, the situation further boiled down to two likely scenarios: the pesky, nosy damn thing had come and gone, which was most likely. Or, less likely, but far more daunting, the damn thing was still in there and, either way, he was going to have a massive mess to clean up, and if the bear was still in there, that eventuality also boiled down to a couple of possibilities. The thing would crash out and boogie as soon as it detected him, or it would decide to stay and fight, either coming out fighting, or holding back for an ambush, and he relished neither scenario and, worst of all, he felt sick at the thought of possibly having to put down an animal that had done nothing more wrong than be what it was: a hungry bear.

In ways he could identify with a bear's way of life and views of its entitlements.

He had no shotgun or rifle, but he was packing a .357 with exploding tip rounds and this would do the job, though he would prefer a 12-gauge slug or some double-ought buckshot. The rifle and shotgun were hidden and locked in his truck and he could go back for them, but he was antsy and didn't want to waste time. Chances are the animal was no longer here.

But what if it was? The rule was to always plan for the worst and hope for the best, and over his very long career, the planned-for worst tended more often than not to be the reality at hand. This was not the time to play stupid. He went back to get the shotgun.

• • •

Shotgun in hand, he first eased up to the camper and took a leak, listening while he peed. Done with this, he moved away quietly and hoped, if the bear were inside, it would smell his little calling card and read it as an invite to get out of Dodge, which it was.

Most bears did not hole up in campers, so this animal was in a small category all its own. Back at the truck he had reluctantly loaded his shotgun. Killing a wild creature for what boiled down to bad judgment or a desperate act did not sit well in his mind. He admired, even liked bears, not damn teddy bears, but the real bears who had a knack of making a life for themselves just about anywhere they landed.

It this bear was inside, he hoped the thing was at a point in life where it had fought enough battles, and just wanted to be left alone, a notion he could get fully on board with, and thinking this, he wondered how Tuesday would handle this situation, and why had he never married her? Was it reticence after the murder of his girlfriend and son so many years ago? No, scar tissue had patched those wounds to the extent such tissue could. No, they were alike, two damn wild creatures, he and this damn bear, old and tired and sick of going all-out every minute, hour, and day of his life, and what woman as smart as Friday wanted to be permanently hooked up to such a wired-up, overamped partner? Good grief, why was he thinking about this crap *now*?

Damn Shakespeare and damn Patty Something too. Shakespeare? In the middle of a damn dicey undercover op? Was he losing his mind? Might be about to have a tussle with a damn bear, and here he was thinking about marriage? And Shakespeare? He had to suppress a laugh.

He flung a piece of campfire wood at the side of the camper and it resounded like a tinny bass drum, and nothing happened. He lit a cigarette and let it hang off his lower lip as he loosely held the shotgun and waited. "Hey bear!" he yelled. Still nothing.

If the animal sought a confrontation, chances are it would lose, but when you had spent so many decades in shit-bucket moments you came to understand just how fickle the third finger of fate was, and how what ought to have looked like and been a certainty could become in a split second the very opposite and could consume you, and the problem was the time between the various outcomes and reality were so small that all odds were nothing but scribbles on paper, and threats looming real *were* real and it didn't matter if the threat was human, animal, or weather, you had to do what you had to do and you had to do it right the first time, with no second chances granted, minimum allowable standard of performance being 100 percent, and thinking this it occurred to him that he was delaying this confrontation with the camper intruder in order to delay confronting Colonel Harlikin and the ROCKs, and this realization disgusted him. Clearly, only four or five years ago, he would have been all over any and all of these challenges and looking for more and breathing fire like some kind of mad dragon.

Grady took a deep breath and walked to the camper, saying "Go bear, go bear," over and over and when he got to the bent door he whacked the camper wall with his boot-toe and nothing happened. He waited, sucked in a deep breath, exhaled slowly, stepped up, and peeked inside, shotgun in two hands like a low spear and ready to be turned to any trouble.

But there was no bear, and no threats except those staring at him from inside his own mind.

He hoped the Harlikin ROCKs situation could be as easily handled, and if Limpy had seen trucks coming and going, was it possible that Harlikin was bailing for elsewhere, and if so, where and why?

Harlikin was a difficult one to figure out. Not your typical gun-toting militiaman, and seemingly deeply interested in money extracted from his men, not by selling them weapons or uniforms of group merch, but by more or less making them take a financial stock in the organization and what militia operated on *this* concept? And why were Harlikin's men willing to pay so damn much money?

He'd once known a successful businessman who, when merch sat too long in his display room, would increase the price as much as three times and whenever he did this, the item sold almost immediately as customers equated higher price with greater scarcity and value, and scarfed up the same thing they could have had for half or a third less a week before. There was no accounting for the ability of humans to fool themselves into thinking logic drove them to do things in which logic played no part at all. Somewhere he had once read something about how humans all look desperately for rational reasons to believe absurd things. True when he read it and still true.

The bear had made a mess, but left surprisingly little damage other than one very fresh pile of scat, meaning it had been in there all the while he made his ruckus outside, and no doubt departed only after he went to fetch his shotgun.

He organized more than cleaned the interior and got out the coffee pot he kept in a cabinet and made coffee and dumped it all into a thermos to carry with him on his hike to Camp ROCK. It was time to hitch up his big boy pants and go deal with the situation, whatever it turned out to be, and Colonel Sane Zane Harlikin, whoever in hell he was, or was trying to be, which was not at all clear.

Some ROCKs he had met clearly were of the whackadoodle school, but most seemed earnest, either about their religious convictions, or their politics, which wanted little to no interference from government or anyone from outside their chosen little group into their lives. Of course, their thinking that their creeds and religious practices were under assault did not make it so. Paranoia was a virus that could quickly infiltrate and sweep through and capture the fears of what was otherwise an essentially law-abiding, largely sensible group of common citizens, caught on their back feet by unexpected moments or circumstances, and unable to get their balance back.

So what the hell was the government all exercised about with Harlikin's outfit? Hadn't the Koresh debacle in Waco, Texas, been enough to learn lessons and handle so-called outlier groups in a different manner?

The bear's gift now made him laugh in a sense of kinship. Service stood on his stoop by the bent-door and said, "Message received, Mister Bruin. Today we both get to keep on, keeping on."

He hoped he had what it took to conclude his undercover assignment, easily the strangest he'd ever experienced. The thought of dealing with Harlikin again sent a chill up his spine and he wondered if he ought to grab a warm puffy vest from his truck.

In the end he took no vest. The chill, he knew, was born not outside him, but inside, and he did not like the feeling of knowing this, did not like it at all.

Hell was other people, lots of them, treating you like a so-called legend, even calling you that to your face (and even more so behind your back). And you knowing that whatever it was they thought you had been, understood nothing. Your knowledge of your own past was vastly different than the account of that same time told by others.

Whatever adrenaline pumped today would not be a product of pleasure. Today was the day some shit was likely to go down and a scorecard was being readied for completion somewhere, whatever the final outcome.

What was his code word, which he now thought of as his George word? *Blue*. Of all the words he could have selected, why that one? He felt behind his left ear and could not feel whatever it was that O'Dell had inserted and this was impressive. "Green Test," he said out loud and heard inside his head, "Five Square." It was O'Dell's voice. Good, he was listening.

As he hiked, his mind locked into a cadence with his boots and nonsensical lyrics of an earworm gone batty, blue skies, true blue and blue taken from the skies and pretty girls' eyes, a deep blue sea for a blue-water navy, blue jacket, blue belly, black and blue, Old Blue, blue chip, blue rose, blue cheese, blue pencil, blue notes, blue funk, blue jay, *Blue Hawaii*, azure blue, Prussian blue, blue grass, blue whale, shocking blue, blue balls, blue lips, toe-tag blue, screwed, blued and tattooed, endless blue, I'm feelin' blue, that's why they call it the blues, and the longer the blue rift went on the surer his step got, and so too, his resolve with his step.

CHAPTER 39

Copper Island

KEWEENAW COUNTY

Hark, how hard he fetches breath.
—William Shakespeare, *Henry IV, Part I*

It was, he thought as he marched, whistling in a graveyard, and eventually he finally shed the riff of blue. It could drive a man crazy to think that he had full command of himself, only to find himself worrying about what others were doing, or would do, and a thought now began to overwhelm him that he needed to meet with his people before he went back into Camp ROCK.

Oddly Grady felt himself needing reassurance. What was his problem? He'd been UC so many times in so many dangerous and potentially lethal circumstances that he'd lost count. Yet this time felt different, less threatening in the sense of how he reacted to Harlikin, but remembering the outfit was a militia, and armed to the armpits, left him feeling raw and on edge. An FBI agent was already dead, and his captain was showing a case of the major hinkies, and he trusted her gut in such matters—usually.

Technically he was alone, albeit with his cavalry near and on standby.

He found himself calling Friday. "Hey," he greeted her.

"I know, you called me to tell me how much you love me," she responded.

"Well, that's certainly part of it," he said.

"Bullshit," she said. "You love your dog more than any human."

"Allerdyce Limpy-napped our dog," he told her.

"What?"

"Brought her over here."

"What is *wrong* with that old man?"

"He thinks she missed me."

Friday guffawed. "Me too, but the old clod didn't kidnap me."

"Those laws are too stiff for a felon to contend with."

"I love that damn dog too," Friday said. "Shigun adores her, and that tells us something about our kid's judgment."

"Have you seen Stealth, or heard her on the radio?" Stealth was CO Harmony Wildingfelz.

"Why do you refuse to call her by her name?"

"Because it bugs her."

"It bugs me too. It's rude. You'll never grow up."

"Not if I can help it," he said. "Seriously, has she been around?"

"For her sometime partner, you are not very damn attentive, are you, Bub?"

"Knock it off. Have you seen her or not?"

"Haven't seen her, but I heard her on the radio day before yesterday. She was in court before me with one of her cases."

"Which one?"

"Boyarleke, illegal deer, no license, shooting from a vehicle at night, the classic after-dark trifecta of stupidity."

"How'd she do?"

"Guilty on all charges, and a twelve-point buck to boot with the trophy buck law applied. Ouchy-ouchy for Mr. Boyarleke."

"Slap on his damn wrist. The guy owns five pharmacies around Lansing, and has more money than God's little sister."

"God has a sister?"

"Doesn't everyone?"

"You don't," Friday said.

"I'm luckier than God."

"That's blasphemy."

"Yet still true."

"You are a far bigger pain in the butt than is God. Why are you trying to bother your sometime partner?"

"You, for obvious reasons, her because I need to talk to her."

"Meaning you don't need to talk to your actual partner?"

"I never said that. Why do you have to be such a jerk?"

"I was home-schooled in emotional maladjustment," Friday said. "Harmony's just back from two weeks annual leave."

"Who the hell's been looking after the Mosquito for those two weeks?"

"That's *her* problem, not yours, Bub. And don't use that tone with me."

"I'm a detective, not a patrol officer. She and I are *not* partners."

"But you tell her you're her partner all the time."

"Just to mess with her head."

"You need to talk to her, give her a bump."

"She on duty today?"

"I don't know. Ask Station Twenty. Probably she's on duty. She's just like you—*always* out and about in her damn truck."

"The Mosquito is a wilderness."

"Uh huh," Friday said, "which oddly enough breeds more psycho game wardens than skeeties."

"I gotta go," he said.

"Coward. Shigun and I will take care of your dog—when she decides to come home."

"That sounds ominous as all get-out," he said.

"Your *work* is what's ominous, Bub."

He hung up and exhaled. Tuesday was usually the model for cool charm and calm. Recently, not so much. Could this job be getting to her *that* much?

He hit speed dial for Harmony Wildingfelz's number. "Yo, Stealth."

"I hate that name."

"Even after two weeks of fucking off?"

"It's called annual leave. You should try it with your family."

"I hear it can be addictive," he said.

"What's up?" she asked.

"You're as smart as you are sneaky," he said.

"Compliments from you always creep me out. What is it you want?"

"Listen up," he said, and brought her up to speed.

"Oh shit," was all Harmony could manage when he was finished.

"I want you with the team," he added. "Where are you?"

"Southwest Marquette County."

"Close enough, put some juice to it, Bruce."

"Is that like a lyric from a Neanderthal courting song?"

"You bet."

"Have you cleared my being over there with upstairs management?"

"When I tell McKower, she'll approve it."

"McKower, huh?"

"What's that supposed to mean?"

"Heard you and her mighta coulda had a thang once upon a time."

"You heard wrong. You need to get your butt up here, PDQ. Let me give you some coordinates. I need you there to help the new kids and keep a leash on Allerdyce."

She laughed out loud. "Even you can't keep a leash on that dickhead."

"There's something else," he said. "A female civilian. I want you to look at her as a possible candidate for the academy."

"Has she taken the state civil service tests yet?"

"Not yet. She's not like our normal candidates."

"No? In what way?"

"She hates to wear clothing."

"Holy crap," Wildingfelz said. "You're still a beaut, partner, one of a kind, and thank God for that. See you soon," she said, and signed off.

"Fly," he told her, but she couldn't hear him.

Stealth was not in the PCOs' command structure, but it wouldn't matter. She was a natural leader and couldn't help but assume command. They could sort out details later.

It was comforting to think in terms of there being a later, he thought as he headed not directly toward Camp ROCK, but to the watching point where Allerdyce and Worm had been stationing themselves. He would enter Camp ROCK from there when it was time.

A quarter-mile farther on, his personal cell buzzed. "Chas," Marschke hastily identified himself. "When I hang up, you will have somebody on the other line who demands to talk only to you. This person appears to have information we've been trying to pin down, but refuses to talk to us, and will talk only to you."

"Who is it?"

When Chas told him the name, Service stopped hiking and took a deep breath. The name of the caller was an assumed name. He had known her for many years as Honeypat Allerdyce, wife of Limpy's late son Jerry. She had once tried to usurp Limpy's poaching biz and he had driven her out. She popped up years later running a chain of call girls in Lansing, women who specialized in state politicians, and she was now among them as a shaker and a mover.

Of all the times. "What could she possibly have for us?" he asked Chas.

"Just listen to the lady, boss. I'm hanging up now. She'll be there."

"Well," a once familiar voice breathed into his ear. "Isn't coincidence sometimes the sweetest charm?"

"Long time," he said. "How are you?"

"Allerdyce close?" she asked. Her tone suggested that even after all these years, she still was wary of the man.

"No, and it's your dime," he said. "Start talking."

"You like phone sex?" she asked.

"This is what you wanted to tell me?"

"Don't be so bloody cynical. I've been told that you're dealing with a guy named Harlikin?"

"You know him?'

"Not biblically," she said. "But I know his wife."

"Know her?"

"I was negotiating with her to buy some of her business assets in Vegas."

"Was?"

"She flew ~~up~~ to Milwaukee and drove from there to her place in Presque Isle, Wisconsin, not far from Watersmeet."

"And?"

"She never made it to Presque Isle."

"You know this how?"

"I was there waiting for her and she was a no-show. I waited until the middle of the next day, and no show and no call."

"Driving?"

"That was her plan."

"Alone?"

"No, her son was supposed to come with her."

"Did *he* show up?"

"Nope, neither one."

"Did you report this?"

"What was there to report? And to whom? It was a business meeting and she was a big name in some circles. I figured she changed her mind or just wanted to buy time to push the sale price up."

"For the record, what was this person's name?"

"She goes by Lady Loire."

"You think something happened to her?"

"I hope not, but my intuition says differently."

"Who was she married to?"

"Fellow named Harlikin, only he now calls himself Gabbart—or he was Gabbart, last I knew."

"Did you know her son?"

"Never met him, but she once showed me a photo."

"Where was that?" he asked.

"We were in Mexico City."

"What did he look like?"

"Nobody. He was so damn tall, the camera cut off his head."

"And she showed the photo to you?"

"She said he's seven foot four and she wanted me to be impressed."

"What else?"

"You and I have unfinished personal business," she told him.

"Never gonna happen," he told her.

"You would not be sorry," she told him.

"I'm already sorry," he said. "Lady Loire and Gabbart slash Harlikin. How old's their kid?"

"Twenties maybe. College kid."

"Their kid from their marriage?"

"That I couldn't tell you."

"He got the same name?"

"I don't know."

"Seven-four, seriously?"

"You should have seen that snapshot. *Beyond* weird."

"How much money were you offering Lady Loire?"

"I don't disclose such details. Do you think something's happened to her?"

"We're looking into it."

"DNR and you in a missing persons case, that doesn't make sense to me."

"Feathers and ore bodies."

"Eagle feathers?"

"What about them?"

Honeypat said, "Lady Loire sold them to Indian tribes so they wouldn't have to get mixed up in the government op that distributes them. The Indians hate having states and feds involved in their religions and in their businesses."

"Cash sales?"

"Some cash, and some trading of mineral rights from Indian lands."

"Active business?"

"A good ten years I'm told. Lady Loire insisted they have first-rate collectors and scouts all over the country. I believed her."

"Your meeting with Lady Loire was in 2009. That's a long time back. You think she's still running the business?"

"I do not. My formal offer was sent back to me unsigned, and without a note, and I never heard from her again. Glad I called?" she asked in a one-in-a-million slithering come-hither voice.

He hated to say it. "I am. And thanks."

"Take care, big guy. You have led one charmed life in a very dangerous job."

So had she. "The day picks you," he told her and he broke contact with her laughter in his ears.

Chas called back. "All set on the land deal. What did she tell you?"

"Talk to you later, Chas. Thanks."

A seven-foot-four son with her the day she disappeared. Now *that* was interesting on many angles, and if White Wilt slash Mesnard George slash Gecko was the colonel's son, that might be one reason for his presence in camp.

He found himself hiking faster through the rocky terrain, his nostrils flared wide.

CHAPTER 40

Outside Camp ROCK

KEWEENAW COUNTY

> There is a history in all men's lives.
>
> —William Shakespeare, *Henry IV, Part II*

Standing back, Service counted five souls at Worm's hideout, four together and another moving toward the four, but not Wildingfelz. He checked his watch. Not enough time for her to get here yet and then he looked and saw the walk, and it hammered him. He could recognize that walk and gait three hundred yards off: It was McKower! And oh shit, and oh damn, and what was she doing *here*?

He sometimes forgot how headstrong she was. Once her mind was set on something, she would fight change unless you gave her overwhelmingly convincing evidence to think differently, and fed it to her as calmly and rationally as possible. What was he going to tell her today, and how?

Of most immediate concern would be her reaction to Allerdyce, never-mind the whole different issues with Worm. By the time he overtook and intercepted her, he found her huffing like a train with a boiler at full steam. "Lookin' good in Class B greens, Cap'n," he greeted her.

She kept moving and barely glanced at him. "Makes me wonder how you'll look in an orange jumpsuit," she retorted.

"For what?"

"For whom and by that I mean Allerdyce. I've already looked down on your little raiding party, or whatever it is. You were to sever all ties with that . . . *creature*."

"He's my friend."

"He shot you."

"It was a long time ago, and an accident."

"He's a damn felon."

Service shrugged. "We have some politicians who are felons."

"What are you *thinking*?" she yelped at him. "Are clots blocking your cerebral blood flow?"

This made him laugh, but she cut him off.

"I mean it. You sometimes act like you're out of your mind."

"I'm just fine," he said in his own defense. He did not mention that he meant most of the time, because there were other moments in his truck where he felt momentarily confused and it took some minutes to sort out where he was and why, and who.

"The classic refrain of nutwads," she said snippily. "You play too damn loose with rules, Grady."

"How's the scorecard and my score on results?" he shot back at her.

"Loose can lead to scorecards being torn up. Think Pete Rose."

"That's rewriting history," he told her.

"History is always being revised," she said, "and the department, the division and the state's resources are better off because of it. You *know* that."

"Using Allerdyce may be unorthodox, but look at our record."

"Achieving results that erode a process can diminish both the results *and* the process. And your emphasis on results is your own interpretation."

"Ask just about any officer in uniform," he argued.

"Your colleagues always cheer stinkers who make Lansing look bad."

Stinkers? "Allerdyce working with me has nothing to do with optics, and *you* know it, Lis."

"It's *Captain* McKower, Detective. You were reluctantly forgiven your trespasses and I told you *then* how damn close you were to having your plug pulled and did I, or did I not, warn you to stay the hell away from that crazy old bush rat? That said, here I am and who do I find? Jesus! Stay in your place and your lane."

"What did he do, grab your ass or something?"

She pivoted abruptly, her face flaming. "I do not allow myself to get that close to known felons."

"Bullshit, Captain. We're in UC and we *all* run felons all the damn time, felons and all sorts of low-life frequent fliers. They always know who the competition is, and have better intel than we can ever develop from the outside."

"That we have to operate so close to such mouth-breathers does not mean I approve of it, but I'm also new to this position and I want to take some time before I even consider sweeping changes, much less implement them."

"I don't pretend to know anything about the upstairs fence lines in the division, but I know pussy-footing when I see it."

"Are you accusing me of political maneuvering?"

"I don't even know what that is," he told her, but she turned away from him, and waggled a finger at Allerdyce, "And you, *old man*! What the hell do you think you're doing here?"

Limpy flashed her his best moronic wood-tick look. "Me?"

"Am I not looking right *at* you?"

"What?" he said dumbly.

"*What* what?" she responded.

"Dunno," he said. "Was you come up barkin' like lab wit' tick on 'is pecker."

"You call *this* barking?" she said with a snarl.

"Don't care what it called," Allerdyce said, "but know it when see it, eh? When da beek bears fight it's da grass most gets beat up."

McKower nodded at Service. "You think he's a big bear?"

"Beekest I ever seen," Allerdyce answered.

"And what am I?" she demanded.

"Beek bear too," the old man said, his eyes gleaming.

"Dammit it, Lis!" Service said with a snarl. This brought everyone to a halt and even the captain stopped to catch her breath.

Service noted that Something and Bapcat did not shrink away and that very moment he saw Wildingfelz running to join them, a stupid grin plastered on her face.

The captain pointed at Wildingfelz. "You're just off annual and what the *hell* are you doing way over *here*?"

"My partner needs backup," she said.

"Your partner needs lock-up, not backup, and he is *not* your partner," McKower said.

"He was, and once partners, always partners," Wildingfelz argued with her jaw jutted out.

The captain sighed. "It was Chief Waco's idea to put you with him," she said, her thumb waggled at Service. "I told him then I thought it was a mistake."

Wildingfelz said, "Actually, I think we've done very nicely so far."

Grady was proud of her resolve, and while McKower was technically correct that he and Stealth were not partners, he loved seeing young COs stand up to senior officers, a great reminder of how the force was at its best when comprised of independent-minded self-starters who only wanted to do their jobs with minimal interference from any direction, *especially* from above.

The captain looked up at Service. "What is this, your posse?"

"Low shot," he told her. "Not fair."

"He don't even know what dat mean," Allerdyce chimed in.

"And you *do*?" McKower said.

"I invent da posse. Was crews before me an' den I make dem posses."

"You are so full of . . . "

"Prove I din't," Allerdyce said cheerfully.

Service groaned inside. Irresistible force had just head-butted immoveable object, result: momentarily silent stalemate.

By now the PCOs had drifted in and it felt like a powder keg, and Service knew it was all his fault.

"This is not a by-the-book formation," McKower told them all.

"You want to run the show, it's all yours," Service told her.

She stepped back and gave him the stink-eye. "You know I would never do that."

"What I know is that you're here and uninvited."

McKower's turn to glare. "This is your show, and your op. I'm here only to help, no more, no less."

At that moment, Worm stepped into view and the captain's jaw dropped.

"Captain McKower, meet Worm," Grady Service said.

McKower stared dumbly at the very tall, very naked woman.

"She's with *us*, Cap'n," Service explained.

McKower nodded dumbly.

"Allerdyce and Worm have been surveilling Camp ROCK, keeping me apprised of comings and goings."

"In writing?" the captain asked, turning her eyes away from Worm.

"We don't waste no trees," Allerdyce told her. "Keep up here in dis t'ing." He touched his head.

Service addressed his captain. "Allerdyce and Worm, in or out?"

"It's your op and your call, Detective, here and now."

Meaning it might be hers elsewhere and at a later time. "Is that a threat?" he asked her.

"Worm does not like this, Her think," Worm interjected.

"It's all right," Service told her. "You know how Limpy and I bark at each other?"

"Worm Her know and Her not like."

Neither did he and now he had landed all of them in a very large doghouse, and no way was he going to even try to explain *that* to Worm.

"When do you have to report in?" Patty asked.

"Technically it's my call," he said, "but not until we get all of our ducks in line."

"What have ducks to do with this dog thing Worm Her want to know."

"Enough," Service said. "You split into two groups. Allerdyce and Worm are scouts. Lis, you and Stealth go with Limpy, Patty and Jordy with Worm."

"This is not what we talked about," Wildingfelz whined.

"Shit happens," he told her.

Worm rolled her eyes and tossed her head and long hair about. "Ducks and dogs and shit," she said. "Worm feeling here much confusion. Worm *not* like confusion!"

The captain patted the strange girl's arm. "Welcome to my world, honey," she said, and looked at Service and Allerdyce. "It's always this way when these two freaks are together."

"Worm like freaks."

"Me too," McKower said, "Unfortunately, and these are words I will no doubt come to regret both personally and professionally."

"Regret only for things Worm do not do, not for things Her do," Worm said.

Service looked at her. "Where did you learn *that*?"

"Worm reads."

"Good," he told her. "Now you and Limpy tell us all about what you've seen in the camp. It's time to green it up and clean it up, people."

"Ah," Jordy Bapcat said, his first words. "The pre-battle prattle, the dance of discord. Let's *get* some."

Service smiled at them. "There's nothing like a looming goat rodeo to spark brains and mouths. Let's get this straight, people. I do not know exactly what's waiting over there, but I do know this: Whatever it is, it is not now and never will be worth one of us not going home when the shift ends, copy?"

Nods all around, even from the captain who now wore her very intimidating game face. Service pointed to his scouts. "How many bodies inside now?"

"Twinny we know of," Allerdyce said.

"Trucks?"

"Two, dey just come back for turd trip today."

"White Wilt and his pal?"

"Have not seen," Worm said.

"But White Wilt's here?"

"Dunno," Allerdyce said. "He come in, but we ain't seen 'im go back oot."

"And the other one?"

"Same. Came an' went oot, den come back and ain't went oot again," Allerdcye reported.

This was new. Nankervus and George were both inside? Were they together? If so, they could present a problem for unmasking him, or worse. "Okay, good. Everyone head out."

McKower walked with Service as far as she could, him talking, her listening.

"The injured kid Something pulled out of the mine shaft is Harlikin's son. The ROCKs are providing eagle feathers to Indians for a small fee and mineral rights. The Indians do the deal because it keeps the government out of their business, and with leases, they can pick and choose. Service looked at his captain. "You with me?"

She nodded.

"Harlikin's wife was in the process of trying to sell some of her assets, or maybe unload the whole shebang. I don't know which and it doesn't matter to us. But I do know she was in negotiations when she went missing. And there's good reason to believe that her son was either last to see her, or actually with her when she went off the radar."

McKower said, "My God."

Service went on. "I have a thing in my head that I just can't shake."

"We all have those days," she said supportively.

"No, Lis, an actual thing, a device an MSP commo tech put into my head behind my left ear. With it, everything I hear they hear—and record."

"Even now?" McKower asked.

Service nodded solemnly. "Everything."

"You never sought approval."

"And I'm not asking forgiveness either. With this thing in my head, the MSP can hook right into whatever commo systems Harlikin has and can in fact appropriate it for our own use." Theoretically. He didn't share this aspect, and continued briefing her as they walked. "If this thing goes south, I'll call for a George from you guys. The MSP's man is O'Dell. He is a very peculiar player, but seems damn good at his job. I have an unrelenting hunch that Harlikin is no military guy and the whole militia thing a kind of front."

The captain's jaw went tight.

"I think this guy is totally about money and I'm going to offer to buy him out, purchase his militia from him. When I make my offer, he'll have two choices, buy in or throw me out by whatever means he uses for that sort of thing."

"You think he's violent?"

"Somebody in his outfit is. Remember what they tried to do to Abel Tooler. If Harlikin lets me leave to arrange the financing, we will call in our Task Force teammates to prepare them for the takedown."

She was shaking her head. "You're out of your mind, Grady."

"Not at all, Lis. I think I've finally gotten this guy's spoor and it is all green."

He didn't tell her the rest of his plan, how he planned to counter the counterfeit colonel if he was reluctant to make a deal, or wanted to play tough guy. "Once this guy and his people are in custody, I'm outta here, color me gone."

The captain looked at him and caught his sleeve. "There will be a lot of downstream details to untangle and deal with," she reminded him.

"You know I'll do my duty on all that, and wrap it up, even give you a nicely written report."

"And then?" she asked and Grady shrugged, gave her a strong hug, wheeled, and headed down into the lion's den, a place he had been many, many times before.

CHAPTER 41

Camp ROCK

KEWEENAW COUNTY

Who makes the fairest show means most deceit.
—William Shakespeare, *Pericles*

The camp's "entrance" was manned by two Mustard Seeds Service didn't recognize, and that didn't surprise him. The personnel situation here seemed strangely fluid, almost a revolving door, more evidence in his mind that this was not about training and preparation for someone's version of God's work, but something different, and he thought he had some inkling now of what it was.

When he identified himself, one of the sentries said, "The old man's expecting you. He calls over to us every hour or so to see if you've showed up yet. You know the way?"

Service nodded. "Let the colonel know I'm here, but I need to put on my uniform and then I'll be over. You two are the only ones I see. Where are the rest of our people?"

"We don't control such things," the talking sentry said.

"How many people have come back before me?" Service continued to press.

"We don't keep a count," the talker answered.

What kind of Mickey Mouse security was this? Early on, it had been formal and seemed formidable, but not anymore, not like this. This was pathetic, amateur, and loosey-goosey by any definition. "Canteen open yet?"

"What canteen?" the second guard asked. "We just got here today ourselves and nobody ain't said nothing about no canteen."

"Wasn't cheap, neither, getting here," the first man added. "We assumed with this high cost, the chow here would be outstanding. Is it?"

"Been all right," Service told them, "if you can stomach MREs held over from Iraq, Afghanistan, and other off-shore forays." He had not thought about this angle before; whenever you were undercover you focused on avoiding detection, not finding the chow line. What had that guard said, "Wasn't cheap neither." Service stepped away but pivoted back. "Question for you guys, the K and C still at twenty-five?"

"*Twenty-five*?" the talker shot back. "*We wish*. It's thirty now, cash-money. *When* was it twenty-five?"

"A while back. You guys on the installment plan?"

"*What* installment plan?" talker said. "Nobody told us nothing about no installments, just thirty grand each, in cash and up front."

How long had the ROCK operation been suspended, four weeks now? He had a hard time keeping a timeline in his head. Whatever it had been, the K and C had been upped by 20 percent, and no terms or accommodations offered, at least to this pair. It would be good to talk to Chas about money here as a symptom. Marschke read money like others read classic novels. The stench of money had been here all through his six months, but seemed even stronger now.

After changing into his mustard seed outfit, Service went to report in and there got another surprise. Harlikin was alone, no body-men in sight.

"John Eben Batanovich," the colonel greeted him. "What avian paradise did we pluck you from on this cycle?"

Service had assumed the breaks were born of caution over security concerns, and now the colonel was calling the breaks part of a cycle. Most cycles were planned. Had this whole thing been, and to what end? "My last job got shortstopped. Bird groups are always scrapping for funding. I took a run out to the Dakotas to pop prairie dogs."

Harlikin leaned forward. "How many you get?"

"About twelve hundred in thirty-six hours."

"Twelve hundred kills is superb shooting. Is there anything more fun than popping varmints?" the insipidly grinning colonel asked.

"My girlfriend prefers the kind of shooting that doesn't involve prairie dogs," Service said, to see what sort of response this would provoke.

Harlikin raised an eyebrow. "She a looker, your girl?"

"The Miss South Dakota people seemed to think so."

"She win?"

"Couldn't," Service told the man. "They did away with swimsuit competition that year. Had they not dropped it, she would have won hands down."

"She look good in a swimsuit, does she?"

"Looks even better without one and the way I figure it, slap a swimsuit on that architecture and the prize was hers."

"What's she do for a living, this girl?'"

"Works on her uncle's cattle ranch."

"A true-blue American woman, your girl. She a good worker?"

"No idea, Colonel. When she and I are together, she doesn't like getting too far from a bed. But she works a whole lot when we're *not* together."

Service decided to fish a little bit. "You'd think," he said, "that God might find some ways to push more cash into the pockets and purses of the brethren."

"Men don't carry purses," Harlikin said.

"Women do and when we use the word *brethren*, we exclude women. Seems like our organization could be a lot stronger with women on board, physically and fiscally."

"Knights never ask Jesus for handouts," Harlikin said. "Real men take care of their own financial obligations."

"Seems the Lord could at least step on the balls of inflation. Word among the men is that K and C has gone up to thirty thousand and if true, that's one big jump from twenty-five in a very short time."

"The announcement may be sudden, but the need has been steadily building up. Hated to do it, but no choice if we're going to keep properly outfitted and kitted."

"The more the K and C goes up, the smaller the pool we'll have to draw from," Service pointed out.

"We're only looking for a *few* good men, not a Roman legion," Harlikin said.

"Few is certainly what I've seen so far today."

"Sometimes the human eyes doesn't take in all there is to see."

Gibberish from the man? "Most people aren't stupid."

"Do not misunderstand me," the colonel said. "I'm talking science and measured capabilities. Our brains use 20 to 50 percent of their capacity to process just what we see and that is extremely *wasteful*. Our standard human visual equipment's pretty outdated. The human eye picks up radiation from visible light that strikes our pupils, and here I am talking a few hundred thousandths of an inch. Just about everything on this beautiful earth can see much better than we can, and can do so without using the high level of brain capacity we eat up. Just to take on raw material. Talk about being trapped naked in the wilderness."

What the hell was the man on about now, and where was this headed?

Harlikin's countenance seemed to grow darker, his eyes narrowing toward slits but the pressure suddenly seemed to open and his eyes popped open. "Fewer people means we can equip them in ways to overcome our natural biological shortcomings. Our focus has to be on our technology and supplies, not numbers of bodies, and when it comes to technology, all magic boils down to money. God gave us these poor eyes as a test of our willpower."

Grady Service had learned over his long career when and how to be silent when someone was in a spilling mood, and Harlikin seemed to be wanting to do just that.

"*Money*," Harlikin said loudly, "and thank you Lord. Money maketh the world move, this world *and* the next one. The better we position ourselves here, the better positioned we'll be up *there*."

Money makes the next world move, and God gave man what sounded like the worst eyes in creation? Whoa. "Money, sir?"

"Indeed. God gave us these lousy eyes as a test. The rest of his animals are stuck with what they they're born with but only humans can improve on what we have, and therein make ourselves better and better. All it takes is cash."

"Sucks to be another animal," Service said, playing along.

The colonel sharply clapped his hands together and laughed sardonically. "Amen, Brother Knight. The Lord gave us the brains to create money which, in turn, helps us improve the other basics he provided us at the starting line."

"Brains are often in short order," Service argued, trying to support the colonel's roll.

"Amen again. Look at how science has given us the ability to own the night in modern warfare. Without that, we're as blind at night as in the daytime, but thanks to science, come nigh now, we're far better off and downright lethal. That's what money does for us."

"And science," Service added.

"Money *is* science, Birdman. Always has been in one form or another. And money's our fuel too. If it's good enough for Jesus, it's good enough for his knights."

If you listened carefully, Harlikin made no sense. But his appeal wasn't intellectual, it was through the guts and prejudices of certain falsely presumed histories.

Charismatic leaders got people jacked up to emotional highs, then took their money and, usually, got them to willingly hand it over. Infected by rhetoric, it often didn't take much to separate listeners into opponents and followers, the latter willingly abandoning healthy human skepticism.

"Thirty thousand is peanuts to become a Knight," Harlikin insisted in a revelatory voice. "It is the best bargain this side of the other side."

Rich ground here, Service thought, exactly what he was hoping for, but before he made his pitch, he wanted more preparation. "I'm back, but not many others are. What's the program here? We can't train effectively with huge schedule interruptions."

"The program is what the Lord says it is," Harlikin said. "You object to that?"

"No sir. Seems to me that He is the ultimate boss."

"Never lose that thought, Birdman."

"I guess what I'm asking then is when does the Big Boss want us to resume our training?"

"That depends on many factors, Birdman."

"Such as?" Service asked.

"Some mysteries lose their elegance if revealed before their time," the colonel said.

"Like great vintages of wine," Service said.

"Surely similar."

Time to start pressing the game. "But some must know the mysteries and their answers," Service said.

"To the most deserving, Birdman, only to the most deserving."

"Who are?"

"One and two steps up the hierarchical ladder from where your boots now stand."

Service smirked. "That sounds like a spiel from Bernie Madoff," Service said. "What's it cost to move up the hierarchical ladder?"

"Well, that's a matter of timing, my friend. You came in at twenty-five and put yourself on the bottom level, and with your next fifty can move up to Level Two, but if that doesn't happen relatively quickly, that price will jump to seventy-five. I'd ardently hoped you'd come home to us with the fifty this time."

"I have the fifty, Colonel, but what I *don't* have is a good idea of what exactly it is I'm *buying*."

"Peace of mind and joy. You're buying in, son. In."

"I have peace of mind and joy whenever the girlfriend rolls off me, and that only costs me a beer or two. And there isn't any sort of financial crap to bother us. You jumped the K and C from twenty-five to thirty, but Level Two now goes from fifty to seventy-five? That feels either like gouging or some kind of weird Ponzi scheme."

"Are you making an accusation, sir?"

"Absolutely not," Service said. "Yet."

"Perhaps you need to look at this differently and not dwell on numbers. At the next levels you will be part of all the decision-making and have access to all our latest intel."

"How many levels? I've heard of only two until now."

"Four in all."

"What's the K and C on Levels Three and Four?"

"The K and C on Level Three is currently at 125, but going up to 140, Level Four, the highest, is on seventy-five, going to two hundred."

Service leaned back in his chair. "Two hundred grand for Level Four. How many Fours *are* there?"

"You are not entitled to know that until you *are* one."

"What about Level Ones and Twos?"

"Also confidential, and not for public consumption."

"I'm not the public, Colonel. I paid in full for Level One. I'm one of yours."

"Not mine, Birdman. You and I, all of us belong to the *Lord*, and let me remind you that you need to go back outside and bring back the fifty before that goes up, and as much as I enjoy your company, which I greatly do, I won't hold you here jabbering like old men over a wood stove."

"Why no body-men today?" Service pointed out.

"I don't need one," the colonel said. "I trust you, Birdman. You have integrity."

"How does one get to be a body-man?" Service asked.

"That's Level Five whom I select from Level Four candidates. Frankly, Four and Five are technically out of your league for now. You should concern yourself with cementing Level Two at your K and C. When you have yourself in good standing at Two, we can then seriously talk about your future and your options."

"I appreciate your concern right now, sir, but to be frank I'm tired and a bit hungry. I'd like to grab an MRE, relax and think on all this before I head back outside to get your money."

"Our blessed Lord's money, Birdman, not mine."

"I stand corrected. Can I bring you an MRE, sir?"

"No thank you. But go ahead and take your break."

Service got to the door and looked over at the man. "Why did you ask to meet with me today?"

"I meet with all Level Ones who come home. And let me ask you this: Has our interrupted schedule played havoc with your bird-count jobs?"

"I'd rather we talk about that at another time, Colonel. Let's leave it at this: I managed to patch together some short stints. I even found a private benefactor who wanted a hammerhead survey on one of his properties."

"Hammerhead?"

"Inside jargon for woodpeckers."

"Where was this job?"

"Not all that far. He paid me what you want for K and C for Level Two."

"Fifty thousand to count birds? That is truly impressive."

"The bird community has a lot of wealthy people who know what they want and how to get what they want, and they are happy to pay what they think it's worth."

"Perhaps that's the business we should be in," Harlikin mused.

Was Harlikin saying ROCK was a business rather than some sort of gun-toting holy calling? Service could feel his hunch glowing warmer.

"MRE time, sir?"

"Dismissed," the colonel said. "This has been a spirited and useful conversation. Have you always told me the truth, Birdman?" the colonel asked, staring at him.

"I'd ask you the same thing, sir. You know what they say among card sharps."

"I'm not a card man, enlighten me."

Service grinned and said, "First bullshitter doesn't have a chance, and now I'm hungry and that's *not* bullshit."

CHAPTER 42

Camp ROCK

KEWEENAW COUNTY

Bait the hook well. This fish will bite.
—William Shakespeare, *Much Ado About Nothing*

Grady Service's mind was ranging like a strike dog hound after a bear.

There was a year, he could no longer remember exactly when, the department sent him to Benzie County to help other officers work fish runs. It was a county where drooling human birds flocked from all over to snag salmon. The CO he'd worked with had a reputation for relentless pursuit of cheaters, and a willingness to mix it up with those who refused to accept their fate with some grace.

"This is the greatest," his partner would chirp incessantly as they worked from group to group in the dark. "The fish are our bait and pull fools to us like magnets. All we have to do is harvest fools."

Unlike facing the decision he was about to make, busting fish snaggers was simple in theory and practice. This thing was neither. Was Harlikin a fish in a river drawing others to him, or something else? The man seemed to trade and traffic in religion, or he tried to come across that way, but in Service's head he heard only empty exhortations to the Lord, and while his ears heard one thing, the longtime CO's gut heard something entirely different.

Like a lot of militia leaders and founders, Harlikin admittedly dealt in guns. The base fix for many such groups, whatever else their angle, was to protect their right to firearms, often against the government, or elements of it they imagined were going to take away their weapons. In most of these groups he'd brushed against over the years, the chorus of all songs was guns-guns-guns, but the ROCKs seemed different in this regard and there were never enough of them gathered at any one time to get any reasonable sense of who they thought they were, or hoped to become. With Harlikin, it wasn't guns blatantly, but wireless high-speed devices or WHSDs, and why the attempt to be so cute? Politics? More importantly, why did everything in and among the ROCKs seem to loop over or back to money? Money *from* his troops, not *to* his troops, and this seemed off-kilter as well. Why train-train-train, then stop abruptly and go on some kind of hiatus, then resume like nothing had happened? This whole outfit seemed an exercise in high-speed wheel-spinning and make-work, with little productivity, virtually no real goals to strive for and no mission to pump up the troops. The weapons, equipment they paid for with their K and C, were real enough but their uniforms were flashy yellow in a way that emphasized their poor quality. They were issued the latest model of commercially available night vision devices, but never trained at night, and what the hell was that about? Did the flashy cheap gold appearance of the unis betray something in Harlikin's character or his creed, or was something else in play? What creed? The group soft-mouthed anti-government rhetoric, but nothing they trained for seemed to point toward any measurable end, only more pointless training and more money, and finally, money was where his mind landed.

If the colonel was a harvester, it was of the Second Amendment's sweetest fruits, guns and money. Or were those two synonymous? Guns *were* money, whether you made them, sold them, or tricked them out, and brought them home to your castle.

Makers risked capital to create and manufacture product; dealers risked capital for wholesale inventory and attendant costs; buyers paid for something they deemed useful, for whatever reason. The common denominator was money from the slipstream of money-making from weapons and ammunition. No other conclusion to be reached here based on what he knew, which was spotty at best, but was pushing him. The gun thing was in essence a money thing and secondarily a matter of constitutionally guaranteed citizen rights. Or more accurately, the right of certain citizens to do as they pleased with their guns and brook no interference from anyone anywhere. Just as the First Amendment gave throat to free speech and words, words, words carried by all kinds of old-fashioned media and now by burgeoning social media where every man could be his own media outlet, and if they chose, use such media to create a revenue stream from their political beefs. A nice package indeed.

Could this be said of the citizen's right to worship or not as they pleased? Had organized religion turned into businesses that ran like bakeries or laundries? Certainly there had been some clowns on TV scamming Social Security for Jesus from the infirm, elderly, and mildly mad. But mainline religions? He suspected but could not prove anything and he decided it was irrelevant what argument or sales pitch Harlikin chose for scamming money. It was the scam that was illegal.

There were also some questions of Harlikin and his missing wife, the role of their son, and given that the son had been seen around here, the father-son connection. And why did the kid have such a different name?

Abel Tooler seemed to believe that the US government was running an underground persecution of Christians. If so, had Harlikin slotted the ROCKs into the middle of this? Their name certainly seemed to confirm it. What exactly did the colonel think he and his little group could do to have an effect on the presumed underground war?

And what was this thing about wanting to be king, and allegedly working to get rid of the governor?

One way or another, the next few hours were going to bring a collision with the counterfeit colonel.

Counterfeit? The word struck like a sledgehammer! Ages before, his old man, a game warden before him, and a true force in his day, especially when he was sober, would tell him, "You want to catch big fish, use the right bait. Big fish eat other big fish *and* little fish, but when they eat mostly big ones they don't have to eat as often or work as hard. You listening, kid?"

He remembered nodding dumbly and the old man churning on, "Here's the real trick to big fish. Give them big baits and dangle them so the fish can grab them without a lot of effort, then hammer that s.o.b. with all you have to bury the hook hard. Once you have him on, don't horse him to you. Let him run but keep constant pressure on him and keep turning his head. Big force to start, steady force thereafter, and never let up until the fish is netted or on the beach. Every time that big bastard tries to dive down and give you a head shake, remind him you're controlling the situation."

"What if my line breaks?" young Grady had asked.

"Then you shoulda checked the damn thing before you put on the damn bait. If you're gonna do a job, do the whole damn thing," his father said with a snarl.

Grady had argued. "We can't catch every fish."

"Why the hell not?" his old man roared back. "Look, boy. A big fish can look and sound big, *or* small, but a little fish can *only* look and sound little. Use your sense and your gut to see what the hell it is you're fishing for."

Was Harlikin a real big fish or a counterfeit?

There was no way to know yet, but for the moment Harlikin was the biggest fish available and he had the attention of several federal agencies. Another pearl from his late father dropped into his mind: "Always wish for a lot, kid, otherwise you're wasting the damn wish."

"How many wishes do we get?" he'd asked his father.

"How the hell would I know?" the old man roared and slapped his son on the back. The blow felt almost like affection.

"But *you* just told me to wish for a lot."

"Kid, where's the rule that says your old man has to make sense all the time?"

Why was he thinking of his father today, here, now? He walked to the edge of the camp property and said quietly, "O'Dell, call Chas Marschke and tell him to ring you, then put it through on this connection, but turn off the recorder, until Marschke says the call is over. You hear?"

"*Ha*," O'Dell said. "I don't have that number."

"Ha. You think this is funny?"

"*Ha* is Vulcan for yes," O'Dell said.

Service said the number. "Do this quickly, I don't have a lot of time."

"You all right?" O'Dell asked in a concerned voice.

"*Ha*. Make the damn call."

A minute later, Chas's voice was in Grady's head. "Got another ask, Chas. Call French Lick, Indiana, the high school or the local paper, and find out if they ever had a seven-foot-four player there named Mesnard George? Second, you remember some years back you put together a balance sheet for me?"

"You mean a statement of net worth. We do that annually. Do you look at them? You never react one way or another."

He hated to tell the man he threw them away or burned them, and rarely read them. "Right, whatever. Pull it out and update it, bring it forward to now, with today's date. How long to make that happen?"

"Minutes," Chas said. "Everything is already in file and easily pulled together."

"I want this thing to scream the bottom-line number."

"Like a poke in the eye with a sharp stick?"

"Exactly. And when it's done, send it to Tuesday."

"You sure about this, boss?"

"Never been more sure of anything."

"You sound like you're in one of your zones," his financial man said.

"One more thing. Tuesday and I are getting married. Take care of the paperwork. She gets everything if I bite it."

"Does she have any idea of the magnitude involved here?"

"She doesn't even know there is a here, here," Service said.

"Oh my," Marschke said. "I hope her heart is strong."

"How long until you can have her as my beneficiary?"

"Minutes. I've got all the authorities and officials I need close at hand."

"Ok, French Lick, numbers to her, and a copy of my will to her."

"On it boss. You want feedback on French Lick?"

"You bet. Call O'Dell, he'll get it to me."

Marschke had once told him his net worth was equivalent to that of a dictator in a moderately large resource-rich African nation. He wondered what it would be now, and how Tuesday would react.

Service went inside the camp's barrack building and got an MRE, which he heated in the kitchen and ate slowly.

With his first taste of the MRE fajita and Mexican rice, O'Dell was in his head.

"Your friend says to tell you a longtime sportswriter in French Lick says there's never been a seven-four kid in town, much less any player or even an adult of that height. And nobody by the name of George, Harlikin, or Gabbart has graduated from the local high school. Good enough?"

"Good work, clear," Service said, and finished wolfing down his meal.

Service walked back to the entry area and found the same pair of sentries on duty. "Any more troops come in since me?"

"No, it's been real quiet," the original talker volunteered.

"You guys on this post yesterday?"

Both nodded. "And the day before, too," this from the talker.

"You seen any groups coming back, you know, four or five at a time?"

"Just singles."

"And only singles going back out?"

"Affirmative," the quieter sentry said. "You must be one of the smart knights."

"Are you saying not all knights are smart, son?"

"I'm just saying we can't all be Firesteins or Einstones," the man quipped.

"You trying to say Firestone or Einstein? Or maybe you mean Harvey Fierstein the actor, and Charlie Einstein, the writer."

"You know," the man said, "the Yids Kids tribe."

"You got something against Yids?"

"Other way 'round, they've got a thing for us. Look what they done to Jesus."

"You need to pay better attention," Service told the men.

"We can't all be brain bombs," the quieter of the two said.

"You both come up with the K and C?"

"You think we'd be standing guard here if we hadn't?"

"What if I told you that this whole operation is a scam. All the colonel wants is your money and your silence. You get nothing in return."

Both men started to laugh, but stopped when they saw Service's stone-serious face.

"Just joking, boys. Lighten up, but don't think you know everything all the time. Surprises come along now and then and bite us all on the ass."

"We ain't so easy to bite," the mouthy sentry said.

CHAPTER 43

Camp ROCK

KEWEENAW COUNTY

> Where be his quiddities now, his quillets, his cases, his tenures, and his tricks?
>
> —William Shakespeare, *Hamlet*

Service glanced at the low ridge where his people were. They would be wondering what he was doing. He turned his back to the ridge and lit a cigarette. "O'Dell, ears on?"

A now-familiar voice said, "*Ha*."

"This is not a joke."

"Calm down, Detective. Remember, *Ha* means yes in Vulcan."

Shit, he'd already forgotten. "Again, I don't speak Vulcan."

"I think best in Vulcan when things get tight. I sense things are about to get real tight, am I right?"

Service found himself smiling. Did nothing knock this kid off balance? "Wouldn't surprise me. Have you looked at their communication system?"

"*Ha*. It's *nenik*."

"English."

"Yes, it's elementary."

"Can you take it over and use it?"

"*Ha*. Just say the word."

"Go blue. You got that? It means send in the cavalry."

"*Ha*. You want the words in Vulcan?"

Service exhaled loudly. Why not? He pulled out a pen and held up the palm of his hand. "Lay them on me."

"*Hal-tar* means Go, and *pla-kur* means blue, *hal-tar pla-kur*."

"Spell that."

O'Dell did and Service read it back to him. "*Hal-tar pla-kur*."

"*Hal-tur pla-kur*. It's written on the palm of my hand. If it gets smudged, I'll just say it in English, okay?"

"*Ha*," O'Dell said. "Be safe, man."

Service dropped his cigarette and mashed it with his boot heel. "O'Dell?"

"*Ha*?"

"Whatever I hear live, everyone here will hear live over the group's commo system, *Ha*?"

"*Ha*. Right on. We've got this, Detective."

Harlikin was still alone, staring at his jars of ticks, which were crawling around inside the pickle jar. Service knocked. "Am I interrupting, sir?"

The colonel pointed to a chair. "Not at all. You headed out for cash?"

"I am, but first I want to settle on exactly how much I need."

"We've been over this. Your K and C for Level Two is fifty thousand."

"That part I know, and that's not my question."

The colonel sat up straight. "Because your bird sponsor covered you on your last job."

"No, that's not quite it, either. Truth is, I didn't need fifty thou from another source. I have plenty of my own."

"You never told us that."

"Unless this is some kind of cult, why would I? It's none of your business where my money comes from."

"Cult is a difficult concept to pin down," the colonel said. "The concept alone frightens and intimidates a lot of folks, but puts iron in the certainty of shared belief in others."

"Listen, Colonel. I don't care if this is a cult or a culinary school. I've played your game by your rules and now we're here alone. What's *really* going on?"

"You know."

"I don't."

Service peeked at the palm of his hand. Skin: Nature's notebook.

Service muttered, "*hal-tar pla-kur*." But he didn't say it so O'Dell would hear it. This wasn't the time to pull the trigger.

"What was that you said?" Harlikin asked.

"Just clearing my throat, Colonel. Sorry. Why am I here? The place seems empty."

"I'm looking for a number two."

"You lost your number two?"

"I'm still looking for the right man."

"Why not promote from within?"

"I am. You're one of us."

"But four levels down and you don't know me, and you can't possibly be certain you can trust me."

"That's a bit harsh of a self-assessment," Harlikin said. "I am a very astute judge of people."

"I deal in reality, Colonel."

The colonel chuckled. "This from a man who counts *birds* for a living?"

"That's not all I do, Colonel. How long have we been out of here now, a month?"

"Not everyone is out. Some are here, some are elsewhere. You lack the big picture."

"Right and all those who *aren't* here, are losing ground in training, and even all those who are here while you're renting to other groups are also losing training time while you rake in cash."

"A leader must first ensure that his organization is fiscally sound."

"I agree, which is what I want to talk about, and here's the gist. What is this place, sir, its real purpose?"

"It's our Fortress, our citadel."

"I call bullshit. I could take this place with a half dozen men in less than an hour."

The colonel stared dumbly at him.

Service said, "You're a smart guy and obviously you understand that to maintain a certain level of operational efficiency, training has to be continuous, not sporadic, and because this place has, so far, seemed to be the definition of sporadic, that suggests to me there are other goals here, other purposes."

Harlikin didn't look nervous and seeing this, Service felt his stomach flutter. "The men here talk like all men talk in a military unit. Some here think you want to be a king, but that doesn't fit in my mind. Kings in reality are rarely absolute rulers, even when they think they are, or claim to be. Other groups get more training time than we do."

The colonel slowly drew in a deep breath.

Calm before the storm? "All this suggests two possibilities to me, Sir. One, this place is a front for something else, or two, the only purpose here is to raise cash through K and C, that this is not so much of a militia as a new take on the old Amway pyramid scams."

Harlikin chuckled sardonically. "I had you down for a thinker, right from the start, but I think you somehow missed the depth of my commitment to our cause, Birdman."

What cause? "I think we're right now in the process of establishing that very thing," Service retorted.

"This is a far more delicate and complex undertaking than you can possibly know."

"You name the price, sir."

Harlikin froze. "What did you say?"

"I said name a price. I want to buy this outfit—the ROCKs."

"You're quite a jokester, Birdman."

"I want to buy the ROCK op, this camp, and your eagle feather business."

"I never figured you for a jokester, Batanovich."

"I like jokes as much as the next man, Colonel, but when I talk money, I never joke. What's your price?"

"In business, sir, one does not pluck such figures higgedly-piggedly from thin air."

"Then bounce it off your balance sheet and pluck it out of the air from there," Service said.

"I refuse to pull figures from vapors," the colonel insisted.

The negotiation seemed to be underway. From here on, all talk would be toward establishing and agreeing on price. "Pull it from where you want, but I need a hard number and I need it now. We'll negotiate based on that, but this is your only chance to move this thing, and if I don't leave here with an agreement, I'm gone period and permanently, and you can find another Number Two."

Harlikin was frozen in place. Were others in the camp hearing all this? Service stood up, opened the pickle jar, scooped out some ticks, and popped them into his mouth like they were sugared nuts.

Harlikin's eyes popped as Service swallowed the ticks and lit a cigarette. After a puff or two, he looked at the colonel. "How big is our force?"

"Competitive secret."

"Bullshit. How about we start at ten million on the nose."

"I never gave any indication that I wanted to sell."

"You didn't have to. All you think about is money. Let's make it twelve million?"

The man's hand seemed to move toward his mouth, but he stopped himself. "Cash?"

"No, a cashier's check."

"A cashier's check means a bank is providing the money."

"True, but I own the bank."

"I don't understand," Harlikin said.

"You don't have to. You want a cashier's check for twelve million or not? Yes or no."

"Twelve million, with 25 percent up front in cash, nonsequential bills, and the rest in a cashier's check, cashable immediately."

"No cash up front beyond the check. That's my offer. If we agree, I'll go out and arrange ~~the~~ financing and bring back the check. If not, I'm leaving now and I'm done with you, this place, and this cause."

Harlikin nodded.

Service said. "Am I to understand that you are nodding your head in the affirmative for the deal, or that you are nodding that you understand I'm leaving?"

"Yes," Harlikin said. "Yes, twelve million."

"And I want a complete membership list as well as the names of contacts from groups you rent to. Agreed?"

Another nod.

"And I'll tell you what. You still interested in that piece of property below Mount Horace Greeley?"

"How do you know about *that*?"

"That doesn't matter. I own the property. What do you want to offer for that? You'll soon have twelve million in your pocket to play with."

"We'll discuss that after this deal is closed and I have my money. How long do you need for this transaction?"

Service looked at this watch. "This late? Overnight."

"I thought you owned the bank."

"I do, but owners don't disrupt their employees for petty business deals."

"Twelve million is anything but petty."

"For you," Service said and went to the door. "Back tomorrow."

Outside, he saw that the sentries at the entry point were gone, and nobody had replaced them, and this made him smile. Those two had gotten the message and voted with their feet. How many others would do the same?

Allerdyce met him at the wood line. "Me and your girlie captain went inside and found us four boxes of eagle feathers," he reported.

"You remove them from the premises?"

McKower stepped out of the woods. "They're still in there, but we now know where. There's like five hundred feathers." She looked at Allerdyce.

"*Girlie captain.*" Allerdyce smiled his toothless smile.

McKower said, "This number alone, from the standpoint of criminal fines, is a small fortune. Did Harlikin not understand the value of what he had?"

"We have until tomorrow to bring a check," Service told the captain, who shook her head.

"What will you do tonight?" she asked.

"Make arrangements for the money. And sleep. Where's Worm?" he asked.

'Grady, you can't do that," McKower said.

"I asked where she is."

"Nabbed her a jamoke," Limpy said, cackling. "Beek bugger, too."

Further in the woods he found Patty Something and Bapcat sitting with Worm, and all three of them looking at a bloodied, cuffed, and trussed up Mesnard George, aka, Gecko, aka White Wilt, possibly Harlikin's son, or his missing wife's son. Either was possible. Neither was clear.

"What's this about?" White Wilt asked and glanced at Worm. "And what planet is *that* thing from?"

"Let's talk about your mother," Service said.

Mesnard George said, "I want a lawyer. I'm not saying any more until I have my lawyer."

"Fine, soon as you're booked."

"We heard the whole thing inside," Bapcat told him. "Way too slick! You didn't even have to kick down a door."

"Yet," Service reminded him. "There's still tomorrow."

"They are coming out of there like rats off a sinking ship," PCO Something said.

Service asked, “You guys help Worm bring down White Wilt?”

Patty raised an eyebrow. “She didn’t need our help. Should we be sweeping up their runners?”

“How many have come out so far?”

“Eight,” Bapcat said, “and this one.”

He shook his head. “Don’t grab runners today. Tomorrow will come soon enough.”

“What if Harlikin pulls out?” McKower asked.

“You guys will be here to intercept and stop him.”

“On what basis?”

“Eagle feathers.”

“Where’s our probable cause?”

“Complaints and allegations from Indians.”

“We can *prove* that?”

“We won’t need to. Just stop him and hold him.”

“Where are you going?”

“Money run and other important unfinished business.”

CHAPTER 44

Houghton

HOUGHTON COUNTY

Our remedies oft in ourselves do lie.
—William Shakespeare, *All's Well That Ends Well*

The manager of the Third Iceberg Bank branch in Calumet complained to Service that he didn't have enough cash to cover his situation, but a call to Marschke set the machine in motion and quickly the manager of the branch in Houghton said he would be happy to facilitate the deal.

Service rarely remembered the names of local banks, his or anyone's, and fell back on Marschke jargon, in which any bank was the Sixty Sixth Most Least Bank. Chas called bankers *BAHhnkers* and sneered whenever he said the word.

Service called Friday as he drove toward Houghton.

"Damn!" she greeted him. "The pool man just shucked his duds, and you pick *now* to call?"

"Give him my deepest sympathies and tell him to go fish elsewhere. You can add, that he can expect to die as soon as I figure out who he is."

"I'll never tell," she said coyly.

"I've got ways," he said.

"I seem to very vaguely remember that," she said.

"Listen up," he told her. "Explain to me why we've never gotten married."

"*What*?" she chirped. "Here I am staring at another man's wee-wee and you suddenly you . . . want . . . to know . . . from *me*, why we've never married? Did you take a round in the hat? Better to ask yourself *that* question, Bub."

"I think I have," he said.

"Did you find an answer?" she asked.

"Something about me being a thoughtless, inconsiderate jerk."

"By Jove, you *have* thought about it."

"So what do you think?" he asked.

"About the pool man's foot-long?"

"I'm being serious and you want to play cute?"

"Sorry, it's not really a foot long, but it's pretty good."

"*Tuesday*."

"*Grady*."

"Shall we?" he said.

"Shall we what?"

"What I just said."

"Now who is playing cute?"

"No," he said, "and I'm thinking when this op concludes, we should get married."

"*You* decided?"

"No, I mean, yes, from my view, but what about you?"

"What, you want *me* to decide?" she came back.

"Geez," he said. "I'm trying to ask you to marry me."

This was met by silence, then, "Do *not* tell me you are having a premonition of getting your big butt waxed in this rodeo you're in."

"That's *creepy*," he said. "I just want to marry you."

"So suddenly?"

"I've always wanted to."

"But you never asked me before. Want to explain past versus today?"

"Maybe I didn't know how to ask."

Friday fired off a maniacal laugh. "Good God, Grady. That is *so* lame coming from a man who can talk the pants off a woman a hundred miles away."

"I can't do that," he said.

"Like hell," she said. "You're just not here to see . . . I *will*," she added.

"Take off your pants?"

"Those are off, Bub. I will marry you."

"You think the kid will approve?"

"Our kid already thinks we are married."

"So how do we explain it to him?"

"We don't. We'll let the judge explain it."

"Big do in a church?" he asked.

"Not for me, that what you want?" she asked.

"Court's good for me," he said.

Friday asked, "You think the judge will be offended if I wear white?"

"The judges we know up here couldn't wear white themselves."

"That's not nice."

"Wear what you want."

"*Could* we do this in the raw?" she asked, "sprinkled with gold glitter and draped in bling?"

"If you want to get married in the nude, we'll find us a judge to officiate."

"You're being very accommodating," she told him.

"You plan the details?"

"Who will stand up for you?" she asked.

"Shigun."

"He's a child."

"Tree, then."

"Also emotionally a child, but at least he meets the age requirement. His behavior is another issue. I'll ask Kalina to stand with me."

"What about Maridly?"

"Flower girl," she said.

"Too gender-restrictive," he said.

"What kind of Kool-Aid are those young female COs serving you over there?"

"Let's let the kids decide."

"What if Shigun wants to be flower girl?" Friday said.

"He can't. He can be flower boy. You *think* that's what he wants?"

"He doesn't even know any of this yet. Who do we invite?"

"The courts have occupancy rules. Just us, and the kids, and the Treebones. Let's keep it small and quick."

"When will your op be finished?"

"Won't be long," he said. "What's with your cold case?"

"Still not sure, but I've learned that the FBI guy died of natural causes. He was a prospector by hobby. Complete coincidence. His heart stopped, the rest of the injuries were solely products of falling, gravity, and impact on nasty rocks."

"He wasn't their inside man?"

"You'll have to ask the Feebs that question."

"They tell you he died of natural causes?"

She laughed. "Not a chance. They told me nada. But I have my own sources."

"So we don't know who the dead FBI man was in his professional role?"

"Only God knows," Friday said.

"And She's not talking."

"Got that right, Bub. What about rings?" she asked.

"They still carry prizes in Cracker Jack boxes?"

She giggled. "Works for me."

"Did you get an email from Marschke?" he asked.

"Yah, what's all that crap about?"

"It's my will and a statement of net worth."

"I didn't even look at it."

"Do it now."

"Is there a problem?" she asked suspiciously.

"You tell me."

A minute or two went by and nothing but silence on the other end. "Are you there? Tuesday?"

"What the hell *is* this?" she said.

"Personal net worth."

"This has got to be a gag."

"No joke, it's real."

"Now I'm about to *gag*! Seriously, you never said a damn word about *this*! *Nothing*, not a damn thing!"

"I don't pay any attention to it."

"Just seeing those numbers in my phone makes me shake and quake."

"Then don't look. The point is, it all goes to you for the kids if you know . . . "

"You *are* having premonitions," she said. "I knew it."

"I don't have premonitions—or post-monitions either. And by the way just what the hell *is* a monition?"

"Dammit, Grady. Where are you?"

"Headed to Houghton. I'm going to crash with Shark."

"You know," she said, "I'd be just fine with rings made from twist ties, and do not get your big ass killed."

"Not planning on it."

"You have pissed off enough people over your career that you don't have to plan for it. Lots of others would volunteer for that chance."

"That's a lousy epitaph."

"Bite your tongue, Service. We shall entertain no further morbid or negative thoughts here. Besides, the pool boy's getting impatient."

"How can you tell?"

"Women are born knowing these things."

"Wives know this kinda stuff too?"

"I guess we're just gonna have to find that out," she said.

"Tell the pool man he's dead."

She laughed and punched off.

An out-of-breath Marschke called. "Harlikin was indicted for running a Ponzi in Colorado."

"Him, or his wife?"

"Him. She had nothing to do with it."

"Get me details."

"Coming soon. You sound your old self."

Service chuckled. "There is no such thing as an old self, my friend. We are sequences of us and when the last sequence stops, we're gone."

"Like totally heavy," Chas said.

"The only heavy things here are my feet and legs. Everything else feels filled with cement."

"Serious enough to talk to your doctor?"

"My doc has retired from medicine to a new career."

"Being?"

"Discovering the world's perfect martini."

"A noble cause."

"Besides his doctor self would just tell me to not work so much."

"Maybe he'd be right."

"Anything he'd say would come through a Bombay filter," Service said and hung up.

He called Wetelainen. "Grady here, I need a crash place. Got a zero nine hundred appointment in Houghton."

Shark said, "Use my office room at the motel. I'll set the alarm for zero seven hundred and synch coffee with that time. You all right?"

"That, I am guessing, is a much-debated topic, depending upon the group consulted."

When he finally pulled into Shark's motel he took a deep breath, thought about a cigarette, thought again, shut off the truck, found his key to Shark's, let himself inside, and crashed, still clothed, where he would remain until the alarm and coffee came on the next morning.

CHAPTER 45

Camp ROCK

KEWEENAW COUNTY

> Our swift scene flies in motion of no less celerity Than that of thought.
>
> —William Shakespeare, *Henry V*

"You're going to *what*?" Captain McKower squawked.

"I'm buying Harlikin's outfit, all of it, feather business included."

"With *what*, your craggy good looks?"

"Not to worry, Cap'n. I've got this and the whole thing's bogus, so it doesn't matter."

"How *much*?" she asked forcefully.

"Fifty K cash for the next level and you really don't need to know the rest."

"Like hell I don't."

"These are not *your* funds, Lis. This is not your responsibility—or your risk."

Her hands went to her hips. "Whose funds then?"

"Mine."

She laughed sardonically. "We're state employees," she reminded him. "You're hourly."

"I inherited something."

"From whom? Your father was an hourly paid game warden, same as you."

"We had a house and land."

"It was hardly a house."

"Leave this alone, Lis. Let it be."

"I will not."

"You will. Have you done anything about search warrants?"

"Thought about them, of course. Done anything, no. I'm still groping for probable cause."

"Wake up: The feds put us into this case based on CITES and feathers, and now you've seen the feathers."

"Not legally, and in the company of a felon."

"Stop nitpicking. I'm undercover. You tell me where the feathers are and I'll swear to having seen them."

"But you haven't and that would be lying."

"Good grief, Lis. Undercover is the opposite of scrupled. We lie to bad guys every day."

"Only when it can't be avoided," she said.

"Bull. We go undercover *on* a lie. We pretend to be someone else." He flashed her his owl eye. "Are you trying to put the kibosh on this?"

"I won't lie," she said. "I'd really like to stop the whole damn thing."

"You'd walk away from all those feathers?"

"That . . . person . . . found them. I didn't."

"That person has a name. It's Allerdyce."

"I know his bloody name."

"Lis, the Feebs, which is to say, Coldbeg himself, asked me to bring him into this."

"Since when do we kowtow to the Bureau?" she countered.

"It's not kowtowing, it's cooperating."

"One direction is not cooperation," she argued.

"Runway behind us Cap'n. Join me and us in the present. I am going inside and that's that. How many more Mustard Seeds did we see boogie last night?"

"Only the two sentries you dealt with and six or seven others."

"Which leaves an estimated ten or twelve over there."

"We don't know how many, Grady. Your estimates come from that thing and that . . . other thing. That *girl*."

"Both are as good in the woods as we are."

"And who is that, whatever that is, she, her?"

"Pretty hard to not see she's female."

"But from what planet?"

"Knock it off, keep your eye on the ball, Cap'n. Let's deal with first things first, leave other issues and questions for after we take care of main business."

"Is she sane?" McKower asked.

"Of course she's sane," Service said, thinking most likely, and added, "Are any of us in this bizarro business? Who is here with us?"

McKower took a deep breath and began to regulate her breathing. "FBI and ATF and Fish and Wildlife, and somehow Homeland Security sniffed out this being some sort of goat rodeo with a militia, and they demanded in."

"The nearness of blood on the water," Grady Service said. "All the scavengers want their share. You might tell Coldbeg the IRS might want a piece of this action too. Harlikin is wanted in Colorado for running a Ponzi. I say invite them all in, and I want to see Coldbeg alone before I cross over. How many bodies on our side do we have?"

"Twentyish so far."

"Then we outnumber the ROCK force."

"You think."

"When do we ever know all we want to know when we're undercover?"

The captain looked at her boots, which uncharacteristically needed a shine.

• • •

Special Agent Coldbeg's complexion was spackled and splotched. Nerves or soap allergies? Service wondered. Either way, the man looked like Eeyore, with the weight of several worlds solidly on his shoulders.

"You have a lot of explaining to do," the special agent greeted Service.

"Not until I finish the job."

"This is *my* task force."

"Good for you, but it's my ass alone inside. The two aren't equal."

"You have all the support you need, Detective."

"I prefer support I can see with my eyes, not try to imagine."

"You want to share your plan for the ROCKs?"

"You first," Service said.

"You misunderstand your position," the special agent scolded.

"Calling a pasty a pizza doesn't make it a pizza. Never has and never will."

"You are forcing me to lodge formal complaints."

"Good, while you're doing that and playing boss-man, we'll be lodging suspects."

"Are we to know nothing of your initiative?"

"As much as we know of yours," Service said. "Such as your dead agent died of natural causes."

"That was a preliminary finding."

"Be nice if we'd been told, but we weren't. And, by the way, we have located the eagle feathers."

Coldbeg's eyes went wide. "Where?"

"Where they belong for the moment."

Coldbeg said threateningly, "You have not heard the last of this, Detective."

"What's true now may soon not be true," Service told the man.

The special agent took a step back, but kept quiet, and Service walked away from him to find his own tribe.

• • •

"You see the fearless task force leader?" McKower asked.

"Heard him too."

"How many people did he bring?"

"I never asked and he never told."

"We need bodies," the captain pointed out.

"We have us," Service reminded her.

"Five of us?" she said.

"I count seven," Service said. "Allerdyce and Worm are with us all the way. Did the George kid get lawyered up?"

"As is his right."

"Others leave the camp last night?"

"Six, maybe seven, plus the two gate guards."

"Seven vee ten or so is doable with surprise on our side," he told her. "It will be up to you and Limpy to make a beeline to secure the feathers."

"And you?"

"Harlikin's expecting me."

"You seem sure of that."

"Money is his perfume."

"Is that all this is, some asshole's attempt to bilk others of their money under a false flag?"

"I like how you put that. It has a deep and long place in American culture and history. But ultimately, someone, or something always shits their bed."

"When do we move?"

"O'Dell will call the George."

"Your go code is go blue."

"Sic 'em," Service said.

"Will you arrest Harlikin?"

"When he shows me the feathers and I hand the cashier's check and cash to him. O'Dell will give us a transcript afterward."

"Did you think about taking a camera?"

"Sure," he lied. Not one thought.

"What if he refuses to make the deal?"

"He won't. This much easy money is too hard to pass up."

"Do you think he knows his kid is in custody?"

"I don't know and I guess I'll find out when I see the man. He strikes me as aloof from reality."

McKower poked his chest with her forefinger. "Don't screw this up."

"Post the feds on the back doors," he said, "Stay alert for bodies moving toward the camp, not rats jumping off."

"Why?"

"The alleged hockey player, Mesnard George's buddy. He's still at large."

"Maybe he's still over there."

"Let's hope not."

McKower looked hard at him. "There's going to be bloodshed, isn't there?"

"Let's make sure it's not ours," he told her.

"You armed?"

"I'm good to go," he told her, offering no details, about which she would be dearly unhappy. He was unarmed, save his wit, experience, and skill with gab. All these many years in a police uniform and he had never shot a civilian, and he did not plan to start now. Risk was a factor in every life. So too was principle.

• • •

Two new sentries were on duty. Service identified himself as Batanovich. "Where're the guys who were on duty yesterday?"

"No idea," one guard said. "We were just told to get out here and do this job."

"You guys trained and experienced Military Police?"

Both laughed. One of the guards said, "Not our can, man."

"The colonel's expecting you," the other guard said. "He's on the horn to this station every twenty minutes or so."

"You hear the big hoohah on the intercom yesterday?"

"We were afield, came back to an empty barracks. What hoohah?"

"How many of our guys are still here?" Service asked.

"Eight we know of."

Seven v. twelve was not even two to one. Good. "Ask you guys a question?"

"Sure," one sentry said, and the other one nodded.

"Why'd you join this outfit?"

"The colonel's spiel made sense."

"As a colonel or as a king?" Service fired back to them.

The men laughed. One of them said, "You been drinking? This outfit is death on alcohol, or any spirits."

But ticks were okay? "Even the *Holy* Spirit?"

The men chuckled at the joke. "Good one," one of the sentries mumbled.

• • •

Sane Zane Harlikin's office door was ajar. Not a good sign. Service put his back to the wall and inched forward, to toe open the door with his right boot. It was one thing to rush a room with a weapon at the ready, but unarmed entry was a whole different deal. He used the back of his right arm to open the door wider and saw Harlikin at his desk, in his chair, slumped backward, his head hanging at an unnatural angle.

Service used two fingers to feel for a pulse, got nothing in the neck or wrist. The body was still warm, Harlikin's eyes wide open. No blood, no obvious wounds. The ME would have to piece this one together. One last look around revealed no pill bottles, and nothing suspicious.

There were ticks all over his head and neck. How the hell did they end up all over the man?

"Go Blue, *hal-tur pla-kur*!" Service said quietly and heard O'Dell broadcast the George to the others.

He leaned over the desk and saw that there was a cheap fountain pen, and it appeared as if the colonel might have been writing a note of some kind, and obviously had been interrupted and most of the ink was smeared beyond legibility. All Grady could make out were six letters, ***r-i-n-e-w-a***. What the hell was that supposed to mean? He left the note untouched, stepped outside the small office and lit a cigarette. There were no interior alarms, no yellow uniforms running around and yelling, no resistance of any kind in sight or earshot. And, within three minutes or so along came Worm, a crudely made spear in hand, and no firearm. She was even clothed, thank God for small things. But she was obviously jacked up on enough adrenaline to twist the head off a bear.

"Whoa," he said quietly.

"Worm She sees no-one, Him Service okay?" she asked, her nostrils flaring.

"Service is just peachy," he answered.

She scowled. "Worm, Her see no juicy fuzzy-skinned fruit of a usually pink-flowered tree related to cherry and plums," she said. "There are plums here, many," she added and made a face. "Not ripe yet. Bitter. She made a foul spitting sound."

"The area's a veritable Garden of Eden," Service said.

Worm smiled. "Eve, she wore no clothes."

"We'll probably never know that for sure," Service said.

"Is written in Good Book," Worm countered.

"The Good Book doesn't cover all good details."

"O.E.D. does," she said.

"Different books, different stories, different facts," he said.

She was so hopped up that she was bouncing like a puppy. "Stay with Him, or help Others?" she asked.

"Stick close to Allerdyce."

"*Please*," she said, rolled her eyes, tossed her mane, and disappeared.

Service lit a cigarette. So far no shots, no screams, no nothing. "Everything copacetic, Click-Clack?"

"*Ha*," the voice behind his ear whispered.

• • •

There was the standard shitload of paperwork every undercover case generated, no matter the case's complexity or duration. Service intended to clear this case as thoroughly as he could. At least they had the feathers and CITES to drive the legal case through the courts.

But Harlikin was dead and gone, his kid lawyered up, and not talking. Natural causes, the M.E. would rule: Heart failure, aortic dissection, a near-instant death. The loose ticks would forever be a loose end, and meaningless. The six-letter scribble ***r-i-n-e-w-a*** would later be interpreted by someone as a partial spelling of Wolverine Watchmen. Why Harlikin had written this, like the loose ticks, would never be understood, though later the FBI, who had an informant inside the Wolverine Watchmen, would charge a number of members of that group with conspiracy to kidnap and perhaps kill Michigan's sitting governor. Apparently the group had occasionally trained at Camp ROCK, but that was the extent of the connection ever made, and even the FBI never disclosed this tidbit publicly.

The justice system, state and federal, had begun its slow crawl toward disposition. He would finish his part, testify if and when needed, but this was the end. After all those years, now had arrived.

Most conservation officers reported in service and out at the beginning and end of every shift, to local dispatchers, and to Station Twenty in Lansing, the DNR's central around-the-clock dispatch center. For years, Detective Grady Service had foregone this procedure, largely to hide who he was, where he was, or when he was on duty.

Grady Service drove back to his home south of Marquette, pulled into the driveway, picked up his microphone, and mashed the transmit button: "Dispatch, Twenty-Five Fourteen is clear of the last." Not that they would know where or what the last had been, and it was moot anyway. For a very long minute or two, he stared at the microphone he had used so many thousands of times, took a long deep breath, exhaled slowly, and mashed transmit again: "Station Twenty, Twenty-Five Fourteen, out of service."

Author's Note

'Tis fiction all.

—William Shakespeare, *Double Falsehood*

Last scene of all, that ends this strange eventful history.

—William Shakespeare, *As You Like It*

Eventful history, indeed! My Dear Readers and Friends: To every end there is a beginning, and, ultimately it follows, to every beginning there must be an end.

Conservation officers live a dangerous, demanding, all-encompassing way of life unlike that of any other member of law enforcement. That way of life can be, and often is, addictive.

After more than twenty years in trucks with officers, I have seen many of my "partners" retire to new currents of life. Few do it easily or quickly, and some struggle mightily. A small few never do make the full adjustment. How will Grady Service handle this major life moment? We don't know, but we shall see, because, like courage under fire, nobody can predict who will be brought to their knees by that unknown monster called retirement. You have just finished reading Grady's final case, but there will be another title in the series, and we shall then see how he greets that imposing beast looming before him.

Omnes exitus.

Joseph Heywood
Central
Keweenaw County, Michigan
September 26, 2023